D1548225

THE GLAD GAME

Also by Rita Louise Kornfeld

Vittoria

THE GLAD GAME

A Saga of Civil War New York

RITA LOUISE KORNFELD

Full Court Press
Englewood Cliffs, New Jersey

First Edition

Published in the United States of America
by Full Court Press, 601 Palisade Avenue,
Englewood Cliffs, NJ 07632
fullcourtpress.com

ISBN 978-1-946989-92-5
Library of Congress Control No. 2021908242

Editing and book design by Barry Sheinkopf

Cover Art, "NewYork Enrollment Poster, June 23, 1863," used by permission from Wikipedia Commons

Author photo by Alex Kornfeld

To my husband, Jay,

who encourages me, tells me like it is—good or bad
—and loves me unconditionally. I love you.

Working on an inpatient psychiatric ward, I ran a weekly group in which I'd go around the table and have each patient identify at least one thing he or she was grateful for. I called it the "glad game." All those patients, most of whom were suffering from devastating mental health issues and had absolutely nothing, had something they were grateful for. It's where I found the title for this volume.

—R.L.K

PROLOGUE

LENA RABINOWITZ POKED HER HEAD *out the window. "Where are your mittens?" she shouted, inhaling the scent of spring on the wind whipping across the plains.*

Layzer looked up with his bright blue eyes and held the gloves for her to see. Bundled in a hat and coat, and a scarf that wound around his face, the eyes were all she could see.

"They're supposed to be on *your hands, not* in *them!" She watched him digging in the earth with two spoons as she stood at the dry sink, scrubbing a pot in a bucket filled with ash and water she'd boiled on the stove. The soil was still winter-hard, and he needed to put all his weight behind the effort. He was a big, strong boy for his age. She could see his shoulders heaving.*

"I'm trying to reach China," he called when he saw her staring at him.

A smile crossed her face. What a beautiful boy, she thought. And, reaching China notwithstanding, so smart. Just six, and not only does he know his full name, he even knows how to spell it. "Thank you, God," she whispered, gazing at the ceiling as if He was in the rafters, "for this light of my life." She lifted the iron kettle from the black water, dried it with a dish rag, put it in place on a shelf hidden behind a floral skirt, and wiped her workspace clean. Though the house was just a step above a hovel and everything in it rickety, she did her best to keep a clean, pleasant home, even brightening it with lovely-smelling wildflowers called Lithuania blues when in season, or branches of red and orange berries, which she kept in jars. I am so blessed. Two healthy children, a good husband. So he's not handsome, and he's old enough to be my father. Her dress swished against the floor of rushes as she turned to the table behind her, to knead a ball of dough that had risen in a covered bowl. It smelled of yeast, and the soft elasticity soothed her fingers, cracked from a lifetime of unending chores—albeit a life of only twenty-nine years. He's a good *man. He has a trade and his own shop, she told herself. He's honest and kind. Too kind sometimes. So what, he doesn't charge enough for his work? I have a roof over my head, don't I? She punched the dough. So it leaks sometimes, but only when it rains—or snows, which is all winter. . .which is most of the year. She was thinking these thoughts, as she often did, to convince herself that she was happy, that her life was more than drudgery, that she should be content. After all, her husband didn't drink, gamble, womanize, or beat her. What more was there to want? If joy she wanted, she need only look at Layzer.* A shtick naches, *my* kaddishel! *Such a child. Those eyes, so blue. And that hair! The thickest, most golden curls she'd even seen.*

The rumble of an approaching coach brought her out of her reverie. Initially, she paid it little attention. Though she lived at the far end of the shtetl, *on a street, not a main thoroughfare—a mere lane, one of many offshoots to the larger dirt road to town—-at that hour of the morning, even when it was barely light, it wasn't uncommon for her neighbors to be out and about. But a moment later, when she* heard the coach come to a screeching halt before her house, she felt her heart quicken. No sooner had she turned to the window than she saw six burly men jump out, burst through her gate, stomp over sprouting snowdrops and crocus, and with ropes and tape in hand set out immediately toward her son. They were Cossacks, not Jews, bare-headed, with sweeping mustaches and high, crinkly boots.

Color drained from her face. Her hand flew to her mouth. "Khappers! Oh, dear God, khappers!" Spinning on her heel and grabbing the rolling pin from the table behind her, she charged out of the house. "Help! Help!" she cried. But no one heard. "Get away! Leave him alone!" she shrieked, rushing toward them.

The men ignored her. Three of them were already upon her son. The stockiest of the lot had him around the waist; another, having already secured his legs, was tying them together; and the third was attempting to gag him with a cloth. Two others stayed near the fence, watching the street, while the sixth man sat on the box of the coach, reins in hand.

Layzer stared at them. He'd never seen gentiles before. They looked different from men he was used to. They dressed strangely, none of them wore a beard, and they even smelled different: like smoke, as if they'd just stepped out of a chimney. What did they want with him? Why didn't they let him go as his mother demanded? Could they be those men who his parents had warned about, the goyim who threw stones at Jews and stole children? "Be a good boy. Don't wander off alone," his father would lecture. "The goyim will catch you and take you to Siberia." But he was a good boy. He hadn't wandered off alone. He was close to home, in his own front yard, only a few feet away from his house.

He didn't want to go to Siberia, whatever that was. He didn't want to be torn from his mother. He tried to free himself, but their arms were too strong. His lips began to tremble.

"Bite him, Layzer, kick him!" he heard Lena command, panic in her voice as she ran to him. He'd never seen her so frantic, her eyes so wild. "Run, Layzer, run!"

But Layzer couldn't run, though he put up a good fight. He wriggled like one of the worms he'd recently dug from the ground and wrung his arms in every direction. Pulling one leg and then the other out of the restraints, he kicked one Cossack in the face, and rammed his head under the chin of the man closest to him, causing his jaw to slam shut and his head to fly backward. Layzer shook his head violently from side to side and sank his teeth deep into the third man's finger.

"Ow! You little bastard!" the man shouted, sucking the wound.

"We've got a real live one on our hands, Boris," the man with the cloth said.

"Damn. He drew blood, Vladimir."

Layzer punched Boris in the face, making him take a step back. When he regained his balance, he twisted the child's arm.

Just then, teeth clenched, knuckles white around the wood, Lena came at them swinging the rolling pin with all her might. Flour dusted the air like snow. Whishing and whistling, it came down with a thud on the head of the man they called Boris, the vibration shooting through her forearms as it met his skull. It so stunned him that he gave up his hold on the boy and fell to the ground, a knot erupting and blood pouring over his ear and into his eye. Layzer squirmed away and again used his head to butt Vladimir. "Hey! Nikoli, Pyetra!" Boris shouted to the two near the gate as he wiped his bruised ear with the back of his hand. "Get this woman outta here, will you, before she murders me. Shit, that hurt!"

What about the boy?" Pyetra asked.

"I can handle him. Just get her off my back."

Lena stood with her feet planted on the earth, whacking and whacking as Boris sat on the ground, warding off the blows.

"Run, Layzer!" she shouted when she saw that he was free. Her words were short and clipped, her breath heavy.

The boy bolted, trampled through the barren vegetable patch, ripping his coat as he jumped over the broken wooden fence that surrounded the small plot, the sound of the tear lost in the excitement, he ran behind the house while his mother stood her ground, fending off the men.

But they were six, and she was one.

It was inevitable.

Four of them had taken off after her son, and though her heart was still pounding, she was tiring. Her arms felt heavy, and her blows were becoming less and less effective. Sometime during the fray, she'd lost her kerchief, and, despite the cold, her cropped hair, wet with perspiration, stuck to her forehead.

As Boris crouched with his arms over his head to deflect the blows, the one who had been watching the street came from behind, clutched her arm, and wrenched the rolling pin from her hands. She spun to face him, tried to retrieve it, but a foot taller than her, he was holding it above his head, out of reach. She pushed him, pounded on his chest with both fists. He threw the weapon to Boris, who had risen and was standing behind her. Spinning again, she leaped on Boris. Both fell to the ground, she on top of him. Pyetra seized her around the waist and pulled her off. She kicked him in the shin. He lost his balance and tumbled onto the two of them, knocking the breath out of her, his legs, the size of tree trunks, pinning her to the ground. Their warm, foul breaths assaulted her. Sandwiched between two hulking men, she could barely move.

She rolled back and forth, trying to break their hold. She kicked

Pyetra's knee with the heel of her shoe. He pushed her face into the ground, where she got a mouthful of dirt, twigs and loosened soil from Layzer's excavation. She spit in his face. He grabbed her by the neck. She managed to bring her hands up and dig her fingernails into his face, tearing away skin and drawing more blood, which was mixed with the soil and spittle and smelled sourly sweet. When he jumped back, she brought her knee up into his groin: he groaned and rolled off in pain, curling and cursing.

Scrambling out of his grasp, she reached for the rolling pin. Her fingers were nearly upon it, but just as they were about to tighten around the wood, he wrenched it out of her hands—and brought it down on her skull. For a moment her head felt as if it had exploded, with flashes of light fluttering before her eyes. Then she lay still.

Vladimir reached inside his belt and pulled out a gun. "You want I should shoot her?" he asked Boris.

"No. Let her be. She won't be giving us any more trouble. We're not murderers, *after all."*

But before he left, he kicked her so hard with his heavy boot that he could hear her ribs crack.

She was able to do nothing as her only son was carried past her, wrapped and gagged like a mummy, and thrown into the waiting carriage. If she had been fully conscious, she would have seen his pale face and frightened, imploring eyes. She would have heard the muffled screams through his gag, the clomping of horses on the hard earth as they tore down the road.

MURIEL GROSSMAN WAS ON HER WAY BACK *from town when she noticed the door to Lena's house wide open and the front gate swinging back and forth in the wind, banging against the fence. "Lena," she called from the street. "Lena? You home?" She entered the property, slowly making her way to the house. "It's me, Muriel." She spotted a kerchief she knew to be Lena's crumpled on the ground and felt a strange uneasiness. ". . .Lena? Is everything. . .alright?" she called, a slight quaver in her voice. "Oy!" Dropping her satchel, her hand flew to her mouth. "Oh, my God!" She fell to her knees beside her prostate, moaning neighbor, noticed blood dripping down her face, her reddened, swollen eye and dirty, ripped dress. "Lena, Lena, can you hear me? Oh, my God! What happened?" She slapped her, shook her. "Wake up!"*

After several more smacks, Lena's eyes began to flutter. "Run, Layzer," she mumbled, "Run!" She opened her eyes, squinted in the sun directly overhead, and saw the big-bosomed woman staring down at her, fear written on her face. ". . .Muriel?"

"Yes. It's me. Oi, Gottenyu. *What* happened *to you?"*

". . .Layzer. . . . Where's Layzer? I have to find Layzer." She tried to rise, to move her legs, but it was as if she were loaded down with lead. Nothing moved. She hurt everywhere. Breathing was an effort. Her mouth tasted of dirt and vomit. Something sticky was trickling down her face. She panted and coughed, clutched the side of her chest where a shooting pain stopped further words.

"I . . .don't see him."

Lena took her neighbor's extended hand and tried to rise, but a wave of nausea forced her back down. Her head was throbbing, the world spinning. Salty tears began to run down her cheeks. Sobs and hiccups overtook her.

"I'll get my son with his cart, and we'll take you to the doctor," Muriel said.

"No. . . . *To town. I have to see the* nemeenha-khal."

AT MURIEL'S INSISTENCE, LENA HAD WASHED *and changed her clothes before leaving home. Nevertheless, with her ashen color her bruised face, her eyes deeply reddened, her limp and her wheeze, she still looked ghastly.*

After a ride that seemed like forever, they stopped in front of the congregation hall, which stood between the synagogue and the yeshiva, the only buildings made of stone. Unlike the rest of the shtetl *where the streets were dirt, cobbles paved the town proper. Muriel's son, a beefy sixteen-year-old, helped her out of the wagon and across the street.*

"I can make it from here," she told him when they reached the building.

"I'll come with you."

"No. Thank you, Sol. I'll be fine."

"We'll wait for here, then."

"I shouldn't be long."

Holding fast to the railing to steady herself, she stopped on each step to rest. The mayor, having seen her from his window, met her half-way up the stairs. "You're hurt. Let me get the doctor," he said.

"I'm fine." She waved him off.

"Please. Sit down," he said as they reached his office, motioning to the overstuffed chair beside the fireplace. Keeping her shawl tight around her body, she eased herself onto the comfortable seat. The room smelled of polish. A log crackling in the hearth threw off a red glow and a pleasant warmth. More books than she'd ever seen covered the shelves of an entire wall. A mahogany desk, cluttered with papers, occupied a space before the window.

He offered her a freshly baked kichel *from a box he kept behind a leather-bound volume of the town records. When he opened the lid, releasing the sweet aroma, she couldn't help but notice a ruby ring on his pinky. "No, thank you," she said in a clipped voice.*

He removed his hat and fur-collared coat, hung them in the closet, and sat on the corner of his desk, facing her. A gold watch chain gleamed from the vest pocket of his worsted suit. He had a mustache and an otherwise shaven face, but she could see a few white whiskers beneath his chin that he'd missed. Other than a yarmulke covering a bald spot, nobody would have picked him out as a Jew. Ordinarily, she would have felt intimidated to be in the presence of someone so above her, but she was too distraught to be concerned. "So, what can I do for you?" he asked.

She told the story of the kidnapping detail for detail, only pausing when she had to stop between words to catch her breath, while he listened in silence.

"You must do something!" she said when she finished. "Organize a search. Go after them!"

He rose, rubbed his chin, and paced. He couldn't meet her eyes. She noticed a flush creep across his face. Reaching inside a drawer of his desk, he removed a bottle of vodka and poured himself a glass. He tilted his head back and took a gulp, then cleared his throat. "There is nothing to be done. No doubt the boy was taken for the Russian army," he muttered. "Even if they could be caught, they are under the protection of the tzar. You know they take four times as many Jews as Gentiles." He downed the remaining alcohol, feeling it burn all the way down his throat, and added in a mumble, "We didn't meet the quota. Someone had to go."

She glared at his expensive suit and the ring that flashed in the firelight.

"It's not something we condone." He stared out the window that overlooked the town square and the crowd that had gathered around Sol and Muriel. The mayor could not hear what was being said, but from the look of the gesturing he surmised the story of the kidnapping was being told.

"We have no choice. Don't you see?" the nemeenha-khal *said, looking at his polished shoes. "If your child is found and returned, they will only take another."*

"One from a wealthy family?"

He turned then and faced her. "What else could I have done?" He put up his arms in surrender.

The log in the fire made a loud pop. "You could have sent your *son."*

LENA FOUND YONKEL BRODSKY WORKING *in his garden. As it was too soon to plant, he was busying himself replacing slats in the wooden fence that had been damaged by the winter storms. A cold north wind blew across the plain. He was wearing a fur hat, a sheepskin coat belted at the waist, its broad collar raised to cover his ears, and woolen gloves with the fingertips cut out so he could work better. His nose and cheeks were cherry red.*

He was not surprised to see her. Bad news travels fast. She was not the first mother who had ever approached him, nor would she be the last. He laid down his hammer when he saw her standing at the gate, bundled in a black shawl, wind gusts whipping her dress around her legs. "I'm Lena Rabinowitz," she said above the sound of her flapping garment.

He nodded.

"My son, Layzer—"

"I know."

The neat, one-room house had a wide-planked floor, a hearth, and a window overlooking the plot of land the government had given him for his service in the army when he retired. A log crackling in the stove warmed the tiny space.

His wife, Natasha, a Russian with a wide, flat, kindly face, stood at the sink. An intricately embroidered apron covered her dark dress. She smiled at Lena when she came through the door, lowered her eyes so not to stare at the woman's bruised, swollen face, and offered her a seat. Yonkel hung his hat and coat on a hook in the foyer. His hair, black with streaks of gray but still thick despite his fifty-odd years, stuck to his head in the shape of the beaver hat he'd been wearing. His chair scraped against the wooden floor as he took his place at the table opposite his guest.

Natasha put a pot of caravan tea and a loaf of freshly baked honey cake on the table. Steam from the kettle moistened Lena's face. The smell of cinnamon and cloves sweetened the room. Natasha disappeared into the storage cellar, returning a few moments later with a shot glass and a bottle of Vishnnyovka, *knowing her husband would need the homemade vodka with sugared cherries to say what he had to. "Thank you, but I haven't been able to eat or drink since the* knappers, . . .*the* knappers *took—" She dropped her face in her hands and began to weep.*

Yonkel inhaled the liquor. "So," he began when he finished his drink, "what would you like me to tell you?"

She raised her head, held her breath, then blurted, "The truth."

He stared at her, twirling the empty glass in his hand. ". . .You will never see your boy again. He is on his way to the training camps. Perhaps Siberia, as we speak." He looked away, for as many times as he had told this to mothers, it still hurt him. He poured more vodka, took another hefty gulp. "If he's not dead already. He may not survive the trip."

It took a minute for Lena to respond, her voice choked in her throat. Finally she managed to say, "You came back. You survived."

"I was twelve when they kidnapped me, not six. And it was summer. I didn't have to march for ten hours a day in the freezing

cold, eating only biscuits. Not half the boys survive the trek. The older ones maybe have a chance. But a six-year-old? And if he somehow survives? What then? He will serve for twenty-five years after reaching eighteen. Until he's eighteen and fit to serve, they'll put him in a re-education camp. They'll teach him to be a Gentile, to hate the Jews. After another twenty-five years, he won't even know who you are."

Lena covered her face with her hands again. "Why my son? What can a baby do for them, in their army?"

Yonkel raised his brow. "Your boy happened to be there. That is reason enough." Another substantial gulp. "In time you will forget . . .or at least the pain will lessen. You're still young. You can have another son."

CHAPTER 1

HANNAH KALISH AND SARAH FRUCHTER exchanged sideways glances. It had been a month since they visited last, just days after the kidnapping, and they could hardly believe the condition of the house. They took in the dust covered furniture and the pots and dishes piled to overflowing in a bucket. Mrs. Kalish couldn't help but stare at the jars, usually brimming with fresh, sweet-smelling flowers, filled only with the smell of decay in the green stagnant water, while Mrs. Fructer's nose was scrunched in reaction to the fusty smell of aged floor rushes. "My mother's not feeling well," Rachel said apologetically. "I'm trying."

Mrs. Kalish patted Rachel's shoulder, and, feeling the bones beneath her rumpled dress that had not seen a washtub in some time, wondered when the girl had eaten her last meal. Or had had a bath. "It's alright, dear. We didn't come to see the house. We came to see your mother."

Hannah placed a bowl of beef stew on the soiled tablecloth, and Mrs. Fruchter lay a plate of still-warm *rugalach* filled with walnuts and raisins, and redolent of cinnamon. "Here." She put a cookie in Rachel's hand, having noticed the girl following the pastry with hungry eyes. "Take one. They just came out of the oven."

"She's up there." Rachel pointed to the staircase behind a lumpy couch.

The stairs were steep, narrow, and dark: for there were only two windows in the house: one above the kitchen sink, the other in the loft, and little light crept up the stairway. Rachel hurried ahead of them. Mrs. Kalish took her time, holding her skirt above her ankles and watching each tread. But Mrs. Fruchter, plump from her baker husband's *humentoshen,* had to stop every few steps to catch her breath. Her wide girth nearly filled the space, and the old wooden steps creaked under her.

By the time they reached the top, she was spent. She needed to sit, but there were no chairs, only a stool, too small and too low, as well as two pallets beneath the eaves. Nevertheless, she lowered herself, albeit with loud moans, and creaking knees, while Mrs. Kalish made herself as comfortable as possible on the edge of a mattress.

Lena was sitting on a hard chair with her back to them, staring out between the open shutters, beyond the muddy street where there was a collection of old, slapped-together wooden houses much like her own. Spring had been slow in coming, and many villagers, having depleted their woodpile, were down to burning whatever they could find for warmth. She stared at the smoke curling from the lopsided chimneys, which vanished in the cold gray sky, yet didn't seem to see or smell it. Neither did she seem to feel the cold or hear the howling wind when it whipped through the cracks in the attic walls and open window.

While the ladies had not expected to find Lena dancing, neither had they expected to find her in such a state. It seemed like yesterday she'd been in the *shul* with Layzer and Rachel at her side, behind the curtain in the balcony, all looking happy and fit. The women were stunned to see how she'd deteriorated. They took in her gaunt face, her sunken cheeks and the dress that hung as loose as a flour sack. Known to be particular about her appearance, not allowing even an errant strand of hair to escape kerchief or her clothes to be untidy, her head was now bare; her hair, unwashed and dull, fell about her face.

"I think she's looking for Layzer, waiting for him to walk down the street," Rachel said. "She sits here all day long. At first, she stayed by the fence and wouldn't move. Papa had to carry her inside. Then she came up here. I guess because of the window. She's been here since. Won't move from this spot. . . . She won't eat anything. I try to feed her, but. . ." She gave them a helpless shrug.

"We brought you *rugalach*, Lena," Mrs. Kalesh said with false brightness.

"Mother," Rachel said, standing beside her under the sloped ceiling, the only space beneath the roof where she could easily stretch to her full four-foot height, "you have company. Mrs. Kalish and Mrs. Fruchter came to see you." She bent over and whispered in her mother's ear, "Talk to them." The wind was coming directly at her, so she tucked her mother's shawl tighter around her shoulders. "*Please!*"

Mrs. Fruchter, still short of breath, couldn't speak. Her head had dropped, and tears began running down her fleshy cheeks. "Have some goulash," she gasped. "Hannah made it the way you like it, with lots of paprika."

There was no response.

"I'm sorry it's so cold. My mother won't let me close the shutters."

The women pretended they were warm enough as they slid their hands inside their cloaks. Luckily, they were dressed for winter in thick woolen hose and undergarments beneath long-sleeved, high-necked garb.

Acting as if all was normal, Hannah made idle conversation. "The ladies from *shul* are all asking for you. The rabbi gave a good sermon this week."

At the mention of the rabbi, Lena dug her fingers into the folds of her dress.

"There was a *bris* for Felga's and Efrayim's new baby boy, Anshel, *kayne hora*, and a *kaddish* for Simon Goldfarb, may his memory be a blessing. . ."

Going on as if all was as usual, they retold their own losses; enumerating their woes. The baker's wife talked about her backaches and bunions. Hannah Kalish told Lena who else had been born and who else died.

There was no reaction.

Sarah regarded Hannah. "May the tzar rot in hell!" the fat woman snapped.

"The *balabatim* and the *pushim*, too, *feh, feh!*" Mrs. Kalish put in. They shook their *sheitel*-covered heads and made as if to spit in their palms to emphasize their loathing. "The pox they should get!"

And at the end of their visit, when Mrs. Fruchter struggled to get herself off the stool, they both agreed that Lena, too, should put her sorrows behind her and get on with life. Mrs. Kalish told her Layzer was in God's hands, and who was Lena to question His will? But all the ladies' cheer did not move Lena from the window or put words in her mouth.

IT WAS RACHEL WHO, THREE MONTHS LATER, when spoon-feeding her mother borscht, wiping the red stains from her chin as the soup dribbled down her face, began to cry. "What about the *rest* of us?"

she blurted out, sobbing. "Do we mean *nothing* to you? We love Layzer, too. We miss him too! It's as if you're already dead!"

Lena finally moved her eyes and opened her mouth. She looked at her daughter as if seeing her for the first time. How sad and tired she appeared. She stared at the tears that streaked her soiled face, the mucus dripping from a nose that tilted left, at her messy hair and dirty apron, her scrawny limbs, and fresh blisters on her palms from the deep wooden bucket she used to lug water and from lifting the heavy iron pots she used to prepare meals for her father when he came home from working all day. Lena knew this was caused by the work she, herself, should be doing. She thought about how selfish she'd been, and that despair was a luxury for the rich. The poor did not have time to wallow in grief. Yonkel's words rang in her ears: "'You're still young. You can have another son,'" she murmured when she heard Rachel's footsteps descending the rickety stairs. "But I swear on my daughter and my dead parents, my next son will never be taken in the army."

That night, Lena washed herself, changed her clothes, doused herself with toilet water, and called Moshe to her bed.

One year to the day after Layzer's abduction, Lena gave birth to a son she named Yussel. It was a bittersweet occasion, for to celebrate the blessings of the new son was also to mourn the loss of the other. To make matters worse, the infant was the image of his lost brother. He had the same face and bright blue eyes; tufts of yellow hair that sprouted on the exact spot of his head where Layzer's had; and like his sibling, even his tiny feet turned inward. Whenever Lena looked at Yussel, she saw Layzer. And every time she saw Layzer, she was reminded of the dreaded Russian army; the *balabatim,* who made up the *Kahalah*; and the most "pious" and scholarly, whose sons were never chosen. She was reminded of the *pushim,* the spies who reported to the *Kabalah* the least "worthy" while lining their pockets in the process. And this made her irate—angry at everybody and everything.

Until his fifth birthday when he started school, Yussel would never be out of her sight. When she worked in the kitchen, he sat on the floor at her feet. When she collected eggs from the chicken coop or toiled in the vegetable garden, she kept him at arm's length. Rachel adored her brother, too. She waited on him as if he were the long-awaited messiah. The pastes of corn starch and buttermilk that she and her mother made to put on their faces so as to keep their skin smooth, she rubbed on Yussel's bottom. She tickled and kissed his little feet to make him laugh when she bathed him in the chipped enamel tub, picked blanket fuzz from between his fingers and toes. If he began to cry, even make a face as if he were *about* to cry, Rachel dropped whatever she was doing, lifted him in her arms, and from her apron pocket a cookie would appear. And when he threw himself on the floor, as he often did, kicking and screaming because he hadn't gotten what he wanted, Rachel rushed to his side and fed him *two* cookies.

Yussel's education began as soon as he spoke his first words. One evening, after donning his fringed prayer shawl as he did before every Sabbath meal, Moshe recited a blessing over the challah and asked Yussel to echo the verse. It was early spring. The house was cold. A fire burned in the cast iron stove, but the heat was spotty. Lena and Rachel wore long-sleeved woolen dresses and shawls over their shoulders. Rachel's wheat-colored hair hung in a braid down her back. Lena covered her cropped blond curls with a kerchief. She only wore her wig when she left the house. The kitchen table, usually covered with a checkerboard print cloth and chipped plates, was set with Lena's finest linens, a linen cloth her grandmother had embroidered in blue and yellow thread in a design of Hebrew letters (which neither Lena nor her mother or grandmother could read), and a Star of David.

Her grandmother's silver candlesticks, the most valuable items in the house, adorned the center of the table. A pot of chicken soup, with matzo balls floating on top, was on the stove, waiting to be ladled into the bowls, though Lena had already put one on Yussel's plate. "Repeat after me, Yussie," Moishe said. "'Blessed are you, our Lord—'"

But Yussel's response was to spit a mouthful of his matzo ball toward his father's face. Lena guffawed openly and Rachel giggled behind her napkin. Yussel, following the lead of his mother and sister, broke into laughter, kicking his chubby legs in his high chair and flinging more food around the room.

"You think this is funny?" Moishe said, picking the mush from his rust and gray speckled beard. He removed his round, wire-rimmed spectacles and took a cloth to wipe the goo off the lens. "He should spit in his father's eye, and you should laugh?"

"He's only a baby, Moishe. *L'azn 'ym zyya.*"

"Will you say 'let him be' when he's a man and spits in his father's face?"

Lena pushed her chair away from the table, wet a cloth in the bucket of water on the floor by the sink and, standing beside her husband, began to dab his prayer shawl. It was the first time she'd touched him since Yussel's conception. He looked up at her then, at her beautiful face, her flawless complexion, her deep blue eyes, striking even without the glitter they once had. He wanted to embrace her once again. How he loved her.

"He's just a baby, a *baby,* Moshe. Don't make more of it than it is."

"This is when the teaching begins. It is never too early for learning. *Now* he must begin to learn the love of God—"

She stopped rubbing, and he felt her body stiffen against him. He felt her resentment toward him. It was in her demeanor, the inflection of her voice, and especially in the fact that she no longer welcomed him into her bed. "Don't talk to me about the love of God! Next thing you'll teach him of the love of the *Kahal* and the *pushim*!"

"I understand your bitterness, Lena—"

"Do you? You go about your business as if Layzer never existed! Reading that Torah of yours, going to *shul* and sitting among those pious hypocrites, listening to their *drek*."

"What would you have me do, crawl in hole like. . . ." He stopped short.

"Like who? Who, Moshe? Say it. Like *me*."

"I didn't say that."

"But you were about to."

"All I meant to say is that we all grieve differently. Some. . .like you, are more. . .open with their feelings. Just because I don't show it on the outside, don't talk about it. . .I understand. I understand your need to protect Yussel, your heartache over Layzer. My heart aches, too."

"Does it?"

"What kind of question is that? Of course it does! Was *Layzer* not my son also?"

"*Was!* He's already dead to you?"

In all the years of marriage, both to Lena and to his first wife, he had never raised his voice in anger. And this, too, he tried to reason in the gentlest tone, but finally even he lost his patience. "My heart still aches for a wife and an infant daughter I lost in childbirth. Maybe I'm more used to losing loved ones than you."

She was about to protest, but he continued. "I'm sorry you married a poor, old, bent-over tailor instead of a handsome *balabos*, who could line the pockets of the *pushims*. But it's the tzar you should hate, not God, or me, or the community. Mark my words, Lena, no good will come of this anger and over-indulgence. Remember the biblical Job—"

"And look what the love of God did for him. That you even talk to that rabbi after what he said!"

"He didn't mean it."

"Didn't he? He should tie a rock around his neck and throw himself in the Volga like those 'pious' boys rather than get baptized?"

"He's old, getting senile—"

"He doesn't seem senile to me! And I'll tell you now. I'll tell you all now, especially you, Yussel. Listen to what I say." Here she faced the boy and spoke to him directly. "You are the most important person on this Earth. And whatever it is you have to do in this life to survive, you must do. What the rabbi and all the other holy ones have to say is *drek!*"

That Yussel didn't understand what she said did not matter, for it was a lecture she would repeat over and over through the years.

"Don't you see what you're doing? It's not just that the boy spit in his father's face, it's *everything*. It's treating him as if were a prince, giving in to his every tantrum, teaching him that he deserves more than anyone, that he's special—"

"He *is* special!"

"Of course he's special. He's precious to *us*. But not to the rest of the world. And it's the *rest* of the world he needs to be prepared for."

"He's just a baby, Moshe. *L'azm 'ym-zyya!*"

CHAPTER 2

LENA STOOD IN THE OPEN DOORWAY watching the cart until it turned the corner and was out of sight. She wiped the tears that were rolling down her cheeks. "*K'nayne hora*," she cried, making as if to spit three times in her palm so not to evoke the evil spirits. "You should go and come back in good health, my kaddishel."

It was the first time Yussel would be away from her. She had to let go. She knew it. But that didn't make it any easier. She'd lain awake all-night envisioning *khappers* behind each bush, imagining a screeching coach with every sound. Her fingers dug into the folds of her dress. A cool breeze snapped the wings of her babushka.

It was a crisp autumn morning, and so bright that even the beaten-brown wheat fields on either side of the dirt road sparkled in the sunlight. Snug in their woolen sweaters, Yussel and his sister swung their feet over the edge of the open-backed wagon. Wind ruffled their hair, lifting Yussel's curls, Rachel's long braid, and Moishe's beard, as the few wisps on his head were beneath his wide-brimmed hat.

"This is a big day for you, Yussele. You must be very excited,"

Moishe said, swaying left than right as the wagon jostled from one rut to another, and the horse kicked up dirt.

"I don't want to go to school."

"Just be a good boy. Heed the *melamed*, and you'll do fine."

"Mama said I shouldn't listen to the teacher."

Moishe sighed. "Your mother doesn't really mean that. She's only joking with you. How can you learn if you don't listen?"

"Uh-uh, Mama's not joking. She says the *alta cocker* will only teach us to say prayers, and it's all *dreck*."

Rachel giggled beside her brother. Moishe snorted. He had hoped that, after six years, Lena would have lost some of her bitterness, yet if anything it had gotten worse. To tell her son the prayers were shit!

He was beside himself over what to do with his wife. They both knew the importance of a good education, not only for its own sake itself, but as a means of keeping Yussel from the draft. Each shtetl was autonomous. So long as it gave the tzar his allotted taxes and met the military quotas, it could run its own affairs. How those quotas were determined were of no concern. Some shtetls used lotteries. Others went by birthdates. In his *shtetl*, scholastic achievement and piety were the deciding factors. Not to say that wealth and power didn't matter. Only a fool would believe otherwise. At five, Yussel was already two years behind those students in the private yeshiva who had begun their studies at three. As Moshe could neither afford to send his son to the favored school nor bribe the *pushim*, their only hope of keeping him out of the army was for the boy to study hard and win a scholarship.

"It's just as important to learn about God as is it to study geography," Moishe told Yussel.

"I don't want to learn geography either. I don't want to learn anything!"

"*Oy*! You want you should be a *nebbish*? A *Yishuvnik*? An ignorant *shaygetz*?"

A cluster of weathered houses came into view when they got closer to town, smoke rising from their chimneys adding a sweet pine scent to the air. Cobbles paved the hub, and the wagon stopped bouncing. Moishe tethered the horse to a pole in the village square, across the quadrangle where the one-room schoolhouse sat opposite the synagogue. Toting his book bag, two hard-boiled eggs for lunch, and holding tight to his sister, Yussel made his way across. It was a hive of sounds, smells, and activity. Water carriers stood in line to fill their buckets from a water pump. Chickens were squawking inside the market. Wagons full of merchandise from larger towns were pulling up to metal-gated storefronts, where women in black shawls were unlocking their businesses. Rachel stopped to look through the window of a fabric store, at the fine silks and brocades meant no doubt, for the more affluent residents who lived in stone houses. Through an open-door Moishe saw the tinsmith tying his leather apron around his waist. Judging from his wide girth, his business was thriving, and Moishe couldn't help but think that he'd chosen the wrong craft. Yussel stared at a peppermint-striped pole in front of the barber shop, then at a toothless man sitting on the steps of the poorhouse, gumming a bagel. The man was unkempt, as if he hadn't washed or changed his clothes in some time.

Rachel pulled her brother along. "It's not polite to gawk at people, Yussie. And besides, you don't want to be late for you first day of class."

"No." Moishe put his hand on her shoulder and shook his head. "Look at him, Yussele. That's what happens to boys who don't study."

The *melamed* greeted them at the door. He was stooped, and his beard, and whatever hair he had left on his head, were gray and wiry. Under a white shirt he wore *tsitsis* that hung over his belt. Yussel stared at the wrinkled face. He'd never seen so many wrinkles. If each one meant a year, the boy figured he must be older than Moses.

The teacher looked down at Yussel from behind wire-rimmed spectacles that sat half way down his nose, his hard eyes magnified behind the thick lenses, pointed his index finger at him, and said, "You're late."

"Make room for your new classmate," he ordered the students a moment later.

Two boys, close in age to Yussel, scooted away from each other, opening a small spot at a table. There were three tables in all, arranged in a U, with backless benches around the perimeter. The teacher's desk faced the children.

Yussel dropped his book bag on the floor with a thud and climbed onto the seat. He kept his sweater on, because it was colder in the schoolhouse than it had been outside. He took in his new surroundings. There were twenty-nine boys, including himself, some younger than he, though he knew they had to be at least five to attend the community school; some much older. The little boys wore yarmulkes; the older ones wore black felt hats; everyone had *peyes* hanging beside their cheeks. The walls, ceilings, and floor were all wooden, making the room dark and dreary. A high, narrow window did not let in much light. The only adornment were Hebrew letters and prayers encased in frames. A chalkboard was mounted on the wall in the front of the room. Before it stood a globe, a trash bin, a big oak desk behind which the teacher sat hunched in his swivel chair, and a long hickory pointer that Yussel soon learned was used more for caning than pointing.

Reb Weischel rose before his pupils. "Quiet!" he thundered, rapping the pointer repeatedly on the desk. The older boys stopped chatting and straightened in their seats. Some of the younger boys, the new students especially, were visibly shaken. Dovid, the little fellow sitting beside Yussel, began to tremble, his lips quivering. "There is to be no talking in this classroom! *Gornisht.* None! Is that understood? *F'arstyyn?*"

No one spoke.

"Is it?"

"Yes, Reb Weischel," the more senior boys answered in unison.

"Avrum, stand up and tell the new students the rules." Yussel watched the teacher's Adam's apple bob up and down his throat with each word.

Avrum climbed out of his seat, pulling one leg, then the other, over the bench, careful not to kick his neighbors. He was skinnier, and taller by a head, than the others. His belt was on the last hole, yet his pants that had been worn by his three brothers before him, were still bunched at the waist. Stubbly facial hair and red pimples covered his face. "Class starts at nine sharp," he said in a voice half man, half child. "Lateness is not tolerated. We have a one-hour lunch break from one to two."

"And?" the *melamed* asked.

"And we're to be back in our seats with our books open at three sharp—"

The hickory pointer cracked against the desk again with a loud, vibrating whistle. "Or?"

"Or Reb Weischel will cane us."

"Go on."

"In summer we stay until sunset. In winter the younger boys are excused at five. We older students stay till nine."

"Thank you, Avrum. You may sit down."

Avrum sat.

"Shlomo!" the *melamed* barked, "Is there anything you wish to add?"

Shlomo rose. He was sitting at the end of the bench opposite Yussel, so he didn't have to struggle, only shift to the edge and rise. He was shorter and stouter than Avrum. He didn't have pimples, but his ears stuck out. "We are expected to sit still."

The hickory stick was back at work. "Or?" the *melamed* asked.

"Or the *melamed* will cane us."

"Thank you, Shlomo. You may sit down."

Shlomo sat.

"Mutty! What else can you tell us?"

Mutty got up. Like the others, he was wearing a white shirt, open at the neck. He was shorter than Avrum but taller than Shlomo. "We are taught to read and write Yiddish. But mostly we study the Talmud. Every Thursday we have to recite a passage from the Holy Book, verbatim."

"And?"

"Those who do not perform adequately have their pants pulled down before the class and are caned."

And so it was that Yussel, fidgety, uninterested, and undisciplined, became intimate with Reb Weischel's hickory stick. More often than not, he could not sit for the Sabbath service. The first few years he took his punishment tearfully, but he took it.

Until one day he didn't.

CHAPTER 3

As usual, Yussel was last to take his seat and had to squeeze between his bench mates. Fat Herschel consumed most of the bench, and Dovid, though skinny, had a shoulder twitch that continually jerked into Yussel's chest. Normally, the proximity irritated him. But, still cold and wet from the downpour outside, he welcomed their body heat.

Half the class was sneezing. Little Shimon, the youngest of the boys, was coughing like a barking dog. Shlomo's eyelids were red-rimmed, his lashes crusted, and mucous poured from his nose. Zelik's snot was green.

The older boys sat across the table. Avrum, opposite Yussel, his neck scrunched into a sweater he wore over his white shirt, already had his book open and was *davening* as he read. "Ass kisser," Yussel whispered loud enough for him to hear as he elbowed his way into place. He got no response. With so much wind and rain battering the building, Yussel thought perhaps he hadn't heard, so he kicked his shin. Avrum looked down at the muddy footprint on his pants leg, then up, and glared at Yussel, who smirked as he muttered, "Oh, was that you? I'm sorry."

Avrum went back to his studies, ignoring the chuckle that followed.

Reb Weischel smacked his desk with his pointer. Startled by the sudden crack, little Shimon jumped in his seat.

"Quiet!" the teacher shouted.

Yussel moaned.

Reb Weischel whacked his stick again and glanced around the room, daring anyone to make a sound. Water from a leak in the roof plinked into a metal pail beneath it. Satisfied that the class was behaving, he turned to retrieve his papers. Yussel threw a spit ball at Avrum. When the *melamed* faced the boys, he found his favorite student leaning across the table, about to grab Yussel. "Avrum! What is this?"

"He threw a spit ball at me," he said, glaring at his attacker.

"Me?" Yussel said, innocence written on his face. "I'm just sitting here minding my own business."

"He's lying. He's always picking on me. Look—" Avrum showed the teacher his dirty trousers— "he did that just a minute ago."

"It was an accident. I thought it was the table. Boo hoo hoo," Yussel mouthed, wiping his eyes as if he'd been crying, when the teacher turned his back. "Poor Avrum. Picked on by boys half his size."

The students stifled their giggles.

The pointer slapped the table repeatedly. "That's enough! All of you." *Whoosh, whoosh, whoosh.* "Quiet! And Mr. Rabinowitz—" the old man scowled— "I'm watching you. "Now," he sighed. "The question of the day:" Morty and Jacob are partners in a business selling horses. A customer buys a horse from them. The next day he comes back, claiming that he was misled about the quality. It's older than they had said, the man insists, and a bit arthritic. Morty thinks that the customer may be right and would like to admit it, but Jacob disagrees. If Morty admits it, they will both lose out. What should they do? Shlomo?"

Shlomo wiped his nose and stood. He rubbed the peach fuzz on his chin. "I would ask the rebbe."

The teacher nodded. "OK. But let's suppose you're the rebbe. What would you do?"

"They should apologize," the boy answered in a gravelly voice, "take the horse back, and give the customer his money."

Reb Weischel nodded. "Tell us your reasoning."

"Well, the customer is always right. And even if in this case he wasn't, even if they would lose out initially, it would be bad for business in the long run if they didn't."

"Itzchak, do you agree with Shlomo?"

Itzchak stood up and thrust out his chest. "I agree they should give the man his money back. Yes, it's good for business in the long run, but it's also the right thing to do *ethically*. They sold the man damaged goods. That's unethical."

Reb Weischel nodded. "Very good, Itzchak."

A smile crossed the boy's face.

"Yussel," the *melamed* sneered. "What is *your* opinion?"

Yussel rose. "I think Morty and Jacob should tell the customer to get lost. He should have checked out the horse before he bought it. Tough for him."

It was lunchtime by the time they finished tossing around the question of the day, and Reb Weischel announced that, due to the weather they would not be eating outside. "Take this opportunity to study your *Mishnah*," he told them.

The boys grumbled.

"And no talking!"

When the hour was up, he clapped his hand. "Open your books to where we left off. Avrum."

Avrum rose and began to recite a passage while the other students sat at attention, following the text. After Avrum, it was Mutty. After Mutty, Menacham. After Menacham. . . . Slumped in his seat, Yussel rested his chin on his hands and moaned. If he had to listen to one more story about smiting Philistines and first-born sons, or Jewish persecution, he would puke. He hated it! At least it was Friday, and they would be released before dusk. Still, three o'clock couldn't come fast enough!

He shifted from one cheek to the other on the hard bench, trying to find a comfortable position. It was no use. His backside ached so, it didn't matter how he sat. Sitting on his hands didn't help either. His fingers were bony and dug into his welted bottom. His sweater cushioned the seat. That helped a bit. But when he removed the sweater he shivered in the cold. The first few years he'd only gotten canings on Thursdays, when he omitted a word in his presentation. Lately, it had become an everyday occurrence. He acknowledged he was no model student. He committed all of Reb Weischel's deadly sins: He talked out of turn, was the last in and the first out, never recited his assigned passage without a mistake, and, he had to admit, often made snide remarks under his breath. Yet it was also true that he couldn't sneeze without the old bastard whacking him. The other boys got their share (except for Avrum), but no one more, or with more passion, than he.

He stared outside. The one window, high up on the wall opposite him, was iced over. The rain had turned to snow, and while he watched the flakes accumulating on the sill, he thought about the hot chicken soup with matzoh balls awaiting him. He could practically taste it.

"Are we boring you, Mr. Rabinowitz?" the *melamed* asked in a sugar-and-spice voice, standing over him. "Perhaps another story would entertain you better?"

Yussel snapped to attention. Lost in the thought of his supper, he hadn't heard the old geezer creep up behind him. The smell of pickled herring on Weischel's breath had melded with his dream. But he did hear the *whoosh* of the pointer and feel the sting across his back that immediately followed.

"You didn't answer my question." The *melamed* gave his ear a clout. "Are we boring you?" The sugar-and-spice tone was gone. "Answer me!"

No."

He seized Yussel by his collar and pulled him backward. "Stand up when I talk to you!"

A series of loud thuds followed as, legs swinging, Yussel kept kicking the underside of the table. If not for Herschel's significant weight holding the bench steady it would have toppled along with Yussel, who hit the floor stinging-butt first.

"*Answer* me! Are we *boring* you?"

Yussel had barely met the floor when the *melamed* was beating him again, the sound of the pointer's steady *swish* magnified in the stunned silence. Yussel was curled into a ball, knees to chin, arms protecting his head. From the corner of his eye he glimpsed the old dog, the sharp-edged features and fringes of hair sprouting from the back of his head and face. *Whoosh.* "Are we? *Are we*?"

"*No.*"

"No *what?*" *Whoosh.*

"No, Reb Weischel."

"No, Reb Weischel, *what?*" *Whoosh*, *whoosh*, crack.

"No, Reb Weischel, sir. You are *not* boring me."

"Liar!" The *melamed* looked over him. *Whoosh.* "You dirty liar!" His voice rose an octave. "I've had enough of you. . .your insolence, your bad manners, your attitude. Enough!"

Yussel staggered to his feet, and in onc quick movement wrenched the pointer from Weischel's hand in mid-swing and lunged at him.

A collective gasp filled the room. Dovid's lip quivered. His shoulder went wild. Little Jacob began to cry. Thick clogs of snot mingled with his tears.

The *melamed* stumbled backward, falling over the globe behind him, the huge sphere clanging as it hit the floor, and crashed into the edge of his desk with a loud *thwack.* Loose papers fluttered off the table and came to rest against the wall, where, seeing a heavy-breathing, enraged Yussel looming over him with the stick raised above his head, the old goat crouched in a fetal position. His yarmulke had shifted and sat on his forehead. "Don't hit me! Don't do it!" he wept, wide-eyed.

Yussel studied the *peyes* bouncing as the man trembled. Then, without missing a beat, he bashed him over and over until his arms ached. He kicked Weischel's belly, stomped his arm, heard it snap, and kicked him again, this time in the mouth.

He might have kicked him to death but for the students who came to the teacher's aid—Avrum, Shlomo, and Mutty first, then four others, who together were finally able to restrain their classmate. Yussel glared at the old man's marred face, at his split lower lip and the blood running from his nose, into terrified green eyes, and snarled, "I don't think you've had nearly enough of *me* as I've had of *you!*" and broke the pointer in two.

CHAPTER 4

MOISHE DIDN'T FREQUENT TAVERNS. He wasn't a drinker. So when the bearded waiter, complete with *peyes*, *yarmulke*, and pad in hand, appeared before him in his dirty white apron, he ordered a coffee.

"Just a coffee? No vodka? Nothing to eat? We got cabbage soup to die for. Or maybe you like borscht? We got herring—"

"Just coffee. Thank you."

"Just coffee. He wants just coffee. . ." the man could be heard mumbling until he reached the kitchen, where the clatter of dishes drowned his voice. It was hot and steamy in there, the walls streaked with grease. A market was scheduled for the next day in a nearby town. In addition to the regulars, traveling merchants had packed the roadhouse inn. Thus, the ovens were working overtime. Between the fire from the stoves and the pots simmering on the range, the air felt wet and heavy. One worker, his shirt sleeves rolled up, was smearing preserves on slices of black bread while another deftly chopped cabbage. Sweat trickled down the cook's nose and dripped into the famous soup.

The dining room, on the other hand, was not hot. Despite heating stoves on either side of the hall, frigid air blew in every time the door opened. It was a dim place with poor lighting, stained wooden floors, and the reek of *makhorka*, the strong, homegrown tobacco. Yet the patrons didn't seem to mind. They danced and drank, oblivious to flakes of ceiling plaster dropping into their drinks.

Two Russian soldiers, notable for their crisscrossed white suspenders and the swords hanging from their waists, were standing at the bar, deep in conversation. The thinner of the two couldn't have been more than eighteen, for he didn't even have facial hair, just blonde fuzz. The other, older and taller, with dark hair that smelled of pomade, waved his thick arm and hollered for the waiter. "Hey. . .Yid, fill these glasses!" Turning back to his compatriot, he went on, "So after the landlord gambled his money away, he demanded three years' rent in advance. Those of us who couldn't pay found ourselves in the tzar's military. And here I am. Twenty years later with five more to go. But I'm lucky. The poor slobs unfit for the army went to Siberia to work in the metal mines."

The ear-locked waiter slowly made his way through the crowd to take their orders, purposely stopping at each table to talk to other customers, before he reached them. "Vodka for both of you?"

"Of course vodka."

"Why is it that all these shitholes are owned by Jews?" the younger one asked, his voice not fully changed.

"The tzar doesn't trust the rest of us to stay sober."

The mood was festive. A fiddler fiddled while Jews twirled in circles, waving handkerchiefs above their embroidered skull caps. Billiard balls clicked when they hit each other on a pool table. Men played cards and laughed in a far corner.

The tavern grew so quiet when a group of Russians in fur hats and sweeping mustaches walked in that Moishe could hear the man behind him slurping his soup. But a moment later as they began chuckling and patting each other on their backs, there was a visible release of tension, and the festivity returned.

Hunched over his brew, staring at the grimy oilcloth that covered the wobbly table, Moishe wondered how in heaven's name he could pay the *melamed* the hundred and fifty rubles a month—double the tuition—he'd promised, to keep Yussel from being expelled. He didn't want to think about it. And indeed, with all the noise in the room, he couldn't hear his thoughts even if he wanted to.

Yet though he might have been in the right place not to have to think, he was in the wrong place if he didn't want to talk. Mordechai Bligman spotted him from across the room.

"Moishe!" Holding his drink above his head so as not to spill it, he maneuvered through the fog of cigarette smoke, rubbing shoulders and stepping on clumsy shoes as he hurried across the plank floor.

"Moishe! What a surprise I should see you here!" He put down his *shtof* and pulled out a chair, the scrape hardly audible above above the clamor. From the smell of his breath and the flush on his face, the glass on the table had not been his first.

Just as he took a seat, one of the fellows hopping about on the dance floor landed on a big Litvak foot. "Hey Jew, watch where you're going!" the burly man shouted, wiping his chin where his drink had splashed. He wore goatskin boots, a red shirt worn outside loose velveteen trousers belted at the waist, and a sleeveless jacket.

"Watch where *you're* walking, *schmuck*!" the Jew yelled over his shoulder. He was considerably smaller than his adversary being only five foot three and about a hundred pounds lighter.

"Who you calling a *schmuck*?"

"You, *putz*," said the tipsy dancer.

No one seemed to notice at first. The room was so noisy. The little man didn't hear the chair smash to the floor or the cracking sound it made when it connected with his skull.

A moment later, the music stopped, squeaky notes dwindling off in mid bar. Russians surrounded the Litvak. The two soldiers at the bar left their *sthofs* half-full to take their place on either side of their landsman, and anxious Jews, wide-eyed with terror, encircled the one who had slumped to the floor. Having just emerged from the cellar with a keg of beer when the commotion started, the proprietor turned white. Dropping the ale where he stood, he hurried to the scene. There was always tension when the two groups were together. They'd hated each other for centuries. Usually they just hurled insults back and forth— "What kind of stupid religion is that that you can't ride on your Sabbath." Which was generally answered with, "What kind of a religion do *you* have when you pray to statues!" On some occasions when the drinking got heavy, the insults grew worse: "Your Jesus is a bastard, born of a whore." But that wasn't used too often, for it was generally followed by a punch in the face, broken teeth, and smashed windows. Except for the worst of insults, such outbursts rarely advanced to physical assault. In this case, however, the proprietor suspected a riot. Putting on his most genial smile and stretching his arms out as if his skinny limbs could stop the catastrophe, he pushed himself between the two groups. He was about fifty, bald, and wore spectacles that made his eyes look like saucers. His apron was stained and smelled of the beer that had splashed on him when he'd climbed up from the cellar. "Gentlemen, gentlemen!" he shouted. "Come, come!" He faced the brute, evaluating his tight smile. Built like a grizzly, he could easily have snapped him in half. "I can see you're a fine fellow," the owner said with a twitching lip. Then, pointing to the prostrate figure behind him, he explained, "He had too much to drink. He didn't mean—"

"What do you know what he meant, Christ killer?" With one swipe, the bear hurled him out of the way and, raising the chair leg high in the air, went to strike the little man on the floor again, who, having regained consciousness, was sitting up and rubbing his head. The door flew open with a blast of cold air, briefly diverting attention. The Litvak lowered the chair leg to his side. But a moment later it was in a swinging position once again.

"I know I have wrinkles," the proprietor shouted from the table where he'd landed, "but do I look like I'm two thousand years old?"

After a moment of silence, the crowd began to laugh. Instead of striking the little man, the bear, too, chortled. The weapon fell out of his hand, thumped and bounced on the floor. The group surrounding their inebriated friend quickly dragged him out of the way before the big lout changed his mind. But when the laughing stopped, the two factions glared at each other again. The peacemaker was in a sweat. Beads of perspiration dripped from his forehead. All he could think of was the cost of new furnishings and plates when his tavern was torn apart. "A free round of drinks for all!" he yelled. And the tension was broken. More barrels of vodka were brought up from the basement. The fiddler took to fiddling again, and dancing recommenced.

Moishe acknowledged his friend, when the commotion was over, as if nothing unusual had happened. "Mordechai. Such a surprise." But of course, it was no surprise at all to see the peddler in the tavern. It was common knowledge that he spent whole evenings draped over the bar.

"Health on your head, my friend." He gave Moishe's hand a hearty shake. "Coffee? That's all you're having? You should try the cabbage soup. It's to—"

"To die for. I heard."

"Or the borscht. . . ." Mordechai couldn't help but notice how haggard Moishe looked. Lines creased his brow. His eyes were sad and his complexion sallow. "What's wrong? Why so glum?"

"Eh. Small troubles."

"So long as you're healthy." The peddler raised his glass. "*L'Chaim*!"

In return, Moishe raised his coffee cup, which, by then, was barely warm, and tapped. A gentle ring passed between them. *"L'Chaim!"*

"Did you hear? About the Cossacks and the Jews? So these Cossacks see these Jews driving their wagons filled with *tchotchkas*. Smuggled, of course."

"Of course."

"The Jews see the Cossacks first. And as soon as they see them, they jump from their wagons, leave everything, and run into the forest. But just as the Cossacks reach the loot, the constable attacks them, snatches the pickings right out of their hands, and even takes their horses." Mordechai's eyes twinkled merrily.

Moishe reacted with about as much enthusiasm as a wet mop.

"This you should hear," Mordechai went on. "You know that bastard Solomon Gerstenfeld."

"The barrel maker?"

"The barrel maker? The *informer*."

"*Chazzer!*"

"To call him a *chazzer* is to insult the pigs! Here he is, on the High Holidays, the picture of piety, parking his *fat tuchus* on the pulpit in the synagogue, *davening*. Such moans like you never heard. Like he's being tortured on the rack. He makes the stone walls shake."

"That two-face."

"Two-face? *Three*-face! So much *tzures* he causes. Reports to the authorities who makes what money, who maybe sells what contraband liquor, who doesn't register his son in the register. Such money he takes in bribes."

"The *chutzpanik*!"

"So the town committee gets together and spreads this story that the *momzer* is responsible for chopping down some old trees, which, as you know, is forbidden." Mordechai pulled out his pipe and tapped tobacco into its bell. "A tragic end he should have."

"He should live a hundred years with only one tooth, and in that tooth he should have a toothache."

Though Moishe did not laugh as much as Mordechai, he at least put a smile on his face. "So how's business?"

"How's business? I sell a little of this and little of that, but not a lot of this or a lot of that. Just yesterday this *goy* buys one button. Can you believe it? One *button.* She spends an hour poring over everything in my cart. Turns over each bolt of fabric. Feels every purse. Smells every ounce of tobacco. Touches every notion in the tin, every single piece. And buys one lousy button. Then haggles over the price! All that for one stinking button. Finally, I say, Take it already. I sell it as cheap as beet soup, and you want it for nothing. Just take it. Take it! Let me get on my way already.' *Vey is mir!*

"But as they say," the peddler went on, "'If one is not able to shit, a fart is also good.' How about you? How's life in the tailor shop?"

"The same. They come in with pants I should fix, but not pants I should make. Ordinarily I would agree that a fart is also good, but I really need a big shit."

"So *that's* what's bothering you. Money problems."

"That should be the least of my troubles."

"Tell me!"

So it was that Moishe told Mordechai about the *melamed* wanting to expel Yussel and the hundred and fifty rubles a month he had promised the teacher to keep him in school, as well as his fears about his family's future: sweet but homely Rachel with no dowry to improve her looks, his son marching in the ice and snow if he didn't straighten himself out, his wife's fragile mental state.

Mordechai commiserated about the daughter's predicament. "Bad enough a pretty girl shouldn't have a dowry."

"She hasn't been the same since Layzer. Lena, I mean."

"How could a mother get over such a tragedy?"

"You should never know from such grief. A whole year she didn't talk."

"I should have such misfortune!"

Mordechai's wife was indeed a nag, the reason, no doubt, he enjoyed his vodka as much as he did. Moishe nodded and continued with his tale of woe. He told him about his wife's paralyzing melancholy after Layzer's abduction, how when she finally came to, she was a changed person, living for the sole purpose of keeping Yussel out of the army, and he worried that, should his son be drafted (which in light of the present circumstances seemed more than likely), Lena would go into that state again and never recover. "She's angry at the world: blames the Russians, the Jews, the rabbi, God, but especially she blames me."

"You got to admit the rabbi telling a grieving mother it's better her son should drown than be baptized is not exactly comforting. It helps like cupping helps a dead person. But why is she upset with *you?*" Mordechai leaned his elbows on the table and rested his fat red face in his hands. He blew smoke rings while he listened sympathetically, shaking his head back and forth, patting Moishe's hand every now and again.

"For not making enough money to pay off the informers, for believing in God, for reading the Torah. She wants I should do everything to keep Yussel out of the army, yet when I show my face in *shul*, like the pious Jew I need to be to satisfy the *Chalal*, she berates me. Because I don't weep openly for Layzer, she accuses me of not loving him. Then she accuses me of not 'loving' Yussel as I should. For not thinking he is the best of God's creations!" He took a sip of coffee and grimaced. Mordechai waved his hands and snapped his fingers to get the waiter's attention, and, when he came to the table ordered. ". . .You sure you don't want vodka?" he asked Moishe. "It's free."

"No. Thanks. Just coffee."

"More coffee for my friend here, and another vodka for me," said the peddler.

"She never said this directly," Moishe went on as if he had not been interrupted. "But I know it. I *feel* it. . . . She hasn't allowed me in her bed since Yussel was conceived."

"*Och und vey*! She expects you should maybe use your seed to grow parsnips?"

"She doesn't care what I do with my seed."

"And you haven't reminded her that it's a *mitzvah*?"

"How could you lie with a woman who doesn't want you?"

"I could think of a few ways. My wife never wants *me*. So what?" Moishe was thinking that he would be happy to sleep on his old lumpy couch if he were married to that loud-mouth Esther.

"I'll tell you the truth, Moishe, those are big troubles you got, not little ones. . . . So what's with the *boychick?*"

"As if you haven't heard. I guess everyone in the town is talking."

"Everybody in the *town*? Everybody in the *country*. In *China* they know already. I'm sure the *momser* deserved it. You remember *our melamed*?"

"Who could forget?"

"Remember we debated a whole day about the man and the cow? 'If somebody borrows a cow and the cow dies, does he have to pay the man who loaned it?' What normal ten-year-old is interested in a dead cow? And if we didn't recite the passages word for word? The smacks in the head we got? No wonder the *melamed* got a beating. I'm surprised he didn't get a beating a long time ago."

Moishe recalled that argument and, too, how the question had intrigued him. But he didn't say so. "It's true. But it had to be *my* son who did it? Such heartaches he gives me. It's even more than that. His selfishness."

"Selfish? What *boychick* isn't selfish?"

"It's little things like taking the last of the food without considering if maybe his mother or his sister, or God forbid his father, should maybe still be hungry. His ingratitude that his mama and sister should go without so he, the prince, should have. His temper when he doesn't get his way. I could say it's all his mother's fault for her over-indulgence. Yet at the same time, I'm responsible for it."

"What did *you* do?"

"I did *nothing*, that's what I did. Trying to keep peace, I didn't put my foot down. I allowed Lena to spoil him. Now he's out of control. It's all my fault. And now with this latest catastrophe. . .If Yussel ever gets drafted—-no, not *if*, *when*—Lena will never recover."

The fiddler still played, but the music was less energetic. Most of the dancers had left the floor.

"I love my son, don't get me wrong. . . ." Then in a whisper, he added, "But I don't *like* him." Tears welled in his eyes. Mordechai passed him a handkerchief he pulled from his pocket, and Moishe blew his nose.

"I'm not too fond of mine either. No ambition. Makes my wife *meshuga*."

"I wish my Yussel was *only* lazy. No. My Yussel beats up his teacher. An old teacher, no less. Not even a youngster. A bent-over old man. But nothing Yussel does or could ever do would upset my wife. Except getting drafted."

"Well, my son didn't do that, I admit. But only because he doesn't have the *chutzpah*. You know what the *goyim* say?" Mordechai downed a big gulp of vodka. "'You should have pigs instead of children—at least you could eat them.' But we don't even eat pigs. Our sons are our sons—whether we like them or not—so we have to do everything in our power to set them on the right path. In your case, if not for the sake of the right path itself, then to keep him out of the army. A major war is coming in the Crimea," he predicted. "And we both know what that means."

Moishe shivered both from the cold draft through the open door and the thought of Yussel fighting in the conflict.

"He could cut off a few fingers," Mordechai suggested. I heard of a boy or two who got out of the service that way."

They were quiet for a moment, Moishe looking even more worried than he had before, not enthused with the suggestion. Mordechai in deep thought, said, "I think I have a solution for you. I heard that the baron recently purchased expensive woolen fabric and isn't happy with his tailor. Maybe you should call on him."

CHAPTER 5

MOISHE FOLLOWED THE SERVANT through the black iron gate as another laborer, similarly dressed in a ragged coat and baggy pants, led his horse and wagon to the stables.

The imposing stone house sat before him at the top of a hill. While the steep incline left Moishe breathless, his escort pressed on exuberantly. Moishe wondered about his age. Surely, he was no youngster, but it was difficult to guess because his face, like his clothes, was stained and rumpled.

"Looks like snow is on the way," the man said.

"Yes."

Moishe panted. "I-I can feel it. . .in my bones." Beside the moisture, he still felt stiff from the long drive, and thanks to the wagon's continued rattle, pain shot from his buttock to his toes.

"Long ride?"

"About two hours," Moishe huffed.

"Came at the right time. A few weeks from now, when the snow melts, you won't be able to get through. The mud gets so deep you could drown. If you'd come a few weeks earlier, you woulda needed a sleigh. No way your horse coulda made it. 'Specially an old nag like yours. And then there's summer, when the dust'll choke ya, and the horse flies eat ya alive. . . . Though maybe ya woulda been better off."

Moishe'd heard stories about the baron, which he'd taken with a grain of salt—but warning from his workers? That wasn't good.

The rumpled-faced man looked up at the graying sky. "Hope you make it back before it starts."

"I guess you live close by."

"Not far. You musta passed it on your way."

Moishe knew exactly where the man was referring to. He had been traveling for more than an hour when he came upon the commune. He'd heard chickens squawking and smelled the rotting garbage and dung before seeing it. Three children, bundled in sheepskin coats, had been running after each other on a frozen pond when he passed. Two girls had had their heads covered with kerchiefs. The boy, bareheaded, his blonde hair cut in a circle and uncombed, appeared to be no more than five, yet Moishe knew he had to be at least eight, because he wore trousers, not a long shirt. All stopped to stare when he rumbled by.

With a round-domed church and a cemetery with simple Russian crosses, a dilapidated building he took for a school, and a collection of equally squalid wooden huts, it looked like be a typical serf hamlet. At first, he'd thought the village was on fire, for each dwelling had its door open, and smoke was pouring out. But then he'd remembered that they used "black" stoves for heat, stoves not attached to chimneys, because they feared sparks hitting the thatched roofs and setting them aflame. Because of that they kept their doors open so as not to be overcome. *Kanye izby*—smokey houses—-he remembered they were called.

The sudden appearance of six thick-muscled, snarling dogs when he neared the house, stopped Moishe in his tracks. They were secured to the porch, he realized after nearly losing his bowels, but pulling against their chains so violently he expected them to bring the thing down.

"You want to stay away from them," the servant said when he noticed Moishe trembling.

"I. . .I want them to stay away from *me*. . . . W-why would anyone keep ferocious animals like that?"

The man didn't answer.

A stout, middle-aged woman was waiting at the door. When they approached, the escort tipped his cap and wished him well before trotting back the way he had come, and Moishe, holding onto the rail for support, climbed the steps and crossed into the stone-floored entrance where the scents of saffron, cinnamon, and fresh bread wafted in from the kitchen.

The woman held her arms out to collect his coat. "So you're the new tailor," she murmured, eying his black hat and *peyes*. "He's never had a Jew tailor." She hung the cloak on a peg. "And he's had a lot."

He heard giggling from the hallway and, when he turned in that direction, saw two young servant girls, in white muffin caps and smocks, staring at him. When they realized he'd caught them, the braver of the two stepped forward. "I, er. . .never seen a man looks like you." She twirled her finger beside her ear. "With curls."

"Ask him to show you his horns," the other whispered from the hallway.

"He's a Jew, Elina." The plump lady sniffed. "And Jews wear curls. Now, don't you have work to finish? Surely, you haven't changed all the linen already."

"Yes, Ponia Malkic, right away." She lifted her hem and scuttled away.

"And you, too, Dalia! Don't think I don't hear you in there."

"Yes, Ponia Malkic. I'm on my way," the younger girl called, her skirts already rustling up the stairs.

Mrs. Malkic turned her attention back to Moishe. "You can wait in here." Her wooden clogs made a tapping sound on the ceramic tile floor in the vestibule as she shepherded him to the parlor.

Despite a warm fire burning in the brazier, it was not a cheerful room. With the candles in the sconces unlit, and the only window—narrow, mullioned, and near the ceiling—letting in a dreary gray light, it was dark. Icons with elongated faces hung on every wall. Moishe took a seat on a stiff-backed chair that smelled of French polish. A bronze clock, the face of Peter the Great, ticked on the marble mantel above the fireplace. Turning to leave, Ponia Malkic muttered over her shoulder, "I hope you're good at what you do. . .for *your* sake."

An hour later, the baron entered the green-papered parlor, his sharp-toed boots sinking in the Persian carpet. Moishe rose as quickly as his joints allowed upon his approach.

"Let us get started, then," the aristocrat said, stopping to fill his pipe from a packet of tobacco he pulled out of his worsted jacket. "Rosenstein, is it?" He took a deep breath, his cheeks sucking into his face, as he lit the bowl and blew out a cloud of hemp-scented smoke.

"Rabinowitz, sir." Moishe bowed. "Moishe Rabinowitz. If you will remove your jacket, I'll take your measurements." He retrieved his tape measure from the box of notions, which a servant had brought in earlier.

"How long will it be?"

"Just a few moments, sir. We don't want to make any mistakes. 'Measure twice, cut once' as the saying goes."

"We?"

"I." Moishe smiled weakly. Beneath his shirt, the baron wore a boned corset to pull in a big belly. Moishe cleared his throat. "Umm, I expect you will be wearing this, um, this—" Moishe touched the bone girdle— "under the suit?"

"Yes, yes, of course. You didn't answer my question."

"Sir?"

"The suit, the *suit*. How long before it's finished?"

". . .That depends on what exactly—"

"How long? How *long*? Just answer the question. I have an engagement next week. I expect it before then."

"Next week? That's rather. . .soon. I have—"

"Your responsibilities do not concern me."

"Yes, sir. One week."

When Moishe finished measuring and recording the numbers in his notepad, the baron called out, "Katryna!"

A moment later came a rapid clacking of wooden clogs on the tiles, and the woman who'd greeted Moishe earlier appeared. "Yes, sir. What can I do for you?"

"Katryna, show Rosenstein out."

"Follow me, Mr. . . .Ros—"

"Rabinowitz. Moishe Rabinowitz."

For the next five days, Moishe worked on the suit. Hour after hour, with his sleeves rolled up, his spectacles low on his nose, and a thimble secure on his finger, he hunched over the fine woolen fabric, sewing until his hands stiffened and his eyes blurred. On the sixth day, as promised, satisfied that the garment was perfect, he pressed and wrapped the finished product, and, with a loaf of bread, a hunk of cheese, and a bottle of water his wife packed for him, left for the baron.

"Be careful!" she called from the door, wringing her hands.

"I will," he answered, knowing her concern had more to do with it being the Orthodox Holy Week when, notoriously, the worst anti-Semitic attacks occurred.

"Come right home! . . . Please. Be safe," she murmured.

FOR THE FOURTH TIME IN THIRTY MINUTES, Lena pushed the shutters open and peered out. Digging her fingers into the folds of her dress, she turned to her daughter. "It's starting to snow."

Rachel dropped her knitting to her lap in mid-row. "What could be keeping him?"

". . .I'm sure he's fine. Probably got a late start."

"He only went to bring the suit. How long could that take?"

"Maybe the baron kept him waiting like he did the last time. And it's a long ride."

"He left at dawn, Mama. Even if it took two hours each way, he'd be back by now."

"Maybe he needed to make adjustments. The baron is a very fussy man.'"

"And nasty."

"Yes. That, too." Lena tucked her lower lip between her teeth. "It could be something as simple as. . .as stopping at an inn for a bite to eat."

Rachel rolled her eyes. "Nice try, Mama. There is no inn on that road. Even if there was, he wouldn't spend a kopek on himself, even to eat. Papa should have been home by now. It's not like him to be out after dark, especially away from the shtetl."

"He'll walk through the door any minute. You'll see." With that Lena went to look out the window again.

"The road is bad," Rachel continued. "Sugar's an old nag. Maybe. . .maybe she fell in a ditch and broke her leg!" She let out a long, loud breath, not realizing she'd been holding it. "Or maybe the cart fell apart and he's walking home. It's as dark as pitch." Her voice rose an octave. "Maybe he's sitting under a tree until daylight, in the freezing cold. Alone. Scared. Maybe his leg is broken." She grabbed her mother's arm. "Aren't there wolves out that way?"

The women stared at each other, wide-eyed.

MORDECHAI AND ISAAC LEFT THEIR WARM HOUSES without so much as a groan when Yussel pounded on their respective doors in the dark of night. Each had dressed in an instant. Mordechai, who had the sturdier of the wagons, insisted they travel in his. Isaac the Rabbiner had the sense to bring a bottle of brandy. "Foul play," Yussel heard them whisper when they thought he was out of earshot.

They'd hardly settled in their seats before Mordechai lashed at the horse with a long strap, and they were on their way. At the edge of town, the pavement ended. From there the road became straight and flat, no more than a logging path through dense forest thick with a woodsy, pine smell.

The wind tore at them, whipping through their coats and the blankets they'd draped around their legs. Isaac blew on his hands. "We should be happy it's freezing cold. At least it's passable. In a few weeks, the mud will so thick we wouldn't be able to get through."

"That's true," Mordechai said, "except that Moishe wouldn't have been able to get through either, and then we wouldn't have to be looking for him. He'd be home safe in his bed."

"Good point." Isaac buried his hands back underneath his blanket, and they both laughed.

On and on the horse plodded, alone on the road for the next two hours, ice crunching under the mare's hooves, and the wind, shrill through the treetops. Lanterns on either side of the wagon did little to light their way. It was so dark Isaac couldn't see Mordechai's anxious face or the frost crusted in his mustache, and Mordechai couldn't see Isaac sitting stoop-shouldered. They could only hear each other's chattering teeth. Snow blew off the trees and swirled in circles around them. They pulled their collars up and scrunched their heads deeper into their scarves, so as not to feel its sting.

Yussel sat in the middle, between the two portly men who took up most of the box, leaving him barely enough room to breathe. The cart rattled and bounced in and out of every ditch, rut, and gully, and they bounced with it—-Yussel first into Mordechai's coarse woolen muffler, which scratched his cheek, then into Isaac's elbow, which poked him in the ribs. Wolves howled. The horse was spooked. Neither man spoke. Yet they shared the same thoughts: Moishe would be dead—if he wasn't already—if they didn't find him by daybreak. And finding him by daybreak would be nearly impossible.

Mordechai shivered. "I should never have mentioned the baron," he said after a long silence.

"Like his wife said, 'A late start he probably got,'" Isaac said.

"Probably."

"Probably he's sitting by a nice warm fire, on one of those nice stuffed chairs in the baron's house, having a piece of cake and a shot of vodka, while we two—" Isaac turned to Yussel and patted the boy's shoulder— "three schmucks, you should excuse my language, are here freezing our *tuchuses*."

Probably," Mordechai agreed, not believing for a moment that that was the case.

"Papa doesn't drink," Yussel said matter-of-factly. "*Probably* he's *dead*."

"You have a crystal ball maybe, you didn't tell us about?" Isaac said. "Probably he's this, probably he's that. We won't know if he's this or that until we find him."

"*If* we find him," Mordechai said. "We can't even see. How are we going to find him?"

"*If* we find him! How are we *going* to find him! No, we'll find him already. He has to be on this road somewhere."

"So you also think he's dead," Yussel said.

"I think nothing."

"It's my fault," Mordechai complained. "It's all my fault. I should have warned him about that man."

"And who doesn't know he's a *paskudnyak*? You think Moishe didn't know? Yussel, did you know the baron's a nasty fellow?"

"Yes."

"See. Even Yussel knows, a boy of ten."

Wolves howled again in the near distance.

Isaac spoke in his *rabbiner's* voice, the voice he used, for a *kopek* or two, to settle disputes. "Let the wheel turn as it will, Mordechai. Neither you nor I can stop it. A problem Moishe had. A problem you tried to help fix." He purposely did not elaborate on the problem, for the problem was sitting beside him.

They were silent again, each in his own head: Mordechai feeling guilty and forlorn, wishing he'd minded his own business; Isaac planning Moishe's eulogy— "A good, honest man, a *mensch,* and a *Kasrilik* who never let poverty degrade him"; Yussel, thinking that this was the most exciting experience of his life and hoping he would get to see a wolf up close.

As the wagon creaked along, Isaac started to sing to break the tension. A popular and catchy tune, Yussel and Mordechai joined in.

Yussel saw it first. "Over *there*!" He stood and pointed, nearly toppling the wagon. "See. There's his horse. And his cart. It's turned over!"

CHAPTER 6

THEY HADN'T COME TO A FULL STOP before Yussel vaulted over Isaac, leapt to the ground, and ran to the overturned wagon. With lanterns in hand throwing small circles of light around them and their boots crunching on the hardened snow, Mordechai and Isaac stumbled up behind them. "Do you see him?" Mordechai called.

"Not yet. It's too dark. . . . Oh, *wait*! *There* he is, in a ditch."

"Is. . .is he alive?" Isaac asked.

"I can't tell." Yussel jumped into the gulley.

"*Oy, Gottenyu*!" Isaac gasped when, minutes later, he and Mordechai reached the scene.

"Must have been wolves," Mordechai whispered. "Look at those claw marks."

"Papa! *Papa*, can you *hear* me?" Yussel shook his father while Mordechai held the light to his face.

Isaac picked up the soiled, crumpled suit a few feet away. "Seems he never made it to the baron."

". . .Mm. . .Mm. . .Mordechai?" Moishe squinted and tried to shield his eyes with his arm. His glasses were gone. The faces leaning over him were blurred.

"Yes. It's us," his friend said. "Me, your boy, Yussel—-" he gestured to the rabbiner— "and Isaac."

Moishe tried to speak, but his words were clipped and too low to hear, so Mordechai lowered himself into the gulley and put his ear close to his lips. He looked even worse close up. His clothes were shredded and bloodied. Gashes ran nearly to the muscle, and one leg was twisted at a freakish angle.

Moishe's teeth chattered.

"You went to work for the baron today and never came home, so we came to find you."

Moishe managed to squeeze his friend's hand and give him a feeble smile. He'd lost his gloves, and his fingers were frigid, stiff, and blue. Mordechai rubbed them between his own, trying to bring them back to life.

"You're on the lumber road," Isaac added, "not far from the serf hamlet. Can't you smell it? Your wagon overturned."

"We thought you were dead," Yussel said.

Isaac let out a deep sigh, his breath a cloud of vapor in the cold air. "We never gave up hope, Moishe. We weren't going to turn back until we found you. Yussel, get the blanket, please. And rags. There's some under the seat," he shouted. Nearby, the sound of wolves.

"Is. . .is Sugar. . . ?"

"Your horse is near your cart. She seems unhurt."

A moment later, Yussel came back with the supplies, and he and Mordechai began to roll Moishe onto the blanket. "Yuck!" Yussel jumped back. "He shit himself!"

"Don't worry about that," Mordechai said. "We'll clean him when we get home."

"Yeah, but he *shit* himself. That's disgusting!"

Let's just get him warm, see to those cuts, and get him out of here."

Mordechai held Moishe's head, Yussel, scrunching his nose, put the bottle of brandy to his father's mouth, and Isaac cleaned and dressed the worst of the wounds.

"Careful with the leg," Isaac said as, swaddled in the blanket, they carried him to the wagon bed and secured the horse to the back.

DAWN WAS JUST BREAKING, the world still and silent beneath a fresh coat of snow, when they rounded the corner.

Lena and Rachel were outside where they'd been watching the road for hours. "Listen." Rachel stopped pacing. "Can you hear it? The clopping?" She tugged her mother's skirt and pointed to the silhouette against a purple sky.

Lena followed her daughter's finger, staring into the darkness. ". . .Yes! I see them!"

"I found him!" Yussel called out when they got closer. "It was just like Rachel said. The wolves!"

Lena threw her arms over her head and wailed. Rachel wrapped her arms around her.

Mordechai rolled his eyes and sighed. "He's alive," he assured them, pulling in front of the house. "We brought Dr. Sussman."

The physician climbed out of the wagon, his advanced years evident in his stooped bearing and cautious gait. "Ladies." He nodded somberly as he approached the women.

"How bad is it?" Lena mumbled.

"It's bad. I won't lie to you," he said in a *prepare yourselves-for-the-worst* voice. "Wolf attacks are particularly grave."

Rachel's gasp sounded much louder in the quiet. She squeezed her mother's hand so hard they could feel each other's bones.

Mordechai and Isaac lifted Moishe from the flatbed, twigs and ice crystals stuck to the blanket, and, with Yussel two steps ahead, lantern in hand to light the way, headed for the house. They moved slowly, Mordechai at Moishe's head, Isaac walking backward holding the feet, one deliberate step at a time so they wouldn't slip on the ice.

"He has some ugly wounds," the doctor continued. "You'll have to be meticulous about keeping them clean. We have to watch for infection. Often the animals have rabies."

In the darkness, no one saw Lena's face drop. She wrung her hands. ". . .Is he going to—"

"It's serious. I won't lie." The physician reached for his satchel of medical supplies, which he took wherever he went, and after excusing himself, shuffled off behind the groaning patient.

For the next week, Moishe lay on the couch before the fire, febrile, restless, mumbling incoherently. He couldn't have had better care if he were in the premier hospital in Vilna. Lena bathed him daily, sponged him with cool water when he felt flushed, changed the linens, administered laudanum when he seemed to be in pain, and slept in a chair beside him. Twice a day, and again whenever the dressing was soiled, she and Rachel attended to his wounds as directed by the doctor. After cleansing them with water and vinegar they'd boiled, then cooled, they let the maggots go to work debriding the dead flesh, applied an herbal salve the doctor had given them when the maggots had completed their task, then wrapped the areas with gauze they'd boiled and dried.

Word traveled quickly in the *shtetl*. By the first afternoon, the whole town seemed to know about the accident. All day, every day while he remained the sickest, the door opened and closed as folks came bringing prayers and food.

On the seventh morning, the fever broke. Moishe awoke to the sound of plates clattering, mumbled conversations, and an occasional titter. The smell of fresh bread and foods he could not identify filled the house. Confused, he opened his eyes and glanced around the room. Without spectacles, his vision was cloudy. But it was clear enough to see that the small space was crowded with neighbors. He saw Eli, the big wheelwright standing near the door, his thick-muscled arms crossed over his chest; Beynish, the simple-minded but sweet milkman; Hyman, the undertaker, grim-faced as ever; Lena's plump friend Sarah Fruchter and her husband Abrasha, the baker, who, Moishe assumed, had brought the pastries the visitors were devouring. At the table he saw his two stout friends, Mordechai and Isaac, laughing.

Still cold after gathering more wood, they were sitting on hard-backed chairs, warming their hands over the stove. Keeping the fire going twenty-four hours a day had depleted the already short supply, and Isaac was reconsidering his jaundiced view of the serfs' smoky houses. "It's not such a bad idea, when you think about it, Mordechai." His face was chafed from the wind. "The heat stays in instead of going out the chimney. Because they have no chimney. That's less wood you have to use." He rubbed a blister on his finger. "And chop. It's almost worth choking to death."

"Almost," Mordechai said. ". . .A party we're having?"

The two men turned toward the scratchy voice. "Moishe?"

"Papa! You're awake!" Rachel shouted, leaving the Fructers, she ran to embrace him.

"Thank God! We thought—*Got zol nur farmaydn*—you weren't going to make it." Isaac left his warm seat to pat his friend's shoulder.

"Ah. So this is a shiva call." Moishe said. "The undertaker, he's sad not because he expects I should die, but because I should live? A missed opportunity, he's thinking?" He smiled ever-so-slightly at the solemn mortician.

"We haven't seen a wolf attack in some time," Mordechai said.

". . .Wolf attack?"

"Just as well you don't remember," Isaac said. "We found you—"

"You didn't find him. *I* found him." From the other side of the room, Yussel puffed out his chest.

"Excuse me. Yes. *Yussel* found you," Isaac acknowledged. "In a gulley. Your wagon was overturned, and the wolves were still nearby."

"They were howling," Yussel added.

"Sugar! How's—"

"Your horse," Mordechai interjected, "a little *farpshadikt* she was when we found—"

"When your *boychik, Yussel—*" Issac nodded to the boy, who nodded back— "found her. But she's fine."

Yussel smiled.

"Like I was saying," Isaac went on. "You were on your way to the baron."

"I'd. . .I'd already been to the baron."

"No, Moishe." Mordechai shook his head. "Isaac found the suit next to your cart."

Lena pulled the quilt higher over her husband's chest. "Don't talk, Moishe. Rest. You're tiring yourself out." She held a glass of water to his cracked lips. He took a few sips, then motioned for her to take it away.

"I was *there.*" Moishe tried to rise, but it took too much effort, and he fell back on the pillow. "I gave him the suit. He tried it on. Said it made him look fat. Then he called me a useless, money-hungry Jew bastard and threw it at me."

"Alright, so you were on your way home when the wolves attacked you," Isaac said.

Moishe shook his head. "No. Not wolves, dogs."

Mordechai lowered his pastry. ". . .*Dogs*? What dogs?"

"He let them loose. All *six* of them. As I was leaving the property."

"Who let them loose?" Mordechai said. "What are you saying?"

"The baron. When I was leaving the house, he unchained them. All I could see were white fangs coming at me. I thought—" tears filled his eyes. His throat felt tight. "I thought. . .they would tear me apart. While he watched from the veranda. Laughing."

The room went quiet. Only a crackling of the stove, and Moishe's sobs could be heard.

"How is it we found you on the road?" Isaac asked.

"Somebody whistled," Moishe answered between sobs. "And the dogs stopped. Just like that. The next thing I knew, two big *goyim* were shoving me onto my seat in the wagon. Then Sugar got spooked and ran wild. And. . .the next thing I remember was you standing over me."

Yussel watched in mortification as his father, this grown man who had shat himself, wept. . .like a sissy boy. And in front of all those people. Yussel didn't know whom he was angrier with, the baron for the attack or his father for humiliating himself—and him. After a long silence, he said, "We have to go there—to the baron, *now*. Kill him—and his dogs."

The room fell silent again. Then, one by one, the men began to chuckle.

Yussel started each man in turn. "What's so funny?"

"We understand how upset you are, son," Eli said in a low-timbered voice. "We all are. But you can't do that."

"Why not?"

"We'll report it to the authorities," Hyman the undertaker offered.

"You're scared! You're all scared." Yussel jutted his chin toward his father, who was still bawling. "Well, I'm not! And I'll go without you if I have to." He stomped to the door.

"Sit down, Yussel." Isaac patted an empty seat beside him. "Let's talk."

"*Talk?*" Yussel's face twisted.

"You have to understand. He's the *baron.* He's a noble and a *Christian.*"

"And that means. . ?"

"It means you can't do anything," Beynish said meekly.

Isaac let out a deep sigh. "We're Jews. This is nothing new. We've been persecuted since before Moses—"

Yussel couldn't believe what he was hearing. "So we just, just let him get away with it? We don't do *anything*?" He pointed to his father. "Just cry like babies?"

"We'll report it the authorities," the undertaker repeated.

"The *goyishe constable*?" Yussel shouted.

"You don't understand—"

"Oh, I understand. I understand that you're all a pack of cowards. All of you!" He stared each of them in the face again, then charged to the door.

Eli stepped into his path as he ran, wrapped his big arms around him, and held him fast. "Settle down, son," he said in his most soothing tone. "Your father is going to be alright. That's what's important."

When Yussel stopped kicking, and Eli let him go, he stormed up the stairs.

When he came down hours later, he came down without his *yarmulke*—or his ear-locks.

On a bright spring morning six weeks later, when Moishe was able to hobble about, he returned to the baron's estate with the suit cleaned, pressed, and refitted, and presented it free of charge.

CHAPTER 7

IT'S GETTING LATE!" MOISHE SHOUTED from his wagon, where he was packing his daughter's soaps. "And be sure to dress warm! Siz zeyer kalt!"

A moment later, he heard the door close and then the crunch of her fleece-lined boots on the ice-coated snow. "Sorry. I couldn't leave without this." Rachel held up a metal can. He could hardly make out what she was saying, as the two scarfs she wore over her woolen hat that covered her face from eyes down muffled her words. But he didn't have to understand the words to understand her meaning. The fire pot: Filled with burning coals and hidden beneath her many layered skirts, it would keep her warm all day.

She secured the cylinder in the carriage, slid beside her father, and tucked a blanket around his knees. Even in his youth he hadn't been robust, but after the dog attack he'd become so frail she worried that the wind gusting across the plains would knock him down. "You shouldn't be out in this bitter cold," she said, pulling his collar up to meet his hat. "Yussel should be helping me to market, not you."

His brows drew together.

"Yes, Papa. I know. My brother would never get out of bed before the sun shines. The prince needs his sleep. Just ask Mama. And even if he did crawl out from under his feather comforter—God should strike me dead—he would be useless anyway." She sighed. "I wish you'd stop working for the baron."

"You know I can't."

"So you can bribe the *melamed* to keep Yussel in school. You're wasting your money. You *know* that. Yussel's only taking up space. He doesn't do any work. He's at the bottom of his class. You know when Reb Weichsel gives his yearly report to the town council, Yussel will be high on the list of draftees."

"I know."

"Then why do it?"

"For your mother. I have to do everything I can."

"Then bribe the informer instead. At least you'll have a chance."

"I can't."

She looked at him. If her scarf wasn't covering her mouth, he would have seen it was open.

"Paying to keep him in school is one thing," he said. "He can rise to the top. . .or not. It's his choice. But paying to have him exempt, only to have another boy take his place, is wrong." Moishe shook his head. "The army might be good for him. Make a man out of him."

"If he doesn't get killed first."

"*Oy*! Don't even say that!"

"Don't let Mama hear you talk about the army!"

"I might be a lot of things, Rachela, but a *meshugener* I'm not. A rabbi I'm not asking him to be. But a little *saichel* wouldn't be a bad thing."

"We should live to see the day."

A blast of wind nearly ripped Moishe's hat off his head. He didn't complain about the weather. Winter was a fact of life. And so was business. Rachel's humble wood-ash-and-lye soap was a big seller, especially at that time of year. With the rivers too frigid to bathe, the bath house open to country folk on market day, and the fancy store-bought Parisian cleansers too costly for peasants, her product flew off the cart.

"I wish you didn't have to work so hard, especially that you have to be deal with those *goyim*," he said. The wagon dipped and rose in the furrows and bumps of the road. "I don't trust one." The ground was slippery. Ruts covered with newly fallen snow were difficult to make out in the pre-dawn dark. He held the reins tightly, afraid the horse would step in a hole. He loved Sugar and wouldn't want to see her hurt—not to mention, if she broke a leg, God forbid, he couldn't afford another.

"Don't be frightened, Papa. The *goyim* I sell to are nice people. . *Smelly*, but nice." Her crooked nose wrinkled.

Moishe harrumphed. "A *goy* is a *goy* is a *goy*. My father thought they were nice people, too. Those same 'nice people'? The ones who came to his shop, smiled to his face, asked about his children? They burned his house down, raped his wife, and murdered his son. The very same 'nice people.'"

She squeezed his fingers, feeling his hand tremors through the woolen mittens. A nervous condition or nerve damage, the doctor couldn't say. Whichever, it was another effect of the dog attack. She looked in his eyes, reddened behind his spectacles, no doubt from his poor sleep and frequent nightmares. "Things are changing, Papa. That was a long time ago."

"Not *so* long ago."

Indeed, it had felt like yesterday when a loud thud woke him from his sleep. The wind had been howling all that night, so at first his father assumed a tree branch had broken off and slammed against the house. But when he felt a sudden heat and saw flames through the cracks of the walls, he had known: *a pogrom*. His father had pulled him out of bed while his mother grabbed the baby. The house was old and rickety, and it hadn't taken long for the wood to ignite. Flames had swirled everywhere; thick, acrid smoke had polluted the air; they couldn't see, hardly breathe. They had coughed, and choked as they crawled along the floor, hurrying to get outside, Moishe holding fast to his father's hand, his mother clutching his brother to her chest.

The stars had all but faded in the sky, a sickle-shaped moon hidden behind clouds. There had been no time to grab coats or blankets, so they'd stood there, huddled together, shivering in their bare feet: his mother, in a cotton chemise and ruffled cap, holding the baby; his father naked, as he had removed his nightshirt to wrap the little one in. Moishe's heart still pounded when he thought of that horrible day, the worst of his life. He could still see the tears running down his mother's face, could still hear her gasps, his brother's screams, the whoosh of the blaze and the dilapidated house crashing in upon itself.

And then—his mother's earth-shattering shrieks as the *goyim* tore the infant from her arms, threw him into the fiery rubble, and raped her. A sound like thunder. His father shot in the back as he ran to protect her. His blood so red against the snow, the smell of his brother's burning flesh. All the while the *goyim* yelling, "Christ killers! Kill the Christ killers!"

Petrified, his heart pounding inside his little chest, Moishe had run into the woods, squeezing through the bramble, as fast as his five-year-old legs would go. Stones and thorns sticking out of the snow had ripped at his bare feet, but he hadn't felt them as he raced between trees, his shoulders scraping against bark and branches until, out of breath, he crouched in a tree hollow. Night had turned to day, day to night and day again, before a neighbor found him curled up and shaking in terror.

The next thing he remembered was being in his uncle's house several streets away, which, for some unknown reason, had been left unscathed. Tante Esther was rocking him, as she rubbed some kind of ointment on his tiny feet by the crackling fire. His toes had stung and burned as they came back to life. "You will be living with us from now on, Moishe," *Fetter* Aaron had said, his voice choked with tears.

Later Moishe had learned that his mother died, too. Distraught and defiled after being violated repeatedly by one after another, she'd killed herself. Some said that she hadn't taken her own life but had been torn and battered so brutally that she bled to death on the frozen ground in front of her burning home.

He remembered feeling guilty for running away, for not saving her. He remembered wondering, even at that tender age, why he alone had been spared. And he still wondered, and still felt guilty.

He reached out and touched his daughter's face. She so resembled her grandmother, her namesake. She had her deep-set eyes and puffy lids, her bent nose, and her rosy cheeks, the same lanky build. Neither could be called a beauty. They were plain yet pretty in a wholesome way. At twenty-two, poor hard-working Rachel should be married and have a family of her own. But she had neither a dowry nor a pretty face. And even for observant Jews who were less obsessed with outward beauty she had been excluded by the taint of her brother's conduct. "No, Rachela," he said softly. "It was not so long ago. Some things will *never* change."

Each of the *shtetl* streets led to the town square, and all of them were jammed. They were behind a wagon filled with squawking chickens, which was behind one filled with grain. The one behind them carried pots and pans that clanged in the wind.

The sky was brightening as they drew closer to town. White smoke had begun to rise from the lopsided chimneys. The air smelled fresh. Merchants came from the countryside and nearby villages with their wares, while peasants who'd camped on the outskirts of town came to buy them. Snow had already turned to slush on the pavement. The iron-rimmed wooden wheels of the wagons made such a huge racket as they rolled over the cobblestones that they drowned out the sound of the clopping horses. Folks babbling in Russian, Polish, Lithuanian, and Yiddish were running up to intercept the incoming goods, looking to get the best picks at the best price.

Moishe helped Rachel position the wagon outside the bathhouse entrance, between the pickle man and the fishmonger. After he arranged the fire pot and got the coals burning, he headed to the coffee vender. "Black?" They bought the coffee more for the heat of the cup in their hands and liquid in their bellies than the bitter taste.

"I'll go. You wait with the cart," Rachel offered.

He pointed his chin to the people already lining up before him. "No. Stay here. I'll be right back."

The wind flattened her rabbit coat against her legs and ruffled her skirt. She sighed as she watched her father go, hunched over like an old man, dragging his left leg behind him. He was no youngster, had many years on her mother, but neither was he as old as he looked. He never complained. Not about his hard life. Not about his pain, though she'd seen him grimace when no one was looking. If Jews had saints, he would be canonized. Saint Moishe. She smiled to herself. She loved him so.

The brew merchant could always be counted on to be set up and ready before the others, for the bulk of his business came from dealers. Enclosed in a canvas tent, a great tin boiler kept hot by a charcoal burner—along with slices of honey cake, and bread, some smeared with butter, some with preserves, laid out on a plank resting on two sawhorses. Fellow salespeople were already dancing from one foot to the other and clapping their hands to warm themselves.

"Where's yours?" she asked when he returned with one cup.

"I already had mine."

She knew he was lying. He wouldn't spend a kopek on himself. With all the fine clothes he made for others, he'd been wearing the same two pairs of pants for as long as she could remember. He wouldn't even buy himself boots. Instead, he'd driven nails through the soles of his shoes so not to slip on the icy ground. While it might have kept him from falling, Rachel knew it did little to keep his feet warm.

"After morning prayers, I'll visit with Mordechai. See what *mishegass* he's selling today."

She kissed him on the cheek, just above his graying beard. "Whatever it is, you need it like you need a wart on your nose!" It was true—his friend usually sold junk, nothing worth buying, but if he sold rubies for one coin, her father wouldn't buy them.

By dawn the market was in full swing. The wagons were parked, the stands displaying their wares. Products from inside stores were outside on tables, each vendor pushing the merchandise.

Women, plump in their layered sheepskins and with baskets over their arms (keeping their money in handkerchiefs tied in knots or inside pouches in their petticoats), went from table to table.

As if immune to the cold, Gypsies in brightly colored skirts and blouses with puffed sleeved jiggled their tambourines, danced for coins, and offered to read palms. Mothers held their children tighter when they approached, and vendors watched their merchandise more closely.

"Towels!" a woman a few carts away from Rachel was hollering.

"I have such towels today. And such a price! You can't believe such a price."

"Fresh pickled herring over here!"

"Pickles! Pickles! Try my delicious pickles!"

Moishe stopped at the preserve table after morning prayers. The treats, ranging from pickled tomatoes to apple jam, were arranged in groups: vegetables with vegetables, meats with meats, fruits with fruits. All were in calico-covered tin jars. Mrs. Shilamova always set up in the same place, close to the synagogue, where bearded congregants were coming out in drips and drabs behind her.

"Good morning, Mr. Rabinowitz." She smiled. Her words came out in a cloud of vapor. She was bundled in a long woolen coat and wore gloves without the fingertips. She was short and squat but had a pleasant face.

"Good morning, Mrs. Shilamova." He doffed his wide-brimmed hat. "And to you too, Hava," he said to the little girl who was peeking out from beneath her mother's skirts. "Are you keeping nice and warm under there?" The tot nodded, then went back under the skirt, where she sat beside the bucket of hot coals.

Mrs. Shilamova produced two jars wrapped in newspaper from under the table. "Pepper jam. Your wife's favorite. They were going fast today, so I made sure to save them for you."

He bought them every week. Lena loved the jam. She could eat it like a meal. "Thank you."

"My pleasure. Regards to Mrs. Rabinowitz."

"And mine to Mr. Shilamova."

"Until next week then." She smiled.

Moishe shouldered his way through the crowd, tipping his wide-brimmed black hat and excusing himself whenever he bumped into someone. It was close to noon by then. The sun had warmed the day, but it was still frigid. His chapped cheeks were the color of the pepper jam he carried. Hungry horses had been unharnessed and were eating oats out of jute feed bags. There were more Gentile merchants on this part of the square. Over in a far corner hogs were grunting and squealing as big strapping men struggled to get them on the scales to be weighed. Moishe could smell the dung through the scarf wrapped around his nose.

Mordechai was set up in his usual spot next to the Russian Orthodox church at the other end of the town square. "What's going on over there?" Moishe pointed to the council hall, where a group of men seemed to be arguing.

"Who knows? Every week there's another rabble rousing instigator."

"Do you have a ribbon to go with his green?" a plump woman in a shawl-collared coat asked the peddler.

Mordechai riffled through his cart until he found a similar color grosgrain braid, which he held up for her to see. "Here you go. A perfect match."

"Um. . .No. Too coarse. Do you have anything—"

"Attend to your customers." Moishe waved. "I'll be back later."

Mordechai nodded. "Here's something that will match. . ."

A cold wind whipped across Moishe's face, lifting his ear locks as he made his way to the group of head-shaking men. He buried his face in his scarf, held onto his hat, and bent into the wind. His black coat billowed behind him.

"'It is estimated that a quarter of a million Russian soldiers, sailors, and civilians were killed in the eleven-and-a half-month siege of Sevastopol,'" he heard a young man read from a newspaper. A communal gasp went through the crowd. The man was standing on a step well above street level, leaning against the building. He was clean shaven and looked to be in his twenties. His cheeks were red and chafed, and he wore a frayed tweed cap with ear flaps that met the standing collar of his equally frayed coat, and a muffler wrapped several times around his neck.

"'Except for the officers,'" the man went on uninterrupted, "'who have their own markers, they're buried in mass graves. This conflict is like no other. It is on a global scale and has a huge significance for Russia, and that area of the world stretching from the Balkans to Jerusalem, from Constantinople to the Caucasus!'"

"What is this war about anyway?" a grizzled old man called out.

"What they're all about?" a man beside him yelled. "*Bupkus!*"

There was a loud chorus of agreement.

"Depends on who you ask," the newspaper reader said with a modest laugh. "The trigger was a quarrel over some church warden's keys. Who should have the first chance to carry out Good Friday services on the altar of the Calvary inside the church of the Holy Sepulcher, the place where the cross of Jesus was supposedly inserted into a rock."

"And our sons should have to die over a set of keys. Could you believe it?"

"I believe it," another man agreed.

"But of course, each power has its own real motives," the young man on the steps added. "The Turks are fighting to maintain their empire against us Russians—"

"*Those* Russians, not *us* Russians. I don't consider myself a Russian," someone else hollered.

"*The* Russians," the newspaper reader acquiesced, "claim to represent Orthodox Christians. The tzar wants to defend them against the infidel Muslims."

"That bald-headed *heslekh*! So our sons are being slaughtered to protect those *goyim* who slaughter *us*?"

"Lower your voice, Isaac. You want some spy should hear you and take you away?"

"My *son* may be one of that quarter million!"

"The British are in this war too, aren't they? What's their story?"

"The British claim they went to war to defend the Turks against the Russian bullies. Truth is they are rivals in Asia. And the French want to reassert their dominance."

"Read the letters!" someone shouted. "Read the letters!"

Several men were waving their correspondence above their heads. The *shtetl* did not have a mail service, but for a fee of three kopeks per piece (and the five-kopek cost of the stamped envelope), Yonkel and Ezra would ride to the nearest post office, about fifteen kilometers away, once or twice a week.

Manny Greenbaum, the town's blacksmith, put a kopek in the scribe's tin plate and handed him his son's.

My dearest father, the scribe read. *I wish I could tell you that all is well. All my letters should begin with the same words: Nothing new. Which is to say we dig trenches every day, and every night we sit and drink around the campfire. But we are to go into battle tomorrow, and we are outnumbered and under-armed.*

We are constantly being shot at. Some of the men—boys, I should say—are going mad. One man decided to leave, and he was shot and killed as soon as he stood up. We don't know if it was the enemy or our own officers. We can only guess, because they are shooting deserters in the back. And if the enemy or the commanders don't kill us, the diarrhea will. Every day soldiers are taken to the hospital. Those are the lucky ones. Most are just left on the battlefield to die.

I love you, Papa. Tell Mama I love her, too. Pray for me.

A long, somber silence fell over the crowd. And then one by one other men held up their letters and dropped their kopeks onto the reader's plate.

Moishe didn't stay to listen. He'd heard enough.

Surely many more men will be drafted to replace those lost. *And surely one of those will be Yussel.*

CHAPTER 8

FROM THE MOMENT THE DOOR SQUEAKED OPEN, it was obvious Moishe was upset. He didn't greet his wife as usual or show happiness at being home. He didn't ask her about her day, even though he passed her in the kitchen where she stood hovering over the paraffin lamp. The temperature had dropped since the sun set, and a draft through the gaps around the old wooden walls caused the flame to flicker. Heat from the stove hardly reached beyond a short radius. Beads of sweat covered Lena's forehead, yet her kerchief billowed and snapped behind her. Without a word, Moishe took the jar of pepper jam from his coat pocket and placed it on the stand by the sink beside a basket of turnips and onions.

Only a few feet away, at the wobbly kitchen table, Rachel, wrapped in a shawl, counted and separated the coins she'd earned selling her soaps. Lena looked to her for a clue to his mood, but her daughter shrugged, the expression on her face that said she didn't know.

Lena attached the globe to the lamp and adjusted the wick. "What were you doing out there all this time?" she asked, her face elongated in the pale light. "Rachel came in almost an hour ago."

"I was tending to the horse. . .cleaning out the stall."

"Wasn't Yussel supposed to do that today?" Rachel said.

"He woke up with a cold," Lena added hurriedly.

Dragging his bad limb behind him, Moishe went to the table where, keeping his good leg bent, the other rigid, and grabbing the tabletop for support, he slid onto a spindle-legged chair, feet facing the heat. After removing his shoes he tried to rub his throbbing, tingling toes back to life.

Lena laid a hot mug of kvass before him. With chafed cheeks and chattering teeth, he looked as if he'd just ridden in from Siberia. "This will help thaw you out." Only one percent liquor, the traditional fermented brew commonly made from black or rye bread was the closest to an alcoholic beverage Moishe ever touched. He closed his fingers around the warm cup and inhaled its scent of strawberry, raisin, and mint, letting the steam moisten his face. After a few minutes of warmth, crusted ice in his pants cuffs and beard began to melt, and his whiskers and trousers dampened. "Our daughter is quite a business woman," Lena said.

"You should have seen the line of people around my cart," Rachel added, as if the heap of copper and silver before her wasn't affirmation enough.

Moishe didn't respond, just sipped his drink as he stared at an embroidered Star of David, in different shades of blue, behind his daughter's head.

"Moishe?" Lena put a hand on his bony shoulder, tight under her grip. "I couldn't send him out in this weather. He's not feeling well."

"Where is he?" he asked. "We need to speak to him."

"Really, Moishe." She sighed. "It's *my* fault, not his. He was ready to go. *I* told him to stay. Blame me."

"Rachel, call your brother, please."

Rachel stopped her counting, and skirt swishing against the rushes on the floor, went to the bottom of the stairs, where she shouted for Yussel to come down. Without her rabbit coat and multiple layers of clothing, she looked as skinny and straight as a reed. Flat-chested and thin-hipped, her only curve was the bump on her crooked nose.

Yussel plodded down draped in a blanket, red-nosed and glassy-eyed, his golden curls tousled from sleep. "What?" he asked in a raspy voice.

Lena hurried to his side to feel his forehead, first with her palm, then the back of her hand. She put her ear to his chest and listened. From the day he was born, his slightest malady had twisted her stomach as her imagination fueled with wild what-ifs: If he had a soft stool he must have cholera; a pimple on his face the pox; if his color seemed yellow in the dim evening light, certainly he had typhus; if he slept too *much,* he must have cancer; too *little,* surely he was getting sick. In fact, he did suffer from constipation, an affliction, no doubt, having to do with using the outhouse.

"*Baruch Hashem*!" Lena sighed, finding him cool and without pneumonia.

Moishe pointed to an empty chair. "Sit. We need to talk."

"About what?" Yussel asked.

Lena faced her husband. "Can't you see he's not feeling well? Could I let him go out in this weather?"

"Sit." Moishe gestured with his raised chin. "You, too, Lena."

Rachel, back in front of her day's loot, rested her hands in her lap.

Yussel eyed a crusty prune tart on a plate next to his sister's money. "You want that?" he asked.

"That's why I bought it."

"Did you buy one for me?"

"Why would I do that?"

"Because I'm your baby brother." He made a pitiful face.

"Give me the money next time, and I'll buy you one."

He studied the three stacks of kopeks. "You're Miss Moneybags, not me."

"If you work as hard as I do, get up before dawn, and stand in the freezing cold all day, you'll be *Mister* Moneybags. Then you can buy one yourself."

Moishe cleared his throat, lowered his legs and leaned forward. The smells of the market were still on him: pickles, horseradish, lemon and almond from fresh cakes, and now the perfume of fresh dung from recent stable cleaning. "I heard some disturbing news today," he said.

They all fell silent. Only the crackle of burning logs and the hiss of the kerosene lamp were audible. Apprehension grew on his wife's face. A lecture about Yussel's laziness was routine, but "disturbing news."

"News from the Crimea is not good."

"What does that have to do with us?" Yussel said, wiping his nose with a snuffle.

Lena turned pale, and she began to twist the handkerchief in her apron pocket.

"It has *everything* to do with us, Yussie." Moishe told them what he'd learned about the Eastern War, the siege of Sevastopol, the tremendous Russian losses, and the heart-wrenching letters the boys at the front wrote home. He looked at his wife, who sat with her head bowed, her hands clenched, fear all over her face.

"So?" Yussel wiped his nose again.

"So?" Moishe looked at him. "So you can be sure the tzar will be drafting more men—and boys—to build up his army."

Yussel shrugged. He was a sturdy youth, well-built and taller than other boys his age. His muscular shoulders rose beneath the quilt he was wrapped in. "I'm in school. We have nothing to worry about."

Moishe stared at him as if he didn't believe what he was hearing. "You're at the bottom of your class! The bottom of the bottom! When the *Khalal* give their list, who do you think they will choose—Avrum?"

Yussel laughed. "Could you see that *shmendrik* with a sword?" He got up to mimic Avrum walking around the room, sniffling, slumped, pretending to lift a heavy sword and not getting it past his knees.

"That's uncalled for, Yussie," his father said.

"Could you picture that pimply-faced *zhlub* swinging a weapon? He'd fall over."

"He's not a *zhlub*!" Rachel snapped. "Not only was he the top student, but he's studying to be a Talmudic scholar!"

"A Talmudic scholar! So he can argue for hours on end whether a widow can eat a pig's foot if she's starving to death. That's what your third pile of coins is for, isn't it? One for the house, one for you, and one so you can marry the *toches-lecher*? Yes, Mr. Teacher. Can I kiss your *ass*, Reb?" He made exaggerating kissing sounds. "So you can support him while he spends his life studying all that *dreck!*"

"Look who's talking, Mr. Lazy Bones himself! And it's my money. I can do whatever I like with it. When you make money—God only knows when that will be—than you can do whatever you like, too!"

"*Zol zein shtil*! That's enough!" Moishe banged the table with his fist. The kopeks Rachel had separated into piles jumped and chimed. "This is nothing to do with Avrum. Avrum's not going anywhere. It's about *you*. Are you not *understanding* what I'm saying?"

"If I have to be like Avrum to stay out of the army, I'll enlist now!"

Lena jumped to her feet and screamed, "No! No, no, *no!*"

Moishe motioned for his wife to relax, and she resumed her seat. "Everybody calm down. I went to see Mordechai before coming home. The way he sees it, we have three options," and up went his index finger with more at the ready. "To go to the army—"

"*No!*" Lena screamed again. "He is not going to live in some ditch—"

Moishe's second finger went up. "Or. . .he can chop off a finger."

"Chop off my *finger?*" Yussel screamed.

"Or a toe."

Lena was about to comment when Moishe continued, "Or. . .we can get him married."

"*Married?*" Yussel and Rachel cried out simultaneously.

CHAPTER 9

When Lena saw the *shadkhn* trudging along the edge of the path, with her black dress lifted to her calves so not to get it splattered, she put up the tea to brew. Spring had finally arrived, and with it the heavy rains that melted the snows and left the unpaved streets awash in mud. She had been expecting the matchmaker, so the table was already set. On a clean cloth, she'd laid her least-chipped dishware and freshly picked Lithuanian blues, aromatic inside an empty jar of pepper jam, and arranged freshly baked *mandelbrot* on a pretty platter.

The blue sky and pleasant breeze did little to dispel the bleakness of the tired *shtetl*, where gray-weathered houses and collapsing fences were everywhere.

The older woman stood at the entrance, scraping the muck off her shoes on the straw doormat. Despite her best efforts, she had been unable to keep clean. Wide swaths soiled her clothes, her cotton stockings were a mess. A few splotches had even managed to land on her bodice. She flapped her skirt as if she were shooing roosters out of a hen house. "I'm so sorry about the streets," Lena said. "Come. I'll help you get clean."

"The streets are *your* fault?" The woman kept to her flapping.

"I'll get a wet towel."

"A wet towel I'll take." She stepped over the threshold. The house was dark as a cave compared to the noon brightness.

Lena hurried inside and returned with a soapy rag. Leaning over and grabbing the other's hem, she began to scrub the dirt away.

"When it's cold, we complain," the *shadkhn* began. "It's so cold I wish it was summer. Then summer comes. And we complain. *Oy*! It's so hot I could die. The mosquitoes, they're eating me alive! Why can't it be spring all year round. But when spring comes, and the weather is perfect, and the smell is *beautiful*—" she took a deep breath and inhaled the scent of budding trees. "Such music the birds make. But the roads are bad. So much mud. And we complain, I wish it was winter. Maybe the Lord should make us another planet to live on."

"Did you find a girl for my Yussel?"

"Ah, *mandelbrot!*" The older woman's eyes widened. Dirty dress and wet towel forgotten, she followed her nose to the table. She was as round as she was short. When she sat, her feet did not meet the floor. It was cooler in the house than outside. She pulled her shawl tighter around her substantial bosom. After tucking the corner of her napkin between the buttons of her dress, she reached for a biscuit with short, round fingers.

"So I saw the doctor about my aches and pains." Her head shook in dismay. "You know what he tells me? He tells me, 'You're getting old.' Like I don't know already that I'm getting old? 'So what should I do?' I ask him. 'Take the alternative and *die*?' He laughed. He thinks I'm funny." Another shake of her head. Another bite from the biscuit. Pointing to Lena with the remains of the uneaten cookie, she went on, her words garbled by chewing. "If my Shmuel were still alive—may he rest in peace—I wouldn't have to work so hard. Now that was a man, my Shmuel. A *mench* if there ever was one. . . . You know, *mandelbrot* is my favorite."

Lena poured tea, making steam and a trickling sound when it hit the cup. "So, Mrs. Rifkin—"

"What's this *Mrs.* business? After all these years, all the matches I made for your family, we're not on first-name basis? It's *Pearl.* Call me *Pearl.*"

"So, Pearl, did you find a nice girl for my Yussel? She has to come from a good family." Lena kept stirring her tea, the teaspoon clicking the edge of the cup.

"A nice girl? A good family? Now Rachel's a *nice* girl. A *jewel.* A little old already. But a hard worker. Men like that. Did you hear that Hershel Greenbaum's wife is very ill?" Pearl made as if to spit to ward off the evil eye. "*Pooh pooh* pooh. May she live to be a hundred. But it doesn't look good, I tell you." She leaned in closer to Lena as if telling her a secret. "Cancer. That's what the doctor says. Such a curse. The poor thing. Terrible. Terrible. She looks terrible. You wouldn't believe it. Such a pretty woman she was." She again made as of to spit. "I tell you, it's not going to be long. Not that I wish it. God forbid! And four children she's leaving. Without a mother." She took another bite of the biscuit and gave Lena a knowing eye.

"Yes. I'd heard about it. I'm sorry to hear it. But can we talk about *Yussel*? Have you found anybody for *Yussel*?"

"Did I find? Don't I always find? Am I not the best matchmaker in this part of the country?"

"And?" Lena held herself back from reminding Mrs. Rifkin that it had been two months since she'd begun looking.

Pearl shook the napkin, propelling crumbs to the rush floor.

"*And?*" Lena's eyebrows furrowed.

"She better not be fat and ugly!" came Yussel's voice from upstairs.

"And who are you, the tzar?" the busty visitor shouted back. "You think gorgeous girls are just waiting in line for *you*? Like such a good catch you are? You who has a . . .history and refuses to wear peyes? If she has warts on her face, you'll marry her!"

If Lena was annoyed with the matchmaker's response to her son, she didn't let on.

"No, I won't!" came the voice from upstairs again.

Pearl turned her attention back to Lena. Lena sighed. "Pearl. Please *tell* me. Who did you find?"

"No pox marks either!" Yussel yelled again.

"She can't be fat; she can't have pox marks. *Oyoyoy*! So much business I have, you wouldn't believe. Everybody is looking for a bride. He not only wants a bride, he wants I should find him a beauty."

"It's this Eastern war," Lena put in.

"And the rumors."

"Rumors?"

Pearl reached across the table and took another pastry. "I like that you're not stingy with the nuts. Mrs. Gogglestein, now *she's* stingy with the nuts. Five matches I made for the Gogglesteins, and she can't add enough nuts in her *mandelbrot*. Of course she *can*. What is it to add a little of this or that. It's just that she *won't*."

Lena realized that she should have set some of the treats aside for her husband. Surely, there would be none left when he got home. She only baked for special occasions, as it was costly and time consuming. Nonetheless, she put the smile back on her face and pushed the platter closer to her guest, who continued talking with her mouth full. "The rumors?"

"Yes, yes, the rumors. The tzar—may he get an itch where he can't scratch—wants to change the rules about married men not being drafted. Bad enough he takes our boys at all. Now, as of next month, he wants to take married men, too."

Lena chewed her lip.

"Not to worry." The matchmaker patted the other's course hand. "It starts next month. Anyone married after next month is in trouble. But luckily you called me. And here I am! Come to your rescue. A thank you, Pearl, would be nice."

"Thank you, Pearl."

Pearl gave a don't-mention-it nod. "So naturally everybody wants to get their sons married before the rules change."

"Naturally." Lena worked her handkerchief into twists and knots. She wondered if this was all leading up to a higher fee. Not that it mattered. Nothing mattered if it kept her son out of the army. Good thing she added those extra nuts. "Take another." She pushed the plate yet again.

The matchmaker stopped for a moment to chew. ". . .Add to that, the need to replace all those poor dead soldiers—-*Gott in himmel!*"

"Poor boys!" Lena was positive this was going to cost her more money. The thought of all those young boys dead and left dying on the battlefield set her trembling.

"*That's* what is sending every bachelor, young and old, nearsighted and lame, to the *chuppah*." Directing her voice upstairs, Pearl screamed, "Even *pockmarked* daughters are already promised! . . . So you see," the *Shadkhn* concluded to Lena, "why too many choices we don't have. Gittel Mishkin—"

"Gittel Mishkin? Daughter of Chaim and Etta Mishkin?"

"One and the same. I know what you're thinking. Such a lucky thing should happen to you!"

But that was not what Lena was thinking. What Lena was thinking was, What could that *macher* and his loudmouth wife want from us?

CHAPTER 10

"MAZEL TOV!" SHOUTED THE CONGREGANTS as the wineglass shattered beneath Yussel's shoe. He turned to his wife, the scent of her perfume filling his nostrils. Hidden behind a thick white veil, her face was a mystery. The *shadkhn's* words rang in his ears: *Even the pockmarked girls are promised*. It did not bode well that her parents and brother were homely. Holding his breath, he began to unveil her.

Ordinarily, wedding ceremonies took place outside. The bride would follow a fiddler, fiddling and dancing, from her house to the synagogue square, where the groom and the rabbi waited. Everyone in the *shtetl* would be invited, and the revelry would last a week. But with so many marriages taking place, often simultaneously, because of the new conscription laws, the usual merrymaking had been dispensed with. Though the table was set with the traditional wedding treats of sweet-and-sour fish, chopped goose liver, pickled meat, noodle pudding, and challah, there were no dancing musicians, and only family and close friends attended.

Chaim Mkin held up his glass and declared in a deep baritone that would have been the envy of any cantor, "A toast to our children!"

"*L'chaim*!" the small group cheered.

"*Mazel tov*, Moishe!" Mordechai clapped his friend's shoulder with the hand not holding his drink. It was his third. His cheeks were reddening, and his speech beginning to slur. "Could you believe this place? It's practically a *dacha*."

Moishe harrumphed.

"I know, I know. Somewhere in the bible it says we shouldn't be impressed with riches. Alright. So I shouldn't be impressed. And *dacha* may be an exaggeration. But compared to the dumps we live in. . .a *stone* house!" He whistled, the alcohol heavy on his breath. They were sitting on hard chairs near the window, Moishe's stiff leg propped out before him. The red velvet drapes had been drawn back, and as the sunlight streamed through the window, diamond designs shone on the carpeted floor. "Why so glum? You look like you're at a funeral instead of a wedding celebration."

"A *celebration*?"

"So a big party it's not."

Moishe raised his eyebrows.

"Alright. A little party it's not either. Whoever heard of a wedding without your neighbors?"

"You noticed the wife studying all of us." Moishe fixed his eyes on the mistress of the house.

"Probably counted the silverware before we got here."

Dishes were clattering as the guests began to fill their plates.

"Like we're animals. Or we smell."

"Don't let it bother you." Mordechai fingered his wiry beard. "At least you found someone for the *boychik*. That's all that matters. Now you don't have to worry about him being drafted. You don't have to pay the *melamed*. You won't have to bribe the informer, that *vos-in-der-kort*, the plague he should get."

"No. I only have to pay *him*." Moishe jutted his chin in the direction of his son's father-in-law. The barrel-chested *macher* was standing beside the *chuppah* he had set up for the service, laughing so heartily that the vodka was spilling over the rim.

". . .Pay him? Why?"

"You should ask *why*? . . . Because he can ask."

"What's this, he can *ask*? He can't find a husband for his daughter either. He may think he's a *goy*. But he's still a Jew. No Jew would have his daughter, and no *goy* either."

"But he knows no one will have my son. And he doesn't have to worry about his daughter going off to war."

They observed the fine house, the plastered walls, the upright piano, cushioned chairs adorned with tassels, the porcelain and bronze objects in a curio cabinet.

"Not bad to be a tax collector," Mordechai said. "And rent collector, let's not forget."

"Who could *forget*? The Shalamovas, could they forget when he put them on the street?"

"Or the Bergmans, or the Feldmans."

"But maybe we shouldn't be harsh," Mordechai went on. "Somebody has to do it. The tzarina needs her jewels, after all."

"After all. . . . Remember Shlomo, the rent collector?"

"A good man, that Shlomo."

"A *shaine mensch*," Moishe agreed. "Would sometimes take the money from his own purse when they couldn't pay. Not like this *sheister*. . . . I'm not stupid enough to think the *ganzer macher* is so in love with my son. Nobody knows better than me that the boy is no prize. I didn't expect—I wouldn't even ask—for a dowry. But this. . .I didn't expect I would have to pay."

"How much?"

"Enough. . . . Enough that I'll still be paying him when I'm in the ground."

"The *momzer.*" Mordechai watched Chaim and Yussel embracing each other, Yussel in a white robe and a prayer shawl. "How did you get your son to wear a *tallis* and *kittel*, I've been meaning to ask."

"It wasn't easy."

"To Gittel and her husband, Yussel!" Chaim clapped his new son-in-law on the back. "Welcome to the family!"

It was a warm day. The house was stuffy. Beads of sweat had pooled on Chaim's forehead. After wiping it off with a crumpled handkerchief, he removed his jacket, unfastened his collar, and rubbed the angry rash on his neck that had erupted from too much starch. Salt-and-pepper curls (more salt than pepper), peeked out of the top of his shirt. "I see we have something in common," he said, gesturing to their absent *peyes*.

"I'll never wear them again," Yussel answered. "Don't expect me to. . . . And I won't wear a beard either."

Chaim guffawed. "When hair grows on your face, you mean? No, no, by boy. I don't expect it. And I wouldn't want you to. You're famous—or infamous—you know. You have quite a reputation in this town."

"The *melamed*? Well—" the new son-in-law puffed out his chest—"I'd do again! The old bastard deserved it. And if I had a gun, I'd shoot the baron, too."

Chaim lit a cigar, inhaled deeply, and discharged a cloud of smoke. "I think you and I are going to get along just fine. I'll teach you the business."

While Chaim again clapped his new son-in-law's shoulder, welcoming him to the family, his wife stood with a stiff posture and a grimace that could frighten the dead. "This he has my daughter marry," she said to no one in particular, in a not-so-hushed voice. She glared at Yussel. "My beautiful Gittel married to. . .*this*. Another mouth to feed. Teach him the business. Ha. His own son he wouldn't take, but this *groisser gornisht* he wants to teach."

Mordechai's wife Esther scooted closer to Lena and squeezed her knee. "Ignore her," she mouthed, rolling her eyes. "Lovely home you have, Etta," she said, turning to the lady of the house, with a faux smile.

"Ah. It's so much work. All these rooms to clean."

"Like she knows from hard work," Rachel whispered to her mother.

"*Hard* work? *Any* work," Lena whispered back.

"You think it's nice to have all glass-pane windows," Etta went on. "But you have no idea what a job it is to wash them. And the curtains. Uh! Just to lift them."

Rachel stifled a laugh. *A gezunte moid*, built like a ditch digger, Mrs. Mishkin looked as if she could lift the furniture single-handed.

All the married women, decked out in their best *sheitels* and sabbath finery, were gathered in an alcove off the parlor. Lena, Rachel, and Esther were sitting together, away from the others, like the poor relatives they were. Rachel wore a simple cotton dress and, being a maiden, kept her hair in a braid that hung down her back. Esther's holiday wig looked as if it had fallen off her husband's junk wagon. Lena had just one wig, which she stored in a drawer. As it made her head itch and sweat, she only took it out on special occasions such as this. But it had seen better days. Unlike the Mishkins' thick, lustrous wigs, made from real hair, hers was made of horsehair, and had wide seams of mesh showing through.

Instead of vodka, the ladies were drinking *gira*, a non-alcoholic beverage made from the natural fermentation of wheat and flavored with fruit, berries, raisins, and birch sap.

"Who made the noodle pudding? It's delicious!" Lena's friend, Sarah Fructher, asked, taking a second helping. "Is that cinnamon I taste?"

"How's your sister, Etta?" Esther asked, purposefully addressing her by her first name again, as an equal.

"*Zei gezundt.* A quick recovery she should have," Chaim's mother said, a remarkably spry woman for a septuagenarian, slicing herself a piece of cake.

"A quick death is more likely," Etta answered. "She's been fading for months. I'm exhausted, having to go over there almost every day."

From the other side of the room, Moishe was telling Mordechai, "He even had me sign a contract agreeing to pay damages if my son runs out on his daughter."

". . .Well, I don't think you'll have to worry about *that.*" Mordechai directed his friend's attention to the newlyweds, who, not having moved from beneath the *chuppah,* were staring starry-eyed at each other. "A *shaine maidel*!" Mordechai whistled. "I know, I know. Somewhere in the bible it says good looks shouldn't matter. But you have to admit, it helps." Then he added what he knew his friend was thinking but too polite to say. "Thank God she doesn't resemble her mother."

That night, after the guests left and it was time for bed, Yussel followed his wife into her bedroom, but before he closed the door behind him, his mother-in-law dragged him out by his ear. "Don't you lay a hand on her, you little *pisher*!" she shouted, loud enough to shatter the crystal in her china cabinet.

"She's my *wife.*"

"And I'm her *mother.*"

"It's my obligation!"

She squeezed his earlobe until it turned red. "It will be your obligation when I *tell* you it's your obligation." She pointed to a steep, narrow staircase at the end of the hallway. "Until then, your room is in the attic!"

CHAPTER 11

CHAIM SLAMMED HIS LEDGER SHUT. "Can you believe it? The Markowitzes are late with the rent again." Yussel lowered his book and watched his father-in-law mop his flushed brow. It was a pleasant evening, a little chilly with the window open, but hot or cold, he always seemed to be in a sweat.

They were in the study, Chaim behind his desk, leaning back in a plush leather chair, his son-in-law sitting beside him. "Tells me 'business is bad.'" He slid a bottle of local vodka across the writing table, pulled the cork out with a loud pop, and poured himself a drink. "A gift from another delinquent taxpayer," he said, bringing it to his lips. "Listen and learn, my boy." After one gulp, his eyes widened, and he began to cough and sputter. Red-faced, jowls jiggling, the alcohol sloshed as he shook. "Phew! That stuff is as powerful as dynamite!" Pushing the ink well, pen, and papers aside, he set the drink down, and swiveled to face Yussel, the seat whining beneath his weight. "Never, *ever*, accept excuses. Remember that. What have you got there?" He pointed his bare chin at the battered book in the young man's lap.

"This?" Yussel held up the well-used volume with curlicue scribbles on the cover. "*Dead Souls.*"

Chaim's eyebrows furrowed.

"It's about this fat guy name Chicikov, who goes from town to town buying dead souls."

"Teitelbaum has you reading that?"

Yussel shrugged. "That and everything else. . .except the Torah, thankfully: Philosophy. History. Literature."

"You like it? This *Dead Souls*?"

"It's pretty funny, actually. 'Satire,' Teitelbaum calls it. And it sure beats reading about stupid cows."

Chaim guffawed so heartily the gap where his molars had been came into view. "The *alte cocker* is still giving the same lessons, I see. 'If somebody borrows a cow, and the cow dies.' . . . Yeah, I remember those debates. 'Who's responsible if the cow dies? The lender or the lendee?' I hated them, too. . . . He must be older than Methuselah."

Yussel chuckled.

"I think he was teaching before I was born. And no doubt he was a dog back then, too."

They could hear the cupboard squeak open and the chink of dishes. The smell of supper wafted into the room. A moment later Gittel was standing in the doorway, calling them to dinner. The loose cotton dress and apron that covered it could not hide the shapely figure beneath it. Neither could the kerchief hiding her cropped chestnut locks take away from her flawless complexion. Strands of hair having escaped their scarf lay limp on her forehead. She lifted her lids and smiled at him. Her eyes were speckled gray, the color of a thin fog. One of them wandered. It didn't matter. She was the prettiest girl he'd ever seen.

Etta was slicing a roast on the butcher block beside the cast iron stove, catching the drippings in a gravy bowl that resembled a steer, when they stepped into the kitchen.

"Doesn't that smell good!" Chaim said, taking his place at the head of the table. Yussel sat to his right, closest to the wall. Cooking made the kitchen hot, so Gittel pushed the window open before laying out the honeyed carrots, toasted barley, and black bread. Her mother brought the beef, carved into thick slices, and the gravy. They lowered themselves across from their respective husbands. Etta grimaced when her bottom hit the cane seat and re-positioned herself so as to sit on one cheek.

"I've been teaching Yussel here how to deal with tenants," Chaim said, as his daughter shoveled carrots onto his plate.

"Mm-hm." Etta scowled. "Pass the barley."

Gittel set the vegetables down with a soft thud and passed the grain. "It was such a beautiful day today," she said. "The trees are so pretty when they're in bloom."

"The heat and mosquitoes will be right behind them," her mother said.

"It's not so bad, Mother."

"Huh. Easy for you to say. You don't perspire like I do, and the bugs don't attack you like they attack me."

Yussel stopped eating. His fork rang on the dish. "I've noticed," he said glancing at his mother-in-law, "that the pests seem to favor. . . large, sweaty people."

Curtains flapped in the breeze. A four-armed chandelier hung over the table, but it didn't need to be lit because the sun was still bright at seven in the evening. Light pouring in from the open window shone on Etta's glower.

Chaim cleared his throat. "How was your day, Etta?" He looked at his wife. "What's new?"

"What's *new*? What could be new? *Nothing's* new. I work. I cook. I clean. I watch over my sister. Every day is the same drudgery."

"And you get mosquito bites," Yussel mumbled under his breath. "Let us not forget that."

Chaim reached for the ceramic bull and poured drippings over his meat. "What's that, Yussel?"

"I was just thinking of those 'awful mosquitos.'"

"Yes, they are indeed 'awful,'" the man at the head of the table agreed.

"God's curse," Yussel concurred into his roast beef.

There was a pause as the mother-in-law glared at him. "Are you mocking me?"

"Leah can't hang on much longer," Chaim said, taking another helping of barley. "Then we'll take Shula in, and she'll help with chores."

Etta ripped off a piece of bread and sopped up the juices. "No. She's got the death rattle."

"Must have a strong heart," he added between bites. "Maybe you should stop giving her the medicine."

"I only give her the valerian now, to help her sleep."

"But shouldn't you give her something for the pain, too? I'd hate to see her suffer," said Gittel.

Etta's silverware chimed as it hit the china. "Of course I give her pain medication. And since when are you the doctor?"

Catching her father's warning glance, Gittel did not argue but looked down at her food. She should have known better than to question her mother when her piles were acting up. It always put her in an especially foul mood.

Yussel couldn't think of a time when her mood hadn't been foul.

He found her remarks invariably caustic. Yet unlike his wife, who backed down, he enjoyed goading her. He looked at her with a glint in his eye. "Papa said you would take Shula in after *Tante* Leah dies, but what of the others? Where will they go? (He intentionally called them "Mama" and "Papa" because he knew she hated it.)

The cutlery chimed again, louder this time. She met his eyes with another scowl. "Am I expected to take in five extra mouths to feed?"

"They're your sister's children. Doesn't it say somewhere in the bible that family should care for each other? Not just the ones who can help with the laundry?"

In truth, he didn't care. Had "Mama" said she would take all five of them, he would have countered that she had no room.

Etta's face reddened. Chaim made a choking sound. Gittel kept her attention on her plate. "Another potato? Carrotts? More meat?" she asked her husband, taking his already full plate from beneath his hands.

"Sure. He gets second helpings while I have to send my nephews—-my own blood—-to other families!" With that Etta slapped her napkin on the table and scraping loudly pushed her chair far enough away to get up, pulled her shawl over her dark dress, and headed for the door. "Gittel, after you clean the table, I want you to practice your Chopin. You have a lesson tomorrow, don't forget. And you—" she glowered at Yussel, her finger wagging, the wattle on her neck swaying back and forth— "Keep your hands off my daughter. *Farshtain*?"

But no sooner was she out of sight and his father-in-law settled at his desk in the next room than Yussel was squeezing his wife's knee under the table and leaning over his roast beef and carrots to give her a kiss. She jumped up before their lips met, nearly knocking over the porcelain bull.

"You heard what Mama said. You shouldn't touch me."

"She's not here."

"That's deceitful. Besides, you heard her. She'll be back soon. And Papa is right next door, in the study."

He reached for her hand, but she pulled away. "You still have meat and potatoes on your dish. Why don't you finish eating?"

He let out a deep sigh. He had yet to give her a peck on the cheek. Many times, he'd tried to get close to Gittel, but, so intimidated by her mother, his wife would never let him near her.

CHAPTER 12

YUSSEL TOOK HIS WIFE'S HAND, buried his face into her neck, and waltzed her to the bed. Her heart was pounding so hard against his chest, he could almost hear it. "Relax." He blew into her ear.

"It's the middle of the day."

He pulled her closer, slipped her scarf off her head and ran his fingers through her cropped curls. Ribbons of light streaming in from between the slats of the shutters highlighted the chestnut hue. "Come on." He caressed her face.

She closed her eyes as he traced the lines of her jaw and turned her head away from him. "Please," she said. "I can't. They're downstairs—"

He kissed her cheeks, her soft lips. "Who cares?" They backed into her dresser, her thigh catching the pointed edge though she hardly felt it. Bottles of toilet water rattled on the oak top. "Oh, God!" he moaned as he lowered her onto the mattress, slid his hands across her bosom, and began to fumble with her buttons.

"*Wait!*" She pushed her palm against his chest, covering her nearly exposed breasts.

He let out a deep breath. "What now?" he groaned, his voice husky.

Wriggling out from under him, she sat up. Blotches of red colored her cheeks. "She might come in," she panted.

"I locked the door." He pressed her down again, kissed her eyelids.

"But they're in the house! They'll know we're here."

"So?"

"I can't." She squirmed out of his grasp again, sat up, and smoothed the wrinkles on the floral printed quilt.

He rolled over and propped himself on his elbow. "What do mean, you *can't*? We've been married over a month. The rabbi gave his blessing—"

"But my mother—"

"Ugh, Etta—*gai kakn ofn yahm*! She should shit in the ocean!"

Gittel retrieved her kerchief, covered her head, stood, and, hand-pressing the creases out of her clothes, started for the door. "I just can't. Knowing what they're thinking. I'm sorry."

"Who gives a *fuck* what they're thinking? For God's sake, Gittel. We're *married*! It's our right. *My* right! It's a mitzvah."

"Tonight. I promise. When they're sleeping."

The door closed behind her with a soft thud.

That night, the house dark and quiet, the supper dishes washed, died, and put away, and the floor twice swept and mopped, Gittel crept apprehensively to her bedroom. Carrying a candle to light her way, she padded through the house. The parlor was thick with cigar smoke, and its harsh aroma followed her up the stairs, not dissipating until she reached the top step. Though her father's snoring was loud enough to raise the roof, and a hall runner would absorb the sound of her the footsteps, she removed her shoes and tiptoed toward the yellow glow spilling out from beneath her door. After standing there for several minutes taking long, deep breaths, she turned the knob.

The scent of sandalwood assailed her.

Yussel was sitting up in bed, his arms behind his neck. A breeze through the open window rustled the thin blanket that covered his nakedness. "Ah! Finally." He patted the narrow mattress and smiled.

Gittel had never seen a bare chest. Once, as a child, she'd wandered into her parents' room when her father was dressing and saw him without a shirt. But that didn't count. *His* chest, flaccid and hairy as a black Russian terrier, was nothing like the smooth, tight, *sensuous* one before her.

She stood at the entranceway for what seemed forever, trying to gather her courage. All was silent, but her senses were on alert. The sound of the lamp, burning on the nightstand, hissed in her ear.

She took a step forward and slowly made her way across the room.

He pulled her into him, on top of him. Through the wall came the strident sound of her father's snorts, the spluttering and whistling preceded by episodes of silence.

"Wait!" she whispered, rolling off him. "They might hear us."

". . .What?"

"They can hear us."

It was true. Their bedrooms were only separated by a thin partition. If someone sneezed on one side, it could be heard on the other.

He pulled her back down, flipped her over so that he lay above her. "First of all, they wouldn't hear the light brigade through that noise your father's making. And secondly, I. Don't. Care."

He lifted her dress, ran his fingers along the inside of her thighs, kissed her lips softly, then fiercely undid her buttons until her breasts were bare, and cupped them, plum-sized, trailed his tongue down her neck, forced her legs apart with his knees. He moaned. He groaned. He grunted. The bed squeaked. The headboard rattled.

And all the while she lay in a state of rictus, watching the candle light flicker on the ceiling and keeping her ear peeled to the wall.

"Can't we be, ah more. . .quiet?" she mumbled when it was over.

"More *quiet*! You want me to stop *breathing*?"

"We don't have to. . .moan so loud, or. . .maybe we could be less . . .you know, vigorous."

"*Vigorous*! I'm already making love to a statue. Any less vigorous, you'd have to be dead!"

YUSSEL MARKED THE PAGE, got off the cot, and, stepping over his clothes, went to open the window. The dormered room was hot and stuffy and had a musty smell. Dust motes floated in the sunlight. Wet with perspiration, his linen under-drawers and night shirt clung to his body. With the low ceiling and sloping walls, he had to crouch. Yet despite the heat and claustrophobia, the attic, once his prison, had become his sanctuary, a place to escape when he quarreled with his wife, or when his mother-in-law's grating voice got on his last nerve.

Whoever painted the window trim last had painted over the latches, so he had to use all his strength to push them out. It was hardly worth the effort. There was no breeze. Only whiffs of horse manure and the clatter of carts on the cobblestones came through.

His in-laws' house was behind the town square, and the best view of the village came from that attic. Standing at the sill to get some air, he took in the gray-bearded men entering and leaving *shul*, and a group of young students gathered outside the yeshiva. Dark-clad women were sitting in front of their shops, fanning themselves, and a boy was drawing water from the pump. A smile crossed his face. For the most part, he was happy living with the Mishkins. Fears about his wife's looks had proved unfounded. His father's concern about Chaim being "an unprincipled crook," and his mother's opinion that Etta was an "uncouth loudmouth," though true, were not important. On the contrary, Chaim was as much an idol to him as the coming messiah was to Moishe. Yes, Yussel's father-in-law was a *sheister.* But he was a *sheister* who didn't care if Yussel wore *peyes*, a beard, or a *yarmulke.* And unlike Yussel's gutless father, who never stood up for himself and accepted whatever life threw his way, his father-in-law took life by the horns. Chaim didn't believe in religious hogwash. He observed the Sabbath and the high holy days out of tradition.

"Three things increase a man's self-esteem," Chaim often told him: "a beautiful wife, a beautiful dwelling, and rooms full of beautiful furnishings." (How Etta fit into Chaim's picture, Yussel often wondered. She was certainly no beauty!) But Yussel had all three.

Life was good. Even his constipation had improved. Besides a more conducive diet, they had a toilet. At home (he still thought of his humble abode as "home"), the privy was a two-hole outhouse behind the chicken coop, cold in winter and inundated with flies in summer, which, despite a liberal use of lime, had the most noxious odor. The Mishkins had had a flush commode shipped in from England. Though not indoors, it was in a shed connected close enough to the heating stove not to be freezing in bad weather or bug infested in the heat, and hardly malodorous.

And goading his mother-in-law had become a source of entertainment.

Gittel was the only fly in the ointment.

He heard clunking footsteps on the stairs.

"Oh!" Shula came to an abrupt halt. "I'm sorry. I-I. . . didn't know anyone was up here." With water sloshing over the rim of the wash bucket, she made an about-face and started back down the stairs.

"Wait," Yussel called, hurrying to grab his pants.

She stopped but did not turn around.

"That's the most I've ever heard you say in the whole two months you've been here."

Indeed, she rarely spoke. She neither gave opinions nor joined in dinner conversation. Except for a muted, "I have enough, thank you," when food was passed in her direction, she picked at her meals in silence. Since the Mishkins took her in after her mother died ("*finally,*" Etta would add), she'd been so unobtrusive, they hardly felt her presence. She performed her chores efficiently, quietly, and without complaint, and retired to her room when her work was done.

"I need to finish my work," she said.

"Or Tante Etta will whip you?"

"Well, maybe not *whip*." Her voice had fallen to a mumble.

"Don't let that battle axe scare you. She's just a bag of wind. If you want to see her cringe, the next time you prepare the apple cider vinegar concoction for her piles, add hot pepper to it." He thought he heard her giggle. "There. I made you laugh."

Her hem swept the step, gathering a dust ball as she faced him. She was a sturdy girl, the very likeness of a milk maid, with big bones, red cheeks, and a thick, dark braid that reached her waist. A full apron, with a scrub brush protruding from a pocket, covered a gray cotton dress. Two buttons were open at the neck, and the sleeves were rolled up above her elbows.

"She tries to intimidate me too, but I won't have it."

"I've noticed how you needle her," she said, keeping her eyes lowered.

"I didn't realize I was so obvious."

She gave him the slightest of smiles, which quickly evaporated.

"Have a seat." He moved a stack of books from the chair behind his desk to the floor and motioned.

"Thank you, but I really have to finish. I'll clean up here when you're done—"

"Don't let me stop you. Talk to me. We live in the same house, and I don't know anything about you."

She shrugged. "There's nothing to know."

"Really?" He crossed his arms, raised his brow, and gave her an I-don't-believe-that-for-a-minute stare. "You've lost your mother. Your father died a few years ago. Your aunt put your three brothers in an orphanage in another town, and you're treated like sweet little Rosy-red in *The Red Slipper*, 'who had to collect firewood for the home, to draw water from the well and struggle along with the heavy bucket whose weight made her arms and her back ache with pain,'" he recited word for word from the fairytale.

"Except that my brothers were put in three different homes, not an orphanage, and I don't have blue eyes or a wicked stepmother."

"Just a wicked aunt."

Her brown eyes began to well up, her shoulders to shake lightly. Tears ran down her cheeks. She wiped them away with the back of a cracked hand. "I should be glad," she began to sob. "I have a roof over my head and food in my stomach."

He went to her then and embraced her. Her skin was moist with perspiration. "There, there. Let it out." He stroked her hair.

She pulled away from him, turned to the wall, dabbed her eyes with a handkerchief she took from her pocket. "I-I'm sorry." She sniffled. "I didn't mean to cry." Lifting her wash bucket, the dirty water swirling against the lip of the pail, she stepped toward the door, her wooden shoes clicking on the floor. "I really must go."

"Wait." He grabbed a book from the pile beside the cot and held it out to her. "Take this."

She twisted, looked at the picture of a boy in a turban standing before large pots.

"*Ali Baba and the Forty Thieves*," he said. "It's a children's book." He stared at her full breasts. "Not that I think you're a child . . . . But I guarantee it will cheer you up." He flashed a deep-dimpled smile. "It's an adventure story about a prince, evil Mongols, and forty thieves. It's fun. We can read it together. Would you like that?"

"I-uh-don't think that's a good idea."

A Chopin nocturne was floating up the attic stairs. Gittel played the piano every afternoon. Yussel nodded in the direction of the music. "It would make her happy, if that's what you're concerned about. She worries about you. . .losing your family and being so sad." He put the book on her palm, wrapped her fingers around it, let his hand linger on hers a moment more than proper. "Go on. It will make you laugh."

She stared at her scuffed clogs. ". . .I really don't have time—there are so many chores, and then when I'm finally done at the end of the day, I just want to sleep." Pail in hand, she started for the stairs again.

"We can read it one page a day," he called after her. "In the afternoon, between errands. What do you say?"

CHAPTER 13

SHULA PULLED HER PILLOW OVER HER HEAD when she heard the birds warbling outside her window. Streaks of blue and gold began to fill the room. Time to get up. She'd only just closed her eyes. She moaned. She'd been so tired when she came to bed the night before, but between Uncle Chaim's relentless snoring and the hot, sticky room, it had been impossible to sleep.

She sat at the edge of the bed with her bare feet on the floor and her chemise crumpled over her thighs. Her chin rested on her cupped hands. She hated Monday. Though not too fond of the rest of the week either, Monday—laundry day—was the worst. "The weekly affliction," her mother had called it.

She poured water from the pitcher into the washbasin, rubbed tooth powder across her teeth then sponged. The tepid water felt cool on her clammy skin. She donned a fresh chemise, threw on her muslin dress and apron, slipped her bare feet into her clogs (It was too hot to wear stockings), combed and braided her hair, and after making her bed, crept down the stairs, careful to tread softly so as not to wake anyone. Yet if her uncle's racket hadn't roused them, surely her footsteps wouldn't. She couldn't imagine how her aunt slept with that noise every night.

Though Shula had separated the wash the evening before and had it soaking in three separate vats, she still had a whole day's labor ahead of her. Though she didn't have to haul buckets of water from the pump at the end of the lane, as she had in her childhood home, and now had the luxury of a hand wringer, the task was no less daunting. Her father had been a farrier who only wore work clothes. Her mother, God bless her soul, had dressed herself and her children in durable, printed fabrics and used colored tablecloths, so that, except for the underwear, all the laundry could be washed in one copper.

Tante Etta was not as practical as her sister, because, until Shula came, there had been a laundress. Etta used white linens, which also required soaking. Small muslin bags, filled with indigo powder, needed to be added to the rinse to brighten the linens, then treated with sour milk and washed again.

The velvet and silk attire worn on the Sabbath needed to be washed in another vat.

The mere thought of the job before her made her cringe. At least it was a nice day.

SHE WAS STIRRING THE LINENS over a fire in the side yard when Yussel snuck up behind her. Her knuckles were still raw and split from scrubbing the floors the day before, and though she used a long washing bat to stir the wash, splashes of boiling water and caustic lye soap on her cuts caused her to wince.

"The witches brew!" he whispered.

"Oh!" She jumped, turned, and raised a quizzical eyebrow.

"You never heard of a witch stirring poison in big, boiling cauldron?"

"...Are you calling me a *witch*?"

"Only if witches are beautiful."

Etta opened the kitchen window and leaned out. "Don't forget the blue bags!"

"Yes, Tante." Shula removed a muslin packet from her apron pocket and held it up for her to see.

Etta gave Yussel a cold stare. "And what are *you* doing there?"

"I'm on my way to meet with Teitelbaum, my tutor."

"The street's that way. Get going." She pointed to the front entrance and didn't take her eyes off him until the gate squeaked open.

He waved at Shula and winked. "Bye, Rosy Red!"

She watched him amble down the street, the sun on his back, his strong shoulders and confident stride. "'Rosy Red... *beautiful*'." She smiled.

Soapy water spilled over the washtub, muddying the ground around the pail and splashed her feet, as she punched the sheets with the wooden oar. *Get a hold of yourself, Shula. You're just imagining things. He's friendly, that's all.* A pillow case with blue-embroidered birds floated to the top, wrapped around the bat tongs. She pulled it out of the basin to untangle it and pressed it down again. The fabric was hot on her skin, not enough to scald her but enough to hurt. *But is it in my head that he stares at me just a little too long? Or that he appears out of nowhere when I'm working?*

At the next vat, she knelt on a towel she'd spread over the soil, rubbed a slice of soap over the metal rungs of the washboard, and began scrubbing her uncle's cuffs. *It's ridiculous to even think about,* she reminded herself. *He's my cousin's husband. And how could he want me when Gittel is so much prettier?*

When the stains were gone, she moved on to the white shirts, pouring lemon juice on countless blots of blueberries. "You're such a slob,

Uncle Chaim," she mumbled. "You should wear a bib!" *Yussel isn't inconsiderate. He doesn't get food on his clothes. He wouldn't give me extra work.* The scent of honeysuckle wafted by from against the stone wall. *What are you thinking, girl?* She chastised herself. *He's a married man*!

There were no trees in the yard, so ropes had been stretched between poles. There were three in all, and even at that, the rags had to be arranged over the fence. She draped the linens up front and concealed unmentionables behind them. Aunt Etta demanded that her underpants had not only to be hidden but folded in half, so nobody would notice she was so fat.

The church bells had just chimed for the sixth time when the last piece of laundry was hung. Shula poured the rinse water into the street, cleaned the tubs, turned them upside down, and, with shoes in hand, trudged to her room. She was hot and so sweaty that her dress stuck to her body. Her chafed hands stung from the caustic soap and rope burns. The back of her neck was sunburned. And her arms ached so badly she could hardly lift them.

She felt Yussel's eyes following her when she entered the kitchen that evening. It had cooled since the afternoon, but the room was still uncomfortably warm from cooking. "Sorry I'm late." She apologized. Her chair scraped on the tile floor as she pulled it away from the table.

"You're just in time," Gittel assured her from the seat beside her. "I just put out the food."

Etta threw her niece a peculiar look. "A new dress you're wearing. . . a ribbon in your hair—" she took a deep sniff and raised an eyebrow— "and *perfume*?"

Shula felt her face flush. Her mouth was dry. She took a sip of water. ". . .I-I squirted on some toilet water to get rid of the lye smell."

Her aunt sneered. "Lye smell?"

"The dress isn't new. It was Gittel's." Shula felt the full linen skirt. Nearly all of her clothing had been Gittel's hand-me-downs. Most had been like new, some never even worn. Being taller and fuller-figured than her cousin, Shula's mother, Leah, had had to move buttons, let out seams, and lower hems.

"Well, you look lovely." Gittel smiled at her cousin. "Green is a good color for you. And I love the matching ribbon you wove into your braid." One eye was wandering, and Shula didn't know which one to focus on.

Gittel addressed the others. "I think I can speak for all of us when I say we are all happy to see you adjusting to your new home."

Yussel's gaze lingered on Shula's bodice, which was just tight enough to outline her generous breasts. "Absolutely."

"Mother? Isn't that right?"

Etta studied her niece. It had been the first time in months she'd taken an interest in her appearance. Aside from the work clothes, she'd worn the same garment every day since her mother had taken ill.

"Isn't that *right*, Mother?"

". . .Yes. Yes, we are."

Had she been asked to prepare a cider vinegar solution, Shula would have taken her aunt's grimace to mean that her piles were bothering her again.

"Doesn't that look good!" Chaim exclaimed, inhaling deeply. "Meat and potato dumplings!"

His daughter, sitting to his right, slid three helpings onto his plate. He'd removed his cuffs, and his sleeves were rolled above his hairy forearms.

"I'll take the beans, and some of that relish, too."

Shula cringed as she watched the bowls pass from Etta, sitting opposite her husband, to Yussel, on her right, to Chaim, spilling bits of diced tomatoes, lima beans, and lemon juice on the white tablecloth each time it changed hands—the tablecloth she would have to scrub next Monday.

Her uncle tore off a piece of black bread and soaked it in the drippings. Crumbs fell onto his shirt. He cut into a dumpling with his fork, which screeched against the plate. "Our son-in-law here is a great asset to our business, Etta." He reached over and squeezed Yussel's shoulder with his oily hand. Shula winced. Another white shirt for the wash.

"Yes, indeed," Chaim said with his mouth full. "A smart one, we got." He chewed his food, swallowed, burped. "Fast with numbers."

Etta harrumphed. "This *shmendrik* you groom for the business, but our Sol—*our own flesh and blood*—you don't teach."

Her husband's cutlery chimed on his hand-painted plate. "Are we going to start that again? The boy—"

"He's not a boy. He's a *man.*"

Shula lowered her eyes and toyed with her vegetables, pushing the beans and relish into separate piles. It upset her that people called Sol "the *dummkopf,*" the dull-witted dunce. It was cruel. He was sweet. But surely, Tante had to know he wasn't capable of running a business, especially one that required ruthlessness.

Her uncle took a deep breath and let it out slowly. "He has a wife, a *shaineh maidele*, I might add. An allowance we give him."

Gittel threw her father a pointed look, then turned to the flushed girl sitting beside her. "Shula! You've hardly touched your food."

"Your tante's dumplings you don't like?" Chaim looked at her. "My wife is the best cook. That's why I have such a belly." He touched it.

"Sure. Blame me," Etta said. "He blames me for everything. The sun doesn't shine, it must be Etta's fault."

"Don't forget the mosquitoes," Yussel mumbled into his relish.

His mother-in-law threw him an odious look.

"I love Tante Etta's dumplings," Shula interjected. "I'm just not hungry."

When the cousins finished cleaning the kitchen, Shula excused herself, saying she was tired and going to bed.

"It's still early. Don't you want to chat for a while before you turn in?"

"Thank you. But I'm really tired." Draping her apron and dishtowel over the sink, she turned to leave. "Good night." The Mishkins went to bed later than she was used to. Having been brought up, like most *shtetl* residents, in a household where oil to light lamps was a luxury, she went to sleep as soon it got dark.

"Good night." Gittel touched the ribbon Shula had in her hair. "I hope you really are feeling more comfortable here."

Shula took the other's hand in hers. It was so much softer and more delicate than her own. "It's nice of you to be concerned." Her smile did not reach her eyes.

She passed through the parlor to the stairs. Gittel followed her in and took her place at the piano, where she began to play a Chopin nocturne. Etta was sitting in a velvet arm chair, the oil lamp casting a pale light on her lap, where a section of a linen tablecloth was held taut in an embroidery hoop. Uncle Chaim and Yussel were on the tufted sofa. "I must confess, Yussel, that I had my reservations about you, but I'm happy to admit I was wrong." With a soft chink, hardly audible against the music, he opened the cherry-wood humidor on the side table, lifted two cigars, snipped the ends with his pen knife, and lit them with metal matches. Wisps of smoke and a spicy aroma began to fill the room. "I think your loan idea might have some merit." He took a deep puff. "I'll consider it. But in the meantime, I must tell you, my boy, I was impressed today. How you evicted the Goldfarbs without even a moment's hesitation. Well done."

"As you taught me: 'Take no excuses.' 'But my son was drafted, and my husband is ill. We have no income. We'll pay you next month,'" Yussel mimicked the old woman's pleas.

Shula listened in horror from the top of the stairs. The hallway was dark. Uttered amid the backdrop of such beautiful music made the words seem uglier. *Yussel could never be so harsh. Surly, he only evicted the couple to impress her uncle. No. Yussel would never do that on his own. Never.*

CHAPTER 14

"Don't leave streaks," Etta said by way of greeting. "And watch how you handle the figurines," she added, adjusting her shawl. "They're quite costly."

"I'll be careful," Shula answered, not turning from the curio, where she was wiping the glass shelves with a mixture of ammonia and vinegar. She heard the swish of her aunt's skirts as Etta made her way to the vestibule, then the door open.

"I'm going to my sisterhood meeting. Gittel won't be able to help you today. I want her to practice before her lesson," Etta called from beneath the lintel. "Make sure you keep the windows closed, so the mosquitoes don't get in." The door shut with a dull thump.

"'Stay all day," Shula mumbled to the knickknacks. "'Be careful with the figurines, they're *quite* costly.'" She wrapped her hand around a figure of a lady in pink and glared at it. "I'd like to smash every one of you!"

"Who you talking to, Rosie Red?"

She jumped, and the china figurine dropped from her hand. "Oh, no!" She stared wide-eyed at the porcelain girl, holding a parasol, with a fractured arm and shattered nose that had come to rest at her feet. Lifting the pieces as if they were baby chicks fallen from their nest, she turned to Yussel for the first time.

If she'd had any thought of berating him for startling her, one look at his handsome form changed her mind. He was wearing high-waisted trousers with suspenders over a loose linen shirt. Blonde curls had fallen across his forehead, his bright blue eyes sparkled, and a musk-smelling cologne surrounded him. All she could say was, "What do I do now?"

"This," he said. In the time it took for the grandfather clock to tick, he'd taken the china doll from her grasp and thrown it against the wall. Shula looked on in horror.

". . .Why did you *do* that?"

"Isn't it what you wanted?"

". . .She's going to be *furious*."

He shrugged. "So?"

"She'll *scream* at me."

"Scream back."

"It's hot in here." Gittel had entered the parlor, her short hair covered with a kerchief, her eyes still crusted with sleep.

"Your mother told me not to open the windows."

Gittel grimaced. "What was that crash?"

Yussel glared at his wife. "*That* woke you up, not your father's snoring?"

She spotted the shards of porcelain on the floor. "Oy oy oy! . . . Is that Mama's pink *lady*?"

"It slipped out of Shula's hands."

GITTEL WAS PLAYING A CHOPIN NOCTURNE when Shula gathered the feather duster, rags, and the bottle of cleaner and climbed the stairs. With the shutters closed, the hallway was dark. Sunshine slipping between the slats cast thin lines of light on the runner. She started in her aunt's and uncle's room. Though Etta didn't do much in the way of housework, she kept her own quarters neat. Other than filling the water basin, wiping down the furniture, which consisted on an intricately carved armoire, matching bed board, and washstand, Shula didn't have much to do. Nevertheless, she could never get out of there fast enough. Between Aunt Etta's aversion to open windows and Uncle Chaim— obviously having a bad aim when it came to his chamber pot—soaking the floor with his urine, it stank. That she would scrub the soiled areas every morning, it still smelled loke cat piss.

Taking a deep breath and still preoccupied with the porcelain figurine, Shula entered Yussel's and Gittel's bedroom. She wiped a tear from her cheek with the back of her hand. *How could he do that? And then blame* me! *Maybe he* is *the scoundrel people claim.* No. She refused to believe that. He'd been nothing but kind to her. In the fifteen months since her mother died, he had been the only bright spot in her world, the only person who understood her grief. He made her smile and even laugh. He made her life bearable.

The room was twice the size of hers. Unlike the other sleeping chamber, it smelled refreshingly of candle wax and jasmine. Brocade drapes were closed tightly, making it more like early evening than afternoon. Still angry, disappointed, or irritable as she may have been with her cousin's husband, she felt a pang of envy looking at the bed he shared with his wife. If only the matchmaker had chosen Shula first.

The Chopin nocturne floated into the room. Gittel played so beautifully. Everything about her was beautiful: her delicate features, her sweet disposition, the way she carried herself with such grace. A wave of jealousy washed over Shula.

From the mirror over the shaving stand, she saw Yussel slip inside. "You're upset with me," he said after pulling the door behind him, shutting out the sound of his wife's piano playing.

Shula turned, stared at him through red, swollen eyes.

"I'm trying to help you," he said.

"*Help me*? By making my life more miserable than it already is?"

He came toward her, the sound of his footsteps lost in the carpet, lifted her chin, and wiped the tears streaming down her face with his fingers. "To stand up for yourself." He tucked a strand of damp hair behind her ear, moved closer, and whispered, "You're not her serf. Not her maid." He stared into her doleful brown eyes. "You're her *niece*. . .her *dear departed* sister's daughter. And you shouldn't allow her to treat you like anything less. . . . Don't be afraid. She's a big windbag."

Then he lifted her mouth to hers. She tasted the bicarbonate of soda he'd used to clean his teeth. It had never tasted so delicious.

It was hard to tell who pulled whom onto the bed, but within moments his trousers, shirt, and underwear lay in a heap, her work dress and apron were off—and fingers were sliding over every inch of each other. He licked the inside of her thigh, caressed her plump buttocks. She moaned. She groaned. The bed squeaked. The headboard banged.

And all the while his wife's fingers fluttered across the keyboard in the parlor.

Shula wasn't as pretty as Gittel, not even close. Shula was plain. Her hands were coarse, her hair dull by comparison, and her legs too chunky for Yussel's liking. But she was there—-willing and passionate. And as the saying goes, every cat is gray in the dark.

That evening at dinner, Shula wore a lavender dress, a matching ribbon woven into her braid—and a new glow on her face. Gittel passed the potatoes as Chaim belched, Yussel ate his beef with gusto, and Etta complained about the mosquitoes. Maybe she hadn't noticed the missing figurine, because she didn't mention it. It didn't matter. Shula wouldn't have cared if she had.

CHAPTER 15

SHULA TURNED HER BACK, grabbed the faded brown dress from the throw rug at the bottom of the bed and slipped it over her head. It wasn't so cold that the windows were iced over, as they were on most winter days, but enough that she could see her breath. Woolen knee-socks kept her feet and legs warm, but her nipples had stiffened when she got out from under the cover, and her bare arms prickled with goosebumps. Winter came early in Northern Lithuania. So did darkness. Dusky light filtered in through the window, setting the room and everything within it in shadow. "I. . .I have something to tell you," she mumbled.

Yussel was sitting on the side of the bed, tightening his belt over a loose tunic. "What?"

She turned, and though she shifted her eyes from her hands to look at him, she could not meet his eyes. "I. . .I have to tell you something," she repeated.

"So tell me."

"I'm. . .I've—" she swallowed— "I stopped bleeding."

A bolt of lightning lit the room. A moment later thunder rumbled.

A gust of wind rattled the shutters.

"So?"

"So. . .I think—I think I'm pregnant."

The cot creaked as he stood up. His arms fell to his sides. His blue eyes widened. "What?"

"I'm preg—"

"I heard you. How?"

"How?"

"Yeah. How?" His face stretched tight as he approached her. She moved back, nearly tripping on a washtub she'd brought in to scrub the floor. Soapy water rippled inside the pail. "How did you let that happen?" They were nose to nose. "You have get rid of it."

"It's too late."

"You missed one period. Throw yourself down the stairs."

"I've missed. . .I've missed three periods."

". . .And you waited all this time?"

"I kept thinking it wasn't so. That I was just late. I've always been irregular."

She could feel his hot breath, his anger. She pushed a stray strand of hair away from her cheek as she took another step back.

"How? How could you not know?"

"How?"

"You sound like an owl. 'How, how, *how'!*" he mimicked. "What are you going to do about it?"

Her mouth opened, but nothing came out. She looked down, twisted a handful of her skirt. "I don't know. I. . .I thought you might. We—"

"Oh, no." He shook his head back and forth, a vein in his forehead bulging. "No, no, no! You're not dragging me into this. . . . I saw the way Izzy Abromowitz looked at you."

"*Izzy Abromawitiz*? . . . You're not suggesting. . . ? That fat old man with a greasy beard? He must be fifty years old. He can hardly walk. You think—"

"I saw the way he looked at you when he came about a loan. And I saw how you smiled at him."

"I smiled at him? He thanked me for the tea I brought him, and I said, 'You're welcome.' How can you question me?"

Before she knew what was happening, he was on her, pummeling her with closed fists.

She stumbled backward, knocking over the tub. The water sloshed over the floor, saturating the carpet. Her head slammed so hard against the wall, she felt as if she might pass out. She shrunk into a fetal position. Her skirt was twisted around her knees, and her shoulders heaved up and down. Blood was oozing from a split lip, warm and sticky on her hands, which were covering her face. Wetness from the bucket seeped through her clothes. He kicked her in her ribs. "You better not accuse *me*, you hear?"

She pushed herself up, getting on her knees first, using the mop as a cane for support. Holding her side and grabbing the galvanized tub, the wire handle cutting into her chafed hand, she shuffled to the doorway. Tears were coming fast. She didn't know if she was sobbing from the physical pain, his betrayal, or both.

Hesitating before starting down the stairs, she looked at him with her one good eye, the other already swelling shut. "You really think when my belly grows—-which won't be long—your mother-in-law won't point a finger at you? This is not just my problem. This is *our* problem." With those words, she left the room, and slammed the door behind her.

Yussel kicked the wall, the chair, the desk, and the iron bed frame, stubbing his toe. He threw his books, one after the other, at the closed shutters, their pages fanning out, until his fury was reduced to seething control. She was right, of course. Everybody would know it was him. His good life would be over. He collapsed on the cot, the bed groaning under his weight, ran his fingers through his hair, and let out a deep sigh. "*That bitch!*"

SHULA WIPED THE BLOOD FROM HER MOUTH as she stumbled into her room. She threw off her wet dress, rolled down her soggy socks and pulled them off, eased into a gray flannel night gown and a pair of booties that her mother had knit, and buried herself under her quilt. Her ribs were so sore that it hurt to breathe. Her head felt as if it would explode.

She didn't know what she'd expected from Yussel. A solution? An 'It will be alright—we'll deal with it together' response? A shoulder to cry on? 'A bad seed,' 'The black sheep,' rose in her mind, phrases she'd heard about him but refused to heed. She'd seen the signs: evicting the Goldfarbs, the sarcastic wit with aunt Etta, smashing the figurine. But she had refused to see.

A few hours later, she heard Gittel's sweet voice at the door. "Shula? Are you alright?"

Shula turned to face the wall, the slight movement causing shooting pain through her body. "*Go away. Please,*" she mumbled into her pillow. A moment later the door pushed open. Light from the hallway and the scent of Jasmine swept into the small space. She burrowed herself deeper under the covers, leaving only the top of her head exposed.

"Aren't you coming down?" Gittel said, standing beside her. "Supper's on the table."

"I don't feel very well. I just need to sleep."

"What's wrong?"

"I'm getting a cold."

"You do sound nasal." Gittel put her hand on her cousin's shoulder. "You're shivering." She sat on the bed, the mattress sinking beneath her, and felt her cousin's brow. "You're cool. That's good."

"I'll be better in the morning."

They heard Etta calling from downstairs. "Come and eat before it gets cold!"

"I have to go," Gittel said. "I'll bring you some dinner."

"No. Thank you. I'm fine. Honest. I couldn't eat if I tried."

"Well, call me if you need anything. No matter what time it is." The footsteps and the perfume retreated. The door closed softly.

About an hour later, Gittel crept across the room, and ever so quietly, left a glass of cider, a bowl of lentil soup, and a chunk of black bread on the bedside stand. "Feel better," she whispered as she tiptoed out.

Shula slept fitfully that night. She dreamed she was in a box and couldn't get out. When she woke, she chastised herself for being so stupid and fretted about her future.

THE NEXT DAY, SHE DID HER BEST to stay out of sight, dusting the parlor when her aunt and cousin were in the kitchen, keeping her back turned when speaking. But she could not avoid them forever.

That evening she went to supper. Walking was painful. She stepped gingerly into the kitchen and stood behind her chair, gripping it for support, until she regained enough strength to sit. Her hair was braided and hung down her back, as usual, but she had not woven a ribbon into it as she'd become accustomed to. Neither had she dressed in her "better" clothes. She was wearing a drab work dress.

"Oh, my God!" Etta's hand flew to her mouth. "What happened to you?" She had seen her niece first, because her seat faced the doorway. Her husband, at the head of the table, and Gittel, with her back toward the entrance, gasped when they turned their heads to see the cause of the outburst. Yussel, at the far end, kept his head and eyes down, and continued to shovel flanken and toasted barley onto his plate. His hands were trembling so that he was spilling grain onto the white cloth.

"Those are some nasty bruises you got there." Chaim pointed his fork at the crusty drainage around her swollen and blackened right eye, then her lips, which, though no longer bleeding, were puffy and moist.

"I fell down the stairs," Shula said.

"That must have been some fall. Leave any blood on the carpet?" her uncle quipped.

"It was the cellar steps. I made the wrong turn on my way to the bathroom last night."

He grimaced.

"Why didn't you call me? I told you—" Gittel faced her. She was wearing her weekday wig, which was shorter and less glossy than her the one she wore on the Sabbath.

"I didn't want to disturb you."

"A fall like that must have rattled the house. Nobody heard it?" her uncle said.

"With the way you snore, Chaim?" Etta turned her gaze away from her niece and focused on her husband. "We wouldn't hear a riot if it was outside our window." Laugher sputtered around the room. Even Yussel, having recovered after Shula's lie, chortled.

"I don't snore."

"And the rabbi doesn't have a beard," his wife answered.

"As I was saying, Yussel," Chaim went on after giving his wife a disparaging glance, "You have exceeded my expectations. I agreed to this match with my daughter with, let's say. caution. But I'll be the first to admit I was wrong to doubt you."

Gittel smiled adoringly at her husband, her good eye focused on his dimpled grin, the other on the pots in the sink.

"Do we have to hear this *every* night?" Etta harrumphed. 'He's so smart.' 'He's so shrewd.'" Every night it's same story how Yussel exceeded your expectations. Yes, Chaim, he's the Messiah himself come to live with us."

Her husband lifted a forkful of his dinner to his mouth, not before sharing it with his white shirt. He'd removed his cuffs and rolled up his sleeves. His belly hung over his belt.

"You and Gittel will inherit my position, this house—"

Etta threw her napkin on the table. Her husband raised his hand up to silence her. "Don't worry. Don't worry. I'm taking care of Sol, too. I've arrangd—"

"I have something I need to talk to you about," Shula said. She was sitting with her hands folded before the plate. Chaim stopped talking in mid-sentence. Etta started hitting Yussel on his back as he began choking on his food. Shula waited for everyone's attention. She watched the color drain from Yussel's face and delighted in watching him squirm before she began. She cleared her throat. "I'm leaving."

They all spoke at once. Chaim questioning what he was hearing and asked her to repeat what she'd said. Gittel wanted to know why. Etta challenged the sense of it. And Yussel asked how soon she would go.

"I'm leaving," she said again. She faced her cousin, who was already tearing up. "Because I'm no longer a child, and I need to make my own way. You've been very kind to me, Gittel." She touched her shoulder. "I'll never forget that." *And I'll never forgive myself for what I did to you.* They were both holding back tears. "But I can't be a burden any longer."

"How could you think you're a burden?" Gittel said. "You do *more* than your share in this house. Please reconsider. You're family. I've come to love you like a sister."

They hugged each other. "And I you."

"I won't hear of it," Etta said. "You're my sister's child. It's my obligation to look after you."

"Where was your sense of obligation when you turned her brothers away?" Yussel mumbled, just loud enough for her to hear. "I guess your duty is somehow related to free labor."

"I heard that!" Etta snapped.

"Where will you go?" Chaim asked.

"I'll work as a servant for the *goyim*."

"That's ridiculous!" Chaim filled his glass with wine.

"Your uncle is right. It's ridiculous. A relative of mine working for the *goyim*? You know how they treat pretty Jewish *maidelas*?"

"If it's because of money we'll pay you a salary—a small one, of course. We're not wealthy people you know."

Etta nearly jumped out of her seat. "Let's not be so hasty, Chaim. Maybe we can talk this through. She does live in a lovely—"

"It's not about money. I just need to go."

"She wants to go. Let her go. She's a grown woman. She knows what she's doing," Yussel concluded, and turned to Shula. "I'll help you pack."

Later that evening when Shula and Yussel passed each other in the hallway, he thanked her. "I really appreciate what you did for me."

"For *you*? I'd see myself paraded in the streets as an adulteress before I'd do anything to help you. I'm doing it for your *wife*. As much of a *momzer* as you are—*and you are*—Gittel doesn't deserve the shame you would bring upon her.I cringe to have to ask, but a few kopecks would help."

"I thought you were going to get a job with some *goy*."

"Who is going to hire a pregnant Jewess?"

"Where am I supposed to get money?"

She stared into his beautiful blue eyes, at his curly hair and dimpled cheeks. But only saw ugliness.

CHAPTER 16

YUSSEL STARED AT THE CEILING while his wife slept beside him. It was cold and drafty, but they were warm beneath a down comforter and with a pan of hot embers at their feet. The rain had turned to snow. An eerie light shone through the window, outlining Gittel's wig on the bedside stand. Why did she have to wear that ugly thing? He looked at her, wrapped in a frumpy flannel nightgown and cap, and sighed. Life would be tough without Shula. She may not have been a beauty, but boy could she move. He was picturing her sweet behind when his mother-in-law's voice came through the thin wall.

"Chaim. Chaim!" he heard her say. He imagined her poking her snoring husband. "Wake up. I need to talk to you. . .wake *up*."

The snorting sputtered. "Huh?"

"I need to talk to you."

". . .Now? In the middle of the night? Go back to sleep. Talk to me in the morning," he grumbled.

Yussel heard the bed squeak, imagined his father-in-law giving his wife his back.

"*Chaim*! This is important."

"What's so important that can't wait 'till morning?"

Yussel heard a long exhalation and imagined another poke. He heard the bed squeak again, a thud that sounded like the headboard hitting the wall, and pictured his father-in-law sitting up.

"Shula is pregnant, and Yussel is the father," Etta said.

On the other side of the wall, Yussel gasped. His heart skipped a beat.

"*What*?" Chaim sounded incredulous. "How in heaven's name did you come to that conclusion?"

"I've been thinking about it," Etta said. "I've had a. . .a feeling about those two. I've been watching them. The way he smiles at her. The way she blushes whenever he looks at her."

"So he smiles. She blushes. That's a bit of a stretch, don't you think?"

"You don't see what's before your eyes because he's your golden boy."

"Here we go again." Another groan.

"Tell me you haven't noticed that she hardly eats, but hasn't lost weight. And she fell down the stairs?"

"How does falling down the stairs mean she's pregnant? Really, Etta, you're just looking for things. I don't see how that has anything to do with it.

"How else would you explain those bruises?"

"Come on. She fell down the cellar steps. The steps are concrete. She got bruises. Simple."

"Or your *son-in-law* beat her."

Another exhalation. "You just told me you think they've making hay under the sheets. Why the hell would he beat her?"

"I don't know. But did you notice that they didn't speak at dinner tonight? How they avoided looking at each other? Maybe, I don't know, it's only a guess, maybe she told him about her condition. Her sudden insistence on leaving?"

". . .I'll admit that is rather strange."

"You didn't happen to notice the dark coloration across her nose and cheeks? In the shape of a butterfly? Of course not, you're a man."

". . .Now that you mention it. . . ."

"It's called a pregnancy mask."

Consumed by terror, Yussel threw off the quilt, sprang from the bed, grabbed his boots from the corner and his clothes from the chair, and hurried across the room, ignoring the pain in his toe, still swollen and throbbing from when he kicked the wall.

As he was leaving, he heard his mother-in-law say, "I'll take her to the midwife in the morning. Then we can deal with *him*."

"Where are you going, Yussel?" Gittel asked in a drowsy voice.

He wondered if she'd heard the conversation, too. He doubted it. She's been sleeping too soundly. They slept spooned. Her leg had been wrapped over his. It must have been his movement that woke her. But it wasn't going to matter. ". . .I-I have to use the use the toilet."

"Use the chamber pot."

"I need to sit. Don't wait up. This may take a while."

"Haven't you taken your castor oil?"

"It didn't work. Go back to sleep."

He closed the door behind him.

After grabbing pillowcases from the linen bureau in the hallway, jiggling the drawer open as carefully as possible so as not to make noise, he crept downstairs. As usual, the parlor reeked of stale cigars. Whatever light come through the windows was poor, but enough for him to maneuver. He could make out the outline of the furniture and felt his way to the kitchen. He lit the lantern that was kept on a hook outside the cold room entrance.

The door creaked when he opened it. He cringed. In his agitated state, it sounded loud enough to wake the dead.

Gripping the bannister tightly with one hand and holding the light with the other, he snuck down the stairs. The larder was half the size of the kitchen. Floor-to-ceiling shelves were stocked with flour, barley, potatoes, and other foodstuffs, vodka and wine. Flickering light bounced off the walls, falling on the stone beneath his feet. A mouse scurried past him. With no time to be choosy, he stuffed his pillowcases with whatever his hand touched and rushed back to the kitchen, where he threw in what was left of a loaf of black bread.

Should he take his father-in-law's fox-lined coat or his own sheepskin? No doubt Chaim's would be warmer. But would it make Yussel a target for assault? Or worse, would dragging his satchels make him suspect, and possibly arrested? In the end he chose safety and put on his own. He set his *ushanka* on his head, the ear flaps tied up, and slipped into his boots.

Before he left the house, he considered taking his mother-in-law's jewelry. Other than the pearls she wore every sabbath, she wouldn't know they were missing—-not that it mattered. But the thought only lasted a moment. She kept them in a velvet lined box under her bed.

Instead he skulked back into the dining room, mindful of every creak and squeak, unlocked the cutlery chest with the key that was taped behind the grandfather clock, and stuffed his deep pockets with as much silverware as would fit. Inching over to the glass curio, he snatched the holiday candlesticks and tucked them in his coat. He put his hand on the menorah. It was cold and smooth beneath his fingers. The alabaster replica of Jerusalem, studded with precious stones, had to be worth a fortune. But it was heavy, and he already had more than he could carry.

With dawn just a few short hours away, pillowcases slung over his shoulder and silverware chiming inside his pockets, he slipped into the snowy night.

CHAPTER 17

SHULA WAS WEDGED TIGHTLY in the bottom of a well. It was cold. She had goosebumps. A monster was glaring down at her, its breath warm and foul. "Get up, you yentzer!" it babbled. "Get up!" She shifted to her side, drew her knees up to her chest to warm herself, and pulled her pillow over her head, trying to quell the visions and drown the awful sounds.

"Whore!"

She felt her face being slapped: jolted awake, she opened her eyes. Her blankets had been wrenched off her. Her muslin gown was wrapped around her waist. *Tanta* Etta hovered over her, features contorted in the quivering light from the candle she held before her face.

"What do you have to say for yourself?"

Half-asleep, Shula didn't answer.

"Well?"

The girl lowered her head and focused on the frost-covered window across from her, where howling snow was accumulating in drifts.

"You're not talking?"

Shula felt a slap across her face.

"We'll just have to take you to the midwife. See what *she* has to say."

"You needn't take me. I'm pregnant," the girl admitted in an almost inaudible voice.

"I knew it! I *knew*!" Etta declared, almost happy to have her suspicion confirmed.

Gittel came running into the room, throwing her robe over her nightgown. "What happened? What's all the shouting about? Why are you screaming at Shula?"

"Get your husband!" Etta demanded.

"My *husband*? What's he got to do with anything? He's not in bed. He went to the bathroom."

"When?"

". . .I don't know. A while ago."

"How much of a while?"

Her daughter looked pensive. "A few hours, I guess."

"*Chaim*! Find Yussel!"

Chaim stumbled down the hall, his nightcap covering his ears, the strings tied under his double chin. "I thought we were going to wait 'till morning to deal with this." He wrapped his arms around himself and yawned loudly. The stove had not yet been lit, and the house was cold.

"What is this all *about*?" Gittel asked again, standing between her mother and her cousin, who was hunched on the side of her bed with her face in her hands, sobbing.

Etta's arms were across her chest. "Tell her, Shula."

". . .I'm pregnant," she whispered.

"*Pregnant*? How can that be? You hardly leave the house. . . . *Oh*!" Gittel gasped. ". . .Is it true? . . . What I'm thinking, is it true?" Shula nodded without saying a word.

Gittel turned white. Her jaw clenched. A vein in her temple began to throb. "How *could* you?" she screeched. "How *could* you?" She dragged her cousin off the bed by her ankles, and when she landed with a thud, pulled at her hair, clawed her cheeks and neck, then started pummeling her, her fists surprisingly strong.

Shula did not defend herself, just lay on the cold floor, curled into herself, taking the beating.

"He's gone!" Chaim announced in his deep baritone voice when he came back in the room. "And so is the silverware."

RACHEL WAS COMING OUT OF THE HEN HOUSE, with eggs in a wire basket, when she heard the front gate creak and saw someone entering her property. Still dark and snowing steadily, she hadn't expected the milk man for at least another hour, and if, for some reason, he was early, she would have heard his clanking wagon. Her heart began to pound. The trauma of Layzer's abduction had never left her. Anything even remotely similar set her nerves on fire.

"Rachel?" the dark figure called.

". . .Yes?"

"It's me. . .Shula."

"Shula? . . . Is something wrong?"

Unable to speak with the lump in her throat, Shula just shook her head.

With the eggs tapping gently against each other, Rachel lifted her skirt above the drifts, and hurried toward her. Powdery snow fell around her ankles and into the tracks she left in her wake. She couldn't make out Shula's features. A shawl covered her head. A turned-up collar hid her nose, and the sheepskin coat met her boots. Only her eyes were visible. But despite the dim early morning light, Rachel could see the tears running down her face.

Rachel opened her arms wide to embrace her. Chunks of ice were sticking to Shula's coat sleeves.

Rachel peered over the girl's shoulder, looked right, then left. The street was empty. "You walked? In this weather?" Her forehead creased. She held Shula's ice-cold face in her calloused hands.

"I-I didn't know where else to go."

"Come. Let's talk inside over a cup a tea. Get you warmed-up." She took her arm and started toward the house.

Shula hesitated. She took a deep breath, inhaling the sweet, clean world. "Maybe this was a mistake." She turned.

Rachel grabbed her elbow. "Come with me. Whatever it is, we'll work it out. We can't stand here in this weather," she said through a cloud of vapor.

A hissing oil lamp cast just enough brightness to outline the kitchen. Rachel left the basket of eggs on the table, draped her shawl over a chair to dry, and slipped an apron over her dress. She shuddered involuntarily. The house was warmer than outside, but not by much. She had only started the fire before going to the chicken coop, and the birch logs had yet to ignite. Only the kindling was burning. The dried mud in the chinks of the walls was failing, and the wind was whining through the cracks. She squatted before the stove, opened the grate, and poked at the crackling tinder with the iron rod. Smoke blew into her face, causing her eyes to tear. "It won't take long to heat up." She pointed to a seat. After breaking through the layer of ice in the water bucket, she filled the kettle and rested it on the burner.

They stared at each other, then at the stove. Shula pulled off her scarf. Her hair was damp, uncombed, and stuck to her head.

"What happened to you *face*?" Rachel gasped.

The girl's hand flew to the angry welt on her cheek. With all her other troubles, she hardly remembered the bruise. "Oh, that."

"Shula?" Lena had stopped mid-way down the stairs.

A low moan escaped Shula's lips: The moment she was dreading. "Good morning, Mrs. Rubinowitz."

The older woman continued down the steps, gripping the railing for support, the rungs creaking beneath her weight. "Is everything alright?"

Shula focused on the embroidered star of David on the wall opposite her. In the dull light, it, and everything else in the room, was muted. She smiled weakly and licked her lips.

"Something's wrong, isn't it?" Lena picked at the knobby wool of her skirt, twirling the fabric around and around. "That's why you're here . . .It's Yussel, isn't it? Something happened to Yussel! *Vey iz mir*!" She sank onto her seat and wiped her forehead with a crumpled handkerchief. Despite the chill she'd begun to perspire.

"Yussel is fine. At least I think so," the girl whispered.

"Oh! Thank God!" Lena looked at the ceiling, clasping her hands to her bosom. "You gave me quite a scare! . . . Wait, what? What do mean, you *think* so?"

"He. . .he left. During the night."

"Who left?" Moishe had entered, his bad leg trailing behind.

"It's your aunt, isn't it?" Lena said, emphasizing her opinion with a wagging finger. "She made his life so miserable. He couldn't take it anymore." She raised her fist. "I never liked that woman. Never. Your mother was such a lovely person, may she rest in peace, but that sister of hers—"

"*Who* left?" Moishe repeated.

"Yussel," Rachel said.

Her father went pale and leaned on his walking stick to hold himself up.

"Papa, sit down." Rachel hurried to his side, pulled out a chair, and eased him onto it. She poured tea into his favorite cup and put it, and a slice of bread with jam, before him. He embraced the mug, letting the heat soothe his swollen knuckles, but didn't take a sip. Steam fogged his glasses. He cleaned the lens with the tablecloth.

Spectacles in hand, he looked at Shula. ". . .Why did he go?"

"She told you," his wife answered. "His mother-in-law—"

Moishe held his hand up. "No, Lena. That's what *you* said. I want to hear what *she* says."

Shula bit the inside of her cheek. She could almost smell her fear. "Um. I'm, ah. . .pregnant." She dropped her head, lowered her voice, and steadied her trembling chin. "Yussel is the father."

Moishe let out a deep sigh, stroked his whiskers. ". . .I see."

Behind them, a log crackled in the stove. The kitchen was getting warmer, the sweet wood smell in sharp contrast with the mood. He removed his sweater and muffler. Underneath, he was wearing *tzitsis* over a white shirt. Rachel opened the shutters a tad. It was snowing harder, spinning in circles. Gray light began to fill the house.

"Oh my God!" Lena covered her ears, waved her arms like a madwoman. "No," she wailed. "No. No. *No*! You—you *whore*!"

From the corner of her eye, Shula saw a brass candlestick about to rain down on her. She crouched in her seat, covering her head with her arms.

"Get out!" Lena screamed. "Get out. Get out. Get *out*!"

Before the weapon came down, Rachel was on her feet, wrenching it out of her mother's hands. "Stop it, Mama. *Stop it*!"

Shula ran for the door. But Moishe blocked her way. "Lena, I've never interfered with you protecting Yussel. But this I will not allow. This girl has no place to go."

"She's a *whore*—"

Moishe held up his hand to silence her. "No. She is no more guilty than your son. Less guilty, in fact."

"My son. Always *my* son. Never *your* son when there's a problem. As if whatever he does is my fault—"

"No, Lena." He shook his head. "I don't blame you. I blame myself. It's *my* fault. I should have acted like the man in the family . . .but I will be that man from now on. This girl stays."

BOOK TWO

CHAPTER 18

Marie Gilbert was sitting across from Walter Hockenberry on the front porch swing, not knowing where to put her hands or what to say. She felt ridiculous in the wide hoop skirt and banana curls her mother made her wear. She'd turned nineteen that year, and, being no beauty (as her mother often told her), until then had never had a proper suitor. None, that is, approved of by her mother—-until Walter.

At seven, the sky was still bright and the air warm and muggy. An occasional horse and carriage clopped along the cobblestones on the quiet Upper West Side block. Roses that edged the yard against the low picket fence released a faint perfumed fragrance into the sultry air.

Walter stared at the oaks and maples that lined the street; at his father's buggy parked in front of the two-storied brick house; at the gas lamps that would be lit in another hour or so. Dinner would be ready soon. The smell the roast beef and duck came through the open windows, along with the murmur of their parents' conversations.

Marie knew her mother was showing off the family coat of arms, which was impossible to miss since, hanging in the center of the wall, it overshadowed everything in the room.

The nineteen-year-old had been listening to the same story for as long as she could remember. Every guest got the same speech-except that in each telling, the family history got more grandiose. Tonight the Gilberts were knights. Yesterday they had been squires. Tomorrow they would be kings. Marie wondered whether the Gilberts were anybody at all or if her mother had found the plaque in a garbage heap and invented the story.

Marie hid her big flat feet under the fifteen yards of organdy-covered hoops. Tall, lanky, and all angles, Walter was sort of cute in an awkward way. She wondered if he liked her. Not that it mattered. Whether he liked her or she liked him, they would be married. Obviously, he didn't care for her. Other than when he spoke about some bug he was studying at college, where his eyes brightened behind his horn-rimmed spectacles, he rarely spoke to her at all, never mind look at her. He kept his eyes on the brick walkway, arranged in a circular pattern, or on the brass door knocker behind her. Understandable. How *could* he like her? How could *anybody*?

The swing made a creaking sound as Marie pushed it back and forth. She cleared her throat. "What is it they call the study of bugs? Does it have an official name?" she said at last, twirling a banana curl around her pudgy finger.

"Entomology," he replied, still studying the pavement. "It's quite fascinating. Did you know, for instance, that insects existed on this planet long before the first dinosaurs? They're very resilient creatures."

"Is that so?"

Walter nodded. "The word 'insect' comes from the Latin 'insectum.' They are the most diverse group of creatures on the planet."

"Are they really?" she said with as much enthusiasm as if she had a toothache. "Is that your major? Ent. . .ent—"

Entomology? No, just my love. One of my loves, anyway. Law will be my career."

". . .Do you like Columbia?"

"Yes, it's quite fine."

". . .You must meet a lot of interesting people."

"Some."

"I suppose the weather is colder up there. Do you get much snow?"

He laughed, keeping his lips closed tight not to show his mouth guard. "Some. Considering it's all the way uptown."

She smiled, too, lifting her eyes from her voluminous skirt. She hadn't realized she'd made a joke. "I hope the war will be over soon. It's just dreadful that it's lasted so long."

"Don't let your mother hear you say that," he said, trying not to grin.

She laughed, careful not to show her horse teeth. He thought she had the most beautiful smile.

Just then they heard the sound of the dinner bell, and the servant, an extra, hired especially for the occasion, dressed in a black-and-white maid's outfit, her hair in a net, emerged onto the porch and announced that it was being served.

Florence had decorated the house. Not one wall was white, each room having been painted or papered a different bold color combination: crimson and purple; yellow and gold; scarlet and blue. Several fireplaces adorned the house, one with a marble mantle, another with a mahogany one. It had piped-in gas and two water closets, not one—-each complete with Italian tiles. The parlor was powder blue. Everything in it was powder blue: the wallpaper, the sofa, the drapes, the over-stuffed, gilded, swirl-legged chairs. Everything was ornate, gold-trimmed, or had swirling lines. A huge oil painting of Louis XVI standing beside Marie Antoinette, in a gilded frame, hung opposite the coat of arms. A lace hanky under glass sat in a curio, among other family relics. French. Everything had to look French. As if being French was some sort of special privilege. Marie often felt she was living in a museum.

In the dining room, their parents were already at the table, beneath the crystal chandelier. It was set with the family's finest gold-bordered china and crystal glasses. A succulent duck, brown and crisp, sat on one end of the sideboard, a roast beef at the other. An array of side dishes filled the spaces in between: mashed potatoes, golden-topped and swirling; creamed cauliflower; string beans almandine; cranberry sauce; brown herb gravy; and stuffed mushrooms. The freshly cut garden roses seemed limp in the heat. The butler poured wine.

"So, are you two getting to know each other?" Florence asked as the betrothed came in. The windows were open, but the air was still. Florence fanned herself and patted her forehead with her lace handkerchief. "Walter, did you know that Marie is a pianist? Perhaps we can talk her into playing s concerto for us after dinner." Florence pointed out the baby grand, glossy and smelling of lemon polish, that occupied an alcove off the room. Sheet music lay open on the stand.

Marie rolled her eyes and whispered when she got closer, "Really, Mother, must you?"

"Now, now, let's not be shy. She plays quite well, Walter."

"As well she should after all the money we've spent on her lessons," her father added with a chuckle. Round and jolly, Gerhard Gilbert was the hundred-eighty-degree opposite of his ambitious wife, not only in the fifteen-year age difference between them, but in every other way imaginable. Whereas Florence was tall and slender, with thick dark hair, he was stout, and the white crop on his head was thinning.

His cheeks were red and beefy; hers were white and prominent. In temperament too they differed—he tranquil and amiable, she high-strung, acutely sensitive, and demanding. His rosy cheeks revealed no sign of his fifty-five years, because he left all the worrying to her. She handled the family businesses. She made the decisions. She ruled the roost.

"I'm sure Walter would be happy to hear you play," she went on. "Isn't that right, Walter?"

Walter smiled without showing his teeth. "Only if she wants to." Steam fogged his glasses as the maid ladled onion soup into his bowl. The course passed in silence.

"Duck? Roast beef, Mrs. Hockenberry?" the butler asked after the soup dishes had been cleared away, standing at her hip, holding two platters, one in each hand.

"Duck, please."

"Breast? Wing? White meat?"

"Dark, and only a little bit of gravy."

"I thought surely those Rebs would have surrendered after Gettysburg," Walter's father said in a stiff English accent despite his forty years in America.

"You would think so, wouldn't you, Edgar?" Gerhard answered, his face redder than usual owing to the heat and the wine he'd drunk before dinner.

"I'd hardly call it a victory on our part," Walter said. "We took almost as many casualties as they did. Nearly thirty thousand men, I've heard."

Walter's mother put her fork down and raised her head. She was a petite woman with a pale complexion made paler by the drab dress she was wearing. In an accent not as thick as her husband's, she said, "Boys, you mean."

"The bloodiest battle of the war so far," answered Edgar, accepting his plate of roast beef with potatoes, mushrooms, and beans.

"All those boys," Mrs. Hockenberry reiterated, shaking her head. "And for what, I ask you? For what?"

"For slavery, Mother. It's an unfortunate situation. But sometimes we must fight for our principles."

Gerhard dug into his meat. "Walter, how can a smart college chap as yourself be so naïve? Do you honestly believe that we would lose all these men—and resources—for a bunch of darkies? The conflict has to do with state's rights and economics."

"With all due respect, Mr. Gilbert, Both the South's states' rights and economics are driven by slavery."

"I think slavery is terrible," Florence added as she topped her plate with mashed potatoes. "It's the dumbest thing I've ever heard. Why on earth would you want to house, clothe, and feed someone, and then have to support them when they're too old and feeble to work, when you can simply pay someone slave wages and be rid of them when they're of no use? Never made any sense to me. But so be it." She bit into a mushroom. "If that's what these Southerners want, all the better for me. May the war last forever."

Unbeknownst to either, both Marie and Walter gave her disparaging looks.

"Well, I hate to disappoint you, dear," Gerhard said, "but I don't believe they can hold out much longer. They've just lost Vicksburg, don't forget; their soldiers are in bare feet and half-starved. The South is in ruins. In fact, I understand that they're selling rats in their butcher shops, and that they've been reduced to eating their own horses and dogs."

"Gerhard, please! Florence scolded. "We're at table."

Gerhard excused himself.

"If they're so badly off," Marie said, soft and quiet, "then we would be winning the war. And if we're winning the war, then why would the president initiate a draft?"

"A draft?" her father questioned.

"Yes. There's to be lottery," his daughter answered.

"Oh, my." Walter's mother put her hand to her mouth as she looked at her son. "You mean to tell me that they can just come in and take our loved ones? Force them into battle?" She lifted the fan from her lap and created a small breeze for herself.

"People such as ourselves will have nothing to worry about, Olga. I'm told there's to be a clause which will allow you to either buy a substitute or pay three hundred dollars. Piddlings to keep out of harm's way."

"So you've heard about it, too. How is it I missed that bit of news?" Gerhard asked his wife.

"How indeed, when you read the *Times* every day. It's been the talk of the town. At least in that part of town where it matters to them. I heard it from a darkie who works for me."

"Well, if it came from one of them," Gerhard said, "it has to be true. You know what they say: 'You want to know anything about the war, just ask a darkie.' It's as if they have a secret line to the White House."

"It's been in the works since spring," Walter added. "A lottery list is to be posted at the Marshal's office. There's quite a stir about it, in fact. This substitute business and three hundred dollars is terribly unfair." He turned to Florence. "Three hundred dollars is hardly '*piddlings'* to the poor immigrant, *Mrs. Gilbert.* He doesn't earn that much money in a year."

Florence's eyebrows arched. After a moment she said, "*Fair*, Walter? I'll tell you what's fair. It's his *duty* to fight for this country.

If he wants to enjoy the hospitality and privileges of our great land, it's only right that he should have to fight for it. If he doesn't like it, he can return to wherever it is he came from. And may I add—" she pointed her fork at him— "if he wasn't out drinking and getting into brawls every day of his life, he might be able to get a decent job and be able to *pay* the three hundred dollars to stay out of the army!"

Walter's knife made a chiming sound as he dropped it on his plate. "A decent job? Working in one of your factories for five cents a day!"

The only sound around the table was that of silverware hitting the dishes and the glasses clinking together. Walter continued, "You talk about hospitality and privilege! To be used and abused by the rich. To live in squalor. To be treated—"

"Hmm." Edgar laughed nervously and patted his cravat. "This is a delicious meal, Florence. I can't remember the last time I had anything so tasty." To the butler, who was standing quietly at the end of the table, he snapped a finger and said, "More wine, please."

"Maybe you should enlist, then," Florence continued.

"Maybe I should. Maybe I *will*."

"Now, now," Edgar cut in. "Nobody's joining the army! Let us not have any more of this war talk. What any of us thinks is of no consequence. We can't change a thing. No sense arguing about it." To his son he shot a hostile look. To Florence he smiled and said, "To be a parent! Walter is young and idealistic. Bad influences out there. He'll learn." Florence would choke on her duck, Edgar thought, if it ever came to light that Walter was an abolitionist who attended weekly meetings at the Black Plymouth Church in Brooklyn. "Let us celebrate what we have come to celebrate, the union of our two lovely children. May we keep our business ventures in the family!"

"Here, here," echoed Gerhard. And in unison the two sets of parents raised their crystal glasses.

Marie climbed the steps after her parents. She watched her father sway back and forth, grabbing the banister for support. He'd had too much to drink again. She could smell the wine on his breath even from a distance behind him. Or perhaps it was his age. . .or his knees. . .or the heat. He was getting old. He was too fat, and she could see he'd put on even more weight in the past few months. She'd noticed before when he was at the table that the buttons on his brocade vest were stretched and popping.

They were speaking as if she weren't there.

"I thought we'd have the reception at Delmonico's." Florence was saying to her husband.

He stopped on the landing beneath a stained-glass window, above a vase filled with silk orchids. "Delmonico's? Isn't that a bit. . .ostentatious?"

His wife's face, bright with excitement a moment before, turned to a scowl. She turned to face him, arms akimbo. "Where else should it be? At some cheap downtown eating house like Columbia's? . . . "Really, Gerhard!"

"Of course not. I didn't mean to suggest. . . ." He started moving again. The heat seemed to be rising the higher he went. He loosened his cravat. "But there are other places a little less. . .expensive."

Florence harrumphed. "This will be the event of the year. Anybody who's anybody will be invited." Her skirt swished on each step. "No. It *must* be Delmonico's."

They reached the top landing and proceeded down the long hallway. A floral runner covered the cherrywood floors. Family paintings hung from the walls: Florence in her teens with a head full of curls, wearing a bright summer dress; Florence in her twenties, sitting side saddle on a horse; Florence in her thirties, beneath a magnolia tree; a portrait of some Gilbert ancestor in a stiff suit; and one of Marie at five, looking like Little Bo Peep with pantaloons peeking out from under a short dress. "Don't you think we're jumping the gun?" Gerhard said. "We haven't even spoken with Marie about it. Maybe she doesn't like the young man."

"Of course she likes him. What's not to like? Isn't that right, dear?" Florence looked over her shoulder at her daughter, who was ambling several paces behind.

"What does it matter what I think?"

"See, I told you. No problem," Florence told her husband.

"And how much will this shindig set us back?" Gerhard went on. "Two dollars, three dollars, a head? It's not as if we're in the shipping business."

"No. But the Hockenberrys are."

"Then maybe we should have *them* pay for it."

She gave him a reproachful look. "It starts at three— without the wine and liquor, of course. That's extra. And naturally we'll have to have something special, different. . .*extraordinary*. Lobster, perhaps."

"Naturally."

She stopped and stared at him. "Since when do you question how I handle our finances? Haven't I invested our money wisely all these years?"

"Impeccably. I'd never question you. I have no complaints, my dear. Certainly not."

"Though I am baffled, I must admit, about what business we should get into *after* the war. In addition to the partnership in the shipping venture, that is." They started down the hall again.

"I'm sure something will appeal to you. You're very resourceful. Getting back to this Delmonico's. . .it is, as I say, grandiose, don't you think?"

"Grandiose? No. *Elegant*. Don't forget, this is a wonderful match. . .despite the young man's liberal persuasions—which I'm confident, will change as he grows up."

"Yes, he's young. He has to grow up."

"And don't forget—how many offers have there been? Marie isn't getting any younger."

"She's only about to turn twenty."

"Soon to be an old maid. . .not to mention she's not exactly a world-class beauty. Those teeth! Where in heaven's name did they come from? Certainly not from my side of the family. . . . She's my daughter, and I love her, but fact is fact—"

"There was this Des. . .Desi something or other fellow. . .whatshisname, you remember?"

"Desislov, wasn't it?"

"Yes. Yes, that's it. Desi whatever. I liked him. He was a nice chap. Polite. Ambitious," Gerhard said.

They reached their bedroom door. Florence stopped before going in to offer her husband a shocked look. "Desislov? You're not serious. He's a *nobody*. An *immigrant, for heavens sake!*"

"Well, the Hockenberrys are immigrants."

"*British* immigrants. That's quite a difference. They're practically American. That Desi fellow, his mother came from Bulgaria or some ungodly place. No. We could never have hoped for anyone as promising to come along as the Hockenberrys. They're wealthy. Aristocratic. Not *old* money, but—"

"I believe the grandfather was a pirate."

"Hearsay. Besides, we can't have everything. And with Edgar in shipping. . .a fine business combination for us." She opened the door, turned on the gas light and entered, the scent of lavender enveloping them. It was a feminine room with flowered wallpaper, a ruffled bedspread, French lace curtains, and a three-mirrored dressing table on which sat a vanity set in a silver case, perfumes, and powders.

She unpinned her hair, letting it fall to her shoulders. Showing her husband her back, she indicated for him to unfasten her gown. "This has to be the social event of the year," she went on. "I want people talking about it for years to come."

His fingers fumbled over the tiny loops and buttons. "When will it take place?"

"October fifteenth. The weather should be perfect. I thought I'd wear apple green. What do you think? Or pink?"

"I always liked you in green." He reached her skin. It was so smooth. He kissed the back of her neck. Her powder tickled his nose.

"I'll wear pink. I have to look young. . .and stunning."

"You *are* young and stunning, my dear, even in a burlap bag."

Marie closed the door to her own room softly behind her, stepped out of her dress, and left it in a heap on the floor for the maid to pick up in the morning. Moonlight through the window illuminated a swath of the Persian carpet. Desislov. She'd never forgive her mother for that. Marie had really liked him. And what's more *he'd* liked *her*. "You want to *marry* him? You're not *serious*," her mother had said when Marie finally got up the nerve to broach the subject—her mother's response to everything she didn't agree with. "Love?" And then her mother had uttered in her condescending, high-pitched laugh. "Let me tell you something about love, Marie. You can't love a nobody." That was another one of her mother's famous adages. Anyone who was not in Florence's circle was nobody.

For a moment that evening, Marie had been in love. Walter had defied her mother. But just as the seeds were planted, they had been uprooted. "My apologies, Mrs. Gilbert," he'd said. "I had no business speaking to you the way I did. Please forgive my bad manners." And Marie's affection for him had curdled like bad milk.

She was in bed, her head on three fluffy pillows, staring at the ceiling in the dark room. She heard the water humming through the pipes when her mother flushed the fancy toilet in the water closet, which was situated between the two bedrooms. Then she heard her call to her father, "This will be the talk of the town. The talk of the town!"

CHAPTER 19

FLORENCE AND GERHARD WERE in the dining room, sipping coffee, when the bell rang. At nine a.m., it was already hot and humid. "Who might that be at this hour?" Florence's cup clinked as she set it on the saucer.

I can't imagine." Gerhard looked over the morning paper to study the clock on the mantel. "Are we expecting anyone? A delivery, perhaps?"

"I don't think so. But I should think they would know better than to use the front entrance."

A moment later, Alfred, the butler, a man of about forty who had been in their employ for almost twenty years, stood before them in his black-and-white uniform. Beads of sweat lined his forehead. "Mr. Gilbert, Mrs. Gilbert, pardon me, but there's a policeman who wants to speak with you."

"A policeman?" Florence dabbed molasses off her lips with a napkin, leaving a red O on the linen. "Did he say what he wanted?"

"No, ma'am, only that he needs to speak with the master of the house."

Florence and Gerhard exchanged glances. "Have him wait in the vestibule," Florence said.

"Yes, ma'am."

The burly young fellow, in full policeman's regalia, was standing in the tiled foyer, twirling his hat and bouncing on the balls of his feet. He had a sweeping mustache, mutton-chop sideburns, and curly red hair, all wet with perspiration. The buttons on his navy-blue tunic glittered in the light from the diamond shaped glass in the door.

"Good morning." Gerhard held out his hand as he entered. "Sorry to have kept you waiting."

The policeman took his eyes off the portrait of Louis XVI and his wife and accepted Gerhard's soft palm. "Sorry to disturb ya."

"What can we do for you, Mr.—"

"Jim. Jim Fitzpatrick."

Wearing a lemon-yellow dress, her hair heaped on top of her head, and engulfed in the fragrance of powder and lavender perfume, Florence appeared.

The policeman nodded. "Mornin', ma'am. I was just about to tell ya husband here that we're expectin' trouble today in the city. We think it would be wise for folks such as yarselves to leave until—"

"Leave? Our *home*, you mean?" Florence exclaimed. "Why, for heaven's sakes? And who are the 'we' you are referring to?"

"For your safety, ma'am."

Florence was about to argue, but Gerhard put his fingers up to silence her. "Please, go ahead, Mr. . .Fitzpatrick, wasn't it?"

The officer nodded. "There's a demonstration going on, against the new draft bill. Maybe you heard about it?"

"As a matter of fact, we were speaking of it just recently." Gerhard turned to his wife. "Walter mentioned something about a lottery, remember?"

"Yes," Fitzpatrick affirmed. "At the marshal's office on Forty-seventh Street. It started out peaceful enough, folks just marching with their *No Draft* signs, but ya know how these things can get. . . . This is New York, after all."

"Yes. I'm afraid you're right, there."

Florence did not seem impressed. "So? There's a demonstration every other day."

"Are the Copperheads behind it, do you think?" Gerhard asked. "Or just those Five-Pointers again?"

"Hard to tell. Some think it might a been instigated by them Reb spies. Others say it's just another excuse for the hooligans to start trouble. Whoever started it, copperheads, spies, Five-Pointers, it's getting pretty nasty."

Florence harrumphed.

"This is particularly bad, ma'am. And they seem to be 'specially interested in government workers, and the upper classes. Which is why we're warning—"

"Surely the troops have been called to the scene?" Gerhard said.

Fitzpatrick shook his head apologetically. "'Fraid not, sir. They been sent to Gettysburg. We're on our own. . . . But not to worry too much. I expect we'll have the incident contained by morning."

"*Morning*?" Florence's eyebrows rose. "I would hope you get it contained before *then!* And you had better put those Five Pointers in jail where they belong when it's over."

Fitzpatrick grabbed the doorknob as he turned to go. The brass was warm in his hand. "Yes, ma'am. We certainly will. We're doing our best. And, ah—" he faced them again— "I'd avoid the main streets if I was you. By the way, that's a lovely picture there on the wall. Relatives of yours?"

After packing their belongings, the Gilberts left for their country home on Staten Island. Though the coach had been parked out of the sun in the carriage house, it was still sweltering inside the square cabin, the leather seats hot enough to sear their flesh. Gerhard sat beside his wife, a cloth behind his head so not to burn his neck, while Florence, patting sweat beads off her face with an embroidered handkerchief, peered out the window, and Marie, opposite them, fanned herself.

Following the policeman's advice, they avoided the main streets. Three big, round hat boxes, one atop the other, wobbled as the carriage dodged numerous holes. One toppled onto Gerhard's lap. "We'll only be gone overnight," he said with eyes closed. "Did you really have to empty your wardrobe?"

"Certainly you don't expect us to go bathing without our sun bonnets," Florence answered.

"Certainly not. How imprudent of me to ask."

"Look at that." Florence turned to her husband. "A few old gents marching with signs is all. See those fellows over there? I don't agree with their sentiments, but they seem benign, not the ruffians that Fitzpatrick person described. Scaring us out of our skin like that, when I have work to finish, orders to get out, huh!"

"When you're faced with adversity, my dear, you have to turn it inside out. Chalk it up as an unexpected but well-deserved, holiday. What do their signs say?" Gerhard asked in a sleepy voice.

"'It's a rich man's war but a poor man's fight!'" Marie answered, her head half out of the window, as she was suffering from motion sickness.

"Say again?"

She pulled her head back inside, her face a sickly shade of green, and repeated what she'd said. While the air made her feel somewhat better, the stench of horse manure in every street made it worse.

"Misguided fools." Gerhard yawned. "*Every* war is started by the rich and fought by the poor. It's the natural order of things. Do they really believe their protesting in this ungodly heat will change the rhythm of the universe?" He unbuttoned his vest and the top of his shirt, pulled a handkerchief from his pocket, and wiped his forehead.

The coach bounced and shook, the big metal wheels dipping and clanking on the uneven cobbles as it made its way downtown. They continued to pass people carrying placards, each message voicing a similar opinion. Except for Marie throwing up, the trip remained uneventful—until they reached Broadway and Chambers.

There they found that Mr. Fitzpatrick had not exaggerated. It was indeed an unruly mob. And it was gaining momentum. These protestors were not carrying placards. They were carrying sticks and pipes. They were smashing windows and setting homes and businesses on fire. Every minute, the Gilberts heard another crash as something else hit the pavement. Gerhard stared out the window with his mouth agape. "Do you see what they're *doing*?" he gasped. "Why, they're tearing up the *streets*! They're using crowbars to pull up the tracks of the railway line. It's worse than that man said."

"Animals. A pack of *animals,*" Florence agreed.

"Women and children, as well." Gerhard looked aghast.

"Oh, my goodness, Mother, look! I think they're setting fire to Orendock's Hardware."

The coach stopped. Florence stuck her head out of the window to see what was happening. The horses were neighing and pissing, their urine making steam as it splashed on the cobbles.

"Thomas!" She tapped the outside of her window as she called up to the coachman. "Why are we stopped? Get us out of here. Turn down the next street."

Holding his high hat with one hand and the reins with the other, Thomas leaned over the side of the carriage and hollered down, "I'm trying, madam. But I'm afraid all the roads are blocked."

An acrid odor began to fill the air. They heard a whoosh and a moment later saw the stores go up in flames. The buildings hissed and crumbled. The Gilberts watched in horror as the mob grabbed shovels, hammers, rakes, and knives. They smashed windows, the glass spilling across the pavement, looting every store along the road. Marie saw women running out of what just moments before had been a jewelry shop, wearing armfuls of bracelets, necklaces, and dangling earrings. A few stores down, a woman struggled with a fancy lamp, and another carried a number of straw hats. An old lady was swinging a cooking pan from each hand. A boy, who seemed no older than seven, was banging a hatchet against a metal pot, making a horrific clanging noise, and laughing.

The fire spread quickly, devouring every wooden building in its path, giving off tremendous heat and blackening the sky.

Marie continued to stare.

Suddenly they felt the coach being rocked from side to side. A grimy face peered into the window.

Florence banged on the outside of the door again, with more intensity this time. "Thomas! *Thomas*!" she hollered, her voice almost a shriek. "Get us out of here this instant!"

CHAPTER 20

ACROSS THE HARBOR ON STATEN ISLAND, the riots continued. Abolitionists' homes and businesses were looted and destroyed. Black men were chased through the streets and, if unfortunate enough to get caught, were beaten, some lynched. Accounts of the events abounded, yet the Gilberts, sunning on the beach, did not see them first-hand. Not until returning home six days later did they learn that the riot had been the bloodiest insurrection in U.S. history.

Florence went to her shop. She didn't relish doing so, going to the loft on Broadway, especially in the dog days of summer, but—aside from her practice of making erratic appearances, so as to keep her employees on their toes—that Monday, the first day the factory would be open in more than a week, she had a lot to catch up on. At six-thirty a.m., an hour before opening, she had long since completed an abbreviated toilette, dressed, had a breakfast of toast, fruit, and coffee. She climbed the three flights of rickety stairs, made her way to the far back corner, and unlocked the four bolts on the door, above which read the legend, in black letters:

GILBERT'S MILLINERY SHOP

IF YOU DON'T COME SUNDAY
DON'T BOTHER TO COME IN MONDAY.

ALL EMPLOYEES ARE TO OBEY
AND RESPECT THEIR FORELADY.
WORK BEGINS AT 7:30, NOT 7:31

Florence Gilbert. Prop.

She entered the tight, airless attic. Dressed for steamy New York weather, she wore a short-sleeved cotton blouse and matching skirt and kept her hair in an upsweep off her neck. With the building closed for the six days, the work place was particularly unbearable. Already, sweat beads lined her forehead and flowed into the creases of her well-endowed bosom. Underarm wetness stained her bodice, and the floral scented talc she'd powdered herself with earlier, felt pasty.

Union hats were everywhere, boxed, packed, and ready to go: Blue cloth, cartons of buttons, blue thread and gold thread in tall cones, all piled high, blocked out light and air from the windows, and obstructing doors and aisles between the four rows of sewing machines that sat practically one on top of the next on old, sagging floors that could barely support the weight.

She studied the calendar of order dates hanging on the wall. "Damned insurrection," she muttered, her sigh audible in the quiet space. So much work. So little time. She supposed she should be grateful. At least her business hadn't been ransacked. Even the two shops on the bottom floor of her building had been pillaged, their windows smashed, army shirts and pants ripped to shreds, strewn about, or stolen.

First things first. She climbed on top of a stool, lifting her hem so not the trip and steadying herself with one hand against the wall, and pushed the fingers of the clock ahead fifteen minutes. Then she settled into the swivel chair behind her rollup desk, turned the lock with a soft click, slid up the slatted tambour, and concentrated on the payroll-a tedious, time-consuming job which, more often than not, left her with a wicked headache. Yet that notwithstanding, she did not trust anyone else to do it.

Before opening the green ledger, she tidied her already tidy workspace, arranged papers in already arranged date orde3, and set them in an already neat pile. Then, after sharpening two pencils she'd removed from the top drawer, mindful that the shavings fall into a wastepaper basket beside her, she opened the record book. Employees were listed in two sections: the piece workers, and the hourly workers.

She began with the more complicated hourly wage earners. The straightforward piece operators would wait for later in the day, when the heat would have undoubtedly affected her thinking. Listed in order of hire, Anne Ryan topped the list.

Florence tallied up the hours worked—fourteen times six days plus five hours on Sundays—and put it in the plus column. Then she accounted for punctuality, deducting one hour's pay for every fifteen minutes late, and factored in fines for talking, singing, and spending too much time in the bathroom. Then she counted the number of hats Anne had completed in the week—fifteen bundles in all—estimated the amount of thread by calculating the number of stitches per bundle and multiplying the number of bundles. Following that she estimated the needles used and subtracted one cent per package. Total weekly pay $3.25.

As she wiped her face with a handkerchief and sorted through the pages, she contemplated again what her next venture should be. Not that she needed one. She and her family would be financially secure for generations to come. (Though one could never have too much!) It was the challenge, the gamble, the excitement of doubling and tripling her money that drove her. The war would be over sooner than later, and her government contract would end. What next? she wondered. Surely Edgar Hockenberry appreciated her managerial skills and would offer her a partnership in his shipping firm. In the meantime, she was looking for something more lucrative and less taxing, something where she'd just have to sit back and collect, a speculation like the ice deal, when she'd made a fortune after the French had the crazy idea of building a canal in mosquito-infested Panama. Though much of ice melted *en route*, the price it sold for was so astronomical she'd made a fortune. Ahh, she told herself, something would strike her fancy.

An hour before closing, the sound of footsteps in the hallway distracted her. Having finished the payroll an hour before, she'd been ordering supplies. The forelady made her way across the room to unlock the door, the groaning boards beneath her feet lost in the whir of the machines. "You're a little late, don't you think?" Florence said, glancing at the time on the wall.

A sweaty bandanna covered Harriet Brooks' tight, bristly curls. Her chocolate-colored face glistened with perspiration. The seamstresses eased their feet in unison off the treadles as she slipped around the boxes, her gingham dress catching dust balls and loose threads, and stood before her boss. Only the tick of the clock could be heard.

"Get back to work. Get back to work!" the forelady snapped, thwacking her wooden stick repeatedly against the nearest tabletop. She was a stout, stern-faced, ram-rod-straight woman in her early forties, a widow with a widow's peak to prove it who took her job seriously. Despite the stifling conditions, and unlike the women and girls behind their machines, who looked as if they were about to die from heat prostration, not a hair was out of place on her severely coiffed head. A diminutive amount of moisture on her forehead, and dampness under the arms of her dark, long-sleeved dress, were the only signs of distress.

"I'll bet me week's pay she won't even dock her," Noreen, a freckled-face sixteen-year-old in the back row whispered. "She favors them darkies, I tell ya. A real bleedin' 'art, she is."

Anne Ryan raised her brows and whispered back, "She's no bleedin' 'art. She jus' keeps 'em here to remind us we can be replaced. Don't matter they can't sew a lick. Ya heard 'bout the labor shortages 'cause of the war? She's afraid we might ask for more than our sixty-five cents a dozen. She don't want us to feel too safe. In case we're tempted to complain or threaten to quit, all we gotta do is look beside us to the four darkies who are happy to be workin' for a pissin' fifty cents."

"Watch out. Here comes the bulldog."

And indeed the swish of her skirt and the jingling of the keys the bulldog (as everyone affectionately referred to the forelady out of earshot) carried around her neck were getting closer. She marched through the cluttered aisles, stepping around cartons, squeezing through the narrow confines, while beating her pointer on the wooden floor with each heavy step. Stopping between the two young women, one eyebrow raised in a V, she glared. "*Quiet,* back here! Do your work. Do your work!" she repeated, through closed lips.

The young women hunched over their sewing, slid their blue woolen hats under the needle, eased their feet back on their respective pedals, and the whirring of the motors began to fill the air in the stuffy space once again. The bulldog turned her back. From behind her machine, Noreen stuck her tongue out. "She didn't shit yet today," she whispered.

Anne and the other girls stifled a laugh. Bulldog spun around, gave them a fierce look, and whacked her pointer again.

"Miss Florence," Harriet said, "I's not come here to work today. I's come to pick up my pay. I wanna thank you for all you done for me, for hiring me. But now me and my family is gonna be leavin' New York, so I won't be workin' fo' you no mo'."

Florence dropped her pen on the desk. The swivel chair squeaked when she rolled around to face Harriet. "Leaving New York? Where will you go?"

Harriet had not been easy to find. There were roughly five hundred free Blacks in all of the city, and of them most worked as domestics. Any boss would tell you that they learned fast, worked faster, and worked cheap.

"It don't matter where we go, so long as we leave here. We ain't welcome no mo'. We never was, but now. . .after what they done to us. . . . Oh, Missy Florence-" she began to sob, her shoulders heaving up and down. "It's terrible what they done. All over the city peoples is gone crazy. They's still shouting, shoutin' and cursin', 'God and niggas and rick folk.' They done burned down the Black chillins' orphanage. You shoulda seen all them little chillin still in their night clothes, no shoes on, running and bein' carried away from the flames. And then. . . with my own eyes, I seen 'em draggin' a po' old Black man, a crippled man, out of his home and. . .Lordy, Lordy, theys hanged him! He was a-kickin' and a-hollerin,' And they hanged him . . . . And all the while they was singin' 'Hurrah for Jeff Davis,' they set his dead body on fire."

She slumped wearily on a wooden stool and buried her face in her visibly shaking hands. "It's all over. All over the whole city," she cried. "Mostly them Irish boys, but womens, too. They hates us, Miss Florence. They hates us 'cause they think it's our fault they's dying in the war."

Fiona Martin jumped up from her seat and came forward. She was a haggard-looking woman, prematurely gray with a face full of wrinkles, who was younger than she seemed. Wisps of wet hair clung to her brow. "Well, *isn't* it, now?"

Harriet's big brown eyes met the other's cold stare. "I's sorry 'bout yo son, Miss Fiona, I really is. I know how it feels to lose someone yo love, 'cause I lost a husband and a brother myself. But it ain't our fault. It ain't. It's that new draft bill they's just put up. That's what's causing all the trouble."

The room fell silent. Even Bulldog did not thwack her pointer. As Gerhard said, 'If anyone wanted to know anything about the war, just ask a darkie.' Their grapevine was faster and more accurate than any telegraph. Harriet knew what she was talking about.

"Draft *law*?" Florence answered. "It's just those drunken Five-Pointers making trouble again."

"It ain't just the Five-Pointers. It's all the people. It's comin' up with three hundred dollars or a substitute. That's the trouble. And to make it worse, they goes and puts the list right next to the list of them boys who was jus' killed at Gettysburg."

"It's unfair, that's what it is!" one of girls shouted.

"That's what them boys is sayin,'" Harriet affirmed. "They's shoutin', 'It ain't fair. How we suppose to come up with three hundred dollars? We don't make that much in a year. We ain't gonna fight fo' no strike-breakin' niggas! We ain't no strike breakers, Miss Florence, we jus' tryin' to make a livin' like everybody else."

Florence was so excited about what she'd heard, she didn't even remember to slow the clock before closing.

CHAPTER 21

At exactly seven-thirty p.m., the forelady blew the whistle. Anne Ryan, along with the other working girls, closed their machines, grabbed their bags, and hurried down the three flights of stairs. Despite the steady stream of employees pouring out of the shops along Broadway, the main thoroughfare was unusually quiet. Many of the businesses were boarded up—some with minor damage, some, like Orendock's hardware store, burnt out entirely. The smell of smoke still hung heavy in the air.

Anne stepped gingerly around torn-up cobbles, downed telegraph lines, and other debris. She dug into her pocketbook, pulled out a handkerchief, wiped her face and neck, pushed away a shock of orange curls that lay limp against her forehead, and blew air toward her face in a vain attempt to create a breeze.

Fiona followed a step behind. "How'd you like that darkie?" she asked, as the two headed downtown. "It ain't *their* fault. Ha! Whose fault is it then, ours? We have it worse than them. At least slaves get fed. And we should go fight and die for their cause. Huh! Who's fightin' and dyin' for us Irish? Who cared when we was starvin'?

And how'd you like the boss? 'Sorry to see you go.' I'll bet she is. I hate this job. I hate this city. I curse the day I left Ireland."

"You don't mean that now, Fiona," Anne said. "We shoulda been born rich instead of beautiful, I'll give ya that, but I thank God every day for bein' in America, and God bless Mr. Ahern fer payin' me passage to get here."

"Bless him? He paid ya passage to get rid of ya, he did, so he wouldn't have to be payin' to bury the whole lot of ya."

"Maybe so, but we wouldn't a been able to get here if he didn't. And we surely woulda been dead. Starved to death with the rest of 'em had we stayed."

"Well, we ain't starvin', I have to admit, but we ain't doing much better. That's for sure." They passed one workshop after another on their long walk home, factories that made everything from billiard tables to umbrellas and china, each having suffered some damage. Some only defaced, some completely demolished. Shards of glass crunched beneath their shoes as they passed a jewelry store where they often stopped to ogle gems they could never afford. The windows, having been smashed, were boarded. A crude drawing of the president was scrawled in orange paint on the crisscrossed planks. Fiona guffawed. Though she couldn't read, the elongated nose and Neanderthal brow ridges made the meaning crystal clear. Anne did not share in her friend's amusement.

On the next block, they stopped to admire dishware displayed behind metal grates, through which the sun glittered on painted platters. "Can't you just see yourself sippin' tea from that dainty cup, Fiona? With your little pinky finger pointed in the air?"

"No."

"Me neither."

They both laughed.

Fiona pointed to a bedroom set, complete with bedside stand and chiffarobe, displayed in the next window. "But I can see meself on one a them beds, all stretched out on that soft mattress. Me, alone, without the husband and the boys. That would be a mighty fine thing now ta have your own bed, it would. And I'd sleep for a week, a whole seven-day week."

As the army had had at last been called in to squelch the insurgency, Union soldiers were everywhere. A strapping fellow in military trousers with yellow stripes down his leg tipped his cap. Underneath it, a thick head of rust-colored hair was wet with perspiration and flat against his head. "Evenin', ladies," he said as they passed him.

Anne flashed her prettiest smile, complete with dimples and fluttering lashes. "Evenin'."

"Anne Ryan, that young man was flirtin' with you, and if I didn't know better, I would think you was flirtin' back."

"Now, Fiona, I already have a gentleman, you know that."

"How *is* that fella a yours, Anne? He gonna marry ya one of these days?"

"Soon."

"Umm. I heard that before. . . . You ain't been lookin' too good these days. I been wantin' to tell ya. You seem peaked 'round the gills, and your cheeks is flushed. . . . You ain't been doing the dirty, 'ave ya?" Fiona looked down her nose knowingly.

"Fiona! I'm a good Catholic girl. You know that. It's the heat. That's all. Cooped up in that shop all day—"

"Ain't it the truth. A damn sweat box, it tis. One can hardly breathe. . . . Not that the air is so much better out here."

"That's fer sure." They stopped at the corner for Fiona to tie her shoe. "I hate the thought of turning on the stove tonight."

"It's too hot to cook."

"That it tis. But Patty and the boys'll be looking fer something."

"I'm just gonna have a piece of fruit." Anne noticed that Harriet Brooks was one block behind her. "I can't walk all the way home with ya today, Fiona. You don't mind, do ya?"

Fiona followed Anne's gaze and shook her head. "Go ahead. I'll see ya in the mornin'. Same place, same time." She started on her way. "Make sure you rest for awhile before ya start out. Till ya feel better, ya hear. You don't look well."

"I'll do that."

When Harriet caught up, Anne called to her. "Would ya mind if I keep ya company? If we walked home together? We're goin' in the same direction, I think. You live in Cow Alley, don't ya? I'm just a few blocks away, on Baxter."

"It's a free country. . . . At least for some people."

"I—I wanted to tell ya that I'm awful sorry 'bout everything that's happened. . . 'bout the beatings. And hangin and all. Really I am."

"Ain't your fault."

"No. But it was a lot of them Irish ruffians, and me being Irish—"

"It wasn't only Irish, you know. And a lot of the people who tried to save us was Irish people, too. Lots of them Irish police was hurt, and even some just plain citizens was Irish."

"Thanks for saying so. But just the same I'm sorry for you and your family. Truly, I am. It's been nice working with ya. . . . Where will you go?"

arriet shrugged. "Don't know yet. Some of the other Black folks in my buildin' is headin' for Long Island. Don't rightly know why. I guess I'll head in that direction."

"What will ya do?"

Harriet shrugged again. Anne noticed the worry lines on her face. "Somethin'."

"Well—" Anne dug into her pocket, pulled out her week's pay, and folded it in Harriet's bony fingers. Her callused hands told the tale of a long, hard life. "I want you to have this. It's just a little something. . .for the trip."

Harriet looked at the money.

Anne thought she saw her eyes beginning to tear. "Is just a little bit, only a little bit, ta help you along."

"It's awful decent of ya." Harriet's voice sounded choked. "But I can't take it." She pressed the money back into Anne's palm. "You need it as much as I do—"

"It will make me feel better. I have plenty of food, and the rent is paid for the week," Anne lied. "At least I know I have a job tomorrow. Please." She pushed her week's wages back into Harriet's hand.

They sauntered along, neither of them in any hurry to get home, where they knew their apartments would be stifling.

". . .They called my friend's name in the lottery the other day," Anne said. "He got drafted."

"I'm sorry to hear that."

"Me, too."

"Is he a *close* friend?"

". . .Very close. . . . I'm pregnant. And I don't know what to do. If he gets killed in the war—" she crossed herself— "God have mercy, I'll be all alone. I can't hide it much longer, and when Mrs. Gilbert finds out, I'll have to leave and—" she sighed. "I don't know why I'm telling you all of this. Maybe because I'll never see you again. . .maybe because I don't think you'll judge me—"

Harriet tried to push the money back on Anne. "You'll need this more than me."

"No. Absolutely not. I insist that you take it. I shouldn't a told you. I don't want it. I really don't."

"Are you sure?"

"Yes."

"About being pregnant, I mean."

"I missed two periods. I'm sick every morning. We took precautions, but. . .when the time comes, he don't like to pull out."

Harriet's bony hand rested on Anne's shoulder. "I got myself three chillin that same way. Not that it's my business, but you're a nice girl, pretty—sweet. How is it this fella a yours hasn't married you yet? Sleepin' with ya all this time like he's been."

"He will as soon as he gets a job. . .a *real* job. He works some, collectin' rents."

"Why, he ain't got no job? There's plenty a work for a white man if he wants it."

"He's educated. Went to school. Even had tutors. He can read and write. He's so smart, and this hard laborin' is beneath him."

Harriet stopped walking, and Anne stopped, too. "Missy Anne. *Honey*. I'm telling ya like ya my own. This here fella a yours is a bum. An educated bum. And that's the worst kind. You get rid of him before it be too late. Before you be sorry fo the rest a you life. I know this woman can help you. You tell her Harriet Brooks sent ya. She'll take good care a ya. She clean and safe."

Harriet started walking again, but Anne did not move. "You're not talkin' 'bout. . .'bout getting' rid of it, are you?"

"I surely am."

"I couldn't."

They stopped to say their good-byes in front of the infamous cul-de-sac known to New Yorkers as Cow Bay, the slum of slums, where the worst of the worst, the poorest of the poor, resided in a collection of dilapidated two-and-a-half story wooden tenements. There were rumors that the city was going to demolish the squalid rat traps and replace them with brick buildings. It couldn't come soon enough.

They smelled the neighborhood even before they saw it. The heavy air reeked with the stench of rot and filth from blocks away, the kind of stink that stuck in your nostrils and burned your eyes. Harriet did not invite her new friend inside. And Anne, though no stranger to the underbelly of society, would not have gone if she had. It was a scary-looking place, packed with unsavory characters. Crowds swarmed the streets. Young and old, black and white, raucous and drunk. A Black boy, maybe six years old, picking through a garbage barrel, caught Anne's attention. He was in waist deep with his bare legs and feet sticking up, the little feet dirtier than the pavement.

A sign outside the tenement closest to the street read, *Boarding House: Six Cents A Night*. Through an open window, Anne could see a number of bunks practically on top of each other.

Harriet dug in her apron pocket and retrieved a handkerchief. "You got a pencil o' something to write with?" Anne went through her bag, its contents clicking, produced a broken piece of clothing chalk she used to mark the hats, and handed it to her.

"'Scuse me if I don't write so good. I ain't never been taught how," Harriet said. Resting the handkerchief on her knee, she scribbled the name and address of the abortionist. "You think about it. Keep this in case yo change yo mind."

CHAPTER 22

INSIDE WAS AS BLACK AS PITCH. There were no windows in the hallway, only a shaft meant to let in light but that only let in the stench of garbage and urine. Holding her skirt above her ankles so as not to trip and a handkerchief to her nose so as not to gag, Anne felt her way to the staircase. Careful to keep away from the loose railing for fear of tumbling off, she started up the five flights of steep, squeaking steps.

If it was ninety degrees outside, it had to be a hundred in the tenement. Twenty families lived in the building, in four flats on each of the five stories. From their open doors she could hear babies crying, dishes clattering, and muted conversations. Sean Monahan in 2C was a nasty drunk, and Anne was sure she heard cursing and the sounds of a beating as she passed his door. She'd often seen his wife, Rose, with bruises, but when Anne had tried to help, Rose told her in a polite way to mind her own business, so Anne just shook her head, kept climbing, and prayed Sean wasn't killing her this time. The fourth floor smelled of fried onions.

"Is that you, Anne dear?" Katie Hare called when she heard the creaking steps. "You're late tonight. I saved your supper."

"Thank you, but I 'ad a piece of fruit on my way home," Anne huffed, looking up at her leaning over the bannister, her checkered dress open at the neck. She was a stout woman in her late thirties, who carried most of her weight in her bottom and kept her straw-colored hair piled on top her head.

"A piece of fruit?" Mrs. Hare followed Anne across through the doorway, her open-backed slippers slapping against the floor. Her stockings were rolled down around her ankles.

It was a two-room apartment, two-and-a-half if you counted the closet-size "bedroom" that Anne shared with Katie's two eldest daughters, totaling five hundred feet, plus a fire escape where husband and wife slept on hot summer nights. Katie was neat. The sleeping pallets were folded and put away first thing in the morning, and their clothing hung on their respective hooks.

Early evening light filtered into the kitchen. A philodendron hanging from a rod in front of the one window was limp from the heat. "You pay me for room *and* board. . . . And while we're speakin' about money, I take it you have the rent."

Anne dropped her purse on the table beside the plate that covered her supper. She knew from the smell it was potatoes and cabbage—-again. She hated potatoes and cabbage. "Well, actually, I'm a bit short this week. I'll have it for ya next Monday."

"Next Monday. Next Tuesday. 'Tis always the same story, Anne dear. You know, when the bad working time comes for my Jim, I won't be able to tolerate such tardiness. I need that rent when it's due. My poor Jim works hard." She pulled a hankie from her apron pocket and wiped the sweat from her scalp.

"Yes. I know. 'He digs sewers and then loads and unloads sacks and crates at the pier when there's no sewer work.'"

"And we wouldn't want my poor Jim to have to go upstate lookin' for canal work in the hard-working times."

"No. Of course not," Anne agreed. Standing on tiptoe, she reached into the high cabinet, grabbed a chipped white enamel pitcher, which she filled from a bucket in the sink, carried it to her bedroom and pulled the curtain across the doorway.

"I depend on the fifty cents a week," Katie said to the closed floral drape. "I have children to feed, and I need a reliable income."

Anne poured the water into a basin on the metal stand beside the bed and disrobed until she stood naked in the semi-darkness with her dress and underwear in a ball at her feet. Her clothes were so wet with perspiration she practically had to peel them off her skin.

And don't give me any of that 'I'm a perfect tenant' speech. You're quiet and clean, and ya eat little when ya eat anything at all, or you're hardly home, I give ya that. But I can't accept this lateness any longer, Anne dear. You have to pay me the rent when it comes due—"

"You're absolutely right, Mrs. Hare," Anne called back as she splashed tepid water on her face. "You've been very kind to me." A bath would have been nice. But the tub was in the kitchen opposite the door and, when not filled with coal, had a board over it to use it as a table. Nonetheless, she had no complaints. With three Hare kids and their parents in the tiny apartment, not every day did she have the luxury of washing in private. As her mother used to say, God bless her soul, "Play the glad game. Look on the bright side. Things could always be worse."

"I'll have the money for you tomorrow, I promise."

"I can't tolerate—"

"Yes, yes, I know. I'll force you to look for a new boarder. And it won't be hard neither, because there are lots of working girls lookin' for a nice, clean, respectable arrangement, 'specially a front apartment that faces the street and not the outhouse.'"

Anne lathered up her wash cloth with a bar of lye soap, washed over her neck and egg-sized breasts, her wing-like shoulder blades, and down her back. She raised one bony foot on the sagging bed that was just big enough for one and sponged between her legs. The cloth went over the belly, not yet starting to show, thank God.

After she toweled dry, she splashed herself with cheap toilet water and put on fresh pantaloons, and a faded blue cotton dress with a neat white collar. She had two outfits, including the one in a ball at her feet, both of which she'd bought in a second-hand store around the corner. She thought she'd seen the dress on one of the neighbors in 3A before she died the week before, but wasn't sure. She swept up her dirty clothes from the floor and dropped them in her laundry bag, which she kept under the bed. Usually she did her wash once a week, on Sundays after work. But expecting it to be just as hot and having only one outfit to change into, she would have to get up extra early the next morning to do her wash at the pump out back.

"I been meanin' to talk to you about all that water you been usin', Anne dear. You know what an effort it is for little Johnny Boy to be carrying those buckets up and down the stairs. I wish you'd be a little more considerate. Why do you have to wash every day, anyway? How dirty does one get working with a needle all day? Not like my poor Jim, who comes home so tired and looks to wash up—"

"Yes, yes. 'And then there's no water.' I know. I'll be more considerate. It's just so hot, and I'm so—"

"I know you will try harder, Anne dear."

The curtain opened. "I'm sleeping on the roof tonight," Anne announced.

Katie Hare looked her up and down. Sniffed her. The mix of cheap perfume and cabbage was practically toxic. "I hope you're behaving yourself, Anne dear. You know my rules. I will not have loose women corrupting my children."

"Mrs. Hare! How could you suggest such a thing?"

"Don't you Mrs. Hare me! Do I have *stupid* written across my forehead? You're going out every night smelling like a flophouse whore. I'll have none of that in my house, Miss Anne Ryan. Ya hear what I'm saying? None of it."

CHAPTER 23

THE FOLLOWING EVENING, ANNE WAS STANDING outside Paddy O'Halloran's bar with her nose squashed against the dirty window, peering in. It was after eight. Though the sun had gone down, it was still hot and muggy. Her orange hair was a flaming ball of frizz, and her faded blue dress clung to her back. Ordinarily, she would have spruced up before meeting Joe, sponge, powder, and don clean clothes. But she was so excited about her news, she'd come straight from work. The perfume-soaked handkerchief she held under her nose did little to blot out the stench of urine, garbage, and horse manure that covered the wide street. She didn't usually come to the Bowery after dark. It was not the best part of town in daylight, but at night the gangs came out in force. Indeed, two thugs were across the street, standing outside a grocery store. Luckily, they were Dead Rabbits—-she could tell by the red stripes on their trousers—Irish lovers, and not Plug Uglies, who though also Irish, were notoriously ferocious.

Her shoes clicked on the wide wooden floor. Gas lamps were hissing on the walls, throwing small pools of pale, yellow light into the smoky dimness that stank of cigar smoke. There were two spittoons, one at either end of the room. Liquor bottles clinked on the counter as the tavern keeper poured more drinks.

Four scruffy men were sitting in a far corner, playing poker and laughing as their cards slapped the table. Five patrons were at the bar, hunched over their drinks. One of them swatted a fly.

The balding, barrel-chested bartender spotted her first. "Hey, Joe," he called from the other end of the counter, jutting out his chin to point in her direction. "You're girlfriend's here."

"Damn." Joe rolled his eyes and let out a sigh.

"A little late today, ain't she? The fellow sitting beside him said.

"I figured I'd find ya here," Anne snapped, approaching him from behind.

"I just came."

"Yeah, sure ya did, Joe Rubin. Ya think I can't tell you're half-cocked? I could smell ya a block away. The only place you've been today is on this stool."

The bartender shook his head.

"Aw, take it easy, Anne," Joe's neighbor answered. "The man's just got drafted, gotta go fight in that nigga-lovin' war. Have a heart. He needs to drown his troubles. That right, Joe?"

Joe tipped his hat and raised his glass. He needed a haircut and a shave: his unruly blond curls were hanging past his ears, and his cheeks were covered in stubble. "Thank you, Brian. I couldn't have said it better myself."

"Yeah. And what was his excuse last week?" Anne asked the ruddy-faced, gnome-like man called Brian, "before he got drafted? And the week before that? . . . But I'm not here ta start a fight. I have good news for ya. My boss is givin' away three hundred dollars so as to pay for a substitute to any respectable, *non-Irish* person who wants out of the army. And since you fit that respectable non-Irish person requirement, bein' educated as ya are, I thought you might be interested."

"Just giving away three hundred dollars? Joe raised his brow.

"Not exactly *giving* it away. She expects to get paid back, naturally."

"Naturally." He took a long, slow sip of whiskey. "But that makes it what you call a loan. And why would I take a loan when the Tammany Hall boys are giving it away?"

"Yeah? Why would he do that?"

"Mind your own business, Brian." Anne turned to Joe's neighbor. I ain't addressin' you. But to answer your question, *Joe*—" she glared at Brian, daring him to interrupt— "because you'll be indebted to the Tammy Hall boys, and takin' it from my boss you won't be."

"Won't have to pay it back? You mean this is charity?" Brian broke in.

"Of course not. There's not a charitable bone in my boss's body."

"Well blow me down, Anne Ryan. You're not thinkin' of stealing' this nice man's money are ya, now? Why, now would you be so willing to stiff this boss of yours?"

"First of all, Brian Higgins, like I said, I'm not addressin' you. Second, my boss is a her, not a him. And third, I'm not thinkin' a stealing nothin'. The way I see it, it's not her money to lose. It's money she owes me, money she stole from my hard work. If anybody's a crook, it's her, stealing our time the way she pushes that clock forward and back to suit herself. I never seen her do it, mind ya, she's too clever for that, but I know she does. I almost caught her once, standing there on a stool. And when she caught me lookin' at her, she tells me she's been dustin' the clock. *Dustin' the clock*. Imagine. I'll bet my first-born son she'd never dusted a thing in her whole life! And I'll tell ya, too, I 'aven't broke nearly as many needles as she claims I did. Ya ever hear the saying, 'The poor get buried and the greedy rich buy banks'?"

The group of men at the table behind them shouted and raised their glasses. "Hey, Annie! A true rebel-rouser is what ya are. How about you joining the protest we be planning? We'll even get ya a club so as you can bust some heads. Whattaya say, fellas?" Another cheer went up.

Anne turned to the men at the table. "I'm not interested in any protests, thank you very much. I'm only interested in myself and my own. I'm interested in getting' this here bloke to finally make an honest woman outta me, and getting' out of this bloody city."

"I thought you liked this shit hole," a tattooed fellow shouted from the other end of the bar.

"I never said I liked it. What I said was, ya gotta make the best of what ya got. . . . And now that we have another opportunity, we'd be fools not to take it. What do you say, Joe? We'll get one of those fancy wagons and go west somewhere. Start a business. You're smart."

"What happened to paying off the army?" Joe said.

"They'll never find ya. We'll be outta here and on our way to God's country before the sun sets."

"What kind of business you thinkin' of startin', Anne?" asked the man sitting next to Joe. "A prostitution business?" All the others laughed.

Anne glared at him. "Come on, Joe, isn't a new life better than spilling ya guts on some God-forsaken piece of Confederate mud? Maybe we could open a general store where we sell, you know. . .everything. Or ya could own ya own bar. I'm sure there are lots of drunks out West like ya friend here Mr. Higgins."

"I beg ya pardon!" Brian said in feigned indignation.

Anne turned to him. "Just wanted to see if you were still listenin' to our conversation."

"Or maybe all them homesteaders would be open to some of that fix-it-all in a bottle? That might be more ya style," a man shouted from the table behind them. Everybody laughed.

"Nah. He'd have to stand in them hot, dusty streets, shoutin' and hollerin'. I see him runnin' crooked card games. That suits him more," another fellow from the same table added. More laughter.

Anne turned to them, hand on her hip, glared at them, and turned back to her intended. "Come on, Joe, say yes."

CHAPTER 24

WHAT WILL MY LIFE BE LIKE *as Mrs. Walter Hockenberry,* Marie wondered as her fingers flew across the keys. Early evening light cast a soft glow through the window behind the piano. The French-lace curtains rustled in the welcomed breeze. Though it was too dark to read the sheet music, it didn't matter. She knew the piece so well, she could play it in her sleep. Her parents were out. Nola, once her nanny, now cook and housemaid, had retired to her room, and Alfred, the butler, was in the cold cellar, checking supplies. Marie was comfortable in a light cotton dress without stockings, petticoats, or stays, and her hair pulled back in a simple queue. Would Walter expect her to dress for dinner every night? To wear corsets, hoopskirts, and banana curls even in the heat? He seemed unperturbed in his starched cuffs and collar.

They were formal with each other—he so polite, hbringing her flowers, pulling out the chair; she, lost for words, stared at anything but his face. He talked quite a bit: about bugs, the evil of slavery, or the War-Between-The-States. She wished the war would end, if for no other reason than to change the subject. That coming fall, he was going to join the practice of Tudor and Hall on Fifth Avenue, specializing in real estate law. Would house sales be the next topic of the day? She hit a sour note.

His parents were buying them a brownstone in prestigious Gramercy Park. Would her mother let her take Nola with her? If not, how would Marie manage? She'd been with Marie since birth, had raised her, comforted her, and tucked her into bed at night.

Florence and Gerhard would buy the furniture. Marie hoped they wouldn't choose stiff, straight-backed chairs like those in the parlor. Her mother had already ordered dinnerware—bone china with delicate pink and blue flowers around the edges, a service for sixteen, along with silverware. Since the day Marie was born, Florence had been filling a hope chest with embroidered linens. She'd already been to the printer regarding the invitations, and to the dressmaker about the gown.

As for the wedding itself, her mother had everything in hand. All Marie had to do was show up. It didn't bother her. The day would be more for Florence than her anyway. Florence being protestant and Gerhard Catholic, they had been denied a march down the aisle, and had had to settle for taking their vows behind the closed doors of the church rectory—a sacrifice she had never let her husband forget.

Marie didn't hear the bell at first, and when, after several more chimes, she did, called for Nola, only to remember that she'd retired to bed. Pushing herself away from the baby grand, heedless of the stool scraping against the freshly polished cherrywood floor, she padded to the vestibule.

"Can I help you?" she asked the man at the threshold. His clothes were worn, he needed a shave, but that notwithstanding, he was a striking figure. Just over middle height, in his late twenties, she guessed, he had an athletic build, with rippling muscles and a flat belly.

He smiled when he looked at her, and she noted adorable dimples. His eyes, however, took her breath away. They were the deepest, brightest, most sparkling blue she'd ever seen.

When he tipped his cap, a moist blonde curl fell across his forehead. Outside, the trees were in shadow. The streetlamp had just been lit, casting a circle of light in the otherwise darkening evening.

"I'm looking for a Mrs. Gilbert."

"That would be my mother," she answered, trying to place his accent. "Is there anything *I* can help you with?"

She seemed to him too plain to be a rich woman's daughter. Plain and homely. Her teeth were too big for her mouth, her eyes too close to her nose, her nose too long for her face. If she'd been wearing an apron, he would have thought she was the maid. But he noticed she wasn't wearing a wedding ring, either. "I understand she is extending loans. I'm sorry to have bothered you. I should have gone to her office. I'll look her up there. Thank you, anyway." He turned to leave. As if on second thought, he turned back. "Moonlight Sonata?"

"Pardon?"

"The piece I heard playing when I came to the door. Beethoven's 'Moonlight Sonata,' wasn't it?"

"Yes."

"It was quite lovely. Are you the pianist?"

She blushed all the way to her ears; her face and head felt hot. "Yes and yes. It was, actually—'Moonlight Sonata,' that is. And yes, I am the pianist. Thank you."

"Well, I'll be on my way." He gave her his most beautiful smile, tipped his cap again, and turned to go.

"Wa—wait! I might be able to help you, Mr.—"

"Rubin. Joe Rubin."

"Mother keeps a contract in the study. If you'll give me a minute."

She left him standing before the porch swing as she hurried into the next room, returning several minutes later with papers waving in hand. "Here it is! I found it!"

"That was quick."

She smiled and chuckled, exposing her teeth. She didn't notice his grimace. About to hand it to him, she pulled her hand back. "Ah. . . . I—I could go over it with you, help you fill it out," she offered, realizing immediately that she had insulted him, since he could not disguise the flash of anger that crossed his face.

But then he smiled and said, "That's most kind of you," and whatever anger she thought she had seen vanished.

"Come in." She opened the door wider. "We can discuss it."

She knew she shouldn't let a stranger in, especially an obviously lower-class person than she, but Nola and Alfred were in the house, and staring at his V-shaped figure and, shame on her, his tight, perfectly round buttocks, her judgment was clouded. If he had had wicked intentions, she reasoned, he would already have attacked her.

His dusty boots clacked on the tile-floored vestibule, then sank into the carpet as he followed her into the powder blue parlor, which was dominated by an overwhelming scent of lemon furniture polish.

He studied the mahogany fireplace and ornate pieces; the lace hankie in the curio, and the huge oil of King Louis and Marie Antoinette. His eyes caught the crystal chandelier hanging over the table and the vase of fragrant red roses. Everything reeked of money.

Marie sat on the sofa and indicated for him to do the same. He settled onto the tufted velvet cushion beside her, close enough for her to smell his sweat, and for him to smell her lavender powder and note once again the bare ring finger. He flashed his most seductive smile. "Your family's coat of arms?" he asked, gazing at the wall.

"Hard to miss, isn't it?" she laughed, covering her mouth this time.

"Yes. The Gilberts," she said.

"Nobles of some sort, I suppose?"

She shrugged. "Who knows? If you ask Mother, she'll tell you they were kings. My bet is that they were peasants. If that much."

"Perhaps attendants of a *totenhaus*," he said.

She looked confused.

"A *totenhaus*," he repeated. "Or *Vitae Dubiae* asylum. An attendant of a putrification house. A death house. Where they waited for the dead to 'wake.' They watched until they were absolutely sure they were dead. You've heard of the 'dead ringer,' or 'kick the bucket'? Comes from the *totenhaus*. The attendant would sit in his little office, listening for bells to go off. Strings were tied on the fingers of all the, um, *patrons,* and the strings were attached to bells. If the bell rang, it meant the person was alive. *A* dead *ringer*. It was one of the worst jobs in town."

"That's awfully ghoulish. What made you think of *that*?"

He pointed to the book on the end table. "*Edgar Allen Poe.*" Thinking of him made me think of premature burial, which made me think of the *totenhaus*. The *totenhaus* made me think of lousy jobs."

She stared at the man in undisguised amazement. "You've *read* him? Edgar Allen Poe?"

"You're surprised?" She caught another flash of anger cross his face but passed it off as her imagination when he replaced it, yet again, with an endearing smile. "How is it a scruffy immigrant like me can read and knows something about history, you're wondering."

Actually what she was wondering was how anyone as handsome and worldly as he could be sitting next to her, smiling at her. And she was thinking about Walter, his obsession with bugs and politics, and how drab a life with him would be.

"Don't be embarrassed," he went on. "I would wonder the same thing if I met someone like me."

"Well, ah—"

"Mind if I take a look at that?" He indicated the document in her hand.

"Oh, yes. Of course." She handed it to him. His fingers brushed against hers. She felt heat rise in her face and was sure she was breaking out in blotches.

Hardly anything repelled him more than a blotchy woman, especially one with a mouth full of horse teeth.

"Would you, ah, like some lemonade?"

"That would be very nice. Thank you."

She disappeared into the kitchen. It was still hot from the day's baking. The windows were open, but they didn't help much. Fresh peach tarts sweetened the room. They were on a platter, on the table, covered with an embroidered linen to keep the flies off. Marie stopped in front of a gleaming pot drying on the drain board to stare at her reflection and ran her fingers through her damp hair.

When she re-entered the parlor, the agreement was lying on the table. "You read all of that already?"

"Fine print and all."

She placed a plate with a peach tart and a glass of lemonade on the end table beside him.

"Fifty percent compounded interest. Ouch. The church accused the Jews of usury for charging far less interest than that."

Crumbs landed on her bodice as she bit into the pastry. She wiped them off with her hand. "You could always go into the army and die for your country. Or lose a leg," she said with more sarcasm than she intended. "I'm sorry. I-I didn't mean to be, to sound. . .to insinuate—"

"No. *I* apologize. I didn't mean to insult you or your mother. Actually, it's very smart of her to charge fifty percent, considering the gentlemen she is dealing with are high risk, shall we say. I wouldn't charge less than seventy-five, myself."

She laughed, grateful for his humor, not realizing that he was not joking. "You seem to know a lot about this sort of thing."

"I have some experience."

She waited for him to continue, but he said no more. After an uncomfortable silence, she changed the subject. "It's too bad about this war, really. Why do people have to fight?"

"War is a fact of life. They have always been, and they will always be. It's one of nature's ways of thinning the herd."

"You sound like my father. You're both such pessimists."

"I'm neither a pessimist nor an optimist. I am simply a realist. Making war is human. It's like love. Neither can be avoided." He seemed to stare right through her. Her hands shook so badly the lemonade spilled over the rim and splashed the front of her dress. She rested the drink on the coffee table, the glass cold in her palms, flushed, once again, and lowered her eyes. "So, ah, Mr. . . ."

"Rubin."

"Mr. Rubin. So, um—" she reached for a piece of paper and grabbed a pen from the coffee table, dipped it in the inkwell beside it— "if you're interested in the—in the loan, I'll take down your information and have Mother get in touch with you. Where can she reach you? Home? Your place of business?" she asked, looking into those eyes.

"I have the address of your mother's shop. I'll find *her*." He finished his drink in one final swallow, put the tumbler down on the table with a soft thud, got up, and started to make his way to the door.

"I'll tell her to expect you."

"Thank you, Miss Gilbert. . . . It is *Miss*, isn't it?"

". . .Yes. It's Miss. You're quite welcome." She opened the door to let him out. It was dark by then and a full moon lit the path. Moths clung to the night light on the patio. Crickets predicted another scorcher to come. She cleared her throat when the front gate squeaked open.

"You seem to know a lot about music," she called after him. "Do you play?"

He turned. "Not as well as you."

She swallowed hard. "I-I, er, I would very much like to play for you."

"I would like very much to hear you play again."

"Next Wednesday?" she asked softly.

CHAPTER 25

MARIE WAS STILL STANDING IN THE VESTIBULE, watching Joe disappear into the night, when she heard her parents' carriage pull up in front of the house. The coach door snapped shut, then Florence's high heels could be heard clicking on the brick walk. "Steak tartare?" Gerhard was saying. "I hope they're charging us less, since they don't have to cook it."

Obviously, they've settled on a menu, Marie concluded. At least her mother had settled on the menu, and her father had acquiesced.

There was a momentary silence except for the chirping of crickets. Then Marie saw Florence turn to her husband, hands on her hips, fancy handbag brushing against her peach voile dress. "You're so uncivilized, Gerhard. Steak tartare is an elegant appetizer." They came through the door, and it closed softly behind them. Florence placed her beaded purse on the table in the foyer and stood before the mirror to remove her hat, a collection of plumes, artificial fruit, and a stuffed bird sitting in a nest.

Gerhard unbuttoned his brocaded vest and undid his cravat. His face looked beefy red again. "Raw meat is what it is," he murmured to his daughter, who by then had taken a seat on the sofa in the living room. "*Expensive* raw meat."

"If it were left to you, we'd be serving stuffed brussels sprouts with cheese and crackers."

"I rather like brussels sprouts with cheese and crackers."

"Sometimes you're impossible, Gerhard. And cheap. Need I remind you how important an occasion this is going to be? It's not as if our daughter is marrying a nobody. Distinguished people will be coming." She managed to loosen the hat pins and rest the wax produce on the table beside the purse. "The mayor. The *commodore*." She undid the three pearl buttons on her kid gloves, slipped them off, and fluffed her bouffant, shiny from the chamomile she used it keep it so. "You must trust my judgment." She crossed the room, her leather shoes sinking into the lush carpet, and bent down to kiss him on the cheek. "Don't I always do what's best for us?"

Marie sighed, sank deeper onto the couch, and rolled her eyes.

"Of course I trust you, dear," Gerhard replied from the chair beside his daughter. He'd unbuttoned the top of his shirt and was rubbing his fat neck where his too-tight starched collar had left an angry irritation. He either had to lose some weight or buy new clothes. "Explicitly. Unconditionally. Whatever you decide is fine with me. If you think raw meat is proper, raw meat it shall be."

"The *maître d'* suggested we have an ice sculpture."

"An *ice* sculpture? Don't you think that's a bit—"

"In the likeness of a ship. A grand sailing ship. What do you think?"

"A *sailing* ship?"

"The Hockenberrys are in the shipping business, after all. I think it would be a nice gesture on our part."

"Well, we're in the millinery business. Perhaps we should have a sculpture of a hat."

She stopped and stared at him, hands on her hips again, and sighed.

"How much is this *gesture* going to cost us?" Gerhard moaned.

"Is that all that concerns you? The cost of everything? Really, Gerhard. Do you want people to think we're—"

"I don't care what people think of us, Florence. . . . A sailing ship, indeed!"

"There you go again."

"And parsimony has nothing to do with it."

"You're talking to *me*, Gerhard. Your wife."

"A man was here to see you this evening," Marie cut in.

Florence turned her attention to her daughter and raised her brows.

"About a loan," Marie said.

"He was in the *house*? You let him *in*?"

"Nola and Alfred were here. And he was only here a minute. I gave him a contract to look over."

"That's another thing, Florence," Gerhard interjected. "I don't approve of this latest scheme of yours."

Florence sighed. "Scheme? If I had listened to you, my dear husband, we wouldn't have invested in that ice venture for the Panama railway. You were against that as well, if you recall, and look at the money we made. Same as the gold rush in California. It was the merchants who sold the fools what they needed who made their fortune, not the ones who did the digging."

"What do you know about these men? These ruffians? What collateral can they give you? How will you collect if they run off?"

"This fellow is *not* a ruffian," Marie interjected. "He is quite educated—"

"Perhaps *this* particular fellow is not, Marie," said her father, "but in general this is a bad risk. I don't like it," he went on, turning once again to his wife. "Besides, I understand these Tammany Hall criminals are *giving* the money away, just to secure their vote."

"I wouldn't worry about that. We don't want to deal with that element, anyway."

"Ah. So you agree."

"I've thought this all through, Gerhard. The Tammany boys can't possibly pay for thousands of New Yorkers getting drafted. And secondly—" she pointed a finger at him— "at fifty percent compounded interest, half of those men could run off and we'd still make a considerable profit. Like shipping ice to Panama. Same principle. Fifty percent of the ice melted before it got there, but we sold it at such a price we still made a fortune. Not to mention that I happen to be an excellent judge of character. So calm yourself." She kissed him again, on the forehead this time. It was hot and wet with perspiration. "Am I a foolish woman? Haven't I always done right by us?"

He gazed at her—still voluptuous in her forties, her lips in a pout—and was reminded yet again of what a lucky man he was. "Absolutely."

Florence kicked off her shoes and picked them up into her left hand. She wiggled her toes inside her stockings. "Come. Let's go to bed." Arm and arm, they went up the stairs. "About that ice sculpture. . . ."

MARIE LAY ON HER FEATHER BED with her three overstuffed goose-down pillows, in her pretty bedroom, unable to get Joe Rubin out of her mind. How handsome. How worldly! Those piercing eyes. That fascinating accent. Alexandre Dumas's d'Artagnan came to mind. And impossible as it was, Joe liked her, too. She knew it. She *felt* it. If only she weren't engaged to boring Walter, what a life of adventure she would have!

CHAPTER 26

NO ONE NOTICED ANNE ENTER THE BAR. It was dark and crowded, and most everybody's attention was focused on an old sailor telling a story. Sitting in the corner, surrounded by a rapt audience, she couldn't see him. But she knew that that raspy voice could only belong to Oswald Beatty. A smile crossed her face as she pictured his bushy eyebrows rising up and down with each sentence. She scanned the group. The usual rabble was there: Brian Higgins, looking like a potted plant on the same three-legged stool, hunched over what could have been the same drink; the bald, fat-bellied bartender in his dirty white apron, wiping the table top; and the same four men, at the same table by the pot-belly stove, still playing cards. "So I'm sitting at this restaurant in Spain," Oscar was saying, "and this guy at the next table orders Rocky Mountain oysters."

"What's a Rocky Mountain oyster? The Rocky Mountains ain't near no water," a young fellow in red suspenders called out.

"Obviously you ain't never been to Spain," the old sailor answered. "They're bulls' balls. In this here Spanish restaurant they serve this dish, quite delicious, I might add."

"*Bulls*' balls! You're kidding me, right?" the same fellow asked, twisting himself around to stare at the gent in disbelief.

"It's a big world, sonny, and people eat a lot of different things. In the Amazon they eat bugs. Bet ya didn't know that neither."

"What kind a bugs?" another young man across the room asked.

"Bugs. What do I know what kind?"

"I thought you knowed everything."

"I know *a lot* of things, but I don't know *everything*. So as I was saying—" he took a sip of his whiskey and smacked his lips— "on this here particular evening, this patron—that's a customer" (he directed this to the chap sitting on the stool at the bar), "ordered the Rocky Mountain oysters. But when the food comes, instead of getting this big dish, he was looking at two little nuggets."

"Little nuggets?"

"Yeah. Nuggets. So he calls the waiter over, and he says, 'Excuse me, sir—'"

"They call a waiter *sir*?"

"Are you gonna let me finish my story?"

"Sorry."

"'Excuse me, *sir*,' he says. 'But why are these balls so small?' And the waiter, he says, 'Sometimes the bull wins.'"

There was a moment of silence and then the room broke into rumbling laughter. Everyone was laughing except for the kid on the stool. "Come on. They don't really do that. . .do they?"

The bartender threw the smelly dishrag at him. It got him in the face. Howling erupted.

When it quieted down to chuckles, the card players went back to their conversation. They were talking about the five deserters who had been executed that week. Everyone had been talking about it.

"Could you imagine," one of them was saying, "they had them sit in their coffins before they shot them."

"Yup. All in a row beside the dug-up graves," his buddy said.

"I heard they was playing the death march while they shot the poor bastards."

"Any a you seen Joe?" Anne called out.

Brian Higgins put his glass down. His eyes roamed over her body from head to toe. Her hair was pulled back, but tight curls escaped from everywhere, sweat beads lining her forehead, and the hem of her skirt was black from sweeping the pavement. "You look like you been shot from one of those cannons in the circus."

"And it's good to see you, too. You have any idea where Joe might be?"

"You don't know where he is?"

"Now, if I knew where he was, would I be askin' you?"

"I ain't seen him."

She pointed her chin to the bartender. "How 'bout you, Bill?"

"I ain't seen him.

She pointed her chin to the bartender. "How 'bout you, Bill?"

"I seen him earlier. Maybe he's on his roof."

She didn't see him. It was too dark. The moon was hidden behind the clouds, and all she could make out were black shapes silhouetted from scattered lanterns and glowing cigars. There were lots of figures. Some were sitting on the ledge, some on chairs. Most were stretched out on blankets. How anyone could doze with the racket from the bawdy house across the street, she couldn't imagine. Then again, compared to the stifling heat inside the airless tenements, what was rowdy music?

"'Ave ye seen Joe Rubin, by any chance?" she asked a man leaning against the chimney, drinking beer.

He took the bottle from his mouth and wiped his lips with the back of his hand. "Joe Rubin, you say?"

"Yeah, is he up here?"

"Hum." He ribbed his chin. "Joe Rubin. Joe Rubin."

"Blond. Dimples. Needs a haircut—"

"Rent collector? Bit of an accent?" he asked in a thick Irish brogue.

"Yes. Yes, that's him! Seen him?"

"No."

Anne moaned.

"I seen him." A big fellow beside the beer drinker pointed. "He's over there."

She couldn't see which way he directed her. "Where?"

He pointed again. "*There*, there. In the back, to the right."

"Thanks."

"Don't mention it."

After negotiating her way around blankets and chairs, she found Joe snoring under a make-shift lean-to. Across the street someone was playing "My Darling Clementine" on a piano, and people started singing and laughing.

"Joe," Anne whispered.

No answer came. Just a soft snuffle.

"Joe," she called a little louder.

Still there was no response.

She bent down and touched his shoulder gently. He swatted her hand away.

"Joe."

Slowly he opened his eyes. ". . .What?"

"You were supposed to meet me," she said. "I was waiting."

"She wasn't home," he mumbled and turned away from her.

"Ah. How come ya didn't tell me?"

"I'm telling you now. Shouldn't you be in bed?"

"I told ya, I was waitin' to hear something. Now what? Will ya go back tomorrow?"

"Next week."

"A whole *week*?"

"I spoke with her daughter."

". . .And? What'd she say?"

"And *nothing*. She gave me a contract to look at. I'll go over it and make my decision."

"What's to decide?"

"What is this, the Spanish inquisition? And what's it to you anyway? It's my life."

". . .And mine. It means we could finally get married. Leave this city. Start our family." She knelt down to kiss him. The roof shingles were rough and hurt her knees. "I love ya, Joe!"

He pushed her away. "We're not getting married."

"We'll go West—"

"Didn't you hear what I just said? I am not going to marry you."

"Start a business like we talked about, and—"

"I am not going *West*. We are not getting *married*."

She stood up, her legs wobbly, and looked down at him, touching her belly. "But. . .the baby."

He put two fingers to his forehead and rubbed between his eyes. "Get off my back." He rolled on his side, turning away from her. "I'm tired, and I'm in no mood to listen to your tantrums. Go home. I had a long day."

"You don't want to listen? You don't want to *listen*? I'm *pregnant*!" She kicked him in the butt. "*You're* the *father*!"

"Nobody forced you to spread your legs."

She kicked him again, harder this time. "Did you *hear* me? I'm pregnant, and you have to do something!"

He rolled onto his back. "Lower your voice. Do you want the whole city to hear you?"

"I don't care if the whole *world* hears me!"

Neither the city nor the world heard hear screaming, but the whole building did. People on the surrounding blankets sat up, turned their heads in their direction, and watched the show.

"I'm not in the mood to talk about this now." He turned away from her again, put his bag beneath his head like a pillow, and closed his eyes.

"No! We'll talk about this *now*, Joe Rubin!" She kicked him again, in his ribs, in his back—-everywhere. "You been keepin' me waitin' long enough, and I ain't gonna wait no more! You're gonna make an honest woman out of me and take responsibility if it's the last thing you do!"

He ignored her.

Another kick in the ribs. "You get your arse up and talk to me!"

In an instant, he was on his feet, glaring at her, their noses nearly touching, his fists clenched at his side. She stepped back, almost losing her balance. "Now we can get married," she said, timidly. "We can leave the city. The baby will be here before you know it. Your baby, Joe."

A long silence stretched out. Finally, he spoke. "Let me put this as simply as possible," he said. "I am *not* going out West. I am *not* going to marry you."

Her eyes glazed over with tears. ". . .Wh-What will I do?" she asked, the words catching in her throat.

"What you do is not my problem."

"But. . .I don't understand. Yesterday—"

"Maybe you will understand *this*." And grabbing her by the scruff of her neck, pulling her so close that their heads nearly touched, he threw her backward. She stumbled over the couple sitting behind them and landed flat on her back on their outstretched blanket. "I'll say it again, more clearly," he snarled looking down at her. "I am not, *not*, going West. I am not, *not*, going to marry you. Do you *understand* that? You are not my problem!"

He dropped back down onto his blanket, stuffed the bag of clothing under his head, and closed his eyes. A moment later he was snoring. He didn't hear the sobs, didn't see the tears running down her face. And if he had, he would not have cared. He would soon be in the midst of a dream, without a single glimpse of Anne or the baby to come to clutter it--dreaming he was living in a big, luxurious house, sitting on an overstuffed sofa beneath an oil painting of Louis XVI and Marie Antoinette.

CHAPTER 27

It was early evening by the time Joe finished his rent collecting and set out for Brooks Brothers, the only establishment in all of Manhattan that sold clothes off the rack. He'd had a busy week tracking down tenants who'd been avoiding him, and it was the first chance he'd gotten to check out the store. He'd have preferred to buy a custom-made suit. But it would have taken weeks for a decent outfit to be made, and even if he had the money, he didn't have the time.

In the third week in August, with temperatures through the roof and air thick with humidity, the heat was oppressive. It had begun drizzling an hour before. Steam was rising from the pavement, and horse-drawn carriages, rattling down Broadway, were splashing filth on the sidewalk. Despite a sore foot, which he'd injured by kicking in a door in his effort to collect a rent, he moved quickly through narrow streets, skirting strewn debris, stepping over a dead dog that lay in the gutter, putrefying in the heat, as if it didn't exist, and ignoring an impending brawl.

Though it was only twilight, the bars were in full swing, and drunks were already flying through saloon doors. Two men were fighting in the street, undeterred by the light rain. One had a knife, the other a bat. The one with the knife had hair everywhere except on his head. His shirt was off, and his chest, muscles rippling, gleamed with sweat. Dark, curly hair covered his arms from his elbow to his knuckles and sprouted from his ears. Striped suspenders held his pants up. He seemed to be doing some kind of dance, getting closer to the other, waving a steel blade. His opponent was just a boy with peach fuzz growing on his chin. Shorter than the other, not as muscled, but quicker, he clutched his bat with both hands. The older man spoke a cockney English and was telling the kid to go back to wherever he came from. Men were gathering behind the two and egging them on. Obscenities flew back and forth. But like the dog, Joe paid them no mind.

Two blocks later, he reached the corner of Catherine and Cherry Streets, where, to his chagrin, he saw that the clothing store was just a two-storied wreck of charcoal and smashed windows. A sign with the legend: *We only sell the finest quality, at a fair profit, and deal with people who appreciate such merchandise,* blackened around the edges, hung sideways from a torn awning. Joe sighed. He should have realized that it would have been targeted during the riot. The company supplied Union uniforms. No matter they were so shoddy they fell apart in the rain. Furious that he'd taken the long walk for nothing, and realizing that he'd have to buy some hand-me-down in a second-hand store, he kicked a charred beam. A thud rang in his ears, and he screamed as pain shot up his leg.

"Want me to kiss the boo boo?" he heard behind him. Following the scent of cheap toilet water, he spotted three whores standing in a doorway. One was prepubescent. He doubted the freckled girl had seen her first blood. She had her bodice half open, trying to advertise the merchandise. But she had little merchandise to advertise, as her breasts were the size of mosquito bites. The other two had more to show—-and did. They all had painted faces. One pulled up her skirt, made a humping gesture, and licked her lips. She wore dark stockings up to the knees and nothing above them. "Hey, handsome, want some fun?" one hollered, holding a newspaper over her puffed-out hair to keep it dry.

"Not today, sweetheart." He smiled and turned away, his sore toe rubbing in his shoe with each step.

"Ah, come on, cutie. Bargain price. We'll give ya three for the price of one."

"Maybe another time."

Joe made it a point not to go with whores. Only first-timers for him. *A night in the arms of Venus leads to a lifetime on Mercury.* He'd heard the claim that the curse of syphilis could be cured by poking a virgin, but he didn't believe it. He didn't believe the mercury worked either. Neither were those French rubbers a hundred percent safe.

"P*sst*! *You*. Come 'ere," a shadow whispered from another doorway, motioning with a curled finger. Joe felt his heart pound. Picking up his pace, he moved to the middle of the street, away from the alley where the figure beckoned. The gangs of the Lower East were notorious. The Dead Rabbits, among others, would as soon kill you as look at you. Usually they only murdered each other. Usually. The street rats and guttersnipes, experts at picking pockets and knife fights, were just as dangerous. And the Plug Uglies were the worst.

A scruffy kid with a dirty face came out of hiding. "I'm not gonna hurt ya. Look." The boy, no more than twelve, Joe figured, held his hands up to show he was unarmed, his palms as black as soot. "I'm alone."

"What do you want?" Joe looked all around, but he didn't see any of the enormous, stuffed hats of the Plug Uglies, or shirt tails hanging over trousers, the signature calling card of the gang so named.

"I saw you going there." He pointed to the burnt-out building. "I have something you might be looking for. Come see."

Joe looked around again, in case others were waiting in ambush. Should he trust this waif? He knew mounds of merchandise had been stolen during the riots and were being sold for next to nothing in dark alleys. But what if this was just a ploy? He wasn't armed. And even if he had a weapon, he was not handy with one.

On the other hand, he needed a decent outfit. It was still light, though barely. And as far as he could tell, no one else was in wait. So he took a deep breath and followed the boy through the alley and into a dimly lit basement. Even with the loads of horse manure that fouled the air, he could smell the unwashed kid. "You have a whole general store down here!" Joe exclaimed as he bent low under the lintel, so as not to bump his head, and took note of the musty chamber. There were racks of jackets, vests, and trousers; tables with shirts, cravats, and socks; stacks of shoes; even a full-length mirror. Against another wall, household goods such and pots and pans and table linens were lined up. Beside them was hardware, and, next to the screwdrivers, pharmaceuticals.

"What size are you?" the kid asked.

Joe shrugged. His father had made all his clothes back home. He was wearing what he'd bought in a second-hand store.

"Try this. It looks like you." The kid took a jacket off the rack.

Joe was about to protest—he didn't like the style, too stuffed shirt with that scissor tail or whatever you called it. But the kid held the jacket and helped him put it on. "It's only for size. Only for size. Naw. Sleeves are too long."

The hangers rattled and pinged together as he found another one. "Here you go. Try this."

After haggling over the prices, Joe bought three jackets, three trousers, socks, shoes, underwear, and silk cravats. The boy wrapped the merchandize in newspaper and, after Joe gave him a tip and promised to return another time, threw in a broad-brimmed felt hat.

"Suppose I steer some fellas here and we split the profits?"

The dirty-faced boy considered this and then agreed with a handshake. His fingernails were black.

With purchase in hand and money left over, Joe went home, limping but happy. It was raining in earnest when he left, drenching his clothes, but he didn't care. Life was good. And getting better all the time.

CHAPTER 28

"MOTHER," MARIE SHOUTED FROM THE BOTTOM of the stairs, "aren't you going to be late?" Gerhard took his watch piece out of a vest pocket and checked the time. His face was flushed, and he was already in a sweat. His stiff white collar was scratching his neck, leaving angry welts. He patted the beads of perspiration on his forehead with a monogrammed handkerchief.

"Florence, dear, I don't mean to rush you, but we are expected in half an hour, and it will take us at least that much time to get there. Forgive my insistence, but what *is* the hold up?"

"Oh, calm yourself, Gerhard!" she called back. "I'll be down in a minute. And it doesn't matter when we get there, anyway. Their dinners never start on time."

Gerhard turned to his daughter, who was unable to conceal her anxiety. "Go upstairs, please, and see what's taking your mother, will you?"

She found Florence sitting at her dressing table, spraying perfume behind her ears and in the crease of her bosom. Jars of creams and oils were arranged neatly on the polished tabletop. "My God! How can you breathe in this hothouse?" Marie said. Though the windows were open, not the slightest breeze came past the lace curtains. The bright floral wallpaper, the yards and yards of white eyelet that draped the canopied bed, and the abundance of intricately carved mahogany furniture made her feel as if she was suffocating.

"It's terrible, isn't it? And to have to put stockings on in this heat. If not for the extra orders I have to get out, we would be spending our summer at the shore like all civilized people. What do you think of my outfit?" The silk lilac dress that lay on Florence's shoulders and plunged low at the neck swished as she rose and spun herself around. Her dark hair was stylishly swept up. She slipped on kid gloves, stepped into her leather slippers, which were scalloped around the buttons, took her feathered hat out of its box, and started to the door. She stopped and looked her daughter up and down. "You're rather primped for an evening at home."

"What time will you be back?"

"We shouldn't be too late—unless the men get caught up in a card game and start their war talk."

"Well, don't hurry home on my account."

"I don't want to leave too late, actually. We have a busy day tomorrow: We have an appointment with the dressmaker, then we need to check on the invitations. . . ."

"My, oh my! Don't you look ravishing!" Gerhard gushed as his wife descended the stairs. "I must say, I married the most beautiful woman in New York."

"Only New York?"

"New York. Chicago. The *planet*!"

Marie opened the door and shooed them into the darkening night. "Alfred is waiting out front on the coach."

"We're coming, we're coming," Florence said. "And why, may I ask, are you in such a hurry to see us go? If I didn't know better, I would think you were expecting a secret visit from Walter."

"Oh, Mother. Please. How could you think such a thing? Walter would never do anything improper. Never. I'm sure he's stretched out in an easy chair, with his head buried in some dull, obscure book."

IN FACT, WALTER WAS NOT SITTING COMFORTABLY in an easy chair with an obscure book in hand. He was standing in a house of worship, mentally and physically *un*comfortable, at a very *un*obscure event. The church was packed. Whites and Negroes, adults and children filled every pew, folding chair, and stool set up in the aisles, and stood in clusters behind the pine benches. All had come to hear the deep voice of Henry Ward Beecher, founder and pastor of the Plymouth Church, who, as ferocious an abolitionist as his sister, Harriet Beecher Stowe, was, perhaps with the exception of the Harper's Ferry John Brown, the most ardent equal rights advocate among White men.

But having come down with laryngitis that morning, the pastor, a robust man with a bulbous nose and bulging eyes, was unable to give the eagerly anticipated sermon. "You'll have to speak for me tonight, Walter," he said in a scratchy whisper.

"What? Me? I-I can't. I've never—"

"Of course you can." The minister patted his shoulder, his hand warm and clammy. "You'll be fine." He wiped his fat red runny nose.

"I'll, I'll s-stutter. I-I do that when I'm nervous."

"Then don't be nervous."

Walter looked imploringly at his mentor. "Look at me. I'm not wearing a cravat, or even a waistcoat. I haven't shaved in two days. I can't stand up there before all these people."

"No one cares. They're here for more important issues than what you're wearing. Besides, you look fine—" The good man sneezed. "These summer colds are dreadful. They come on so suddenly and at the most inconvenient of times. Just say what's in your heart. I have the utmost faith in you." He gave his young protégé a gentle shove up the few steps to the speaker's platform, which, more like a theater than a church, had a curved stage instead of a pulpit. Walter couldn't help but feel intimidated thinking of the anti-slavery giants who had spoken from this very pulpit: Walt Whitman, Sojourner Truth, Fredrick Douglass, Charles Dickens, Mark Twain—and the great President Lincoln.

Dusky light was pouring through the windows, giving the enormous space a grayish tint. He cleared his throat and kept his eyes focused over the heads of the crowd for fear he might stammer if he met anyone's gaze. "Wh—what kind of world do we live in where we can treat the Coloreds so shamefully?" he began in a robotic squeak. "The president freed the slaves last January, yet life for our brothers and sisters is no better. In New York City, it is actually worse."

"Yes. Yes!" someone shouted.

Encouraged by the response, Walter raised his arm and pointed to the four individuals standing beside him. "Who will help this family reach the free soil of Canada?"

"I will!" came a voice from a middle row.

"As will I!" someone else shouted from the opposite direction.

"These good people, our neighbors," Walter roared, "have been burned out of their home. . .lost everything they owned! Three thousand of our twelve thousand Colored neighbors have been left homeless since the July 13 riot. Yes. Three *thousand*! And they were some of the lucky ones. How many were killed, lynched? *Lynched*. Right here in New York City. Not Alabama. Not Mississippi. Right *here* in a so-called *free* state. What kind of freedom is that, I ask you!"

"That is no freedom at all!" a plump woman, blotting her perspiring forehead with a lace hankie, declared from one of the front benches.

"You're right, Madam." Walter nodded, approvingly. "That is no freedom at all. Does anyone know how many were slaughtered? Anyone?" He looked from face to face. No one spoke. "I'll tell you. One hundred and counting."

A collective sigh went through the audience.

"It's an abomination!" a gray-haired gent cried out.

"And these people. . .those fortunate enough not to be dead—continue to be clubbed, stabbed, and mutilated when seen on the street—merely for having dark skin." He pointed to the sign above the pulpit, and he and the congregants chanted in unison: "Let us do unto others as we would have done to us, and let the human being however varied the color, be justly entitled to freedom!"

"It's an outrage what our fellow citizens are doing to our Negro brothers!" a deep voice exclaimed from the balcony.

"The sins of the father will be visited on the children!" someone hollered from a folding chair in the aisle.

It sounded like thunder. The walls seemed to vibrate as the crowd stomped their feet and howled, "Amen!"

"It is our Christian responsibility to come to their aid!" Walter continued, looking directly into their eyes. "We must assist them to Henson's Dawn colony, the ultimate safe haven in Ontario."

The heat was brutal. Windows were open, but that didn't help. Hand-held fans had no effect. Many men had removed their jackets. Women were sorry they had worn their corsets.

"How much? How much is justice worth?" Walter boomed, emulating the pastor's mock auctions. "Who will buy their freedom?"

Two young men took that as a cue to pass the baskets, and as the wicker vessels went from hand to hand throughout the church, and people dropped in coins and bills, gold rings, cuff links, necklaces, brooches, metal could be heard clicking and pinging throughout the church.

MARIE HURRIED TO THE MIRROR IN THE VESTIBULE the moment the door closed behind her parents. "If I were only a blonde. . .or a red-head. . .or had anything but this mousy brown. And these teeth! Why are they so big?" She pinched her cheeks until they were sufficiently red. "And why couldn't I have blue eyes, or green, or anything but mud?" She turned this way and that, critiquing her outfit. She couldn't wear her fancier dresses, as her parents would be suspicious, and she also didn't want to appear too eager. But she wanted to look . . .alluring. She had chosen a yellow gingham with short puffy sleeves and a square neck, adorned with matching ribbons. It was too hot for petticoats, but she wore them anyway. She didn't know if Joe Rubin would come. She didn't even know if he'd heard her when she whispered, "Wednesday."

Ten minutes later, the doorbell rang.

CHAPTER 29

MARIE TOOK A DEEP BREATH, straightened her shoulders, and, fighting to control the butterflies in her stomach, opened the door. The sun had set, and with a half-moon hidden behind thick clouds, near total darkness had descended.

Standing on the brick patio, the lamplight outlining his features, Joe looked even more handsome than she remembered. She opened her mouth, but nothing came out. She was only able to stare—first, at his striking blue eyes, then at the starched standing collar, still stiff despite the humidity, and the wide silk cravat that matched the handkerchief in the pocket of his brocade waistcoat.

"You *did* say Wednesday?" he asked, giving her a dimpled smile.

"Y-yes. . . . . Please. Come in."

Flaxen locks fell onto his forehead when he lifted his new felt hat. A wide smile crossed his face. He followed her through the blue parlor into the dining room, his clean, masculine scent trailing behind him.

Before coming to call, he'd soaked in a big metal tub at the bath house, where he'd tipped the attendant to add extra hot water and scrub his back, gotten a shave and a haircut, had his fingernails clipped and polished, and doused himself with expensive cologne he'd bought especially for the occasion.

"Have you thought about the loan?" Marie asked, because she couldn't think of anything else to say.

"I'm still considering my options."

"I didn't realize there were any."

"We always have options, Marie. We may not like them, but we always have them. The question becomes, can we live with the consequences of the ones we choose?"

Hearing him call her by her name had caused her heart to flutter. She felt his eyes boring into her. Ridiculous, she knew, but it was almost as if he were regarding her as one of those choices. They moved into the alcove. The windows were open, but the French lace curtains did not move in the still air. "What would you like me to play?" she said nervously, looking at the piano.

"Chopin's 'Nocturne 9'? I know Mozart and Beethoven are considered greater geniuses, but I've always preferred Chopin." He pulled his pant legs up a notch and lowered himself onto the bench beside her.

His closeness flustered her. Once again, she couldn't speak. Without a word she began to play.

Her fingers rolled over the keys. Her feet pumped the pedals. Lost in the crescendos and trills, her body swayed. It had been a long time since he'd heard the great composers—and never had he heard Chopin played so exquisitely. The music transported him to another time, another life. The girl beside him was as beautiful as the melody she played, her nose was not too long for her face, and her teeth did not belong inside the mouth of a horse—as long as he kept his eyes closed.

Lost in the romantic nocturnes, he moved closer to her, sliding easily on the polished mahogany. Their hips touched. She could feel his breath on her neck. She hit the wrong notes.

Just then, the kitchen door swung open, and the aroma of freshly baked bread wafted into the room. "Oh, me Lord!" Nola screamed, silverware clanging as she dropped a tray of cutlery she was bringing to the china closet.

Marie jumped up, her face as red as the roses on the dining room table. "Ah, this is Mr. Rubin. He came here this evening. So we could play together. I thought you were in bed."

"I'm sure you did!"

Marie pointed to the baby grand. "The piano. Mr. Rubin plays the piano, too—"

"Does he now?"

"And, and I thought—"

He rose and extended his hand. "How do you do, I'm Joe Rubin."

The woman scowled. She was round and shapeless. Her eyelids were fleshy, and deep creases lined her cheeks. Her usually crisp uniform was limp with humidity. Strands of damp gray hair that had escaped from beneath her cap stuck to her plump, flushed cheeks.

"And you are, I take it. . .the *maid*?" He raised his eyebrows.

ola positioned her arms across her belly. "Indeed, I am, Mr. Rubin. And I'm also put in charge here to watch over Miss Marie." She squinted, considering him more closely. "And how old might ya be? Close to thirty? You should be ashamed a yourself, tryin' a take advantage of a young girl. Did she tell ya she has an understanding with a fine gentleman? Soon to be married, they are. A gentleman her own age, I might add."

"Nola! That's enough!"

"You're getting married?" Joe couldn't hide his alarm.

"She is indeed. October coming."

"This October? In three *months*?"

Marie glared at her housekeeper, who, huffing, turned on her heel and charged back to the kitchen.

Joe had paled. "You're engaged to be *married*?"

"I-I—"

"You *can't* be!" He blurted. "You can't. I *need* you!"

NOLA WAITED UNTIL SHE NO LONGER HEARD Joe's footsteps on the tiles before entering the vestibule. She put her calloused hand on Marie's arm. The girl turned from the glass portal where she had been watching him until he disappeared from sight and glared at her. "How could you!" she cried.

Nola pulled herself up to her full five-foot-two. "I'm sorry if I embarrassed ya. I spoke *outta* turn. But what might ya be up to entertainin' a gentleman—"

"Joe Rubin is a friend. Only a *friend*."

"A rather *handsome* friend, I should say."

"He's *not* just a pretty face. He's smart and cultured and—"

"Has a sweet bum?"

"Nola!"

"Don't be so shocked. I may be old, but I'm not dead."

"Well, it's more than his looks. He's—" Marie paused contemplating the appropriate adjective.

"'Dishonest' be the word ya looking for."

"How can you say such a thing? You don't even know him."

"Do you? What kind of accent is that he 'as? 'Tis none I never 'eard. Where's he come from? How'd ya meet 'im?"

"I know all I need to."

Nola sighed. "Then you also know that your mother would not take kindly to yer *friendship* with Mr. Whatshisname."

"Don't call him that! His name is Joe Rubin. And my mother

doesn't have to know. *I'm* certainly not going to tell her." She stared at her old nanny. "And neither are you."

Nola's eyes widened. "And how is that?"

"Because, if you do, I'll tell her about the liquor you've been tippling from the cabinet."

Nola gasped. "You wouldn't."

But from the look on Marie's face, she knew she would.

CHAPTER 30

ANNE PUSHED THE FLORAL CURTAIN ASIDE with a swish and entered the kitchen. Wearing a wide-brimmed straw bonnet to mask her tear-stained face and holding a drawstring purse over the beginnings of a belly, she hurried across the squeaky floor to the door. She felt dreadful. She hadn't slept. The mattress sagged in the middle, and the sisters, one on either side, rolled into her. Rose, the elder sibling, must have shifted positions every fifteen minutes, and while Colleen stayed in one spot, she whimpered all night! Anne wanted to scream—when she didn't want to cry.

It was only six a.m., but the night soil had already been dumped, the floor swept and mopped (the warped wood still wet and reeking of ammonia), and the sleeping pallets folded and stacked against the wall. Mrs. Hare was at the table, sorting beans, which were making a pinging sound as she slid them into a big pot she kept on her lap. Her stockings were rolled down around her ankles, as usual, and her hair was pulled away from her face. "This heat is unbearable," she said without looking up. She pointed to a hanging plant with her chin. "See my poor philodendron. No matter how much water I give it, it just dries up." The window was wide open but little air came through.

"'Tis rather limp," Anne acknowledged.

Mrs. Hare looked up at the sound of her quavering voice. "Would ya be cryin, now?" She pushed her chair back, got up, and took a closer look. "Are those tears I see in yer eyes? Why, Anne dear, you '*ave* been cryin'! Sit down here and tell me what it 'tis that has ya so upset." She pulled a chair out for her, but Anne kept standing.

Despite her best efforts the big silver drops rolled down her cheeks. "I. . .I. . miss my ma." It wasn't a lie. Though not the reason for her distress, at that moment she missed her greatly

"'Tis very sad, dear. Such a tragedy," said Mrs. Hare. "So young."

"Yes," Anne managed to say. Her shoulders shook as tears rained down her cheeks and pooled on her chin.

"Ah, to leave two small children as she did to fend for themselves." Mrs. Hare clicked her tongue and moved her head from side to side. "So very sad. But that was a long time ago, Anne dear. I would think you would have come to terms with it by now. Like I always say: 'Count ya blessings, not ya heartaches.'"

"Some days are just harder than others."

"Yes, of course, I understand. Ain't you working today, Anne dear? And here I am holdin' ya up. You'd better be on your way!" She pointed to the door, which was already open, in hopes of better ventilation, and shooed her out. "You don't want to be fired, now, do ya? Hurry. Hurry."

The hallway was stuffy and dark, as usual. As Anne began to make her way down the creaking stairs, Mrs. Hare leaned over the bannister and cried after her, "Should I expect ya for supper, Anne dear?"

A few tenants, sitting on the stoop and in chairs they'd brought from around their tables when Anne pushed the door open, scooted closer together to make way for her to pass. "You're all up early this mornin'," Anne said, trying to act normal.

"Who could sleep in this heat?" Rose Monahan answered, looking up from the infant dandling on her knee. "Liam's been up all night cryin'."

Anne imagined the young mother leaving her apartment in the pitch dark so the baby wouldn't disturb her drunken, wife-beating husband. A wailing babe would be just enough to set him off. Indeed, she saw that Rose's hair fell conspicuously over her left eye.

"Hot it tis," Anne acknowledged.

When she was far enough away from her neighbors for them not to notice, she pulled a wrinkled hankie from her pocket and stared at the address written on it. Luckily, she'd had the foresight to remove it before washing her dress, so the pink chalk scribbles were still legible.

The first week after Joe left her, she'd been in a fog, too distraught to think rationally, and behaved as if her "problem" would disappear. Only when Fiona had told her she'd better do something sooner than later had Anne snapped back to reality. Her friend wished she could help her, but she had her hands full with Paddy and the boys and couldn't spare a nickel. "I coulda told ya that fella a yours was a scoundrel. Never did have any good intentions," she'd declared. "And you, a good Irish catholic girl. Tsk, tsk." But for all her condemnation, she had given Anne the name of a pushcart lady on Broadway who sold "something that should do the trick."

Anne had bought the Brewer's yeast and pennyroyal tea the woman sold and drank it three times a day as directed. It had cost her a week's pay—and another verbal lashing from Mrs. Hare for not having the rent again. But it had only given her cramps. After that, she'd contemplated using a coat hanger but didn't have the courage, the morgues being filled with women who'd died that way. Fortunately, she'd saved the address Harriett Brooks had given her.

Or was it so fortunate? God might forgive her sexual indiscretions with Joe, but *this*? *Abortion*? Would it have been any less of a sin to do away with it earlier? Was it ever alright to murder it? *It*. Not the *baby*, or *he*, or *she*. Just *it*. About to commit a mortal sin, she would be doomed to the everlasting fires of hell. "Saint Bridget, help me," she prayed. "I know what I'm about to do is wrong, but what else is there? I'm four months pregnant, starting to show. I have no one to help me. I'll lose my job, my room, I'll be sleeping on the park bench. And the baby? What would become of the baby? I 'ave no options, don't you see? You understand, don't you? Can you forgive me? Will *He* forgive me?" she asked, staring up at the hazy sky. When a woman walking beside her clutched her toddler closer to her breast and gaped at Anne as if she'd escaped from an asylum, she realized she'd been talking to herself.

Four weeks had passed since the draft riots, and New York City had returned to its bustle. The streets and sidewalks were crowded with folks going about their business. It was a Monday, wash day, and across the alleys women were leaning out of windows, hanging their sheets to dry on the clotheslines between tenements. She couldn't help but think of her mother as she passed one rope where pantaloons, socks once white, and crotchless drawers were dangling. Kathleen Callahan Ryan would be turning over in her watery grave. "Shameless!" Anne could hear her say. "To have your unmentionables blowing in the wind for the world to see." Of course, there was no wind. The air was as still as her da when he was too hung over to get out of bed. Thinking of her long-gone parents brought smiles and tears to her face. How disappointed they would have been over her predicament. And yet, Anne knew, they would not have turned her away.

She kept close to the buildings, trudging along under store awnings to avoid being doused with night-soil, which was too often thrown from the top floors, or be splashed with manure and other filth from the street.

Traffic was chaotic. Horns honked, and wheels screeched and rattled as horse-drawn trucks, wagons, and delivery carts speed by, zigzagging in and out of their respective lanes. Immersed in her own misery, she hardly noticed. Neither was she paying attention when she crossed the street in the middle of the intersection.

"Hey, you *stupid* or somethin'? Watch where you're going!"

A driver raised his fist and let out a string of curses after nearly slamming into her. Horses whinnied. A milk truck skidded to a stop. She looked up, startled.

"Ya just gonna stand there? Tryin' to get yourself killed?" the man who nearly ran her over shouted.

Get yourself killed. The thought hadn't occurred to her before. She stood paralyzed.

A driver with muttonchop sideburns, wearing goggles, hollered, "Move, lady!" More riders cursed. Finally, she hoisted her dress above her ankles and, stepping carefully around the horse shit that covered the granite blocks, made her way to the other side.

Peddlers were everywhere. Fruit vendors weighed potatoes and onions in hanging metal scales that glittered in the emmerging sun. Full-skirted women gathered around the produce, squeezing peaches and plums. A rag picker was making his way up the street, chanting, "Rags, rags, any old rag!" again and again until his voice was hoarse. Behind him a scissor and knife grinder blew a bugle to announce himself.

Anne held her handkerchief, saturated in cheap toilet water, tighter under her nose as she drew closer to Cow Alley. Street cleaning and garbage pick-up in that part of the city were practically nonexistent.

Everyone in the neighborhood must have been outside. She had never seen so many people in one place. There were bordellos and saloons one after another from which painted women, young and old, called out to passersby. *'Tis very convenient for them to have the abortionist just around the corner,* Anne thought.

She ventured farther onto the street, maneuvering between fast moving wagons, when she passed the rat-killing pits. The mere thought of the place made her shiver. She'd been there once with Joe. It was one of his favorite pastimes. She remembered holding her ears for fear they would burst with the sound of dogs yelping and men screaming until they lost their voices, while they wagered on which dog would kill the most rats.

She remembered navigating a rickety wooden staircase, finding herself in a dirty sub-cellar full of smoke that burned her eyes, and the stink of sweat and flat beer. Sconces had hissed. Glasses had clinked behind a counter while men laughed, talked, and argued. The cigar smoke in the murky light had given her a coughing fit that nobody seemed to hear.

But most of all she remembered the terriers, bitten and bleeding all over their bodies, pitted against a hundred rats in the ring.

It was a disgusting place even for Five Points, and if for no other reason, she was happy to be rid of Joe never to have to go there again. She'd threatened to leave him if he continued to join in such brutality. If only she had stuck to her guns.

She turned the corner, and another, until she came to a back alley behind a dilapidated cluster of two-story buildings, where she found the door with the sign that read: *Relief to women who are temporarily indisposed.*

Clutching her draw-string bag to her chest, she proceeded down the crooked steps to the basement. It cost ten dollars, Harriet had told her—an exorbitant amount for a person in her position, but she could pay it over time.

The room was too small for the number of people in it, and uncomfortably quiet. Five women and two girls were squashed together on two benches that faced each other, their knees and elbows tucked close to their bodies so as not to poke each other.

When Anne came in, two of them shifted over to make room for her. A woman, and a girl Anne assumed to be her daughter, were on her left, a pretty blonde on her right. The girl on her left had pink, cherubic cheeks. The blue smock she wore outlined a tiny bulge just starting to show below her breasts. She was resting her head on her mother's bosom, while her mother finger-combed the girl's hair. The girl was crying softly; the older woman had dark circles under her eyes and an angry expression. "It will be alright, Maureen," Anne heard her whisper. "Everything will be alright." The other youngster, on the bench across from Anne, just stared at the low ceiling, her arms folded across of her chest. Anne tried to read her. She must have been in her mid-teens. She seemed angry, not scared. Probably not the first time, Anne concluded

In addition to the blonde, there were three other women in the room. No one spoke. No eyes met. Everyone had a somber expression. Each sat in her own world, with her own secret, as if no one else in the room knew why she was there. But of course, they all knew that they all knew, that they were all there for the same reason.

Anne wondered about each one's story. Was she single, married, involved with a married man? She imagined the child on her left had been raped by her father. The poor child. Anne wondered whether in fact everything *would* be alright for her. Would the mother be able to keep the beast away? In a small way, the girl's plight made Anne feel less despondent. At least her troubles were of her own doing.

She looked out the basement window because she couldn't look at *them* anymore. The window was close to the ceiling and secured with iron bars. She could see shoes and skirts passing by.

A clanging of metal on metal erupted from the other side of the wall, breaking the silence. The women started. A door creaked open, and a woman emerged from within the office. She looked pale and worn out. She was bent over as if she had cramps. The nurse, or midwife, or whoever was behind the door called, "Next." Anne gasped when she saw her. She was colored! Of course. Why should she be surprised? Harriet Brooks had given her the name. Anne had never thought to ask. And so what, anyway? She looked around. All the patrons were white. They didn't seem to mind. And then she remembered seeing the colored and whites living side by side in the Five Points

A haggard-looking patient who appeared to be too old for such issues got up and lumbered in. The occupants on the bench where she had sat spread out and stretched their legs. They didn't stay comfortable for long, though, as two more subjects soon came through the door.

That woman was in there a long time. The walls were thin, and through them could be heard the sounds of crying and an occasional scream. "It's almost done," they heard the voice of the other say, and added, "It will be behind you soon. The cramps will go away in a day or two. Expect to see bleeding. You were too far along, so I expect there will be clotting. You should have come sooner. Stay in bed for a few days, until it stops. Don't lift anything heavy for a few weeks. Don't take baths. No sex. *And don't get pregnant again.*"

"I have five children at home," Anne heard the patient say. "How can I stay in bed?"

"Perhaps the older ones can help out."

"The oldest is six."

"Is there anyone who can help you? Your husband, maybe?"

"He works all the time. He's never home."

Anne laughed despite herself, and she noticed that the irony of the woman's husband never being home struck a chord with the others in the room as well—suddenly all those somber faces were hiding smiles.

The girl with the cherubic cheeks went next, her mother holding her hand, then the angry adolescent.

The door creaked open over and over until finally it was Anne's turn.

CHAPTER 31

"Nola, have Thomas get the coach ready," Florence called from the dining room. Platters of scrambled eggs, slices of ham, biscuits still warm from the oven were sitting appealingly in a cloth-lined wicker basket. Sliced cantaloupe and peaches had been laid out on the buffet behind the dining room table. Beside the food stood tubs of butter and strawberry jam, a crystal pitcher of freshly squeezed orange juice, and a silver carafe of coffee.

Nola came in from the kitchen when she heard her name, a blast of heat following her as the door swung open behind her. Ninety degrees notwithstanding, it was the humidity that made the house unbearable. Sweat streamed from beneath her cap down her red, flushed face. "Yes, ma'am. I'll have him bring it around front."

Florence, having bathed, perfumed, and powdered shortly before, was quite fresh in a short-sleeved organdy dress. A wide-brimmed fuchsia hat adorned with silk flowers, and satin birds, rested atop her hair, which was coiffed in an upsweep off her neck. She held up her cup. Nola poured more coffee, careful not to spill any on the embroidered tablecloth. "Mr. Gilbert, more coffee, sir?"

He looked up from his *New York Times* and smiled at her. "Yes. Thank you. And Nola, your biscuits are mouth-watering, as usual."

"Thank you, sir. Kind of you to say so."

Florence turned to her daughter, who was wearing a plain cotton day dress in apple green. "I hope you're going to change into something more presentable."

"We're only going to the seamstress."

"Actually, I thought we'd go to Steward's after the dressmaker, and there one certainly needs to be dressed appropriately."

"This isn't going to be an all-day affair, is it?"

"I expected that you would be more excited, Marie. It's not every day a girl shops for her wedding gown and touring outfits."

"What's wrong with the clothes I have? And who wants to go to Paris, anyway?"

Florence nearly choked on her coffee. "Did you hear that, Gerhard? 'Who wants to go to Paris, anyway!'"

Gerhard laughed behind his newspaper.

"I suppose you would be happier with Walter's idea of honeymooning on the Galapagos Islands!" Florence said. "My God, but you're impossible!"

"I'm not interested in going there either."

"Well thank God for that at least."

"And why do we have to go the seamstress, anyway? I already had a *fitting*."

"Ahh." Florence pointed her long, nail-polished finger. "One fitting, dear. There will be many more before it is finalized. And if you would stay still, and not wriggle about, it will go a lot quicker."

Marie made a face. Being fitted for the wedding gown was bad enough. The thought of her upcoming vows tied her stomach in knots. And while shopping with her mother under any circumstance was a chore, Stewart's, with its five stories of merchandise, would be an agony. No doubt Florence would go through every single item, try on every single hat and dress twice.

"Stewart's?" Gerhard dropped the paper to his lap. "Isn't that the fancy new store at Broadway and Fourth? Just across from Astor Place?"

"It's only the largest, most elegant retail store in the *world*. Honestly, Gerhard, have you been living under a rock? Anybody who is anybody knows Stewart's."

"The place with the staggering prices."

Florence's cup clinked on the saucer as she glared at him. "The prices, the prices. It's always about the cost of things with you, dear."

"Just saying, that's all. Have I ever denied you anything? You have my permission to spend what you like."

"Your *permission*?" Florence's eyebrows had risen.

"A poor choice of words. My blessings. You have my *blessing* to purchase whatever tickles your fancy."

Florence turned back to her daughter. "You'll need a decent wardrobe, traveling outfits, for your honeymoon." She stared her daughter in the face. I won't hear another word about it. And better take your corset with you to the dressmaker." She noticed that the egg on Marie's plate had not been touched. She was playing with it, twirling the fork, shifting the ham from side to side, and staring into space. "Are you not feeling well, Marie? . . . *Marie*?"

"Yes?"

"Are you not feeling well?"

"I'm fine. Why do you ask?"

"It's not like you to dawdle over food. You haven't eaten anything."

"I had some biscuit."

"Hardly."

"It's this God-awful heat," Gerhard interjected from behind the paper. He turned a crisp page. "Will it never end? It's affecting all of us." He loosened his collar as if to make the point and dabbed beads of perspiration off his forehead with his napkin.

"Anything of interest happening in the world?" Florence asked.

"The usual mayhem. The war. . .it's been raining in San Francisco, in case you're interested."

"How was your dinner last night?" Marie asked.

"Dreadful. Your father lost at cards, and the ladies talked about the gift packages they've been sending to the soldiers, competing over who could make the most pairs of socks. As if I cared. Next time anyone invites us over in the middle of August, we will send our regrets."

"There will be no 'next time,'" came Gerhard's voice from behind his paper. "We are spending *next* summer in Saratoga. No excuses. I insist."

Marie perked up. "Maybe you can still go, for a week or two! The only thing keeping you here is your shop. And you said yourself, Mother, the forelady is quite responsible in managing things."

The paper crinkled as Gerhard again rested it on his lap. "That's a *capital* idea, Marie. We can go for the rest of August."

"I have to deal with the payroll—"

"So it will be late. Surely the workers can survive a week or two without their pay."

"Then I'll have double the work when I return. You have no idea how time-consuming—"

"I'll help you, Mother! I'm good with figures. Think of those bubbling spas. Just what you need after all the tension you've been under . . .and Father can spend his time at that new racetrack while you socialize."

Florence looked dubious. "What about the wedding plans?"

"What about them? You can finish the invitations there. I can keep an eye on things at home, you know, if anything should come up. And who knows the people you may bump into: Lillian Russel. Or J.P Morgan. You can ask his advice about your next venture."

Gerhard chuckled. "As long as you don't comment on his nose."

"I understand he is quite sensitive about it," Marie added.

"I would be too if I had something like that growing on my face," her father replied.

"I've heard said it's some kind of tumor," said Marie.

"Well, whatever it is, it's disgusting," Florence added.

"Talk about ventures, and noses aside, dear, how is that loan business coming along?"

"Not well, I'm afraid. A few of those Five-Pointers applied, but they're such unsavory characters I wouldn't consider loaning them one of Nola's biscuits, never mind $300.00. And as if that isn't enough, I believe the governor has asked Lincoln to suspend the draft."

"That doesn't seem quite right. Rewarding the hooligans for their antics."

"It was a poor idea, Gerhard. I'm afraid you were right. And don't tell me you told me so."

"I wouldn't dare."

Florence turned to her daughter. "Marie, did I understand you to say you would stay home?"

"Well, I—" Marie buried her eyes in her empty juice glass, the pulp stuck to its rim. "I thought it could be like a second honeymoon for you. I'm perfectly comfortable here," she said, wiping the sweat on her forehead. "I. . .I thought perhaps I could get to see Walter."

Florence looked stunned. "I know it's been a while since you saw him, but it's hardly proper to visit with him while we're away. And you will be married soon enough."

Nola re-entered the dining room and was collecting the bowls of food.

"I'm quite aware of that," Marie said in a low voice. "But we won't be alone," she said more brightly. "Nola will be here. I haven't seen Walter in a while and I—I do miss him so."

Nola let out a choking cough.

"Are you alright, Nola? Do we need a pat on the back?" Gerhard attempted to rise from his seat.

"N-no, sir. Just a tickle."

Florence turned back to her daughter. "Well, I suppose if Nola is home and keeps an eye on you. It's true Walter has been awfully busy lately."

Nola spun around. "Excuse me, ma'am. Not that it's any of my business, but does Mr. Walter have time to visit? Is he not busy studying for his bar exam?"

"That's true, too, Marie. You don't want to take him away from his studies."

"An hour or two of distraction may clear his mind," Marie said.

"Not too much distraction, I hope."

"Papa!"

"Just kidding, dear. I trust you absolutely." Turning to his wife, he said. "I don't see any harm in it, Florence. A few hours of distraction. A walk in Central Park, perhaps, with Nola behind, of course, might be just what the chap needs."

"Pardon my saying," Nola cut in hurriedly, "I can keep an eye on the house, and any messages. Miss Marie doesn't have to sacrifice a nice summer retreat. After all, it's only two weeks, and I'm sure Mr. Walter can live that short a time without seeing the lovely Miss

Marie."

Marie threw her a scathing look.

"Thank you, Nola, for your advice," said Gerhard, "but if she doesn't want to come, she doesn't want to come.It's not as if she needs to look for a husband anymore."

"I suppose you're right, Gerhard. I would feel safe leaving her in Nola's good hands."

CHAPTER 32

It must have rained while they were inside, because the pavement was wet, and water had pooled in the cracks between the cobbles. It didn't kill the heat, though. If anything, it made it worse. While summers were hot in Lithuania, it wasn't as muggy as New York. Or as rancid. Joe wrinkled his nose. Horse shit smelled like horse shit no matter where you were. It was just that there was so much more of it in Manhattan.

He flashed Marie his best smile. She was standing on the sidewalk behind him, before the Barnum museum, wearing a pastel voile dress. Her hair was braided, looped around her ears, covered with a bonnet, and a light shawl crisscrossed over her shoulders. Her fingers were fretting over its edges. She smiled back, dropping her eyes bashfully. He watched the color rising up her face, like a glass being filled with tomato juice. Her earlobes were hidden inside her hat, but he suspected they had reddened as well.

Men in top hats, and women clothed in a similar manner as she, sauntered past in both directions. Behind her, people stood in a line, laughing and chatting as they moved slowly toward the ticket booth.

Some were pointing at the animals and banners painted on the five-story building, others at the illuminated panels or the line of American flags flapping on the roof. It was said that P.T. Barnum had hired the worst musicians he could find to serenade the museumgoers in the hope that they would not linger outside but pay their twenty-five cents and enter so as to avoid them. Indeed, the clanging, discordant sounds coming from the balcony above the entrance were painful to hear.

The noise vibrated into the street, mixing with the traffic sounds. Joe grimaced, then smiled. Soon his ears would be exposed only to the finer acoustics of The Academy of Music and the Astor Opera House, where the Gilberts owned a box.

He stepped into the gutter to hail an omnibus. Though there was little chance of running into anyone he knew, he would have felt safer taking a cab. Marie, however, never having used public transportation before, wanted the "common experience". He'd tried to dissuade her, citing the crowds and her penchant for motion sickness. But she would hear none of it. "Please, Joe!" she'd begged. "This is the first time in my life I've been in Manhattan without my parents or a chaperone. I want to savor every smell and feel of the *real* New York City."

Joe had laughed. "Oh, you'll smell it alright."

He studied the street, scanning the hidden corners of St. Paul's Chapel and the Hotel Astor on the other side of Broadway, when a milk truck sped by, splashing filth on his expensive trousers. "*Oy! A klog oyf deyn kup.*" He jumped back. "*Putz!*" His fist raised in the humid air.

He heard the two-decker bus clacking up Broadway before he saw it, and gripping Marie's hand, they squeezed through close-packed bodies and bumping elbows. "Hold on tight," he told her as they climbed the steps onto the bus. Grabbing onto the rope overhead, one hand over the other, they inched along until they found a sliver of space to plant their feet. The bus moved. They jerked and swayed. If not for being squashed among the commuters, she would have fallen. Whatever little breeze came through the open windows was blocked by the mass of people.

Luckily, more people got off than got on, and after a few stops, two seats side by side became available. Marie sat by the window. The bus continued to move in fits and starts, as did her stomach. She concentrated on the sights and sounds outside so as to ignore impending nausea. They stopped in front of Plaff's restaurant and, through the glass above its simple half-curtains, she saw customers sitting at tables with plates of food and drink before them. Further down the street, she watched a couple standing at a pushcart, eating hot corn on the cob.

When the queasiness passed, she turned to Joe. "What language were you speaking?"

He paled and cocked his head as if he didn't understand.

"When you screamed at the truck driver. It didn't sound like anything I've ever heard."

"Oh, yes, that. That was—" he cursed himself for the gaffe and coughed. "It was. . .ah, Yiddish," he mumbled.

"Yiddish!" Her eyes opened wide, and she sucked in her breath sharply. "As in *Jewish*? You're a—a *Jew*? Not that I have anything against Jewish people," she added hurriedly, raising her hands and showing her open palms as if to accentuate the point. Indeed, she was so taken with him, it wouldn't have mattered if he were green with purple polka dots.

"Bite your tongue!" he snapped. "One of *them*? How could you think such a thing? Of course I'm not! You don't see a big bent nose on this face, do you?" He gave her his handsome profile. "Do I look like a sniveling, frightened, money-hungry fool?"

"I'm sorry. I didn't mean—" she lowered her voice apologetically. "But. . .why were you speaking—"

"In Russia, they're all over the place, like flies on stink."

"Russia! You're Russian? I've never met a Russian. Why. . . ."

Joe had to think fast. He could smell her wheels turning. The Irish came in numbers because they were starving; the Germans came because-well, he didn't know why they came, but they came in numbers. But if others came alone, people suspected they were criminals, or running away from something or somebody. He couldn't claim to be German. She might know the language. He wouldn't be able to fake it. Having failed to come up with a reasonable answer, he leaned over and kissed her lips. "You've captured my heart," he whispered in her ear.

She was mortified at being caressed in public, felt every passenger staring at her, though in truth not a one took any notice. Yet despite her embarrassment, and the distress from the stays of the tight corset pinching her ribs, she'd never felt so wonderful. She inhaled deeply, having forgotten to breathe. "Joe Rubin doesn't sound—"

"I—it's. . . . Can I trust you to keep a secret?"

"Of course!"

"You have to swear never to tell."

"Cross my heart and hope to die." She crossed a hand over her bosom.

"My true identity must never be divulged."

"You can trust me. I promise."

"Well—" he leaned into her and lowered his voice— "I'm on a very covert diplomatic mission."

"Oh!" Her breath caught in her throat. "A secret mission!"

"*Shh*!" He put his fingers to his lips, looking around as if spies were behind him. "Sent by Tzar Alexander himself."

"A secret mission?" she whispered.

He nodded. "My real name is Josef Rubinovsky. . .*Baron* Josef Rubinovsky."

Marie's eyes widened even more. "A *baron!*"

"*Shh!*"

"Sorry."

He wanted to leave it at that, but he could see her curiosity. Besides, it was getting to be fun. "I shouldn't tell you."

"I crossed my heart!"

". . .I suppose. You did promise."

She nodded.

"Tzar Alexander wants to sell Alaska to your government. We—the tzar and I—understand that Mr. Seward is quite interested. I'm here to negotiate."

Her mouth dropped so far he could practically see her tonsils. When it closed, she asked, "Why?"

"Keep your voice down," he warned.

She lowered it to near inaudible. "I mean, we're in the middle of a war. And. . .*Alaska*? There's nothing there but snow and ice and Eskimos."

He hadn't thought of the war. "Well. The war won't last forever."

She seemed to consider this and accept the answer. "I can understand why Russia wants to sell it. But why on Earth would *we* want to buy it?"

Joe had no idea. He knew that Russia needed money after the Crimean War. He knew Russia couldn't afford to support the few settlements it had on the Southeast Coast, or the money to defend them. But he didn't have a clue why Mr. Seward was interested in buying it. *Deflect. Stall*, he told himself. "I think I'm in love." He leaned in and kissed her again while he tried to think of a reason. And when the fuzz above her upper lip tickled his nose, he was reminded, thankfully, of the rich *goyim* in their seal and sable coats, and he broke away and said, "Actually it's quite rich in furs."

This time she didn't care who would be looking. She tingled all the way down to her flat feet.

The bus stopped. About ten passengers got on and pushed and shoved their way to the few open seats. Those who weren't quick enough were left to squeeze in the aisles, grabbing on the ropes and poles to keep their balance. After an initial jerk, the bus was on the move again.

"What's it like to be a baron? Do you live in a castle?"

"A *dacha*."

"A *dacha*?"

"A small estate, only a hundred acres or so. It was given to my family by Alexander for their loyalty."

"Alexander?"

"The tzar."

"The Romanovs? Oh, my God!"

He told her about the galas he had hosted, his personal friendship with the tzar, his travels to Paris and Florence, and the Russian sleigh he rode in, drawn by a team of three white horses, called a *troika*.

This time when her jaw dropped, he *could* see her tonsils.

He was leaning back in his seat, feeling pretty good about himself, sure that the line of nonsense had won her over, when the bus stopped in front of John Allen's Dance Hall, one of his favorite haunts. Music and bawdy laughter floated through its open door. Ladies of the night, in red-topped black boots, were standing outside, smoking and making cat calls to the men who passed by. Several drunks in various stages of ossification stumbled out of the bar and onto the bus. One of them had such slicked hair it was a wonder his hat didn't slide off his head.

And one of them was Brian Higgins. He was wearing checkered pants with suspenders, cracked shoes, and a peaked cap. He stank of whiskey.

Joe groaned audibly when he saw him and crumpled into himself, dropping his head in his lap.

"Are you *alright?*" Marie asked in a panic.

He tried to keep his voice down. "My stomach," he grunted. "It will pass."

"Maybe your appendix is bad. It comes suddenly like that. My father had a bad appendix when he was in his twenties. Had to have emergency surgery. Let's get off and hail a cab, get you to the hospital." She reached for the rope that was attached to a bell near the driver, but Joe batted it away before she could reach it.

"It will pass!" he insisted. He put his bowler back on his head and tried to yank it over his eyes, sank deeper in his seat as if that would hide him, cursing his stupidity. He should have *insisted* on taking a cab. To hell with what she wanted. *Stupid, that's what I am, Goddamn stupid.*

Despite his efforts, Brian spotted him. "Hey!" He poked one of the other drunks in the ribs. "Ain't that Joe?"

"Huh? Who? What?" the other said

"Ah, go back to sleep," Brian said. Leaving his inebriated companion wrapped around the pole, he stumbled down the crowded aisle until he pushed his way close enough to stand beside Joe's seat. There was so much alcohol on Brian's breath that if anyone had lit a match there would have been an explosion. The smell of him set Marie's stomach in motion again. She put a perfumed handkerchief beneath her nose.

"Well, I'll be damned if it ain't Joe Rubin," Brian slurred, grabbing onto the rope above his head. His armpits stank. Marie gagged behind her hankie. "And all dandified. Ooo-hee, look at them duds! Fancy hat and all. Where you been keepin' yourself these days, Joe? Life just ain't the same without your company. Annie's been lookin' all over—"

"Listen, mister. I'm afraid you've mistaken me for someone else."

"Mister? It's *me*, Brian Higgins! Your drinkin' bud. You got one a them amnesia or somethin'?"

"I'm sorry, Mr. . . .Higgins, but you have the wrong man." Joe tried to make him understand with his eyes, opening them wide and nodding his head ever so slightly to warn him off.

"What's a matter with your eyes? You havin' a fit or somethin'?"

Joe turned to Marie, whose expression was a mixture of horror and confusion.

"Let's get that cab you suggested. My stomach is getting worse."

CHAPTER 33

When Nola heard a carriage pull up in front of the house, she pushed herself out of the overstuffed chair, shuffled to the window, and lifted the drape to look out. Though the gas lamp outside lit a circle of light, the cab was not within its narrow compass. There was no sound for a long time, and she could only imagine what was happening in the back seat. Finally, she heard the carriage door close. A few moments later the gate squeaked. Then she saw them strolling up the brick walk, arm in arm, aglow beneath the moonlight, Marie, her head on his shoulder, was holding on to him as if she might fall if she let go. They stopped. He kissed her nose. She giggled. When they approached the porch, Nola dropped the curtain. There was a distinctive crinkle of satin and a nervous titter. Then the sound of the bolt sliding out of place, followed by the whoosh of the door opening and the tapping of leather heels on the Italian tiles in the vestibule.

"Kinda late, don't ya think?" Nola said, glancing at the ticking French clock that told her it was one-fifty-three. She lit the lamp and, waiting with hands on her ample hips, watched Marie stumble into the parlor.

"Are we going to start this 'you're home late again?" Marie shielded her eyes with her lace-gloved hand and hiccupped.

"We most certainly are." Nola was in a loose cotton night shirt. Her silver-streaked braid hung down her back. Waking at five every morning to begin her chores, she very much looked forward to being in bed by nine and snoring by nine-ten. She was not happy to be missing her sleep. "I'm supposed to be watchin' over you."

"I'm an adult. An. . .an *adult.* And being an adult I don't need watching *over.*" Another hiccup.

Nola crossed her arms above her large bosom. "Your mother would differ."

"I'm twenty-years-old. Old enough to be married—"

"To Mr. *Walter*! So, where did Prince Charming take ya tonight? I guess his appendix didn't explode, after all."

"Turned out, it was only something he'd eaten, a cup of hot tea and a good night's sleep cured it."

"Hmm." Nola grunted. "Sounds fishy ta me."

"Everything sounds '*fishy*' to you."

Nola stepped closer and sniffed. "BeJesus, you smell like a bawdy house! You've been *drinkin'!*" She glared at the cluster of red blotches above her scooped neckline. "And doing God only knows what else!"

"And if I have?" Leaning on the wall so as not to fall over, Marie pulled her shoes off and rubbed her sore feet. "And dancing too, if you must know!" Just the thought of Joe's arms around her, his breath warm on her neck, set her tingling again. "And for your information, he is *almost* a prince. He's a *baron*!"

"A baron is he? And I'm Queen Victoria! Ahh." She threw her arms in the air. "May the curse of Mary Malone and her nine blind illegitimate children chase him so far over the hills of Damnation that the Lord Hisself can't find him with a telescope! 'Ave you lost *all* your senses? Can ya not see the man is a scoundrel? Do ya not realize what you're getting yourself into? Take your head outta your pantaloons! You're to be married in two months to Mr. Walter, a fine young man if there ever was one. A man who loves ya."

"How do you know he loves me? He's never said so. Besides, I don't love him. I love Joe. And he loves me. He told me so."

"Jesus, Mary, and Joseph!" Nola smacked her forehead. "A man does not 'ave to tell ya to feel it. And a man does not 'ave to *mean* it to tell ya. Sweet Jesus, if the Missus ever knew!"

"But the Missus is not going to know, is she?"

"Child, I hope for both our sakes she will not."

"I know, I know, I *know*!" Marie covered her ears and hurried to the staircase on unsteady legs. "Don't I know!"

"You know, you know, you know—but what are you gonna to *do* about it?" Nola yelled after her. "Ya had your two weeks of fun. Get yaself back together, now. Need I remind ya that your parents are expected home *tomorrow*? Mr. Walter came by this evening."

Marie stopped and looked over her shoulder. "Where did you tell him I was?"

"Don't worry. I covered for ya. Though, don't ask me why. I told him you was suffering from your monthly."

"You didn't!" Marie spun around. The room spun with her.

"A course not. 'Miss Marie's not been feeling well the last few days,' is what I said. 'She's nappin' right now.' He was quite concerned about your health, poor boy. But I assured him it weren't nothing serious. 'I'm sure she'll be recovered by the morning.' He'll be here tomorrow afternoon to look in on you."

Marie sat on the step, not straightening the satin dress beneath her, and sighed. She pulled off her bonnet, catching her amethyst earrings, and toyed with the grosgrain ribbon.

"He brought roses and candy." Nola shook her head and tutted. "I put the flowers in a vase on the dining room table and the chocolate in the ice box."

"Chocolate? Do they have nuts?"

"Covered almonds."

"Ummmmm. My favorite."

MARIE COULDN'T SLEEP. IT WAS HOT. Crickets were making a racket outside the open window, moonlight was painting strange figures on the wall, and the room spun with her every move. Yet it was not the heat or the noise, the scary images, or even her spinning that kept her awake. The past two weeks had been the most exciting of her life, and as she lay across her featherbed, with her chemise pulled up around her plump thighs and a cool towel on her forehead, she relived every moment. "Oh, My Darling Clementine," the song she'd heard for the first time that evening in the dance hall, played over and over in her head.

She'd never been in *demand* before. Other than the Bulgarian (whose name and countenance she could hardly remember!), she'd never even had *one* suitor. Now she had *two*. And they were both in love with her! Incredible! She wiggled her toes. Her feet were still on fire from dancing. The new shoes had not been broken in, and her pinky toes were red, sore, and swollen. Just to remember Joe's arms around her, those magnificent muscles holding her close on the dance floor, that masculine scent, his warm breath on her ear, set the blood racing in her veins.

It's not that I don't like Walter, she was thinking. *He's sweet, kind, and so thoughtful. But compared to Joe. . . .* Well, there was no comparison. An exciting date with Walter was a history lesson and nature tour. "Over a quarter of all the bird species found in the United States have been seen in Central Park," he'd told her.

That aside, she and Walter had spent a lovely Sunday afternoon together at an outdoor concert. Lovely but *hardly* exciting. The weather had been perfect, more like mid-September than steamy August, with a bright blue sky, light breezes, and air heavy with the scent of honeysuckle. Nola had packed a delicious lunch of fried chicken, homemade biscuits, corn on the cob, strawberry tarts, and a jug of lemonade. They'd spread a blanket on a grassy knoll beneath the boughs of a chestnut tree and there they ate their food. On the paths below them, elegant carriages had clopped and clattered—barouches, and, the lighter two-wheeled calashes with their roofs rolled down, their occupants facing each other in their Sunday best. The drivers wore top hats. Couples had ambled by, men in straight trousers, stiff white collars, and waistcoats, ladies hiding their delicate skin beneath ruffled parasols that matched their wide-hooped skirts. Though no fashion connoisseur, Marie had enjoyed watching them.

Nevertheless, she could not help but imagine the Russian nobility, decked out in emeralds and rubies, coming in horse drawn *troikas* to call on her at her *dacha*. They would have exotic names like Count Alexandrovich and Countess Irenavna. Of course, the guests would not be carrying parasols. They would be draped in mink, fox, and seal. *Dacha. Troika.* Even the words were thrilling!

Walter had watched Marie watch the parade. "Central Park wasn't supposed to be for the rich, you know," he'd said, his voice bringing her back to New York.

She had turned her attention away from the fancy outfits and glanced at him. He'd been sitting against the tree trunk, his long gangly legs stretched out before him, holding the chicken, his face freshly shaved, and every hair on his head in place and slicked down with pomade. "What?"

"The Park," he had said, speaking through closed lips to hide his mouth guard and pointing at an especially well-dressed pair strolling by.

Isn't one supposed to be finished with wire cribs in their teens? she had been thinking.

"To give them fresh air and get out of the slums for awhile. But it didn't work out that way."

"Mm." She had turned her attention back to the couple in point: the woman's ostrich-feathered hat, and her spouse's mutton-chop sideburns.

"It's too far uptown," he'd gone on, as if she were interested. "Not within walking distance of their tenements."

She'd hoped he wasn't going to go on and on about the "shameful conditions" they lived in. She had opened her mouth to respond, but as if he knew what she was about to say, he'd answered first. "Train fare is more than they could afford. And after working six and a half days a week, who has the time?"

"Mm."

"Worse than that. In order to build this park they evicted close to two thousand people who had been living here."

"It was only *swamp* land. And they were only *squatters*. I would think they would have been happy to leave." She turned her attention to the picnic basket, where she rummaged in search of a tart.

"Is that you or your mother talking?"

She had gasped. "That was a nasty thing to say!"

He'd taken her fingers in his. She'd pulled them away quickly.

"I'm so glad you think so," he had said between tight lips. "I always knew you were more sensitive, and more socially conscious." Lowering his voice to a mumble, he'd added, "That's why I love you.

Only *some* were squatters. Some were legitimate renters. And included in the eviction were a convent and school, a Negro settlement with close to three hundred people, which also had a school and churches, and residents of the Seneca Village."

"The city must have paid them."

"Yes. They got paid—a lot less than the properties were worth. But it's about more than money. They lost their community, their homes, their history, their livelihoods."

The sound of drums had been like distant thunder, cellos and violins warming up floated through the air. He'd taken a bag of peanuts with the express purpose of feeding the squirrels, and they'd both laughed as the little creatures came up to him, stood on their hind legs, and took the treats from his hand. He had taken such pleasure in feeding them, she remembered thinking. And then she remembered Joe kicking a stray dog they'd passed one night on the way home that lay on the sidewalk.

"Did you ever visit the Barnum museum?" she'd asked Walter.

"Never have, and never will. I understand it has some very interesting exhibits. I admit I would like to see the Beluga whales, but just the thought of the freak show turns my stomach. . . . It's hard to believe that people actually find the misfortune of others funny. Hard to believe." He had stood up awkwardly, brushing dirt and grass from his pants.

She'd thought about the day she'd spent there with Joe. Tears had come to her eyes when she passed the bearded lady, and a dwarf, General Tom Thumb wearing a bandmaster's suit. Worst of all were Chang and Eng, two distinguished gray-haired men, impeccably dressed in tuxedos, joined at the sternum. *Siamese* twins, the sign below them read, and went on to state that they were each married, had a bed made for four, and fathered twenty-one children between them. There had seemed to be much conversation and snickering about that fact. "How could people *laugh* at them?" she remembered asking Joe. "It's not funny. Being on display like that!" And then she'd turned only to see that Joe had been laughing, too. "Not *so* hard to believe," she had whispered to Walter.

But as she lay in her hot room, unable to sleep, she didn't dwell on the stray dog or Joe laughing at others' misfortunes. She thought only about those piercing blue eyes and the thrill she felt at his touch. Neither did she question why he'd been interested in a loan, the improbability of his "cover mission, or the encounter with that Higgins fellow on the bus, who had called Joe by name. "It's a coincidence, a common name. The man was drunk," Joe had told her. "Every other bum you meet is named Joe Rubin." And she had believed him. . .because she wanted to.

CHAPTER 34

WALTER WIPED THE PERSPIRATION from his forehead with a silk handkerchief that matched his socks. He checked his watch again. *What could be keeping her?* The scent of the gardenia in his lapel and the baskets of calla lilies and heather decorating the nave behind him were making him queasy. *Must be the traffic—not an accident, God forbid?* He shifted from one foot to the other. *Could it be she intends to stand me up? . . . What a silly thought. Or is it?* His mouth went dry. She had been rather cold lately—distant, pre-occupied. Nothing seemed to excite her, not even the three-bedroom brownstone his parents had bought them in Gramercy Park. *But she's not demonstrative by nature.* He chewed his lip.

The white-steepled church was packed. As well as occupying every seat in every pew, people stood three rows deep in the back and along the side aisles: men in their morning attire, top hats in hand, ladies in bonnets and colorful hooped skirts. Though a cool autumn day, the size of the crowd made it feel stuffy. They were getting restless, fanning themselves, chattering, and turning their heads toward the door with every new sound. Walter looked at his parents, who were sitting in the first row: his mother, paler than usual in an unpretentious dark dress and hat, raised her eyebrows. His father's head was bent, chin on his striped cravat, studying the time. Walter checked his watch—again. One minute had passed.

Finally, the heavy oak door swung open, and Marie, on the arm of her father, entered the marble vestibule that smelled intensely of frankincense. She wore a wreath of orange blossoms under her veil, a voluminous cream-colored, puffed-sleeved, silk taffeta gown held out with layer upon layer of petticoats. Rose-bud stockings were fastened at her knees with blue embroidered garters. Elbow-length kid gloves covered her hands and arms. Her silk slippers were adorned with silver buckles. Her eyes were red and her lids swollen. Her hands and shoulders trembled so that the ringlets on either side of her face bounced, and the bouquet she held, with a small porcelain horseshoe, which Nola had tucked in for good luck, shook in her fingers. Gerhard removed one of his white gloves, dipped his fingers in the font filled with holy water, and crossed himself.

Initially, the priest had refused to marry the couple at the altar because Walter was protestant. But after Gerhard—-at his wife's behest—-threatened to withdraw his financial support, the monsignor had acquiesced. Florence would have preferred that the wedding take place in Walter's Episcopal Church. It was unfashionable to be Catholic. What would people think of them, after all? Yet despite Gerhard not being devout, the difference over religion was the one battle she could not win. Still, the church's opulence delighted her.

The organist hit a chord. The congregants rose and turned to the vestibule. Lifted in unison, the wooden kneelers sounded like distant thunder. With her nose high in the air and her emerald jewelry sparkling in the sunlight that poured through the stained-glass windows,

Florence glided down the aisle. She wore a pale green *crepe de chine* studded with beads that clicked with her every move, matching satin shoes, her upswept hair beneath an ostrich-plumed hat. Though she kept her eyes straight ahead, she noticed every person in the church. All the best families were there.

The bridesmaids came next, one slow step at a time, then, with a collective *awww* from the attendees, the flower girl and ring bearer. Dressed as were the others in blue taffeta, she carried a basket of rose petals, which she scattered along her path; a blonde tot bore the ring on a white satin pillow.

Gerhard pulled Marie closer to him and gave her a reassuring hug. "Don't be nervous," he whispered. "I'm beside you. Just look straight ahead as if nobody were here."

As the soprano in the choir loft belted out the "Ave Maria," Marie took her first steps down the long red aisle.

She wept all the way to the altar. Several times she'd tried to speak with her parents about Walter, but her mother had intimidated her so, she hadn't been able to get past "I don't think I'm ready to be married."

They never took her seriously. "The jitters are normal, dear. Every girl gets them before the big day," her mother would respond, and carried on with the wedding arrangements.

Her father kissed her wet cheek, handed her over to Walter, and left to take his place beside his wife. Marie stepped onto the nave. Walter smiled from ear to ear, mouth guards finally removed, his straight white teeth gleaming. Her gown rustled as she turned. When they faced each other, he took her hands in his, squeezed her gloved fingers, and gazed into her reddened eyes. She kept her head bowed. "I love you," he whispered before the priest began to read the vows. "And I promise I will make you happy."

Marie broke into sobs. The priest waited until she calmed a bit to recite the vows. Another collective sigh came from the congregation as the tot in his page-boy haircut stepped up. Walter took the diamond-studded gold wedding band from the silk pillow. Marie removed her glove. The priest sprinkled holy water, swung the incense, and began his marriage sermon: "To live as one, forsaking all others .... Do you, Walter Alistair Hockenberry, take Marie Antoinette Gilbert, to love and to cherish. . . ."

"I do," said Walter, loud enough for those standing in the vestibule to hear.

The priest turned to Marie, who was still in tears. "And do you, Marie Antoinette Gilbert, take this man, to love and to cherish, forsaking all others, to be your husband?"

He waited. Coughed. Waited. Coughed again. Walter's wide grin began to fade. "Marie," the pastor whispered, "do you take this man?" Silence. "Marie?" he whispered. She could hardly find her voice.

And then, after what seemed like an eternity, she murmured, "I. . .I .... *No.*"

Pulling her hands from Walter's, eyes still downcast, she turned on her heels and, not hearing the collective gasp or seeing her mother's stunned face, ran out as fast as she could.

She flew out of the church and down the steps, the ringlets on either side of her face bouncing and her veil flapping behind her in the autumn breeze. "Hurry, Edwin, *hurry*!" she cried. Holding the voluminous wedding gown above her ankles with one hand, she threw away her bouquet of buttery ivories, which came to rest in Saint Anthony's outstretched arms.

Edwin dropped the hand-rolled cigarette from between his fingers and rubbed it out on the cobbles with the tip of a black leather shoe.

He raised his eyebrows to the other drivers with whom he'd been socializing and hurried across the street. He was tall and fit, except for a paunch. The monk's bald spot in the middle of his head glistened in the sunlight. Like the other chauffeurs, he wore a stiff-collared shirt under a black suit. No sooner had he set on his top hat than she was ripping the orange-blossom mantle off her head and vaulting into the open chaise carriage her parents had rented, along with the driver.

"Hurry!" Breathing as deeply as her corset would allow, the word came out clipped. She threw her veil on the plush seat beside her.

"What about the others? The groom, and—"

"Never mind them." She checked behind her, her vision still blurry from the tears she'd shed since parting with Joe.

No one had come out yet. But they soon would. The carved oak doors were opening. She squinted at the sun, not directly overhead, thankfully. She had some time. But not much. "Just go! *Please.*"

"I'm afraid we're stuck, Miss." Edwin pointed to the vehicles blocking their path on both sides of the street. "We can't get out."

"*Try!*"

He shrugged as he climbed onto the box. When he stretched his long legs out before him, his trousers rode up above his socks to expose hairy shins. He took the reins in his gloved hands and pulled the straps. Nothing happened.

Guests had begun trickling out. She could hear talking and laughter, heels clicking on the pavement. Though she couldn't make out what they were saying, surely it was about her. She shut her eyes, wishing she could melt into the roadway, disappear. But sitting there, in plain sight, in a sparkling white coach, so flamboyant among the other luxurious but more sedate barouches and broughams, she was about as inconspicuous as Lady Godiva. The best she could do was crouch on the floor and cover herself with the marabou cape she'd left before entering the church. Her arms were goose-bumped, and her teeth chattered whether through nerves or cold she couldn't tell. It was cool but not enough to shiver.

"Go. . . *Please*!" she begged, her voice breaking.

She felt the coach edge up a few inches, stop, back up, jar forward, back up again. Back and forth, back and forth, her body rocking on the wine-colored carpet with each jolt. She could hear people strolling on the sidewalks, what sounded like children traipsing through piles of leaves, a dog barking in the distance.

And then at last they were moving.

NOLA SCANNED THE HOUSE ONE MORE TIME to assure everything was clean and in order. The house wasn't in order, it was in obsessive order, so clean that not even one dust mote floated on the sunbeams.

After deciding to host a wedding brunch (in addition to the dinner at Delmonico's), Florence had been fanatical. From that day forth the residence had been a beehive of activity. The walls, already freshly painted, were re-painted. Woodwork was polished and polished again. Windows were washed, summer curtains removed, and new, custom-made (and very costly) brocade draperies installed in their place. So many flowers had been set out in each room, it smelled like a botanical garden. Madeira linens that covered the tables and buffet matched the color of the walls; on them lay silver trays filled with bacon, cheese-deviled eggs, French toast strips, sliced apples with a honey, and fruit cake, divided into individual pieces, wrapped and ribboned, for the guests to take home.

Lizzy, one of three domestics employed to prepare for the big day, was putting out platters of petits fours in the parlor, when she heard horses clopping outside. Putting the last of the miniature cakes down, she pulled the window covering aside and looked out. The sky was a deep blue with faint streaks of white. There was a brisk wind, and red, orange, and yellow leaves were dropping on the lawn and pathway to the house that had been raked and swept clean two hours before. "I think they've come," she said to the others.

"It's too soon," Nola answered. "They shouldn't be back for at least another hour. Must be another delivery."

"Probably another one of them crystal ice buckets," Lizzy added.

"How many of them she got so far?" Nola asked.

"Six. Includin' the silver one."

"How many ice buckets can one use?"

Packages had been arriving for the past two weeks, wedding presents from out-of-towners who'd sent their regrets. The parlor was stacked with them, each catalogued and displayed.

"Nope, it ain't no present. It's them. They're *home*.

"Already?" Nola re-arranged the aperitifs in size order just to calm her nerves, the decorative bottles clicking as they passed each other.

"Wow! I've never in me life seen a coach like that," Lizzy said. "It looks like Cinderella's pumpkin. Except it's white, and doesn't have a top."

"That sounds *exactly* like it, alright," answered Nola.

"Oh, what a beautiful gown! Wait 'till ya see those puff sleeves. I want one just like it when I get married!"

"Keep dreamin', Lizzy. You'd be lucky to be wearing a potato sack. Besides, you ain't even got yaself a boyfriend," Aileen pointed out.

"Not yet. But someday I will."

"Who wants t' get married, anyway?" Claire said, "Ya just has to work twice as 'ard."

All three girls were in their late teens and had different shades of brown hair, all of which were tucked beneath their ruffled white caps. With their pale complexions, rosy cheeks, and brogues, each looked and sounded as Irish as leprechauns. The maid's uniforms they were wearing were probably the finest clothes they'd ever had.

"Here she comes. Here she comes!" Lizzy called, dropping the curtain, and hurrying to take her place at the door where she'd been instructed to greet the guests as they entered, and take their wraps. "But I didna see the groom. Wouldn't they be in the same carriage?"

The color drained from Nola's face. "Oh, Mother Mary!" She crossed herself, reached for the bottle of whisky she kept hidden behind the mantel, filled half a glass, and drained it without so much as a grimace. "Sweet Jesus, don't let it be so."

But a moment later, when the door swung open and she saw Marie storm into the house with her gown rumpled and her hair askew, her worst fears were realized.

Nola followed her with her eyes, then with her feet.

She found Marie in her room, with her arms twisted behind her, tugging frantically at the back buttons of her gown. Her silk slippers, rose-bud stockings, and garters were on the floor, the edge of the eyelet bedspread wrinkled from where she'd sat to remove them. "Look at the state ya in! Jesus, Mary, and Joseph!" Nola huffed, red-faced and out of breath from mounting the stairs. "I might as well a been whistling jigs to a milestone. What did ya do? If you was not intendin' on marrying Mr. Walter, why did you not tell them afore now! Embarrasin' the young man like that. And Lordy, Lordy, not to mention your mother. O, me God!

"Please don't lecture me, Nola. Not now. Just help me get out of this gown!" She held her curls up while Nola's thick fingers fumbled with the tiny silk loops that ran from the neck to the small of her back. "I feel badly for poor Walter—"

"Don't feel bad for Mr. Walter. He'll be just fine—once he can show his face in public again. Feel bad for *yerself.* You're the one you need to feel bad for."

Marie groaned but didn't answer. What could a fat old maid know about love, or the exciting life she was going to have among Russian royalty? "I meant to tell Mother. . . . I mean. . .I couldn't. Every time I tried, she was busy making table arrangements or adding outfits to my trousseau. It's not that I don't *like* Walter. I *do.* I was *going* to marry him. I *was.* But then, at the last minute. . .at the *altar.* I just, just . . .I just couldn't. Not with being in love with Joe. What's taking so *long*?"

"Hold still! The buttons are too big for these little loops. And there's so many of 'em! Stop movin'!"

"I can't. *Hurry.* I have to get to Joe before he kills himself."

"Kills himself—-oh, mother Mary! I'd be more worried about your mother killin' *you* when she finds ya here."

"That, too."

The bedroom faced the back of the house. They wouldn't be able to hear her parents approaching. But Nola told her that Lizzy would warn them as soon as they did.

The gown fell to the floor. "Thank you, Nola."

"Thank you, Nola, ha." She picked up the slippers, hose, and wedding gown. "Will ya be thankin' me, I wonder, when we're both sleeping on the park bench? I shouldna a listened to you from the beginnin'."

"You didn't listen to me. I threatened you." Marie sniffed. "Have you been drinking?"

"Indeed I have. And I'll be needin' a whole lot more when the Missus gets home."

Marie stepped out of layers of pink-trimmed petticoats and frilly pantalets. The crush of the corset against her ribs had been stifling, so when Nola unlaced it she let out a sigh of relief.

"What now, I'm afraid to ask?" Nola folded the slips and pressed out the wrinkles with her hand, placed them neatly in the drawer.

Marie was about to open her mouth.

"No. Don't tell me. He loves *ya*. Can't *live* without ya. He's gonna take ya back to his ice castle in Timbucktu and smother ya with jewels, he is."

"It's called a *dacha*. And there are no ice castles in Timbucktu. Timbucktu's in Africa."

"Oh, pardon me. A *dacha*! A *shithouse* is where he be takin' ya! I'm not gonna tell ya I told ya so. But someday soon your gonna say it yerself. 'Nola told me so. I shoulda listened to the old crone.' Well, I'm not gonna tell ya. No, I'm not."

Clothes rustled and hangers thumped as Marie went through her wardrobe, trying to decide what to take. She didn't have much time to choose as carefully as she would have liked, so she pulled two simple day dresses out at random, one rust-colored, the other a brown-and-green check. After slipping one over her head and throwing the other on the bed, she put on stockings, and a pair of brown ankle high tie-up shoes. Then, grabbing an over-night case from the back of her bureau, she threw in the second dress, three pairs of long batiste underwear, a shawl, and stockings she seized from her dresser. She didn't have the room or the time to pack her winter clothes, but she was confident that, when she got to Russia, Joe would buy whatever she needed and more.

She was almost finished when they heard Lizzy's alarm. Moments later, the front door slammed shut with such force it nearly shook the house. "Where *is* she!" Florence screeched. "I'm going to *kill* her!"

CHAPTER 35

WALTER BURIED HIS FACE IN HIS HANDS and sobbed. He could hardly recall watching his bride run out of the church, the gasps of the startled guests, or his father hurrying him through the crowd and into the family coach. Nor did he recall jumping out of the carriage before it came to a stop, or ripping off his suit jacket, starched cuffs, collar, and silk cravat, and falling onto the over-stuffed chair in the parlor.

The room was clean and neat yet lived in. Elegant but not ostentatious. The walls were painted in soft hues, and plants hung in front of a south-facing window. A basket of needlepoint sat on the carpeted floor beside a Chippendale sofa. A pile of magazines lay on an ottoman.

Olga tucked an afghan around his shoulders. They'd left the windows open when they walked out that morning, and the house was chilly. She kissed the top of his head, his hair still stiff with macassar oil. "I know you're hurting," she whispered. "In time it will just be a bad memory. You can't believe that now. But it will." She stroked his cheek.

"Mother is right, Wally. There will be other girls. Best it happened now, *before* you married."

"Thank you, Malcolm." Olga turned to her older son, who was on his knees before the marble fireplace, lighting crumpled newspapers beneath two logs. Though brothers and separated by only two years, they looked as if they'd been from different parents. While Walter was tall and lanky and had a full, thick mane, Malcolm was stocky and balding.

"But did the moment have to be at the altar?" Edgar muttered. Having shed his wedding attire and two-toned spats, he was stretched out on his favorite lounge chair. A sudden flame from the fire cast a golden light on the portrait of his father, Alister Hockenberry, ship builder extraordinaire, that decorated the wall above his chair. "Malcolm, I think a hot toddy might be in order. I could certainly use one."

His son nodded, found the brandy in the liquor cabinet in an alcove across the hall, and went to the kitchen.

"The honey is on the third shelf in the pantry," his mother called out.

"Did she have to humiliate him in front of the whole world, and make him the laughingstock of the city?" Edgar asked.

His wife shot him a *you're-not-helping* look. "Who cares what people say?" she sighed. "It will be old news as soon as something more salacious comes along." She, too, had kicked off her shoes and changed into casual wear.

"Drink that," Edgar advised when Malcolm brought the glasses. "It will make you feel better."

Walter took a careful sip, feeling the alcohol burn his lips and throat.

"Atta boy." Edgar smiled. A clunking came from the fireplace as the wood settled. He turned the tumbler back and forth between his fingers, the brandy sloshing against the rim. "Who does she think she is, anyway? She's too good for my son? Ha. Let me tell you, *he's* too good for *her*. . .and her whole family! Could you believe that mother of hers had the audacity to approach me outside the church: 'We shouldn't let this incident interfere with our plans for a partnership,'" he said, mimicking Florence's high-pitched voice. "*Incident.* Well, I told her—"

Olga rolled her eyes at her husband.

"What?"

"Please don't talk about Marie," Walter said. "She's a wonderful girl—"

"What's so wonderful about her?" Malcolm said. "I don't know what you see in her, to tell you the truth. She's nothing to look at with those ugly teeth and big feet."

"Stop! *Please*!" Walter shot back, covering his ears.

"Really, brother, with our family credentials and you soon to have a law degree, you're what people would call a "catch." Any girl would fall at your feet. And prettier ones than her, I'm sure."

"Stop it. *Stop* it! I will not have you speak badly of her!" Walter banged his fist on the end table with such force the Tiffany gas-lamp rattled; then he shot out of the chair and headed for the stairs.

Malcolm, Edgar, and Olga exchanged glances. "Walter, darling." His mother followed him, nearly running to match his steps. "Your brother didn't mean any harm. He loves you. He's just concerned. We all are." She caught up with him and grasped his arm.

He pulled away. "I don't need your concerns! Or your sympathies. Keep them to yourselves. All of you!"

She watched him hurry up the stairs and listened to his bedroom door slam behind him.

The next morning, at first light, when she went to check on him, the room was empty. The bed hadn't been slept in.

A note lay atop the blanket: *Don't look for me. I've joined the army.*

WALTER WINCED WHEN HE FELT a cool wet rag on his forehead. He was burning up. His head pounded. His leg throbbed. Nausea consumed him.

"Ah, you're awake."

The voice sounded far away, but it came from a thick-set woman standing beside him. He looked at her through blurry eyes. She was middle-aged and plain, with dark circles under her eyes. Graying hair was tucked inside a white muffin cap, and an apron stained with blood and body fluids covered a brown-checkered dress. "You're in a field hospital," the woman told him when she saw his confusion. "Been here for three days— unconscious 'till now."

He looked around, gingerly moving his head from side to side, and saw that he was in a big white tent. There were four rows of cots—two against the walls, two in the middle—-and boards on the floor, each occupied by coughing, retching, and groaning men. The air was foul with the smells of urine, diarrhea, and death.

"You were shot in the leg." She smiled sadly, patting his arm, hot beneath his nightshirt. "They had to amputate it."

"You've mistaken me for someone else," he muttered, his voice weak and hoarse. "I can feel my legs. Both of them." He tried to lift his neck and peer under the sheet but, overcome with dizziness, dropped back on the pillow.

"I wish it weren't so." Two days before, she'd read instructions to a doctor who, until that battle, had never seen a gunshot wound or performed surgery, as he sawed Walter's limb off. "I'm sorry."

"I'm going to be sick."

No sooner had she grabbed a basin from under his bed and held it beneath his chin than green bile began splashing into the metal pan.

"*Ohhh.*" He licked his cracked lips. "I'm so dry. My mouth feels like cotton."

Holding his head up, she put a glass of water to his mouth. "Just a sip, now. You don't want to vomit again."

"Thank you." He was only able to wet his lips before everything began to spin.

"Close your eyes. Rest."

He tried to remember, but his brain was foggy. Events were only coming in disorganized glimpses: gunshots, and the acrid, sour smell of the powder. Men lying on the ground with their guts spilling out. Body parts strewn across the battlefield. The putrid odor. The blood-soaked ground. Moaning. Arms waving. Cries for help.

"Welcome back to Earth, Captain," the patient beside him said. "We all thought you were a goner."

"Captain?"

Their cots were so close they were practically in the same bed. "I'm Jim."

". . .Walter."

"Try to see the better side—"

"*Better side*?"

"You're alive. If you were shot in the chest, they would have left you on the battleground to die. You weren't captured and taken prisoner. I'm told the conditions in one of them camps is so bad the soldiers dig holes to sleep in to keep warm. A course, you bein' an officer, they'd ship you out of a place like that. Just like here. Soon as you're in decent shape, they'll send you up north to a hospital for officers," he sighed. "Be happy you only lost one leg, not two. See that fella over there? He lost both *arms*. Imagine that. Can't even wipe his own arse. That poor guy on your right is blind. *And* you get to go home."

From one of the cots on the floor they heard retching. Someone else was screaming for morphine.

"I have nothing to go home to," Walter murmured.

"She's not worth it."

"Who said anything about a *she*?"

"You did. You kept calling, 'Marie, Marie,' when you were out of your senses."

"*She* has nothing to do with it. I came here to fight for the cause, to do my patriotic duty."

Jim started to laugh. It had a husky sound. "Patriotic duty? The *cause*? Seriously?"

Walter looked at his neighbor for the first time, the world spinning as he turned. He and Jim seemed to be close in age, and, measuring from the length beneath the sheet, the same height. Except for one pale blue eye, his nostrils, and mouth, his entire face was covered in linen bandages. Brown hair sprouted on his head in all directions. If Walter felt uneasy at his appearance, he was still groggy and in too much pain to express it.

"Why did *you* join?"

"Not for the *cause*! My buddies were joined up, some for the glory." He laughed. "Some for the twelve bucks a month—which they hardly saw. Me, I didn't want my sweetheart to think I was a coward. The fine howdy-do is that she married someone else. A deserter, no less. And I'm left with one eye and a burned face so ugly even a mother couldn't love it. How about you? How come you have nothing to go home to, if you don't mind my askin'? If they made you a captain, you either have a college education, come from money, or both. That sounds like plenty to go home to, if you ask me. If you don't mind my sayin'. We won the battle, by the way, if that makes you feel any better."

An orderly filled Walter's water pitcher. "Glad to see you improvin', Captain. We were all worried 'bout ya." The young private in hospital-issued pajamas and slippers smiled, showing his crooked teeth. "And how are your headaches today, Corporal?" he asked Jim.

"As well as can be expected, Timmy. Thanks for askin'. How about you? I dare say, you're getting more chipper every day."

"*Too* chipper, sir. The doc's discharging me this week, and I'll be going back to my unit."

"I'm sorry to hear that."

"Thanks. Me, too."

The wheels clanked as Tim pushed his cart to the next row of patients.

"He almost died from the shits," Jim told Walter. "I don't know what's worse: a battle, or the months of *waiting* for a battle in them filthy camps with the stinkin' latrines and rotten beef," he went on. "Or the marching. . .marching and drilling. And waiting. Waiting's the worst."

The closest Walter had come to experiencing any of that had been the enlistment process at Riker's Island. First there was the physical exam, which had consisted of walking naked across the room to check for flat feet, jumping up and down, and a few taps on the chest. "How do you fail a test like this?" he remembered asking the doctor, who had responded, "You don't."

From there he had been off to another tent to sign some papers, swear in for three years or until the war ended, whichever came first, and receive his three-hundred-dollar enlistment bonus (which he'd given to Preacher Beecher to help the Blacks). In the third tent he'd picked up his uniform, knapsack, heavy socks, and boots. Two days later he was on his way to meet up with the 42nd New York Tammany in Virginia.

No sooner had he arrived than his corps stumbled upon a Confederate contingent and was thrust into battle. He'd never even fired his rifle.

"Let's take a look at that leg, shall we?" a man Walter presumed to be a doctor said to a woman he presumed to be a nurse standing behind him.

"Yes, doctor," the woman said. She wasn't the same person he'd spoken to earlier, but she too was middle-aged, stout, and plain. He remembered his neighbor calling the nurses "Dix's girls": the nursing superintendent only hired Northern women old enough to be considered spinsters but young enough to have strong backs—-and the homelier the better. She turned to Walter. "Captain, I'm going to change your dressing. Ben is going to hold up your leg. It might hurt a bit. I'm sorry."

Walter nodded.

While the silver-bearded physician felt Walter's forehead with an age-spotted hand, checked his pulse, and listened to his chest with his stereoscope, she, with the help of a pajama-clad orderly, and after smearing mint oil under their noses, unwound his bandage. The mint was obviously not working, for Walter saw their noses wrinkle.

The doctor peered over his round spectacles to examine the angry suture line oozing pus. "Mmm." He sighed. "I'm afraid your wound is infected, son. You're still febrile. Your heart is racing. And I'll be honest with you—that's not good."

The nurse threw the soiled bandage into a burlap bag, holding the soiled wrappings by the tip of her fingers, washed and re-dressed the draining stump. Walter grimaced at the touch.

"Am I going to. . .die?" he asked, studying the troubled expression on the old doctor's face.

"Can't say for sure. Most men with as bad an infection as this don't make it." He patted his arm. "But you have youth and otherwise good health on your side. . . . I'll have the nurse give you more morphine."

"I'd appreciate a pen and paper."

CHAPTER 36

THE WINTER WAS PROVING TO BE AS COLD as the summer had been hot. And the shop, stifling in the heat, was bitter when temperatures dropped. Bolts of fabric and boxed hats that blocked the ice-crusted windows and doors lessened the draft but did not eliminate it. Sitting in the row near the window, Anne adjusted her scarf to keep the wind off her neck. Like the other seamstresses, she wore long underwear under a long-sleeved, high-necked woolen dress, two layers of socks, every sweater she owned, and fingerless gloves.

She jumped when the forelady thwacked her tabletop with the hickory pointer. Shawl wrapped around her shoulders, a grimace on her stern face, she looked down her nose at her. Even with her ears covered, Anne should have heard her coming, should have heard the swishing skirt, jangling keys, and creaking floor as she squeezed between the aisles. Other than the sound of the sewing machines, to which the operators had become so accustomed they hardly noticed, the shop was quiet: this, in part, because it was difficult for whispers to be heard through draped mouths, and in part because the boss lady herself was there—and being in the foulest of moods (as she'd been for months), the operators were afraid to breathe. But, preoccupied with her own thoughts, Anne hadn't heard.

"Stand up!" the bulldog growled. As, one by one, the girls lifted their feet off their treadles, she spun around, whacked her stick again, and in a cloud of vapor, snapped, "Get back to work. Get back to *work!*"

Anne left the cap under the lever, pushed herself out of her seat, and keeping her shoulders rounded, her sweaters tightly in place, and her arms across her belly, rose.

"Stand up straight! Put your arms at your side. Open your sweaters."

Anne did as she was told, albeit slowly, unfastening each button as if it didn't fit through the hole.

The machines stopped. Complete silence descended. All eyes turned to the forelady.

"Hurry up. Hurry up. I haven't got all day."

Other than Fiona, who silently put her head down, all the girls stared and sighed.

"Just as I suspected," said the sour-faced supervisor. "You're up the pole! And not married either, if my memory serves me correct."

Of course her memory served her. It was her business to know everybody's business. And she did.

Anne had known the day would come. Her only surprise was that it had taken as long as it had. Carrying small and wearing extra loose clothes had enabled her to hide it. But she seemed to have exploded overnight. Now only a blind man would not have noticed.

"Gather your things and get out, you *slapper.*" The manager pointed to the door. "This is a respectable business, not a bordello." She stared at the others and, smacked the tabletops again. "The rest of you, get back to work. The show is over. Let this be a lesson." One by one, heads turned to their respective machines, and the whirring recommenced.

Anne left the Union cap under the lever, grabbed her purse, re-buttoned her sweaters, put on the tattered coat that had been resting on the back of her chair, strode down the aisle, and came to a stop before Florence, who was buried in her ledgers. Holding her head high and restraining the tears that stung her eyes, Anne extended her open palm. "I'd like me week's pay, please."

It was still morning when Anne left. It was cold outside but not much worse than in the shop. Instead of going home, she went to Tompkins Park. Very few people were there: an old woman feeding pigeons and a couple of raggedy-looking boys, who Anne assumed had no place to go, playing some sort of hop-scotch game, throwing a pebble and jumping where it landed. Since most of the benches were unoccupied, she was able to find a seat in sunlight. Beyond the leafless trees, traffic were rumbling and horns honking, but she hardly noticed.

If, dressed in many layers and hunched over a machine, her supervisor could see her condition, surely her landlord would, too. She'd avoided discovery thus far thanks in part to the season, leaving for work at five, before sunup, tiptoeing out while the family was still asleep, and returning when the Hares were already snoring loud enough to wake the dead. Mrs. Hare would realize eventually, but until that time came, Anne would have a bed to sleep in, food in her belly, and a roof over her head. She'd refused to think about her predicament, made no plans, and avoided contemplating her future—-until now. The tears she had not allowed her boss to see were flowing down her cheeks.

She counted the coins in her pocket, the silver, bronze, and copper bits clinking as they slid over each other. She had one dollar and three cents in all. That, the clothes on her back, and the few items in her shared bedroom comprised her total worth. The narky-witch of a boss had only given her half of what she was due. And when Anne held her hand out and told her she owed her more, the bitch had told her she was lucky to get that. She didn't look kindly on loose women, and if Anne didn't get out of her sight right then and there, she would take the money back and have her *thrown out.*

Anne considered her options. There were none she could live with. No one could be hired without references, especially a person in her condition. As a child, before she learned the pickpocket trade and before living in an orphanage, she had scavenged nails, screws, rope, broken glass, and anything she could sell to the waterfront dealers. But there was a lot of competition lately and not enough money to buy a meal at the end of the day, let alone rent a room. She'd been a good thief, but that was long ago. She'd be rusty now if she chose that, and she most certainly would not. There was always prostitution. Surely some men enjoyed lying with pregnant women. But she would just as soon hang herself as subjecting to such indignities.

"*Ahhh!*" she sighed, "*you've gotten yourself into some mess, Annie.*" Why she had jumped off the table just before the woman was about to abort her, she couldn't say. Her dress had already been hiked up and her bare feet cold in the stirrups. Was it fear of being probed? Fear of dying? Guilt? God's wrath? Stupidity?

Nothing to be done about it now. She would go home, sleep in a bed, and worry about her predicament tomorrow.

She waited for nightfall to leave the park. The temperature had dropped about ten degrees since morning. Her backside, not well padded despite the layers of clothing, and her feet, were cold and stiff from sitting for so many hours. She rubbed her bottom and wriggled her toes inside her thin-soled shoes to bring them back to life. Then she pulled her hat further down her ears and tightened her muffler. She buried her face deeper in her collar and, with the scarf snapping behind her and dead leaves swirling around her feet, bent into the wind and started on her way.

Her landlady was leaning out the window, a blanket wrapped around her shoulders, the chill air coloring her pale cheeks. When Anne approached the street, Mrs. Hare pulled her arm out from under the cover, wagged her finger, and began shouting for the whole world to hear, "When was ya plannin' on tellin' me you was up the pole? Thought ya could pull the wool over my eyes, did ya? Took me for a *dummy*? Well let me tell ya, Anne Ryan, it will be a cold day in July before someone can pull the wool over these eyes!" Anne's blue cotton dress came floating down to the pavement, followed by her pantaloons, underwear, sleeping gown, and an orange hat with fake cherries and feathers that she'd bought on impulse at the second-hand store. She watched them land, one after the other, like parachutes, folding onto themselves. Next, her hairbrush came hurtling down, clacking against the wooden building before it bounced into the gutter.

"I knowed the first time I smelled that hussy toilet water you was nothing but a common thing. Shoulda put you out then. Sleepin' on the roof because it was too hot. *Ha*! Been shaggin' some tom cat, is what you was doin'! A bad influence on my girls, ya are! A *slapper*. Nothing but a common slapper!" With that, the angry woman pulled herself inside, and Anne heard the window slam shut.

After she collected her belongings, picking them up one by one, she sat on the stoop, with everything she owned in her lap, and rocked back and forth.

Had to be the old hag in 5C, Anne reasoned. *That nosey hole.* She and Mrs. Hare spent their days passing gossip back and forth as they did their chores. That morning, when Anne left the building to go to work, she'd come face to face with Mrs. Murphy as she was returning from the outhouses in the back, where she'd emptied her night soils. The bucket still stank. Her son, Johnny Boy, had been up all night with the flux, she'd explained, and the pail, filled to overflowing, couldn't wait another minute to be disposed of. Just as she'd been about to go inside, a gust of wind had blown Anne's coat open, and she had noticed Mrs.Murphy staring at her stomach.

What am I to do? Anne wept. *Play the glad game*, she told herself, remembering her mother's words. The way she had complained about the color of her hair, and her mum would say, "To be red-haired is better than to have no hair." "Be strong," she'd heard her say just before she died. "Remember, when a heifer is far from home she grows longer horns." The thought of her mother's adages put a smile on her face. But only for a moment. Panic overtook her. Her heart hammered against her chest. "But I'm afraid, Mum," she said aloud. "I'm alone and afraid." She burst into tears, sobbed into her hands, her shoulders heaving up and down, snot running down her face.

She heard a crash. Following the noise, she saw her chamber pot smashed on the sidewalk. And despite her desperation and the flowing tears and snot, she laughed, and mumbled: "Now I truly don't have a pot to piss in."

CHAPTER 37

MARIE HID BEHIND A SYCAMORE TREE, waiting for her mother to leave the house. It had been no small feat to get home. The Third Avenue streetcar only went as far as Sixty-second Street, so she'd had to walk twenty blocks. She couldn't afford a cab. What little money she'd had was all but gone, barely enough for another bus ride.

"'Tisn't much, but God knows you'll be needin' it." Her old nanny had wept as she forced her rainy-day savings into Marie's pocket. Touched by the gesture, she thought it laughable—-both that the money would be needed, and that the minuscule amount could help her even if it was. But now, standing in the rain, wet and shivering, she realized how wrong she'd been.

Everything had been glorious—-for the first three days. After being married at city hall, they'd honeymooned at the opulent, three-dollar-a-day Hotel Astor. A bell boy in a flat hat and high-collared jacket had taken them up in the lift and showed them to their room on the sixth floor. They had dined in the courtyard, beneath a vaulted cast-iron-and-glass ceiling and had cocktails at the curved mahogany bar.

She'd been deliriously happy, he affectionate and exciting. He'd made love to her as if she were the only girl in the world—until she asked when they would be leaving for Russia.

After lobster and a fine wine, they'd returned to their room. A soft light had cast a romantic glow. The sheets had been turned down, and a mint had lain on each pillow. Joe had settled in the wing chair, kicked off his shoes, unbuttoned his jacket, and had his legs stretched out on the mattress.

"I'm so excited," she'd said, almost giddy. "Living in a *dacha*—"

"I love you too much for that. It wouldn't be fair to take you away from everything you know. My conscience won't allow it. We'll stay here, in New York."

"Oh, Joe." She'd padded across the room, her gait unsteady from two cocktails, and kissed his cheek. "That's so sweet of you. But I'll be happy to live wherever you are. You have your work—"

"Your happiness is all that matters." He'd caressed her fingertips that still smelled of fish. "I'll give up my mission, work for you family—"

"Work for my *family*?" She'd thrown her head back and guffawed. "No, no, no. That would never happen. You don't know my mother. She will never accept our marriage. I'll be lucky if she ever speaks to me again."

"Your father could—"

"My father does whatever my mother tells him. If she says jump, he asks how high. No, Joe, it's not possible. But don't worry. I'll be happy in Russia. I'm excited about it!"

He'd pulled his feet off the bed and sat up straighter.

She went to kiss him again. But instead of meeting warm lips she'd been met with a cold, hard slap.

The next thing she remembered was her head pounding and morning light streaming through the window. Without moving, she'd looked around to get her bearings. She'd been lying on the floor. There was no trace of Joe. The bed hadn't been slept in. His clothes were gone, the dresser drawers open and empty. After struggling to her feet, she'd hurried as fast as her bruised body would allow to the front desk.

Despite the early hour, the lobby had been busy. A pretty maid in a bib apron had been putting out fresh flowers, which floated a delightful smell. Mumbled voices, and the sound of laughter, had come from couples sitting on plush sofas. Bell boys in crisp uniforms had been scurrying across the marble floor with luggage in tow, and a cleaning lady had been on her knees in a corner, wiping up a spill.

A dark-haired clerk had pulled his head out a ledger and gasped when Marie presented herself before him at the front desk. "Ah!" He couldn't help but stare at her purple, swollen face, her black eye nearly shut. "Are. . .are you alright, miss? I call for a doctor." He'd reached for a bell from a shelf below the counter. Marie had put her hand up, waving away his suggestion.

"Have you. . .ah, seen my husband by any chance? Medium height, blond hair. . ."

"Ah, actually, yes. He, ah, left last night. Are you certain I can't ring for a doctor, miss?"

"Did he say anything? Where he was going?"

"Only that he would be checking out, and that I should see you about the bill."

It had been as if she was stabbed in the heart. She'd almost felt the blood drain from her face. Tears had begun to well over the edges of her lashes and roll down her cheeks. She'd begun to tremble. The clerk had caught her before she hit the floor.

After the initial shock, her response had been to go home. What else could she have done? She'd never been on her own. She had no way of supporting herself. But it had only been three days since she'd run away, and surely her mother would still be apoplectic. Her stomach had twisted at the thought of crawling back. She didn't have the courage to face them, to admit her mistake, to beg forgiveness. The longer she stayed away, she'd reasoned, the more time they would have to regain their composure, the more worried they would be, the more forgiving. She hoped. A year would be about right.

Her feet hurt. The custom shoes her mother bought for her to accommodate her fallen arches had been stolen. The replacement pair she'd bought in a second-hand store were too tight and gave no support. The pointed tips crunched her toes. A blister rubbed against her heel. She didn't have a warm coat or hat, only the shawl she'd taken when she left home and the cotton dress, which was shabby and faded from constant wear and cheap lye soap. Nola's rainy-day savings had been pretty much depleted after paying the hotel bill. Putting aside enough money to rent a room, there'd hardly been enough remaining to eat, never mind buy new clothes—-even from a second-hand store.

Not quite three months had passed. But that morning, claustrophobic in that tiny, windowless room, huddled on a lumpy mattress beneath one thin blanket, fully dressed because of the cold and in fear of having her clothes stolen, she'd realized she couldn't wait a year. She couldn't wait another day! She thought she would die if she had to spend one more night there.

So there she was, cold and wet, knowing her mother went to her shop on Wednesdays, praying she would stay out long enough for Marie to persuade her father to take her back.

The sky had been gray when she left that morning, but it hadn't begun raining until she was in transit: not an icy downpour but enough to chill her to the bones. Hiding beneath the leafless branches, rubbing her arms and rocking back and forth to generate heat, it seemed like hours. Finally, she saw her mother, hunkered under an umbrella with her arm looped in the crease of Alfred's elbow. Taking small, deliberate steps on the slick pavement, she made her way down the brick walkway, came through the metal gate, and, after Alfred opened the door, climbed into the waiting coach. Only when they disappeared around the corner did Marie emerge from behind the tree and cautiously cross the ice-crusted ground.

She wiped her feet on the mat at the back door as she slipped her key into the keyhole. It slid into place easily enough but didn't turn. She knocked, waited a few seconds, and knocked again, harder than before. With one hand above her eyes, she peered through the glass into the kitchen. It was dark and still. Could it be her father wasn't home? It wasn't like him to be out at that hour, particularly in bad weather. What would she do if he wasn't there?

Just as she began to bang again, she heard footsteps on the tile floor, an Irish brogue hollering, "I'm coming, I'm coming," and then the clack of the deadlock slipping out of place.

A gust of warm air engulfed Marie when the door opened. A girl in a white cap and apron looked her up and down. She had seen plenty of beggars and wretches in her short life, but never in that affluent neighborhood. This one was so thin her dirty dress hung like a sack. Her cheeks were pale and drawn, and her hair, tied behind her head, seemed not to have been washed in weeks. "'Ow can I help ya?" she asked.

Marie stared at her rosy cheeks and freckled face.

"I 'ave no money ta give ya, but if ya come in I'll make ya something to eat, and dry ya up. Look a ya. All wet and drippin'." She grabbed Marie's arm, skinny enough to wrap her hand around, guided her into the room, and closed the door. "Take a seat, why don't ya?

Careful on the floor. I wouldn't want ya ta slip. I just mopped. But don't ya worry 'bout dirtying anything," she advised as she led the unfortunate soul to the table, where she pulled out a chair and pushed a bowl of apples out of the way to make room for a plate of food.

Though everything was the same as the last time Marie saw it, she seemed to appreciate it all for the first time. She'd never noticed how shiny the copper pots and pans were on the open shelves of each wall, or how delightful the heat felt that was pumping out of the cast-iron stove ensconced in a brick wall. Where was the bowl, piled with muffins, Nola baked every day? At that time of year, especially, Christmas cookies sprinkled with cinnamon or red and green jimmies would be cooling on a rack, the sweet scent permeating the whole house. Marie hadn't had a pastry—or juice, or fruit, or meat, or *anything* that tasted like real food—since her honeymoon. The beautiful smell of simmering pea soup made her stomach rumble loud enough for the girl to hear.

"Take one if ya like." The freckled girl nodded toward the apples. She tip-toed across the damp floor to the ice box, from which she removed a platter of left-over turkey and a crock of mayonnaise. The door closed with a soft thud, but not before Marie saw that it was crammed with food. Once again, her stomach grumbled. The servant sliced the bread she'd removed from a slatted box and began piling meat between the slices. "You came at a good time." She jiggled the utensil drawer open to pull out a butter knife. "Whenever it rains, this drawer sticks. Oh, will ya looka that. It wasn't the drawer atall but this 'ere corkscrew causing all the trouble. My boss lady wouldn't look kindly on me givin' away her food. Or find ya sittin' in her kitchen. But don't you worry. She shouldn't be back for hours. Has some kind of factory, and goes there once a week. If ya ask me she just wants to make sure nobody's stealin' nothin'. She's a tough one, that one. You know, they're royalty. Some relative was the king of France. His coat of arms is hangin' in the living room." She shook her head as the knife clicked against the stoneware jar.

"Somethin' 'bout you seems awful familiar. Like I seen ya someplace afore. But a course that's ridiculous. Where would I 'av met you afore? Hmm . . .maybe we came through Castle Garden together? Been on the same ship maybe? Wouldn't that be a hoot?" She put the sandwich on a plate and added a pickle. "This should hold ya for a while," she said after she left the dish. But when she noticed Marie gulping down the food as if she'd never eaten before, she filled a bowl of soup from the cooking pot and placed in front of her. "This ain't completely done yet. The carrots are still a bid 'ard." She studied Marie more closely. "You sure do look like I seen ya before." Then she stopped short and spun around, and a few strands of brown hair escaped her cap. Her hand went to her mouth, and the silverware chimed on the floor. "Oh my God! You're Miss *Marie*! I'm sorry. So sorry. I di'na recognize ya, bein'. . .you look so—"

"I couldn't get my key to turn."

"All the locks 'av been changed. I'll get a towel so ya can dry yourself. You must be freezin'." She turned and hurried off in pursuit of the cloth from the cedar linen chest outside the pantry.

Marie waited at the table, holding the bowl to her mouth, licking it clean.

"I guess ya don't remember me. I'm Lizzy," the girl was saying as she re-entered the room a few minutes later holding a fluffy bath towel. Marie rose, the chair scraping against the floor, and took it from the girl's outstretched arms. Tears filled her eyes when she pressed the soft fabric against her cheek, the smell of lavender water that her mother insisted be added to the detergent. She'd never imagined what a luxury something as insignificant as a towel could be. "It was me who called upstairs when they got home. I loved your gown. Those puffed sleeves—"

"It's yours. Help yourself."

"Well, I thank you for that, but the missus ripped it up and threw it in the fireplace.

"Where's Nola?"

"Nola? Nola hasn't been 'ere for months. I always wondered 'ow you disappeared. If you don't mind me asking? You was 'ere one minute and gone the next."

"I climbed out the window. Why did she leave? Did she say where she was going?" Marie feared she already knew the answer.

"I don't rightly know. 'Twas the same day you, ah. . .left. The missus was doin' a lot of screaming, and tearing up your dress, and the next thing I knowed, she was gone. Nola, that is."

Marie tried to step around her, but Lizzy stopped her. "Sorry, Miss. I been given strict orders not to let you in." She bent her head apologetically. "Mrs. Gilbert—"

"Well, she's not here. I'm going to change my clothes and speak with my father."

"She gave me strict orders: 'Miss Marie is not to enter this house' is what she told me." But Marie had already pushed her aside and was hurrying through the dining room, living room, and up the stairs, passing the enormous portrait of her mother that hung in the stairwell. "Well, I suppose—" Lizzy's voice trailed off. Then to herself she said, "But I would na do that if I was you."

Marie stopped on the landing, beneath the stained-glass window, to breathe in what had once been her life, the scent and warmth of home. She inhaled the pine smell of logs burning in the fireplace. Everywhere she looked was decked out for Christmas. Her mother fussed over the holiday, paid a designer to come in and adorn the house. The silk orchids in the vase where the girl stood had been replaced by poinsettias. Boughs of pine were wrapped around the banister. The oil of Louis XVI standing beside Marie Antoinette, the family coat of arms, and the curio with other family relics were similarly encased in evergreens. A huge, perfectly symmetrical balsam fir, stood before the front window, reaching the ceiling. It was bedecked with angel hair, bells, red bows, and crystal ornaments that twinkled in the light of the candles that rested on the branches. An angel in gold lame adorned the highest bough.

She hurried down the second-floor hallway, her bare feet sinking in the carpet, her wet shoes in her hands, passing the familiar photos and oils of her mother, the aroma of a vanilla-scented eau de toilette growing stronger as she neared her parents' bedroom. The portrait of her five-year-old self was missing. It should have alerted her what to expect. But it didn't. More than clean warm clothes to change into, she wanted a decent pair of shoes. She entered her room.

If not for the fading scent of marjoram that had been sewn into her pillowcases, she would have thought she was in the middle of a weird dream. Everything was gone: her canopied bed, her dressing table, the feather quilt. Even the walls had been re-papered in a peach floral print. Thank God, her cherry dresser and wardrobe were still there. She opened the intricately carved door, catching the strong aroma of cedar, and stared at her mother's coats. She pulled out the top drawer, where she had kept dozens of pantaloons, chemises, gloves, and hose. Empty. Spotting her trousseau in the corner of the room, she lifted the lid. What had been filled with silverware, china, and embroidered linen contained ledgers.

"Where are all my things?" she asked Lizzy when she hurried down the stairs as fast as she was able to with her sore feet. "Where did she put them?"

"She gave them all away."

"My clothes?"

"She threw whatever she could in the fireplace. Then a truck came, and men emptied out your room."

"The oil of me as a little girl?"

"The one where you look like Little Bo Peep?"

Marie nodded. Lizzy lowered her head. "After she tore the picture to shreds, she threw it on the fire, too."

"I need to speak with my father."

"'E's nappin' right now." Lizzy followed her into the parlor. "'E 'asn't been feeling well."

Marie ignored her.

"Maybe I should wake him first," Lizzy suggested. "So's 'e won't be startled. Don't want him to get a shock or somethin'."

Marie stopped in mid-step and nodded. ". . .Maybe that *would* be best." Tears clouded her eyes. There were so many questions she wanted to ask but she was unable to speak.

Gerhard was sleeping in his favorite chair. Double chin resting on his chest, his mouth half open, drool hanging from his lower lip. He was snoring in arrhythmic grunts. New lines had creased his cheeks, she noticed. A crystal tumbler rested on the coffee table beside him, with three fingers of something that resembled whiskey. The smell of cigar smoke engulfed him.

Around the corner, in the alcove, she saw her piano. More tears broke through and ran down her cheeks. At least her mother hadn't destroyed that. She sat on the polished stool, raised the hood, and stroked the ivory keys.

"Mr. Gilbert," the freckled-face girl whispered in his ear. "There's someone 'ere to see ya, sir." He didn't respond immediately, so she touched his shoulder and whispered again. "Mr. Gilbert?"

". . .What?"

"Someone's 'ere to see ya."

He dabbed his eyes, lifted his spectacles from the side table, wrapped the wire earpieces in place, and turned in his leather seat. "Is that the piano? *Marie?*"

Hurrying through the rooms, she knelt beside him, her dress damp beneath her knees, took his hand in hers, and ran her fingers over his puffed-up blue veins. He stared at the bone-thin girl in soiled, oversized clothes.

"Yes, Father." Her lower lip trembled. Her voice cracked. "It's me."

CHAPTER 38

GERHARD WRAPPED HIS ARMS around her and rocked back and forth. His eyes were moist, his throat so choked he could hardly speak. "Marie, Marie," he sighed as his fingertips brushed her hair. "How I've worried about you. Where you were, what you were doing."

She lifted her head from his sweater, so soft and comforting, but he held up his hand, shushed her, and gently pulled her back to his chest. "Don't tell me. I'm just happy you're here. Safe."

"Father," she whispered, "I want to come home."

She felt his warm breath on her cheek.

". . .Your mother would never allow—"

"You can talk to her."

"Talk to your *mother*?" He almost laughed, shook his head. "No, Marie."

She pulled away from him, looked at his haggard face. "You must! *Please!*"

He continued to shake his head. "I can't go against her. She will never—"

"I. . . I *need* to come home. I have no place to *go*. . . . You *can't* send me out." Tears streamed down her face. "I'm your *daughter*. Your *flesh and blood*. . . . Try to make her understand, have her forgive me."

"Understand? Why you ruined your life? Forgive you for humiliating her before the whole city? No, Marie." He sighed. "*I* can't forgive what you did to her. I love you. I will always love you. I will help you financially—but that's all I can do."

He took a handkerchief from his pocket, wiped his eyes, and called for the servant girl.

Lizzy padded into the room so quietly they didn't hear her until she spoke. "Yes, sir?"

"I want you to draw a bath for Miss Marie." He blew his nose, a loud honk. "And help her scrub her hair, will you, get the tangles out."

"Yes, sir. I already 'ave the water heatin'."

He looked at his daughter's shabby dress, too thin for winter weather. "And find something among Mrs. Gilbert's things for her to wear."

"Yes, sir."

Marie followed her up the stairs to the bathroom, a stranger in her own house. Lizzy had filled the tub, added bath oils to the water, put out a fresh bar of lavender soap, and draped a plush bath towel and robe over a chair. Marie took in the combination of white tile and white marble, with a marble sink, and a marble floor, intertwined with forest green accent tiles—a palace compared to where she'd been. The room was steamy, the glazed surfaces damp.

She undressed and immersed herself in the hot water, letting the warmth engulf her. She hadn't luxuriated in a tub in months. Until leaving home, she'd taken bathing for granted. Though the Astor

Hotel had tubs, they had to be shared by hundreds of guests. In the boardinghouse, she'd had to wash in a basin in her room.

Gray light filtered through the stained-glass window. The wind had picked up. She could see the branches of a tall oak swaying, could hear the gentle tapping of the rain. The gloomy day added to her despair. "I don't want to be alone." She wept. "I'm so afraid."

Downstairs, Lizzy held a plain long-sleeved, high-necked wool-flannel dress for Gerhard to inspect. "Will this do, Mr. Gilbert?" she asked.

"Perfect, perfect. My wife hates brown. She'll never miss it."

"I found this, too." She felt the scalloped edge of a fleece capeo

He nodded. "And shoes?"

"Not so good, sir. Miss Marie's feet are bigger than Mrs. Gilbert's."

"That will have to do, then."

"Yes, sir." She turned to leave, the clothes draped over her arm.

"And Lizzy. . ."

"Sir?"

"Ah, one more thing."

"Yes, sir?" She faced him.

"This is just between you and me. Understand?"

"Oh, yes, sir." She pulled a finger across clenched lips. "I won't say a word. Not me, sir. On my poor ma's grave." Transferring the garments to her left hand, she crossed herself. "May she rest in peace."

After she laid out the clothes and helped Marie wash and detangle her hair, Marie joined her father in the parlor.

Gerhard let out a sigh of relief when she entered the room. Having lost weight, the dress fit her well, and she appeared less gaunt. Her hair was damp and lay in flat braids against her head, but clean and smelling of herbs. While her eyes were still red and puffy from crying, the hot bath had added color to her cheeks. "You look like a new person," he said, a full glass—scotch, no doubt—in hand. After setting his drink on the end table, he pushed himself out of his chair and made his way to the staircase. Sliding Florence's portrait to one side, he opened the safe behind it with a few quick turns and removed a stack of cash, which, with his eyes everywhere but on her face, handed her the money. "Your mother will be home soon. It's best you go now," he told her, his voice cracking. "Buy yourself a decent pair of shoes." He cleared his throat. "Get a room somewhere, the St. Denis Hotel maybe, until I find someplace suitable." He wiped his eyes. "Did you eat?"

Marie nodded. "Lizzy made me—"

"Good. She's a—" he blew his nose "—a. . .good girl," he said, staring at the carpet. "Take care of yourself. Lizzy," he called out, "Be sure to find Miss Marie an umbrella, and. . .and anything else she. . .might need." Reaching inside his pants pocket he retrieved an unopened letter, and, still focused on the floor, held it out for his daughter.

She studied the onion-paper envelope, her name written beside care of Mr. Gilbert, and at the return address of an army hospital in Virginia. ". . .Walter? He joined the *army*? . . .He wrote to *me*?"

Gerhard nodded. "A month or so ago. I've kept it here—" he indicated his pocket— "waiting for you."

"Father." She tried to make eye contact, but he wouldn't look at her. "Father, please. Don't send me away! I made a mistake. A *terrible* mistake. I'm sorry. *Please*!"

"Sometimes being sorry isn't enough, Marie. Some mistakes we make we have to live with."

CHAPTER 39

HOLDING HER HEM ABOVE HER ANKLES and a newspaper above her head, Anne stepped over a drunk lying face down in the gutter and splashed her way across the street. Laughter and curses from the saloon behind her were muted by the clatter of the icy rain. It was coming down almost sideways, and though she buried her face in the collar of her coat, it was stinging her cheeks. "Any beds left, Marge?" she asked when she reached the building. The former slaughterhouse now flop house, with its sagging roof and rotting clapboards, was one of many in the Five Points.

Marge spit out a wad of tobacco. She had a port wine birthmark that covered the left side of her face. From the shadow of the entranceway where she was sitting on a stool, it appeared to be the same color as her watchman's cap. "Good you got here early. Usually they fill up when the bars close," she answered. "But when the weather is like this!" She looked up at the sky, shrugged, and stuck her hand out to collect the fee. Dirt was crusted underneath her fingernails.

Anne held the three-cent coin above the scrawny palm but hesitated.

"You'll get two cents back if you have to sleep in the cellar."

Anne shivered, whether from the cold and wet or the thought of the subterranean warrens she couldn't be sure. "Better to freeze on the sidewalk," she said.

Marge smiled, displaying missing teeth.

Inside was no palace. Plaster was peeling from paper-thin walls. There was no insulation. Kerosene stoves, used for both cooking and heating, were a fire hazard and stank. Though each of the place's five levels was separated into cubicles, privacy was non-existent. Double, and in some places triple, bunks took up every inch of space. But the cellar, where people crowded together on a dirt floor, which flooded on rainy days when the outhouses overflowed, could have frightened the Devil himself. Divided into about twenty chambers by cardboard walls, the largest was the infamous Den of Thieves. Everyone remembered the story of a little girl who had been stabbed to death after showing a penny she had begged. The body had lain in a corner for five days until her mother buried her in a shallow grave dug in the corner.

"Try the top level," Marge suggested. "The beds up there are always the last to go. Too many stairs. . .and the roof leaks."

Anne thanked her and dropped the money into her hand. Out of habit, she scraped her feet in the hall before disappearing inside, a gesture hardly necessary for mud was the least she had to worry about.

The corridor behind the door was dark and malodorous, the stink of piss and feces so strong she covered her nose with a camphor-soaked handkerchief and tried not to breathe. She threw the saturated newspapers into a corner and shook the wet out of her hair. Sounds of singing, dancing, and fighting were coming from downstairs.

Once her eyes adjusted, she made her way up. There was a lamp at each level. Some threw off light, but most didn't. They all hissed.

At every landing she stopped to check. Each bed was taken. She recognized several faces, those who rarely left for fear they would lose their spot. They were holding their belongings as if they were things of value: a few rags, cracked shoes, items nobody wanted but them, though Anne realized all too well what was trash to one might be a treasure to another. She thought of her chamber pot, which she missed so very much, a mere piss pot of no value to anyone but herself.

Marge had been right—the only beds left were on the top floor. Two were in one room, one in another, and each on the third tier. As the chambers were equally foul, Anne took her chances with the one farthest from the stairwell.

Though a tiny window facing the back alley was stuck shut, it didn't drown out obscene catcalls from the bordello downstairs. But it let in enough light to see that much of the plaster was falling off the walls, the gaps covered with newspaper. She scanned an article from 1859 about a Mormon conflict; an advertisement for Nautilus Mutual Life Insurance that offered policies on slaves, allowing their owners to claim funds on their lost property when they died; and a story from 1862 with the headline *The Death of Prince Albert; The Event and Its Influence on the Queen and Its People* in bold black letters. Anne didn't know much about Prince Albert, but she was happy that his wife and children had been at his bedside when he took his last breath.

She saw people's scrawled names and comments on what plaster remained. From that she learned that Suzanna, Sean, Mary Pat, Concetta, and Kevin had slept there; that New York City was the "asshole of the world"; and that Sou Chin prepared and sold the best opium in the city from his laundry on Mott Street.

Of the seven occupants in the room, two had obviously read the wall. Anne didn't have to be a user to recognize the drugged-out look or distinctive, pickle-like smell. On one bunk, a skinny teenage girl, with greasy brown hair and glassy eyes, was smoking a long pipe over an oil lamp. On another, a stubbly-faced man with a sour odor lay still as a corpse.

Drugs were not the only vice or malady. One couple was copulating on a cot against the outside wall. No one seemed disturbed by their grunts. On a middle bunk a young woman, with a raucous, body-shaking cough, seemed to be dying of consumption. In the dim light, Anne could see she was perspiring profusely and that a handkerchief in her hand was stained with bloody sputum. Another occupant, so tall his booted feet hung over the bed, was talking and laughing to himself. The seventh, a fortyish brunette, was just staring at the ceiling, lying stiff, unblinking.

Anne threw her few belongings on an empty pad and climbed up. The mattress was as thick as a pancake, damp in the center from the leaks in the ceiling, stained, and probably crawling with only God knew what.

In the more than two weeks since her eviction, she'd passed herself off as a war widow in a failed attempt to secure benefits, eaten restaurant scraps, and slept in alleys, abandoned buildings, and seedy flop houses, all of which housed knife-wielding thugs who would slit your throat as easy as steal your bread—and she had lifted a ragged blanket off one such casualty.

She draped that bloodstained blanket over the dirty cushion and closed her eyes. Yet as exhausted as she was, sleep wouldn't come. The consumptive on the cot beneath her was hacking without pause. The copulating couple were at it again and sounded like rutting moose. And the stench of body odor—-her own included—-was making her gag.

She sat up, rested her head in her hands, and tried to play the glad game. But she couldn't think of a single thing to be glad about.

CHAPTER 40

THE SUN WAS JUST COMING UP when Anne left. Fighting the urge to throw up because of the assortment of odors, her roommates' snoring and coughing, the howling wind, the hammering rain, and her own dark thoughts, she'd spent the night staring at the ceiling. She could hardly remember the last time she'd had a decent sleep. Apart from her mother's death, she was as miserable as she'd ever been. She couldn't, wouldn't, accept such a life any longer.

She wrapped her few belongings in the blood-stained blanket, threw it over her shoulder, and negotiated her way through the dark, still-somnolent building.

The rain had stopped, but the wet smell remained in the air. The temperature had fallen. Cold stung her cheeks when she opened the door. The drunk she'd stepped over the night before was still lying face down in the gutter. He was stiff and blue. Ice and mud were encrusted in his beard and mustache. "Mister? . . . Can you hear me?" She nudged him with her foot, bent down, put her hand on his chest and her ear to his mouth. The smell of alcohol was so intense it nauseated her.

Eventually she felt a cloud of vapor on her face. He was breathing. The ice that covered the streets cracked beneath him as she rolled him over. She turned his head, undid her bundle and tucked her blanket around him, crunched up her spare dress and put it under his head. "Here," she said. "I won't be needin' this no more." After rubbing his nearly frozen hands back to life, she dug in her pocket, removed her last forty cents, and placed them in his hand. "I wish you good luck, Mister."

Then getting up off her knees, she headed toward the river.

She hadn't expected the pub to be open so early in the morning, but the metal gate was up, and she could see patrons inside. The bartender had his back to the door when she came in. The breeze she brought with her lifted the few strands of hair he had left on his head.

Brian Higgins, sitting at the bar, wrapped his arms around himself. "Close the door, will ya. You're bringing in the *cold*!"

She studied the hat pushed to the back of his head, the striped suspenders that hung loosely around the waist of his checked pants, and the worn-out shoes at the end of his short legs on the footrest. "I'd a thought all that alcohol woulda pickled ya by now, and ya wouldn't a felt the cold."

He shifted on his stool, looked at the offender, and squinted. "Is that *Annie Ryan*?" He looked her up and down, at her muddied dress and coat and dirty hair. "What happened to *you*? Ya crawl out of a sewer or somethin'?" He scrunched his red, bulbous nose, waved his hand in front of his face. "Ya sure smell like it. *Phee-ew*!"

"Nice to see you, too, *Mr.* Higgins. I see you're still glued to that same stool, lookin' like one of them gargoyle statues."

"Oow-ee! Hear *that,* fellas?" He faced the two gents at the table behind him. They were leaning against the wall, their legs stretched out before them, the chair's front legs hanging in the air. "Gar goyle. I bet ya never heard a fancy word like that."

"I can't say as I ever have," one guffawed, his whole body shaking.

The other banged his hand so hard on the table his drink rippled inside the glass. He had a wiry beard and smelled of stale cigars even though he wasn't smoking.

The bartender turned around. "Joe's not here."

"I can see that," Anne said.

"Want me to give a message when I see him?"

"You can tell him to drop dead. But I ain't come here for him. I come here to see you."

"Me?"

She thought she noticed a crease between his eyebrows. "I need a favor."

"A *favor*?" Brian Higgins exclaimed. "What kinda favor you be needin'?"

"Do you see me addressin' you, Brian Higgins? Turn back to that kerosene you're drinking and let me talk to Bill here in private."

"Oh. Pardon me." Brian tipped his hat. "The lady needs *privacy*."

"Bugger you, too." She looked at Bill. His beer belly had gotten bigger, and he'd lost more hair since she last saw him. The buttons on his shirt were straining. His sleeves were rolled up to his elbows, displaying hairy arms.

"Can we go someplace where we can talk—*alone?*"

The bald proprietor threw a dishtowel over his shoulder and motioned to the end of the counter. Watching that Brian minded his own business, she followed.

"So, what is this favor you need?" Bill asked without preamble.

She sat on the stool nearest the far wall, bent over the counter, and lowered her voice to a whisper. Her face was so close to him he could smell her bad breath. "I need a loan."

"Why come to me? I don't have money."

She looked him straight in the eye. "I'm not stupid, Bill. I seen how you tap the till."

His jaw tightened.

"You can pick your chin off the floor. I ain't in the blackmailin' business."

"Why not go to Benny Eggs? That's his profession."

"His *profession* is breaking legs. Besides, I ain't lookin' for much. Ten dollars is all, and I'll pay ya back tomorrow. Promise."

Bill licked his lips, scratched his bald crown. ". . .How do I know I can trust ya?"

She let out a deep sigh. "Have ya ever knowed me to be dishonest? Come on, Bill. Help a girl out."

CHAPTER 41

ANNE STOOD ON THE CORNER OF CHAMBERS and Reade among tripled-parked carriages, watching a crowd of jeweled women enter and exit the department store that occupied an entire city block. Rule number one: It is easier to pick from a man than from a woman. She found this to be true because men kept their money either in their pants, vest, or jacket pockets, while women generally kept theirs buried in the bowels of their bags. But then came rule number two: Work with what you have. With Christmas a few days away, and shoppers more concerned with buying gifts than the money in their purses, it was the ideal situation for a rusty pickpocket.

She didn't blend in with Steward's rich clientele. Her freckles and orange hair alone marked her as suspicious (though Mr. Steward, the founder of the store, was himself Irish).

She'd found a long-sleeved, dark woolen dress with ruffles at the neck and wrists at a second-hand store. It was a bit tight around the waist, but that didn't matter, because the cloak she'd picked was roomy. But she hadn't been able to find a pair of shoes to fit. She'd had to shine the ankle-highs she wore and insert more cardboard to cover the holes in the sole. The shop keeper had asked for fifteen dollars for the outfit because the cape had satin lining. She had put eight dollars on the counter, and when he wouldn't come down on the price, she'd promised to pay the balance later that day. Having done business with her before, and knowing her to be honest, he'd agreed.

With new used clothes in hand, she'd gone to a bath house, where, for her remaining two dollars, she'd scrubbed and de-loused herself. It had taken three hot tubfuls to wash off the grime and a metal comb to untangle her hair. When she stepped from the bath, her skin had been as raw as uncooked beef.

Noise was coming from all directions. Horses clopped and snorted, and horns honked non-stop. Carolers were advocating peace on Earth and good will toward men. On Anne's left, a chauffeur was sitting on the box of a coach, scanning through the *New York Times*. In bold black print: *General Braxton Bragg Replaced by Joseph E. Johnston.* Beneath, in smaller print: *Renowned for his significant Confederate victory in the Western Theater at the Battle of Chickamauga in September 1863, but later defeated by General Ulysses S. Grant at Chattanooga . . . .*

To her right, a driver was holding a carriage door open. It was a blustery day, gray, and windy, with the threat of snow in the air. His tailcoat was ruffling behind him. "You couldn't find a farther spot, Robert? In Brooklyn, perhaps?" came a voice from inside the coach.

Anne saw a muscle twitch in Robert's otherwise stoic face as he answered, "I'm afraid we had little choice, madame. The queue stretches as far as Park Row."

"Well, don't just stand there like a statue, help me out." A gloved hand emerged from the passenger seat, followed by the tapping of an ivory-handled walking stick and ankles wider than the shoes. "You don't want me to fall on those cobbles, do you? . . . Or maybe you do." A matronly woman in a black gown, mink cape and bonnet, and a Mary Lincoln hairdo, stepped out. Anne immediately noticed the oval cameo that adorned her standing lace collar, and a brocade handbag, the same color of her dress, dangling from her arm. "I shan't be very long, Robert," the pinch-faced woman said, pressing the creases out of her skirt with her hand. "I only need two items."

Robert nodded. "However long you need, madame. I'll be right here."

"You'll take my wrap when I go inside. It will be too cumbersome."

Robert nodded again, took her arm in his, and escorted her to the building.

A stiff breeze whipped Anne's dress around her skinny legs. She hoped no one would notice her shoes. Sweat began to build the back of her neck and underarms. She didn't want to do it—not so much out of fear of being caught—-though that, too—as for the theft itself. Stealing repulsed her.

But she'd spent her last penny, and having no place to sleep, not even enough money for the flop house, nowhere to wash, no food to eat repulsed her more.

She followed the dangling purse.

"Why is that lady sitting in a sleigh, Mommy?" a little girl in a plaid coat and hat asked as Anne squeezed through the bottleneck of the double doors. She heard laughter and mumbled conversation. Then the little girl's voice. "She's not a real lady."

Sandwiched between a plumed hat and the Mrs. Lincoln imitator, Anne squeezed against her as her fingers crept to the handbag. Just as she was about to reach inside, the doors flew open, the richly clad woman pulled her purse into herself, they were propelled inside, and

Anne was left empty-handed.

She had hoped to complete the task before entering the store and was tempted to turn around and hurry out. But the bag swinging before her was too tempting.

Her heart was pounding so hard she could feel it pulse in her head while she followed the pocketbook past the fresco work and white marble columns, a floor-to-ceiling Christmas tree decorated with ribbons, bows, and bells, a nativity scene with life-size porcelain figures, to a glass-encased display of cuff links, where a group of perfumed ladies was perusing the gem-studded items.

"What do you think, Martha? The silver or the gold?" a middle-aged lady smelling of jasmine was asking as Anne insinuated herself close enough to smell their breaths.

"Oh! I'm so sorry," she apologized profusely as she "accidentally" stepped on an old lady shoe. The cameoed crone turned and grimaced. Her facial powder was too heavily applied, giving her a ghost-like appearance. She looked Anne up and down, from the orange frizz to the cracked shoes, and scrunched her nose as if she detected rotten fish. "Watch where you're going."

Anne put her hands on the woman as if to steady her, feeling the bones of her corset through her black velvet dress. "Yes, ma'am. I'm so sorry. So, so sorry. I hope I didn't hurt you. . ."

Flailing, the woman took a step back, bumping into Martha's friend, who was still contemplating her choice of silver or gold. "Take your hands off me!"

"Is this person bothering you, madame?" A thick-necked man in a dark suit had appeared out of nowhere.

"I'm so very sorry," Anne said to him. "I-I was just trying to look at the, ah, jewelry—"

The security guard raised an eyebrow. "Interested in emeralds, are you?"

"Well, actually, I—I just wanted to see. I was looking to buy a pair of socks, a present for my boss, such a lovely person, but as long as I was here I thought I'd—"

"Pick someone's pocket!" the crone butted in. She reached into her bag to check.

Anne feigned horror. "Oh, no, absolutely not! I would *never*!" She spun around and put her hands on the powdered woman. "How dare you accuse me of such a thing! Just because you're rich, you accuse a poor girl like me of *theft*? A good Christian, a war widow?"

A crowd had begun to form around the scene. Those behind the immediate circle stood on tip-toe to see.

"I'm afraid I'm going to have to search you, miss." The security guard said as he wrapped a muscular hand around Anne's arm. "Come with me." He pulled her through the throng of onlookers, past a counter of silk scarves, leather gloves, and men's colognes, to the office at the back of the store. It was a small room with one window. The floor was of white marble, like those in the rest of the store. There were two cushioned chairs, one behind and one in front of a mahogany desk, on top of which sat stacks of papers. Floral pictures hung on the wall.

"I demand to see your superior!" Anne said. "Search me. Go 'head. Search me!" She raised her hands in the air. He patted her down, had her empty her pockets and remove her shoes. And found nothing. "Satisfied?"

"I—I'm so sorry, miss." He blushed. "You can go now." He opened the door for her to leave.

"Sorry isn't good enough, and I'm not leavin' until I see your boss!"

"I'm afraid he's not available."

Anne made herself comfortable in the seat behind the desk, crossed her arms over her chest. "Then I'll wait until 'e is."

A few minutes later, the supervisor came in. He was bald, like his subordinate, but taller and thinner. He must have lost weight recently, Anne thought, because his belt was on the last loop and his trousers were bunched at the waist. "I understand there has been a mistake."

"A mistake? I was *humiliated*!"

"My sincerest apologies, miss."

"It's missus. And your apology is *not* accepted. You insulted my honor. He—" she shook her finger at the younger man— "*violated* me!"

"It was an honest mistake—"

"An honest mistake, was it? I'll go out there and tell every customer what an *honest* mistake you made. I'll tell them how a war widow whose husband, God rest his soul—" she bowed her head and crossed herself— "died for his country, was attacked and molested on the word of a nasty woman!"

"Now, now. Let's not take that route." The thin man put his hand in his pocket and pulled out a ten-dollar hill. "Perhaps this will help you forget it ever happened."

"Trying to bribe me with a measly ten-dollar bill! What an insult!"

"Maybe fifty would be better."

"A hundred would be better still."

The thick-necked guard, still blushing, began to escort her out.

"Before I leave, I want an apology from that witch."

The guard looked at his boss, who shrugged. "Just make sure there isn't a scene."

When they reached the gaggle of jeweled women, the guard explained to the lady that he had performed a thorough search and found nothing. Perhaps she had misplaced her money. The woman admitted her purse was intact. Anne looked her in the face. "You owe me an apology!"

". . .I'm sorry."

"Being the good Christian woman I am, I accept your apology."

The muscled man let out a sigh of relief.

Anne gave the woman a long, tight hug. "I forgive you."

"The socks are that way." The guard pointed to the left. "I'll take you."

"No, thank you. I've had enough for one day." And out of the store she hurried before the old biddy found her purse missing for the second time.

CHAPTER 42

SHE STOLE MY PURSE! Go after her!" the old biddy screamed as Anne hurried toward the door. Anne recognized the security guard's voice.

"Perhaps you misplaced it, madame. I did a very thorough search. I can assure you she had nothing."

"I'm telling you, she stole my purse!"

"Madame. . . ."

Anne made it to the exit before he finished his thought. Once outside, she picked up her pace, pushing people out of her way as she barreled through the throng of gawking window shoppers. "Hey, watch where you're going!" someone hollered.

"There she is! That's her! Stop her!" The woman and store manager had come through the double door. She pointed to her coachman, who was leaning against the carriage. "Robert, grab her! She stole my purse!"

Anne ran between the waiting cabs, darted around the corner, and hurried down Chambers Street. The baby kicked a few times, as if telling her to slow down. She made a right on Broadway, blended into the crowd, and disappeared down Park Row, where, with heart pounding and out of breath, she finally sank onto a bench opposite a recruiting station.

The seat was damp. It had begun to drizzle. Her hair was frizzy as it always was in damp weather, her woolen dress smelled like a wet dog, and the pieces of cardboard she'd stuck over the holes in the bottom of her shoes had worn through. Despite the raw day, she was sweating.

Not until she'd calmed herself did she pull out the purse and run her fingers over the brocade. It smelled of rosewater and almond oil. She reached inside, removed a round hand mirror encased in silver, a colorful fan in a Japanese design, some kind of facial paste—which, when she put it to her nose, smelled like gardenias—a pencil, a white lace handkerchief monogramed with the initials APG, and a tortoiseshell case, inside which were calling cards.

But no money.

She could have cried. After all that, she sighed, burying her face in her hands. She tried to play the glad game: She had the cash from the store manager. The purse, the mirror, and the fan were surely worth something. Nevertheless, she was disappointed. She shook the handbag inside out.

And then, just as she was about to toss it into the weeds, bills flew out—one hundred dollars in paper money! It had been folded inside a pocket of the satin lining.

When, after several minutes, she realized that she wasn't seeing things, she threw her head back, letting light rain mingle with the tears that were rolling down her cheeks, and exploded in laughter. "Mother Mary! Baby Jesus!" she shrieked. "Let me not be dreamin'."

The contrast from the warmth of the cab, where she'd been wrapped in a lap robe and had her feet perched on a metal coal-ember warmer, to the cold night air hit her like a punch in the face. The temperature had plummeted since morning. The drizzle had changed to sleet. Wind whipped the tassels of her angora scarf.

Stepping around ice-skimmed puddles, craters, and horse manure, she tottered toward the restaurant. The cobbles were slick. Her new leather shoes, with their chunky curved heels, and her seven-month-pregnant belly, made the short distance to the eatery treacherous. She should have bought more practical footwear: winter boots, something with rubber soles, or those ugly high wooden-soled French *sabots* that housemaids wore to mop floors, along with metal cleats that strapped on over the shoe for walking outdoors in bad weather. But she loved her new shoes, the scalloped design, the faux pearl buttons, and that they were maroon, not tan, brown, black, or white. Only the rich wore color and ornaments on their feet. She didn't want to be practical. Not today. Tomorrow she would worry about tomorrow. Today she wanted to feel like a queen—even if only a queen for a day.

A uniformed doorman reached for her hand, while beads of ice pelted the umbrella he held over her head. The night air was dense. Streetlamps cast hazy yellow light. On a building adjacent to the dining hall there was a tattered poster of the president. In the picture, Mr. Lincoln was wearing a crown. His features were exaggerated to resemble those of a Negro, and beneath the sketch ran the legend *King Africanus*. Someone had given him a mustache and blackened out a few teeth. Though she wasn't surprised to see the poster, New York City's sympathies regarding Confederate versus Union were pretty much split down the middle. But she would have expected that sentiment closer to Fulton Street, at Sweets Hotel and Restaurant—a well-known hangout for Copperheads and slave smugglers.

"Good evening, madame. Welcome to Delmonico's." The maître d', a tall, distinguished man with flecks of gray in his thick black hair, smiled at her. "The name of your party?" He went to a counter and opened a log book.

". . .A *party*?"

"A reservation, madame. You *do* have a reservation?"

"I. . .no."

His lip curled. "I'm afraid we're rather full this evening." He rolled his thumb over the tips of his manicured nails. "But perhaps I could re-arrange—" he lifted a brow and tapped his chin. "Let me see what I can do. Hm. Mm." His fingers drummed on the podium. "Table for two. . .table for two."

Anne peered over his shoulder into the dining room. Marble pillars outside the building were impressive enough, but the inside was beyond her wildest dreams. The dining hall was not especially large, but mirrors on the walls made it appear so. There were chandeliers, satiny wall coverings, a bubbling fountain, and a vase of fresh flowers on every table. Most were unoccupied. "The place is almost empty. And I only need one seat, not two."

"Your husband will be joining you, I assume?"

"No. Just me."

He took his eyes off the daily register and stared instead at her abundant belly and bare ring finger. The ledger closed with a thud. Looking down his nose at her without even a pretense of a smile, he said, "I do apologize, madame. But it is our policy not to serve unaccompanied women."

"I see an unaccompanied woman right there." She pointed to the back corner of the dining room. "I can sit with her."

She pushed past him, getting a whiff of his freshly laundered shirt and vetiver-scented cologne, and, with her feet sinking into the plush carpet, made her way across the hall, past a well decorated Christmas tree. Singing, laughter, the clink of glasses came from a room off the main dining hall. Despite the sour notes, she recognized the song as "Jingle Bells." A waiter in white gloves and tails, carrying plates on a round silver tray that he held above his head, entered the area. The scent of steaks freshly grilled in butter made her mouth water.

The maître d' followed her. He cleared his throat. "That, madame, is not your concern! She does not want to be disturbed."

Anne turned on her heel, hand on hip, and having realized that "unaccompanied woman" was a subtle way of referring to prostitutes, said, "And just for your information—not that it is any of your business—I am *not* an *unaccompanied woman.* I am a widow. A *war* widow." She raised her chin and puffed out her chest. "I lost my dear husband, a colonel, he was—at Gettysburg. And what, may I ask, have *you* lost for the Union cause?"

"I am terribly sorry for this intrusion," the tall, dignified man said to the young woman sipping a before-dinner orange cordial when the two reached her table. "I will have her removed immediately." He motioned for two rather large men.

"My apologies." Anne nodded at the young woman. "This gentleman will not allow me to sit at another table. Would ya mind very much if I joined ya?"

Two thick-limbed men appeared.

People at a nearby table began to whisper to each other.

"That won't be necessary, Claude." The young lady smiled.

Anne couldn't help but notice the big teeth she had.

"Please." The seated woman indicated the cushioned silk seat across from her. "It would be my pleasure to have you join me. My name is Marie."

Marie wouldn't be pretty even without those ugly teeth, Anne thought, but she wouldn't be quite as homely. Her hair, pulled into a knot behind her head, did nothing to enhance her looks. The way she held her pinky out when she sipped her drink, sat with perfect posture, and spoke the King's English told Anne she was well-bred. Well-bred but far from stylish! It was obvious her clothes were of fine quality. Yet the drab navy dress she wore was more befitting somebody's grandmother.

"Are you certain?" Claude asked. "She is—"

"A colonel's widow." Marie raised an eyebrow.

Claude nodded to the guards, who uncrossed their arms and lumbered off.

Marie looked him in the eye. "Have someone take her order, please."

He bowed and motioned to a waiter against a back wall.

Anne unwound her scarf, shrugged the imitation mink cape off her shoulders, and draped them across the back of her chair. Her seat faced a mirrored wall. In it she could see a group of diners behind her: four couples dressed to the nines. Women with meticulous coiffures, their jewels glistening in the beveled glass, sat in the company of distinguished men. She admired her own reflection. She'd brushed her hair into an upsweep, all but a cluster of tight orange curls peeking out of her bonnet. The room was delightfully warm. Her chafed cheeks stung from the change in temperature.

"Welcome to Delmonico's, madame. May I take your wrap?" The waiter, striking like all the employees at the restaurant, had a proud bearing and wore tails, a white shirt with stiff cuffs, a standing collar, and highly polished shoes.

"I'll keep it. Thank you," she said, holding it tight.

"As you wish." He stepped to her side. "May I suggest you try the steak? It's traditionally prepared with salt and pepper, broiled to order, topped with herbs, and commonly served with Delmonico potatoes—a baked and slightly mashed potato dish with cheese."

She was dipping a warm roll in oil and garlic.

"I can also recommend our lobster Newberg, chicken a la king, eggs benedict, baked Alaska, and Manhattan clam chowder. Each is *magnifique*."

Anne had never heard of lobster Newberg, chicken a la king, eggs benedict, or *magnifique*, and though she'd heard of steak, she'd never eaten one. Ordinarily, she'd have ordered the "regular dinner" of liver and bacon, beef or mutton stew, ham and eggs or corned beef and cabbage (well, not the cabbage), which cost twelve cents. But she would celebrate. "I'll have the steak and potatoes, the lobster Newberg, and the soup."

He took in the woman before him. Apart from a round belly, she was as thin as a pole. He coughed. "Steak *and* lobster? Are you certain you want—"

"And more bread, please. . .and butter."

His brow knit as he considered the empty bread basket and the crumbs on the linen cloth.

"And to drink? May I suggest a claret? We have an excellent—"

"Beer."

She heard his breath catch. "*Beer*? With *soup*?"

"Yes. Beer!"

Anne heard a nearby patron exclaim, "Beer!"

If she had been watching the group behind her, Anne would have seen the smirk on the lady's face, though even if she had, she would have seen little else, as the room was engulfed in cigar smoke.

"How is it Claude let ya in unaccompanied, if ya don't mind me askin'?" Anne asked after the waiter departed.

"He knows my parents. I was supposed to have my wedding reception here." Marie pointed to the frescoed ceiling as if she could see through it. "Upstairs. In one of the ballrooms."

"Supposed to?"

"I left him at the altar."

Anne's mouth fell open. "Oh, my!"

"The biggest mistake of my life."

Anne reached across the table and put her hand on Marie's arm. It felt as bony as her own under the woolen sleeve.

"Look at the bright side. You're still young. You'll make a lot more mistakes in ya lifetime, and some may be even worse."

They both laughed, Marie through tears. "That makes me feel better." She wiped her eyes with a lace-trimmed handkerchief. "He was such a good man."

"Was? Is he. . .dead?"

Marie rested her face on her steepled fingers. "Not yet, anyway. He joined the army the day after the wedding—-the wedding that never was. Shot in the leg at the battle of Bistoe Station. She broke into sobs, her shoulders trembling. "He wrote to me after they amputated. To think how. . .how I. . . *humiliated* him. And after all that, you know what he wrote? He wrote he still loves me. He's not angry. 'A beautiful girl like you shouldn't be tied down to a nothing like me.' *Beautiful*. Can you imagine? He thinks *I'm* beautiful, and he's a nothing."

"If he's so wonderful, why did ya leave?"

"Because I'm stupid. I was taken in by a scoundrel. Taken in by his good looks instead of good character. His blond curls and bright blue eyes. His charm. His *lies*. Nola—she was my old nanny—tried to warn me. She saw through him, predicted exactly what would happen. But I wouldn't listen. I refused to see what was in front of my face. Can you believe anyone could be so naive?"

Anne glanced at her belly. "Yes. I can. My scoundrel has blonde curls and bright blue eyes, too."

"The colonel?"

"What colonel?"

"Ah. The one you were married to?"

"Oh, that one." Anne laughed. Marie did, too.

The waiter whisked the breadcrumbs onto a plate and off the table, put out a tub of butter, replaced the empty bread basket with warm rolls, and cleared space for the first course. "It's quite hot, madame," he said to Anne as he placed the steaming bowl of clam chowder before her. "And your *beer*." He sneered, set down a stein of golden liquid topped with white foam. "Your shrimp cocktail." He nodded to Marie. "May I get you another aperitif, madame?"

"That would be lovely. Thank you."

He disappeared.

Anne was nearly finished with her clam chowder, soaking bread in the broth and downing each spoonful with delight, when she noticed that Marie had not yet begun. "Aren't ya goin to eat?"

"I don't have much of an appetite. Would you like one?" Marie slid the silver dish with the enticingly arranged prawns across the table. Anne started to put one into her mouth. "You need to squirt the lemon on it then dip it in the sauce," Marie added.

"Oh my God, this is *so* delicious!"

"Have more."

"If ya don't mind me askin', why would you come to this restaurant if ya weren't hungry?"

"I just needed to get out and didn't know where else to go," Marie explained. "I was hoping, if the food was in front of me, I'd get my appetite back." Dishes clattered at the table behind them. A party in the room off the main hall was belting out "Hark, the Herald Angels Sing." "But I haven't," she continued. "I'm too upset. It's my fault. I ruined him."

"You can't beat yerself up. Ya did not tell your intended to join the army. 'Tis only a stepmother would blame ya for what happened."

"It's more than Walter's predicament. It's—" tears welled in her eyes- "It's everything. My parents won't let me come home. My mother even threatened to have me committed if she ever sees my face again."

Anne put a half-eaten shrimp back on the plate and stared at her. "Committed? Like to a *crazy house*? . . . Your own *mother*?"

Marie nodded.

"The cheek of 'er. The only person I know that mean is my ex-boss. Fired me, she did, right on the spot, soon as she realized I was pregnant." She picked up the shrimp. "Didn't even give me my proper pay."

The waiter brought the entrees. The aroma of the steak made Anne's mouth water before she even saw it. "Another beer?"

"Yes. Please."

"Enjoy your dinner."

Anne dug into the steak, lightly charred on the outside, browned around the sides, and dripping in its own juices, while Marie dawdled over her chicken a la king, segregating the noodles from the peas. "I don't know what I'm going to do," she said above the sound of her fork tapping on the plate. "My father rented an apartment for me—in *Brooklyn*—so I have little chance of running into mother. I've never lived alone. I've never learned anything useful. I was trained to be a socialite, to play the piano and read classic literature. All my needs—every *wish*—was taken care of for me. I've never peeled a carrot, or made my bed, or washed or ironed my clothes. I hardly know how to boil water." Tears stung her eyes, ran down her cheeks, and wet her dowdy bodice. The navy-blue wool turned inky where the drops fell.

Anne's cutlery chimed on the china plate. "Think of the good things in your life."

"There *are* no good things in my life."

Anne stared at her, lips parted. Here she was, rich when so many were poor. Her father was supporting her. She wasn't sleeping on the street. So many people would die for an opportunity like she had. "Marie, love, you have to play the glad game."

CHAPTER 43

"May I hail a cab for you, madame?" the doorman asked through chattering teeth, when with valise in hand, Anne left the St. Nicholas Hotel. The sky was gray and the wind fierce. He was holding his top hat down with a white-gloved hand so that it wouldn't blow away. His ears were ruby red. She could hardly hear him above the of horn blasts and scraping shovels just feet away.

"Thank you." She smiled. "But I only have a few blocks to go. And I doubt too many cabs will be out today." She would have preferred to ride had she been able to afford it.

Indeed, there were few vehicles on the road, and those that were were skidding. The streets were a mess. The snow, white and lovely when she watched it fall during the night, had turned to slush. Gangs of street cleaners were out in force, pushing the snow into mountainous piles.

Stupidly, she'd bought those fancy shoes she couldn't walk in, and would probably never wear again, which had cost her a whole $2.50, and was then compelled to spend another $3.00 on boots. At the time, she had bemoaned the expense, but it had been her only *sensible* purchase. She could hardly believe how much money she'd spent. And on what? she asked herself. She could have bought a winter coat for what it cost for one night at the world-class hotel. It had been a hoot, she admitted. But she didn't need to sit on satin-upholstered furniture to be comfortable, eat in the tearoom beneath chandeliers and painted ceilings, or be entertained by a rosewood baby grand with pearl keys. Eggs were eggs whether they were served in a tin bowl or on a gold plate. A rosewood baby grand with pearl keys didn't make better music than a simple upright piano, at least not to her ears. Having central heating, on the other hand, and a room with a fireplace and its own bathroom—-supplied with hot and cold water—was stupendous. That had been worth every cent.

She sighed. It had been fun playing queen for a day. Now it was time to face reality. Tomorrow was today.

With a big belly and no references, she had no way to get a job. She'd counted her money the night before and, after calculating and re-calculating, determined that if she were very frugal and didn't squander another penny, she'd have enough to make it through until the baby was born. What would she do after that? One hurdle at a time.

A blast of cold air whipped at her hood, lifting the edges of her cape. She pulled her scarf higher on her face, so that only her eyes were showing. Then, while offering a silent prayer of thanks and asking forgiveness for the money tucked inside her chemise, she bent into the wind and stepped onto the sidewalk.

Street cleaners were only assigned to major throughfares, so when she turned onto Thompson Street, only the tenants were outside sweeping their stoops, and groups of boys were pelting each other with snowballs. The Greenwich Village neighborhood was far from luxurious but not nearly as seedy as the Lower East Side. There were no stores or bars on the block, no dark alleys or piles of garbage (though, to be fair, Anne thought, the snow on the ground could be hiding it), only decent-looking tenements. The room she came to see was going for seventy cents a week, twenty cents more than she had paid Mrs. Hare, but Anne would have the whole room—-a whole *bed*—to herself.

Trudging through the slop and carrying high, the short walk winded her; but it was climbing the three flights of stairs that did her in. She stood outside the apartment, waiting to catch her breath, before knocking on the door.

The hallway was clean and bright. An opaque window at the end of the landing added light to white plastered walls. And the hallways did not stink of urine.

She heard footsteps and locks releasing. A moment later, the door opened, and a woman in a shawl was standing before her. The smell of frying garlic and onions wafted into the corridor. "Can I help you?" she asked.

"I've come about the room ya 'ave for rent."

The landlord looked her up and down but focused on her protruding belly. "Your husband working?"

"I'm a widow." Anne hadn't anticipated such a hostile response. She'd thought that her new boots and expensive angora scarf would look more acceptable. Perhaps it was her accent. But she removed her mittens and flaunted a silver-plated ring she'd bought in a pawn shop.

"Mm. A common story." The woman smirked. With her hair parted down the middle and braided around her head, a long face, and a long black hair sprouting from a chin mole, she reminded Anne of a witch she'd read about in a childhood fairy tale. Or maybe it was just her scowl.

"You have a death certificate?" Even the voice was shrill.

"He was killed at Gettysburg."

"I'm sure he was." She tsked. "No family to go to?"

"My parents are dead."

"And *his*?" She raised an eyebrow. "They can't take you in?"

"Um. . ."

"I didn't think so. This is a respectable neighborhood. I don't rent to the likes of you." She started to close the door.

Anne put her foot in the way. "I 'ave money for the rent." Reaching inside her dress, she pulled out a purse. "Here. See!"

The braided lady kicked at Anne's foot. The door slammed, just missing her toe.

"I'll give you *eighty* cents!" Anne yelled to the closed entryway. Slumping onto her battered suitcase, she added, "I can pay in advance!"

Several women peeked into the hallway, shook their heads, and went back inside.

"Pull yerself together," Anne told herself. "Who wants to live in that nasty woman's house, anyway? Ya have four more places to check." Surely, she'd have better luck. She stood up, grabbed her luggage, and, head high, started out to the next of the addresses on her list.

But it was the same with each: *no*, but not in such polite language. After the fifth rejection, her back ached and her fingers were numb. She could hardly walk. Her new boots kept her dry, though they had been rubbing against her pinky toes. Valise in hand, bumping against her thigh, she dragged herself to an empty bench to rest. Her eyes welled with tears. *Play the glad game, Annie*, she told herself. *Ya still have money. Ya don't 'ave to sleep in the street. At least not tonight.*

You can go back to the hotel. She smirked. If she had to stay at the St. Nicholas much longer she'd be penniless in no time. The regular three dollars a night was bad enough, but she'd had to bribe the hotel clerk double that to allow "her kind" to stay. She pushed the thought out of her head. *Soak in the tub. Get a good night sleep. You'll think better in the morning.*

She didn't feel better in the morning. Despite the hot bath and comfortable mattress, she'd hardly slept, tossing and turning for hours, and when her eyes finally closed, she'd had nightmares. At seven a.m. she had awakened with her heart pounding. She was in a sweat. Though check-out wasn't until eleven, she got herself out of bed, washed, dressed, threw her few belongings in her cloth valise, and left the hotel—-this time, she swore, for the last time.

It was a nice day, still cold, but the wind had died down, and the sun was bright. She'd never been to Brooklyn. Though it was an easy enough trip, only a short ferry ride across the East River, she'd never had reason to go there. She had taken the Staten Island ferry often as a child, and then as an adult on Sunday summer afternoons, just to ride back and forth to get away from the heat, but she rarely got off.

It was as if she'd entered another country when the boat docked. A commuter suburb, Brooklyn Village was one of New York's premier residential addresses. The low-rise architecture and brownstone row houses were nothing like Manhattan. She stopped a passerby for directions when she landed; he told her that her destination was only three blocks away.

Chestnut Street was less built up. The big multi-gabled Victorian house was set back from a gravelly road and surrounded by hardwoods and pines. Icicles hanging from the eaves were dripping onto boxwoods. Much of the snow had melted, but there were still some slick spots in the shaded areas of the footpath where large trees filtered the sun. She stared at the scalloped siding and conical peaks. Then, holding her breath and slinging her valise over her shoulder, she made her way up the walkway. This was her last hope. She was prepared to beg.

It was a three-story building. The apartment was on the second floor. Anne stashed her baggage in a corner, out of sight, smoothed the wrinkles out of her skirt, and pushed loose strands of hair off her face. After a deep breath, she knocked. And waited.

A harried woman with three small children in tow tramped down the stairs. She was tall and spindly and couldn't have been past her late twenties. A bright-eyed toddler in a Little Red Riding Hood cape, ankle-high shoes, and stockings held her hand as she negotiated the stairs. The middle child, similarly dressed, jumped from one step to the next, the treads groaning under her weight.

"Good morning." Anne smiled.

"Morning," the young mother answered. "*George!* Get off the banister! What did I tell you? *Off!*" The banister creaked and squeaked as the boy, plump backside first, slid down the wooden railing.

There was a loud thump followed, a moment later, by a wail. Anne turned to see the chubby boy sitting cross-legged on the landing, holding his knee, peaked cap askew on his head.

"Mama!" His curly-haired sister pulled her thumb out of her mouth. "George fell again."

The woman picked up her son and started to smack his rump. "How many times do I have to tell you? How. Many. *Times!* This is not a *playground*!"

He continued to wail.

"Children," she sighed, looking at Anne. "This one will be the death of me."

"Who's there?" came a voice from behind the door.

"Anne," Anne said, turning away from the distracted mother.

"*Anne*?"

"We met at Delmonico's last week," she said to the closed entryway as the woman and children continued down the stairs. "We sat—"

A chain rattled, and the door swung open. "*Anne*!" Marie wrapped her arms around her. "Come in. Please. I can't tell you how happy I am to see you!"

"Really? . . . I woke you," Anne apologized, seeing that she was in her night clothes and her hair was hanging loose around her shoulders. "I'm sorry."

"You have nothing to be sorry about. I should have been up by now. But I haven't been sleeping well. I didn't close my eyes until the sun came up. You know how it is. Strange surroundings. Every noise startles you. Take a seat." She pointed to a kitchen chair. "Let me get dressed. Oh, I'm so happy to see you!" she continued, padding through the parlor into the bedroom.

Anne glanced around, wide-eyed. Katie Hare's whole apartment could have fit into the kitchen with room to spare. Marie's place needed curtains and wall hangings to cozy it up, but, that aside, it was *wonderful*. Except for where a cast-iron stove and bucket of wood stood on a square of bricks, a hexagonal-patterned linoleum covered the floor. Sunlight pouring through double hung windows gave the room a pleasant feel—though some heat would have made it more pleasant. It was so cold, she could see her breath. Though she'd removed her coat, she kept it draped over her shoulders.

"I would offer you tea if I knew how to work the burner," Marie said as she re-entered the room. She'd changed into a house dress and swept her hair into a loose bun. A shawl was wrapped across her chest.

"I'll make it, if you like."

"Ah, that would be *lovely*!"

Throwing off her outerwear, Anne crossed the room, thrust an armful of wood into the oven, lit it, and waited for it to heat. "What have you been eating?" she asked, noting the absence of ashes under the grate.

"Anything I don't have to cook. You thought I was joking when I said I didn't know how to do anything. Now you see it's true."

"*I* can make you something. Do you have any food in the house?"

"Some. My father saw to it that I had the basics."

"How's a potato and egg omelet sound?" Anne asked from behind the ice-box door, where a melting block was dribbling into the drip pan beneath it.

Soon, butter sizzled in the skillet. The potatoes, cut into cubes, hissed. Once they were brown, she added the eggs. "Salt and pepper?"

"No, thank you. Mm! That smells so good!"

Anne filled a plate and brought it to the bare oak table.

"What about you?" Marie said before taking a bite. "Make yourself some. I know *you* don't have an appetite problem."

Anne returned with a full dish and pushed the chair far enough away so as not to press her ever-expanding belly.

Marie removed her shawl, rolled up her sleeves, and opened the two top buttons of her shift. "That stove really warms the room."

"So, how 'ave ya been since I saw ya last? Ya 'ave a beautiful apartment."

"Well, it's nowhere as dreadful as the boardinghouse, but it isn't what I'm used to. The people upstairs are noisy. The children stomp. The mother shouts."

Anne laughed. "Yes. I met George."

"And I have to *share* a bathroom."

"With them?"

"No, no, no." Marie shook her head. "With a tenant on this floor."

"*One* tenant?"

"A widower, I understand. I haven't met him."

Anne knitted her brow. "Marie, love, ya don't know how much ya 'ave to be glad about."

Marie's fork chimed as she dropped it on her dish and its scarcely eaten food. She covered her eyes with her hands and began to sob.

Anne pushed herself away from the table, got up, went over to her and wrapped her arms around shoulders. "I'm sorry. I didna mean to hurt ya feelings."

"Oh. It's not that. You're right. I know how lucky I am. But. . . it's, it's *everything*. I'm so homesick. The mess I've made of my life. I think about Walter. Is he dead or alive? What a terrible thing I did to him—and to *me*. The colossal *mistake* I made."

"Now, now. Let's not start again. Have you written to 'im?"

"And ruin his life more than I already have? *If* he's alive, he should meet a girl who deserves him. He doesn't need to be entangled with a married woman." She dried her eyes. "How rude I am. I never even asked how *you* were doing. Is everything alright?"

"Actually, no." And Anne proceeded to tell her about her predicament.

When she finished, Marie clapped her hands. "I'm so happy!"

"What?"

"I hate being alone. Come live with *me*."

CHAPTER 44

Having lost her taste for coffee (just the smell of it made her nauseous), Anne heated water for tea. She was due any day and wobbled when she walked. The baby hadn't dropped yet, and the slightest exertion took her breath away. Her legs were swollen. Her feet didn't fit in her shoes. Open-backed slippers were all she could wear. Even her face was fat. Some women loved being pregnant, she'd been told. She wasn't one of them.

Fear of the birthing notwithstanding, how had they tolerated the last month with all of its discomforts? She crossed herself, as she did every day, and thanked God for her good fortune. It had been two months since she'd moved in with Marie: two glorious months of eating her fill and sleeping between clean sheets and beneath a warm comforter. The mere thought of where she would be if Marie hadn't taken her in gave her chills. She was blessed and had so much to be glad about.

The kettle had begun to whistle when she heard a knock on the door. She shuffled to the entryway, wondering who could be visiting. Marie had secured a midwife for her, but the highly recommended Mrs. O'Mara wasn't expected until that evening. Concerned about

Anne's bounding pulse and bloated limbs, she'd been making daily visits. "Toxemia, possibly life-threatening," Anne had heard the woman tell Marie. "No salt anderabsolute bedrest," she'd ordered. It was funny, Anne was thinking, how good things came from bad, how her condition had turned the table. Until the midwife voiced her uneasiness, Marie had been in an ever-deepening melancholia, moping about the house, going from the bed to the couch, had even stopped playing the piano, which was her one love. Anne had prepared the meals, had had to encourage her to eat and see to it that she washed. And now, it was Marie who was nursing her. To think how much Marie worried about her put a smile on Anne's face. Not since her mother was alive had anyone cared if she lived or died.

Light from the hallway filtered into the vestibule when she opened the door. Though it was a bright apartment, with sunshine pouring through its many windows, the alcove was only lit with a wall sconce. An adolescent girl in a well-worn coat, with red, chafed cheeks above a woolen scarf, smiled at her from the hallway. "Hi. I'm Lizzy. I 'av Miss Marie's groceries." She looked at the shopping bag that dangled from the crux of her arm.

Anne could smell the fresh bread and feel the cold coming off the girl's coat when she opened the door wider and stepped aside to let her pass. "Yer frozen."

"'Tis *cold* out there." Lizzy shivered. Once she settled the package on the table, she removed her outerwear, stuffing her muffler in the sleeve and gloves in the pocket, and hung her wrap on the hook in the foyer.

"A nice cup a 'ot tea will warm ya right up," Anne called from the stove, where she was pouring the brew into two thick mugs.

"You sit down." Lizzy burst into the kitchen. "You're 'avin' a baby. I'll serve *you*." She pulled out a chair to make the point.

"I'm fine. It's good fer me to move around."

Lizzy took the steaming cups from Anne's hands and carried them to the table, the porcelain warming her fingers. "You'll be movin' around plenty when the baby comes. Rest yourself while ya 'ave the chance. Milk and sugar?"

"No, thank ya. I take it plain," Anne said as she plodded across the room, her scuffs slapping against her heels with each step.

"Oh, my God! Look at ya *feet*."

"'Tis nothin'."

"*Nothin'*?" Lizzy set down the drinks and hurried into the parlor, returning a moment later with a pillow. She pulled another chair across the floor, fluffed the cushion on top of it, and lifted Anne's legs, her fingers leaving indentations in the swollen ankles. "There. That's better. Ya keep those feet up. Ya want a girl or a boy?" She pulled a lemon cake out of the grocery bag and cut them both a piece.

"Don't matter."

"As my mum would say—" Lizzy crossed herself— "may she rest in peace, 'as long as it's healthy.'"

Anne smiled.

"'Ave a name picked out?"

"Not yet."

"Superstitious, are ya? My ma was too, bless her soul. Ten children she 'ad, and she wouldn't prepare a thing 'till after they was christened. Nellie, call her Nellie if she be a girl. 'As a nice ring to it, don't ya think? Ya must be wondering who I am. I work for Miss Marie's parents."

"Marie mentioned that her father 'ad someone come every week or so to see that everything's aright. I don't know 'ow I've managed to miss you. Well, it's nice to meet ya now."

"Pleasure's mine." Lizzy nodded. She put a second piece of cake on Anne's plate.

Anne waved the dish away. "No. No more. I've 'ad enough."

"Shouldn't deny yaself. You be eating fer two, ya know. Nice people, the Gilberts." Lizzy licked her fingers. "At least *Mr.* Gilbert is. The missus—" she puckered her lips and whispered— "isn't nice atall."

It occurred to Anne that, though she and Marie had become fast friends, they didn't know each other's surnames. "*Gilbert,*" she said. "That must be a common name. I used to work for Gilbert's Millinery shop."

"That's them. The missus owns it." She lowered her voice, leaned toward Anne. "I hear she's a *witch* to work fer."

Anne's mouth dropped open, and her fork fell from her hand onto the dish, making a chiming sound.

"Are you aright? You 'avin' a spell or somethin'?"

Just then, the swish of Marie's skirt announced her arrival. "Lizzy!"

"Miss Marie." The girl rose and curtsied. "I brought ya groceries. I'll get ya tea."

"Thank you." Marie took a seat. She looked at Anne, at her face, milk white. "Why aren't you in bed? You heard what Mrs. O'Mara said: 'Complete bedrest.'"

". . .I'm. . .I'm fine." Anne lowered her eyes, realizing that she had been staring. "I-I'm losin' my mind stayin' in bed all day."

Marie frowned, then turned her attention back to the teen. "How is my father?"

"Drinkin' too much, if you want a know the truth," Lizzy said, placing a mug before her.

"And. . .my mother?"

"Sound as a bell, she is." Lizzy pulled a packet from her purse and handed it to her.

Marie eyed the plain white envelope. "Is there nothing else? A letter?"

"Lizzy shook her head. "No, Miss Marie."

Tears welled in her eyes. "Would you know if my father spoke to Mother about. . .about me coming home?"

"I wouldn't know. I'm sorry. 'Ave a piece a lemon cake. Mr. Gilbert had Cora bake it special for ya."

"Cora?"

"I almost forgot. You don't know the new cook."

"What happened to the other one. . .Emily, wasn't it?"

"Well, the Missus 'asn't been happy with anybody since. . . since—" she mumbled— "ya wedding. Been firin' the 'elp left and right. Which reminds me, I have to get back before she gets home, today bein' Wednesday—"

"Yes. Payroll day."

"If she realizes ya father sent me—" her voice disappeared in the hallway where she was lifting her coat off the hook. "Nice meetin' you, Miss Anne," she called from the doorway. "Make sure ya keep those feet up!"

"I'll make sure she does, Lizzy," Marie answered. "Thank you for coming. Thank my father. And please, tell him. . .I love him."

After the girl left, Anne and Marie retired to the parlor. Marie fed the Franklin stove, beside which stood a stack of wood on a brick platform, while Anne relaxed on a floral button-backed sofa, her feet on an ottoman. It was a furnished apartment. Along with the settee and hassock, there were two tasseled armchairs, and end tables covered with thin sheets of blue glass. Though the fabric was fading, all the pieces were clean and comfortable. Near the wall adjacent to the window sat the upright piano Gerhard had had delivered before his daughter moved in.

Marie took a seat by the window that faced the gravel street. Sunlight bounced off the ceiling fixture, casting diamond-shaped patterns on the linoleum floor. A draft ruffled her lace collar. She pulled the shawl tighter around her shoulders, took *Madame Bovary* from the end table, and opened it to a dog-eared page.

"Marie. . .how did you meet your husband?"

Marie lowered the book to her lap and stared.

"I'm just curious."

Marie sighed. "I hate to even think of him. It was my mother's fault, actually. She had another one of her money-making schemes. She'd made a bundle selling ice in Panama when the French were trying to build a canal, you see. And since then she'd kept her eyes open for a new windfall. So when we had that terrible riot in the city, and she saw how desperate the men were not to be drafted, she came up with the idea of lending three hundred dollars to every man who wanted to pay his way out of the war an interest rate of fifty percent. The scheme didn't pan out. But *he* came to the door to apply—"

Anne gasped. She knew what the answer would be. She didn't have to be a sleuth to put it together: Joe's change of heart after he went to apply for the money, Mrs. Gilbert's ire after her daughter's wedding, Marie's description of her husband's blond hair and striking blue eyes. But to hear it made it real. It hurt more than she thought possible. Thoughts swirled through her head. What were the chances? One in a million? One in *five* million? And why was she feeling. . .*jealous*? Joe had left her for Marie. He'd *slept* with her. Anne's whole calamity was her fault. . . . Yet she was also her savior. Never in her life had Anne felt so secure. . . . But Marie was also a victim. They were both victims.

"You look terrible, Anne. You really must lie down."

"Yes. I think I will," she said as she pushed herself off the sofa.

CHAPTER 45

"BREATHE, LOVE, BREATHE," SAID THE MIDWIFE from the stool where she was sitting at the foot of the bed. "Deep and slow. In. Out. In. Out. 'Atta girl. Ya doin' fine."

Mrs. O'Mara was a plump woman in her forties with a round, red face. Anne's water had broken that morning; her labor had begun twelve hours earlier, at noon. The room was dark except for the flickering light of two gas lamps.

Though the parlor was roasting, the heat didn't reach the bedroom. The midwife and Marie, who was standing beside Anne, wiping perspiration off her forehead, were wrapped in heavy sweaters, though Mrs. O'Mara's was rolled up above her elbows. "It won't be long now," she said.

"Ya told me that an *hour* ago!"

"'Tis the curse of Eve, child. Just a wee bit longer now. Ye'r almost there." Despite the late term complications, the birthing was going well. The middle-aged mother of seven, having had delivered hundreds of babies, exuded an air of calm and competence. "Here she comes. *Puuush*!"

Anne grabbed Marie's hand, squeezing her fingers so tightly she could feel bones crunch, and pushed with all her might.

A moment later they heard a healthy wail. "It's a girl!" Mrs. O'Mara exclaimed. After being cleaned and swaddled, the mid-wife placed the little bundle in her mother's arms. "She's a pretty little thing."

"That she is," Anne agreed as she stroked the infant's pink cheeks, and ran her fingers through the orange tufts sprouting from her scalp.

Anne was sitting in bed with the baby in her arms when Marie, garbed in a ruffled sleeping cap, a flannel nightie, and a robe came into the room. It was early morning. Mellow dawn light was drifting into the bedroom.

"How's the bleeding?"

"I 'aven't 'ad to change my pad for hours. Why are you awake?"

"I wanted to check on you." She crossed the room, her slippered-feet shuffling on the linoleum floor, sat beside her on the mattress and brushed the baby's cheek. "She's so beautiful."

"Isn't she though? I. . .I can't believe that I almost—" Anne's voice quavered— "almost. . .did away with her."

Marie patted her arm. "But you didn't."

"I thought about it. I almost—"

"But you *didn't*! Have you decided on a name yet?"

Anne wiped the tears that were beginning to streak her face. "What do you think of Marigold?"

"It's. . .unusual."

"But pretty, don't ya think? Orange flower, like her hair. "Marigold *Kathleen*. . .for my mother."

"It's lovely."

"Yes. I think so, too."

"I'VE BEEN THINKING," ANNE TOLD MARIE a few days later as they were sitting in the parlor, the swaddled infant in Anne's arms. It was early morning. Anne had lit the stove an hour before, and the room was comfortably warm. Steely blue light was coming through the window. Anne was dressed for the day. Marie was still in her night clothes, her hair hanging loose down her back. "How long have you been up? It's practically the middle of the night." She rubbed the sleep from her eyes.

"She's got 'er nights and days mixed up. I couldn't get back to sleep after she woke me. I'm sorry if we disturbed ya."

Marie made a don't-be-ridiculous gesture. Marigold began to whimper, and Anne pulled her closer and gave her her breast. The pink lips found the nipple and latched on.

"I'd been 'hopin' to find a job after deliverin'—"

Marie sighed. "Are we starting that again?"

"But I musta been dreamin. Unless I 'ire a wet nurse, 'tis impossible. Makes no sense atall. Why would I pay someone with the pay I could get? Besides, I've 'eard some terrible stories about some of those women. Miss Lydia from upstairs told me 'bout a woman she knows of who gives the babies rags ta suck on that 'ave been soaked in laudanum to keep 'em quiet."

"I'm glad you came to see the light. How many times did I tell you that you don't have to work? There's no need—"

"I know, I know. You need me as much as I need you. I appreciate ya carin' and generosity, Marie. You can't imagine 'ow much. My own ma could not a treated me better. But—"

"Oh-oh!" Marie rolled her eyes. "Here it comes."

"Try ta understand. I need to do this for me, *meself*. I can't be a freeloader no more—"

"You're *not* a freeloader. How many times do I have to tell you? You do more than your share—"

Anne held up her hand. "I *'ave* to pay my way," she said emphatically. "I'll take in piece work. But it's even more than that."

Marie opened her mouth to speak, but Anne shushed her again.

Marigold finished. Anne wiped drops of milk from around the baby's lips and re-arranged herself. "'Tis about more than ya generosity and me making money," Anne went on. "We 'ave to face the facts. Your father won't be 'ere forever. What'll 'appen—"

"He's still a young man!" Marie broke in indignantly.

"I'm only sayin'. We, you *an* me. . .'ave to be prepared for when . . .financial support ends."

"He'll provide—"

"He's missed sending you money a couple of weeks already. Ya heard what Lizzy said 'bout him, ah. . .drinkin' too much and gettin' forgetful.

"It only happened a few times. And besides, I'm sure he'll make proper arrangements—"

"Will he? In his *will*?"

"Yes."

"Ya really think ya ma would allow that? Ya said yaself that 'if she says jump he asks how high'."

Marie's shoulders slumped.

"And since it doesn't seem like either of us will be findin' 'usbands—"

Marie gasped.

"We don't *need* 'husbands, Marie." She smiled reassuringly. "We just need ta be smart. We 'ave to be more careful with our money. Well, *you* do, anyways."

"Careful with my money?" Marie stiffened. "How could I possibly spend less?"

"Well, for starters, instead of 'avin' Lizzy buy the groceries, let *me* do it. I've always been good with a farthin'. When I was just a child, my ma 'ad me do the shoppin' cause even then I could split an 'alf-penny three ways. We don' need to be buyin' the better cuts of meat. Cheaper ones are just as good. And I can make lard and soup from the fat and bones. Besides, we don't need to be eatin' meat but maybe once a week, anyway. We can buy day-old fish and bread—"

"Day-old bread?"

"If we heat it on the stove it'll be just as tasty."

Marie made a grunting sound.

"And we don' need no fancy cakes neither."

"No cake!"

"I'll bake if ya like. Then there's the newspaper—"

"Oh, no." Marie shook her head. "I won't give up the paper."

"Ya don't 'ave to. But ya don't 'ave to have it delivered when ya can buy it on the street corner."

Marie sighed. "Are you going to tell me I have to get rid of my perfumed powder and lavender soap, too?"

"No. You can keep those."

"Well, thank *you!*"

"We need to do somethin' about the heat, though."

"The heat?"

"There's no reason we have to keep both stoves going day and night. We're only in one room at a time."

"I'm used to a warm house in winter. I don't like walking into a cold kitchen when I wake up in the morning."

"As long as we're talkin', ya didn't 'ave to 'ave ya room re-papered neither when there was nothin' wrong with it."

"The wallcovering was horrible. The red velvet drapes! It was like sleeping in a brothel. And before you say it, yes, the lamp and the duvet cover didn't blend in, so they had to be replaced." Marie's voice was rising, and Anne knew she'd gone too far, so she didn't cite other extravagances—like the finer dishes when those provided with the apartment were perfectly serviceable, or Marie plastering every wall with pictures she'd bought (each at full price), or that she'd purchased new curtains for all the windows.

"I can take in piece work until I'm able to leave Marigold. If it's aright with the landlord, I'll plant a vegetable garden this spring. You can invest, maybe, or give piano lessons."

"Invest? With *what*? And *how*? I don't know anything about managing money. I never had to."

"Your mother didn't know anything about investin' until she invested."

"But she *did* know enough to marry a rich man."

"Well, I can't argue with you there."

They both laughed.

"As for the music lessons?" Marie argued. "Nobody around here has a piano or is interested."

"You don't know that. And even if it's true, let people hear you play. They'll be so wantin' to learn they'll be knockin' down the door."

ANNE PUSHED OPEN THE CURTAINS IN THE PARLOR to let in the light. It was a beautiful day—cold but clear—and sunshine flooded the room. Marie was sitting at the piano beside George. Her little upstairs neighbor had been the first of five students. Anne had been right. Once the neighbors heard her play, word spread, and soon Marie had more students than she could handle. "One and two and three." She tapped a pointer with each dreadful note. "Pay attention. Sit still," she told him as he swung his legs and wiggled on the seat. He was rounder than tall. His backside hung over the edge. With every movement, the bench creaked. She looked at the clock on the wall. Only five minutes had passed. Giving him lessons was a waste of time for both of them. He had no interest. She had no patience.

"I'll see you later," Anne whispered, when she, with Marigold tucked in a pram, left the house to go food shopping. Without stores or push carts on every corner, as in Manhattan, she had to walk several blocks to the avenue. A light snow had fallen during the night, and stones, roots, and cracks in the sidewalk, hidden under a layer of white powder, made pushing the carriage a challenge. Nevertheless, Anne loved the walk. It was a beautiful neighborhood, clean and quiet, a delightfully boring, stable, working-class enclave where women smiled in greeting and men tipped their hats. Blocks of freshly painted Victorian homes alternated with row houses of brick and stucco. Mature trees lent shade to the streets. In front of one detached home, hedges had been trimmed in shapes of animals. The air smelled sweet and fresh. Life was good. She had so much to be glad about.

CHAPTER 46

MARIE DROPPED THE *NEW YORK TIMES* on her lap. (Despite Anne having offered to pick it up on the street corner, Marie insisted on having it delivered.) "Walter would have been so happy today," she said, wiping her eyes.

It was a clear, cold January morning. From the kitchen table where they were sitting with their coffee, they could hear the wind howling outside. The windows rattled. Sunlight shone through the ice-crusted panes. Though wood was crackling in the stove, it was still chilly, and they were both wearing shawls. "Why is that?" Anne asked.

"Congress passed an amendment to abolish slavery." Marie sniffled.

"I thought the President already did that."

"He had called for it, but now it's the law. Walter was an abolitionist, you know." Marie's eyes were getting glassy, and she had to pause to get her voice back. "He risked his life bringing slaves to safety. Gave the Negroes free legal aid. He lived for this day." A choked sob rose in her throat, and Anne got up and put her arms around her. Marie had filled out since they started living together. Beneath the lambswool sleeve, Anne could feel that the arms weren't as scrawny.

"What's this 'woulda been'?" Anne went on. "You already have him dead and buried. You don't know that."

Marie made a face. Tears were flowing freely down her cheeks. "What are the chances? I never got another letter."

"You never answered *his*. Maybe 'e thought—-thinks, *thinks*—you're not interested."

"He's dead," she whispered. "I know it. I can *feel* it."

"Why don't you find out fa sure?" Anne went back to her seat, sipped her coffee, and grimaced. "I made it too strong. Write to his family." She got up to make another pot.

"His *family*? Oh, my God, I could never face them. Never!"

"Then ask the army. I'm sure they 'ave records."

"Go to *Manhattan*?"

"You're still afraid ya ma will find ya and put ya in an *asylum*? Tis a big city, Marie. What are the chances? 'Specially on the Lower East Side?" *Then again, what were the chances that she would be living with the woman who had married her Joe?*

Marie didn't answer.

"Come on. I'll go with ya. Cover ya face with a scarf, if it'll make ya feel better.

THEY WERE RED-FACED AND BREATHING HARD when they arrived at army headquarters. Having been re-directed from one office to another, they had spent the past four hours navigating the city streets and transit. The wind slammed the door behind them. A burly man in a Union uniform was sitting on a swivel chair that creaked with every movement. His outsized boots were crossed at the ankles and rested on the desk, which was overflowing with papers. Metal file cabinets covered the walls. A thirty-six-star American flag hung above a cabinet. Green linoleum covered the floor. A pot belly stove warmed the small space.

He looked up when Marie, and Anne pushing the carriage, entered the room, quickly removed his feet, and gathered up the papers that had begun to flutter in the cold breeze that came in with them.

"Morning, ladies." He nodded.

Anne gave him her best smile. "Mornin'."

"Have a seat." He gestured to the other side of the table, where two chairs sat empty. He was a big man in every respect, easily over six feet, with broad shoulders and long, thick legs. He gazed at the rosy-cheeked child, snug inside a fleece-lined blanket that Marie had had Lizzy buy in Little Germany. Marigold had outgrown the pram and was settled into a high-wheeled wicker stroller lent to her by her neighbor, Mrs. Iacono, who only used it when her grandchildren came to visit.

"Pretty baby," he said.

"Thank you."

"What can I do for you?"

Marie kept her hands in her lap, squeezing her fingers together. She'd pulled the scarf from around her face. Her hair was mussed. "I hope you can help me. We've been to just about every army recruiting station in the city. I'm looking for information about my. . .uh. . .*fiancé*. I don't know if he's dead or alive. He wrote me a letter after he had his leg amputated. He was in a field hospital in South Carolina." She lowered her voice. "I haven't heard since. . . . I was hoping *you* might have. Please tell me we're finally in the right place."

He nodded sympathetically. "His parents would have gotten a notification if. . . . They would have gotten a letter. Asking them would be your best bet."

"I'd rather not."

He raised his eyebrows.

"It's a long story."

"All right, then." He rose and lumbered over to the file cabinets. "Let's see what we can find. What's the name?"

"Hockenberry. Walter Hockenberry."

"What unit was he in?"

"The 42nd Volunteer New York Tammany Hall. He was injured at the battle of Bristoe Station."

"Well, you're in the right place. We have the records for that unit—"

"Thank God!" Marie said, visibly relieved.

The soldier went to the H cabinet. They heard the metal drawer squeak open. His thick fingers walked through the files. "The 42nd,' you say. You're sure? That's a notoriously Irish regiment. Hockenberry doesn't sound—"

"He volunteered late in the war."

"Uh. That may be why. Hockenberry, Hockenberry. Here we go. Walter Hockenberry." He waved the file in the air.

Marie held her breath as he opened it and began to peruse the report.

"Is he. . .dead?"

"Not that I can tell." He turned the page. "He *was* injured. Leg amputated. Was sick with fever." He turned the page again. Continued reading. "His parents had him picked up and brought to a New York hospital—-or home. That's all I can tell you." He closed the folder and put it back in place. The drawer rang shut.

"Now what?" Marie asked when they got outside. The sky was clouding up. The temperature had dropped while they were inside. Snow was in the air.

Anne pulled Marigold's hat further down over her ears and pulled the blanket up higher. "Write to his mother if you don't want to go to the house."

"I can't. I just *can't.*"

"What's the worst that can happen? She'll call you names? You don't have to see her. And either way, you'll *know*.

Marie crumpled another sheet of paper and tossed it into the wastebasket. A dip pen, an inkwell, a stack of fine linen paper, and a mug of steaming coffee sat on the kitchen table before her. A warm breeze blew through the open window, lifting the edges of the violet-scented stationery. The morning light caught the gold medallion of the Virgin Mary around her neck, a gift from her father after his most recent trip to Italy. Lizzy had brought it to her, wrapped in newspaper, on her last visit. From the wrapping, Marie knew he'd bought it on the sly, probably slipped into a jewelry stall on the Ponte Vecchio when her mother was trying on a pair of shoes. Had *she* bought it, it would have been cloaked in ribbons and bows. To Florence the presentation was as important as the item. *Wear it knowing that I will love you forever*, said the note attached to it. *But you don't love me enough to let me to come home*, she'd thought when she read it, and had been tempted to throw it across the room. Instead she'd wept. Between her father's gift and the Walter situation, she was becoming more and more melancholic.

Her head was resting in her hands when Anne entered the room. "Tryin' to write a letter?" she asked, eying the nearly full pail and picking up, and adding, a few more smudged balls of paper that had fallen to the floor.

"I don't know what to say."

"Marie." Anne rested her hands on the hips of her grieving attire. "It's been more than two months. In all that time, can ya think of *no-*

thin' to say? Just tell him ya received his letter. Ya hope 'e's well. You're sorry. Can he ever forgive ya. Something like that. And why don't ya try usin' a writin' pad and a pencil first? Instead a wastin' all that ink and expensive paper." She looked at her friend's frumpy nightgown and matching robe, her hair hanging loose and messy down her back. "Ya gettin' dressed? We should get there early, so we can get a good spot."

Marie removed her hands from her chin and shook her head. "Go without me. I'll watch Marigold."

Anne sighed. "Stop *loligaggin'* already! T'only makes things worse. Wash ya face. Brush yer 'air. It looks like a rat's nest. Get dressed and come with me. It'll make yer feel better."

"How is seeing the President's dead body going to make me feel better?"

"It won't. But 'tis a lovely day, and you'll get some air. God knows, ya hardly left the house all winter. And we could stop for oysters. Make a nice day of it."

"It's rather hypocritical, don't you think, for New Yorkers to put on a show for a President they hated, didn't vote for, even tried to kill?"

"Ah, Marie, the whole city turned out for the Union Jubilee when he got re-elected. I guess a spectacle for his assassination isn't *so* outrageous."

"New Yorkers will throw a party for anything. And since when are you willing to spend money on eating out? . . . Have a good time. Bring some oysters back for me."

Though Anne arrived hours before the procession began, she did not get a good spot. The crowd was enormous. Everywhere she looked was packed. She had had to squeeze herself in, sandwiched fifteen rows behind the barricades four blocks from City Hall, where the

President's body lay in state. Maybe it was the warm weather. Or that people had the day off. Maybe it was because everything—including the bars—were closed, and people had no place else to go. Or maybe Marie was right: 'New Yorkers will throw a party for anything.' Except no one was in a party mood.

The city was in mourning. Buildings draped their windows in black crepe. Black streamers fluttered from the top of City Hall along with a pennant declaring that *The Nation Mourns.* American flags, and banners that read *Death to Assassins,* waved in the breeze. Men and boys bared their heads and adorned themselves with black arm bands or remembrance badges. Nearly all the women were dressed in full mourning. Those who weren't garnished their hats with ribbons. Even the poorest of the poor wore some kind of memento. "Get your arm band here!" Anne heard a young voice calling out. "Get a likeness of the best president who ever lived."

A lady near Anne gestured to the lad, who, after pressing through the crowd to reach her, pulled a burlap bag off his shoulder. He couldn't have been more than twelve. His mouth was full of bad and missing teeth. His breath was foul. His britches were patched. He needed a bath. The woman peered into the sack. She was wearing a dove-gray dress and holding a shawl, because, though there was a delightful breeze, it didn't reach the tightly packed throngs. "That looks interesting." She pointed to a little paper item.

"Yes, ma'am. It's a best seller." He picked up a three-dimensional paper White House.

"I'll take two." She turned to Anne. "One for each of my grandchildren. How much?" She faced the hawker, reaching for the purse she kept inside her sleeve. When the boy told her the price, she grimaced and replaced the purse. "That's absurd!"

"I'll take 'em," Anne said, her hands already in her pockets to pull out the clinking coins.

"Are you certain, dearie?" said the woman. "You can buy the same exact trinket in the store for half the price. He probably stole them."

Anne smiled at the youngster and pressed the money into his dirty hand. "But the stores are closed today," she said to the woman.

"Wow! *Thank* you, ma'am!" He tipped his cap, exposing tousled hair, when he realized she'd given him a tip.

"Did you happen to see the Barnum museum?" the lady next to her asked. "It has a large black urn of smoking incense. And, my God, you should have heard the singing as the coffin was carried inside City Hall. It was chilling. Just chilling. A German musical society, I was told."

"You came here yesterday, too?"

"Oh, yes. There were so many of us who filed past the coffin." She leaned so close, the feather on her hat tickled Anne's nose. Her voice faded to a hushed whisper. "He looked *terrible*. Shrunken, shriveled. But then, he was never a handsome man, was he? Not outwardly, anyway. But inside he was beautiful, and that's what counts."

Anne studied the crowd. "No place in New York for Copperheads today," she said.

The older woman's eyes teared. "Oh, they're around. Just keeping low. I heard a man was thrown off the Brooklyn ferry for saying something like 'Good, the bastard is dead.' Excuse my language."

"Did he drown?"

"No, unfortunately. A passing boat picked him up."

"Shame."

The procession started. Small talk was replaced by muffled weeping. Sixteen horses dressed in black pulled the glass-walled hearse down Broadway, each stallion led by a Negro groom. The hearse was immense. Even from her spot in the fifteenth row, Anne could see it. White satin trimmed the inside. A golden eagle on the roof glistened in the mid-day sun. The slow clopping of horse never sounded so sad.

The city militia, and a seemingly endless line of groups representing the businesses, lodges, labor unions, and civic organizations, solemnly marched. Some had built mourning floats. Two hundred freed New Yorker Blacks brought up the very rear of the line. Throughout the whole long march, church bells tolled and cannons boomed. Viewers were hanging from every lamp post and tree as it passed. Thousands more leaned out of every window. The woman beside Anne told her that some landlords along the route were charging admission of up to forty dollars for folks to poke their heads out of their windows.

The ferry, crowded with Brooklynites on the best of days, was jam-packed that evening. It had begun to rain, and every seat and square inch of floor space inside the cabin was taken, so Anne pushed the heavy door open and clattered down the metal steps to the deck outside, where, even if wet, there was more room. A strong, cold breeze slapped her face and whipped her skirt against her legs. After wiping beads of water off the seat, she lowered herself onto the slatted bench beneath the overhang. "Ah! It's so good to sit," she said to the girl beside her. "My feet are on *fire*. Not that I'm complaining, mind ya. I'm 'appy to 'ave witnessed it, though, sad as it was."

A pale moon shone through a patchy fog. The water was choppy and lapped against the boat. She closed her eyes at the sound of cawing sea gulls and the feel of rumbling beneath her feet, removed her bonnet, and inhaled the salty fish smell.

"Did ya ever in ya life see such a hearse? And all those flags," Anne said behind closed lids. "Terrible that a wonderful man like Mr. Lincoln should be assassinated. And don't you find it interestin' that the sky got black at three o'clock? Just like Jesus's crucifixion." She crossed herself, opened her eyes, and turned to her neighbor. The girl was curled into herself, her shoulders heaving up and down.

nne stroked her arm encouragingly. She was a pretty little thing on the verge of womanhood, with breasts the size of walnuts and hips hardly noticeable. Anne guessed her to be about fourteen. When she looked up, Anne noticed her eyes were red and puffy.

"Now, now. Let it out. It was a terrible thing. And I'm sorry the world is not a better place," Anne said. "But 'tis the only world we have. We 'ave no choice but to live in it. You 'ave to think about the good things in ya life. Play the glad game."

"I—" the girl hiccoughed. "I . . .I don't have *anything* good in my life."

"A course ya do. Spring is 'ere. Just look around. Flowers are startin' to bloom." Anne pointed to the girl's drab cotton dress covered with a full-length bib apron. In the thick fog it looked gray like everything else. "You 'ave a job."

The girl shook her head and sobbed louder. "No. I don't."

"Well, you can find another job." Anne took the girl's calloused hand in her. "A better one! One that pays more." "And one that doesn't work you so 'ard."

"No. I can't. . . . I'll never be able to find another job." The sobbing got louder. "I don't know what to do. I have nowhere to go. I been riding the ferry back and forth since this morning. . .since he fired me."

"What happened? If you don't mind me asking."

"I told him I didn't want to. I told him I wasn't that kind of girl."

Anne sighed. "He told you he would fire ya if you didn't."

The girl's eyes widened. "How did you know? I didn't want to. I didn't. But I had no place to go. So every day he. . .you know. And then—"

"You got pregnant."

". . . Yes."

"And when he realized it, he fired ya anyway."

"He said that, if I told anybody, he would say I stole his wife's pearls and have me arrested. That nobody would believe me anyway, because he's an important businessman and I'm just a—a cheap, lyin' whore. He didn't even give me enough time to take my belongings! I'm so scared." The sobbing resumed. "You can't imagine how scared I am!"

CHAPTER 47

MARIE AND MARIGOLD WERE ASLEEP on the sofa when Anne got home, Marie in the same frumpy robe and rat's-nest hair, Marigold in her nightgown, snug beneath her favorite blanket, her curly red hair splayed on Marie's lap. Anne left her wet shoes by the door and draped her damp shawl over a kitchen chair. It smelled like wet dog. Then she padded across the room and bent over to kiss her daughter's forehead. Marigold's lids fluttered open. "Mama!"

"Yes, sweetness." Anne lifted her up and hugged her tightly. "Oh, ya're gettin' so heavy!" She kissed her cheek. "I love ya *so* much." Thinking of the girl on the ferry, the future she faced, how close she herself had come to doing away with this beautiful child, she felt her eyes gloss over with sadness. "Were you a good girl while I was gone?" she asked.

"Anne?" Marie stretched, set her feet on the cold linoleum, and sat up. "You're home late."

"Sorry. I hope she wasn't too much of a handful."

"Of course not. She's a delight."

"Marigold pointed and said, 'Piano.'"

"You played the *piano*?"

"More like banged the keyboard." Marie laughed.

Anne had been tempted to chastise Marie for not getting dressed or caring for herself but realized it was the first time in months she'd seen a smile cross her friend's face. Perhaps her melancholy was lifting. Better not to hound her. Besides, she had bigger fish to fry. "You wouldn't believe the crowd," she said. "The buses were full. Four passed me by before one stopped. Then I 'ad to wait for the ferry—"

"Did you bring the oysters?"

"Ah. No. But I did bring ya a lovely souvenir." From her pocket, she pulled out the paper White House, a bit limp from the rain. "It's three dimensional. Look." She pulled it open and showed her the cut-outs of the president's residence.

Marie looked at her suspiciously. "You bought *this* instead of the oysters? And paid *what*? You, who will only buy day-old bread?"

Anne chewed her lower lip. ". . .And, ah. . .I brought something else." She turned to the vestibule, nodded, and the girl from the ferry came out of the shadows. "This is Julia."

ANNE GAVE JULIA ONE OF HER SLEEPING GOWNS, heated some left-over chicken soup, and made up the couch.

She was still asleep in the morning when Marie and Anne sat at the kitchen table staring into their coffee. Marigold was sitting cross-legged on the floor, playing with wooden blocks. Anne blew into the cup and watched the coffee ripple. Marie picked up her cup, brought it to her lips, and put it down again. It rattled on the saucer. In the living room, the clock ticked. "She can't stay," she finally said, staring into her brew.

"We can't send 'er out. She 'as no place to go."

"She's not our responsibility."

"Whose responsibility is she?"

". . .I don't know. But not ours. The church should be able to help her. She can go there."

"The *church*?" Anne's head jerked up, and she looked at Marie for the first time. "The church is the last place she should go."

"We can't have her *here*. I'm not trying to be mean, but how many pregnant widowed cousins can I have? The neighbors will think we're running some kind of house. . . . And if my father finds out, he may stop supporting me."

"Of course, you're right. I'm sorry." Anne pushed her chair away from the table and got up.

"Where are you going?"

"Wherever Julia goes."

Marie let out a long breath. "Ahh, don't be like that. You know I don't want to put her on the street. But what can I do? And what's wrong with sending her to the church, anyway? Isn't that what the church is supposed to do? Help people in need?"

Anne sighed. "Marie, I know you're a good person. You wouldn't a taken me in if ya weren't. God knows where I'd be if you hadn't. I thank the Lord every day for you." She crossed herself. "But you're naive. You only see the world from the eyes of your privileged bubble."

"What is that supposed to mean?" Marie stiffened. "I'm hardly living a *privileged* life now."

"I didna mean it as an insult. We all see the world from our place in it, is all." She sat down again, and patted Marie's arm. "Let me tell ya something about the church. About them nuns. 'Cause that's where she would go, to the convent. Somethin' my ma once told me. A friend of my ma's daughter got in a family way, raped by her fecken da, who got hisself horned up every time he drank—which was every day. Poor girl would hide in the closet whenever her da were about."

"Didn't her mother notice what was happening?"

"Oh, Marie, love. I'm sure her mother knew. But she *chose* not to know."

Marie gasped. "What kind of mother doesn't protect her child?"

It was on the tip of Anne's tongue to say, *What about wha your mother did to you?* But instead, she said, "A mother who 'ad nine little ones, no means a making a livin', and no family ta run to." She sighed. "Anyway, the bastard da had to get rid of the girl quick so as not to bring shame to the family. Ha! So he 'ad her committed to a convent and signed over all her rights.

"He coulda dumped her on the street, that's true. Mighta been better off if he 'ad." Anne sipped her coffee, grimaced because it had cooled. "The place was *clean* enough. Too clean, according to my ma. Sterile like. No rug on the floor. No pictures on the walls. Just a white metal bed and night stand you see in a hospital, a white basin and pitcher, and a big crucifix above the bed. They treated the girls like prostitutes, all of 'em, no matter if their condition was their fault or not. Shamed them, they did. Worked 'em like slaves in the laundries. Worse than the prisons and work 'ouses. And then they sold their babies."

"That happened in Ireland. Surely, we don't do those things in America."

Anne stared at her friend and sighed. "I can't say from first-hand knowledge how those unwed mothers are treated in this country. But I do have first-hand knowledge how they treat orphans. And I say, she's not going to a church or a convent." Marigold began to wiggle, and Anne realized she was wet. She lifted her off the floor and took her into the bedroom to change her diaper.

"Then what do we do?" Marie asked when they came back in the kitchen, both smelling of the calendula salve that Anne used on Marigold's bottom to prevent nappy rash.

"I don't know. But I can't put her out. I won't. You'll 'ave to put me out, too."

Marie's jaw dropped open. "You can't mean that."

"Indeed, I do. I understand what ya saying, I respect ya position. But I can't let the poor thing go out alone."

"Well, maybe. . .maybe she can stay until she shows."

Anne threw her arms around Marie. "I knew you'd understand."

"But only until she starts to show!"

JULIA WAS THE PERFECT HOUSE GUEST: quiet, clean, and unobtrusive. First one up in the mornings, she started the stove, put up the coffee, folded and put away her bedding, and cleaned their shared bathroom. The rest of the day she kept a low profile, especially around Marie, who, polite but not warm, seemed to study her belly whenever their paths crossed. Conversations consisted of everything and anything—except the embarrassment in the room.

And Julia played the glad game, too. She thanked God for being taken in, thanked Him for the warm apartment, the comfortable couch she slept on, the food she ate. She thanked him for Anne, and even Marie, who she knew took her in reluctantly but took her in. But she couldn't glad away the inevitable. What she was going to do after consumed her thoughts.

Anne did her best keeping up a happy façade, yet she too was preoccupied with Julia's predicament. Day and night she puzzled over a solution. Two weeks after the girl's arrival, she had an answer.

She was adjusting her bonnet when Marie came through the doorway. "Where are you going?"

"To raise money."

"Raise money?" Marie was standing between their bedrooms. Anne had opened the doors to the balcony. The outside furniture was wet with dew, but the sky was clearing, sunshine flooding the room, and birds were chirping noisily. Marie kept her sleeping place dark, and the sudden change in light hurt her eyes. She pulled her bathrobe over her night gown. "How do you suppose to do that?"

"I'll ask people to donate."

Marie stared at her. "Who's going to give you money? With so many wounded veterans needing help, no one cares about pregnant girls."

"Maybe. Maybe not. I won't know until I try. The worst they can say is no." Anne studied her friend and sighed. "Ya gonna brush yer 'air and get yourself dressed today? How long ya going to mope around feeling sorry for yourself?" The words came out harsher than she'd intended.

Marie seemed about to cry. ". . .I'm sorry."

Anne lowered her voice to a near whisper. "Ya worry me so. Look at the state o' ya. Nothin's gonna change in ye life unless ye change it yerself."

CHAPTER 48

IT HAD BEEN A LONG DAY, and Anne was tired and hungry. Her feet hurt. She'd knocked on every door in the neighborhood, spoken with every woman she passed in the street—and had achieved little more than sore knuckles and a scratchy voice. How is it that women felt such little compassion for their sisters' troubles? she wondered as she lowered herself onto a stone wall. Well, that was completely fair. Most of them expressed their sympathy but said they had their own troubles. One woman even invited her in, and gave her a cup of coffee, a piece of cake, and a few coins. But then there was the nasty, gray-haired crone who had swung a broom and chased her down her porch steps as she hollered, "Tell her to keep her legs crossed!" that made Anne cringe.

She'd been at it since dawn. It was five o'clock, the sun was setting, and the rock was cold beneath her. Discouraged but not deterred, a long, exasperated breath escaped her lips. "Maybe I'll have better luck with men," she said into the darkening sky.

O'Halloran's was packed. "What are they givin' away?" Anne asked a young man standing in the doorway.

Loud with shouting, laughing, singing, and clinking glasses, he had to lean into her to hear. "The ports are open again," he said, cupping his hands and speaking directly into her ear. "A ship from the Caribbean pulled in this morning." Anne stepped inside, her shoes catching on the sticky floor. The smell of sweat was thick in the tight space. Smoke curlicues drifted in the dim light.

"'There were two lofty ships from old England came,'" a glassy-eyed sailor in a loose shirt and wide-legged trousers was singing from where he stood on a chair.

A group of similarly dressed men held up their glasses and sang out in unison, "'Blow high, blow low, and so sailed we!'"

"'Aloft there, aloft, our jolly boatswain cries.'" The sailor on the stool waved his arms like a conductor.

"'Blow high, blow low, and so sailed we!'" the men responded.

Above the noise, Anne thought she heard Oswald Beady's booming voice. Sure enough, when she looked in that direction, she saw him sitting on a high stool at the end of the bar, his shoulders topping those of the audience around him. The hard-boiled mariner looked older and more worn than the last time she'd seen him. His wrinkles were deeper, his skin more leathery, and his hair, grayer and scragglier, had receded to the middle of his head. What was left was tied in a queue. His eyebrows, however, were as bushy as ever, and his eyes still twinkled.

"So these three old guys are sitting on a bench," he was saying to a gaggle of shipmates.

"I hope they were in the shade. It's pretty hot down that way," said a fellow salt with a red bandana.

"*Yes*, the benches were in the *shade*. Under a big palm tree, if it's important for you to know."

"Well, I'd like to think the three old-timeys were comfortable is all," the other replied, puffing a cigar and blowing rings into the already smoky air.

"So these three old gents are sitting on a bench *nice and comfortable* under a really *big* palm tree," Oswald went on. "'How ya been?' they asked each other. So, the first guy says, 'Not so good.' 'Why's that?' the other gents wanted to know. 'Well,' said the first old guy, 'every morning, I get up after seven and try to pee. I try and try, and nothin' happens.' So the second fella says, 'I get up at seven-thirty every morning and try to move my bowels. I try and try, and nothin' happens.'" Beady took a gulp of beer, the white foam wetting his soup-strainer mustache, and set the mug on the counter behind him with a soft thud. "'How about you?' the first two old timers asked the third. 'Not so good either,' he says. 'I pee and crap every morning at eight, like clockwork.' 'What's so bad about that?' the other two asked. 'I don't get up 'till nine.'"

After a short pause, there was a lot of leg slapping and guffaws, none louder than Beady's, whose laugh came from deep down his throat.

During the story, Bill the bartender, his big belly jiggling up and down, and Brian Higgins, like a potted plant on the same stool as always, his head turned in Beady's direction, hadn't noticed Anne's arrival. "Can't a girl get any service 'round here?" she said, standing before the bar.

Beady was in the middle of another story, about a woman at the beach with her grandson. Bill and Brian looked Anne's way at the same time. Brian was too far in his cups to recognize her—or anybody else. "Hold your damn horses," he said. "Can't ya see we're enjoying some storytelling here?"

But Bill whacked his dirty dishtowel on the bar when he looked at her. "Anne Ryan! I haven't seen you in a dog's age. What can I get for ya? A loan, maybe?" He gave her a big smile, exposing a missing tooth. "Look at you." He eyed her up and down—her blue bonnet, matching dress, undamaged shoes, and new womanly figure. "Looks like ya doing pretty good for yaself."

"Can't complain."

He gave her his back, displaying suspenders that pulled the seat of his pants high above his waist, reached into a cabinet beneath the liquor bottles where he kept his longer-aged scotch, and poured her a glass. "On the house," he said, placing the drink before her. "So. Ya need a loan? Ten percent interest sound fair?"

She shook her head, her curls swinging from side to side. "No. Not a loan. A donation."

"*Donation*?" He jumped back, knocking into the bottles against the wall that clinked in response.

Everyone stopped and stared. Brian Higgins rolled his head around and squinted at Anne.

The sailor in the red bandana gave a wolf whistle and told the men, "Show the pretty lady some respect. Let's hear what this *do-nation* is all about."

"Maybe she wants to send nappies to the three old-timeys!" suggested another mariner with buck teeth in a floppy straw hat. Hearty laughter again erupted.

Beady silenced them all with a commanding hoot, smacking his hand on the table so loudly that glasses of whisky shook. "Give the lady the floor."

The guy with the bandana waved a tattooed arm in her direction, a silver-finned mermaid peeking from beneath his rolled-up shirt.

Anne's initial intent had only been to ask Bill. But who better to make her case to than these old salts, who'd no doubt planted many seeds in their day? She'd never spoken before a group, never mind a caboodle of such caliber. She stepped forward. At least her trembling knees were hidden beneath her skirt. Though she was looking down, she could feel all eyes on her. She folded her fingers together to stop them from shaking. "I'm. . .I'm Anne Ryan, for those of ya who don't know me." Her voice quavered. "I-I don't know where to begin."

"How 'bout you begin at the beginning," Oswald said.

"O.K." Anne took a deep breath. "After my da died in the Great Hunger," she began, "our landlord, Mr. Ahern, bless 'is 'art, sent ma, me, and me brother, Timmy, to America. Paid our passage, he did." She held her hand up, expecting the comments to come. "I know what you're gonna say: 'He probably didn't want to pay to bury ya.' And me answer to that is: He coulda let us rot in the fields, too. Whatever 'is reason, he saved our lives. Well, me and Timmy, anyway, and I bless him fer that. Ma died on the way over. Buried at sea, she was. I can still 'ear the splash when she was dropped inta the ocean."

A collective sigh erupted.

"So I grew up on the streets. In the summer, me and Timmy slept in alleyways. In winter, we snuck on the ferries and went back and forth, back and forth, to stay warm." Her eyes twinkled as she laughed. "We thought we were *sneakin'*. But in truth, the workers musta felt sorry for us. They always seemed to be lookin' in the other direction when we slipped past 'em so as not to pay the fare." She became animated, bending and imitating how she and her brother used to crawl under the ropes.

"We begged. Timmy did, anyway. He was younger, and, with those big doe eyes, that angelic face, and the cowlick that stuck out of the top of his head, he looked more pathetic." Her voice fell, and she studied her shoes. "I picked pockets."

"She was damn good at it, too!" one in the crowd who knew her shouted.

"I'm ashamed to say, 'tis true. And I became better and better the hungrier we got." She took a deep breath and let out a long sigh. "But even the finest are not the finest a hundred percent of the time. I got caught."

The crowded bar moaned in unison.

"But—" she held up her hand — "lo and behold, the gentleman whose purse I stole brought me and Timmy to an orphanage instead of to the police."

"Nice to know there are at least a few decent people in the world," a buck-toothed sailor called out.

"Yes. Very decent, he was. Not only did he na take us to the police or yell at us, he took us to an eating house across the street and bought us plates of ham with carrots and kidney beans and a big bowl of ice cream for dessert. Timmy had chocolate and got it all over his face." The memory forced a smile. "He was a sweet boy, was Timmy."

"How was the orphanage?" Oswald asked. "I heard some nasty stories about those places."

"At first I thought we died and gone to heaven. We were warm! First, we were scrubbed, had our heads shaved and doused with kerosene to get rid of the lice. I can still smell it." She scrunched her nose. "Like coal oil."

"Good thing nobody lit a match!" the man with the bandana said.

"Stop interuptin', will ya. Let the lady finish," Oswald barked. He motioned to Anne. "Please, continue."

"We were given new, clean clothes, and we slept in beds—with real mattresses—for the first time in our lives. Our bellies were full. At least at first. But after the first few days, every night for supper it was only thin soup and a piece of bread. . . .

"The next thing I knew, me and Timmy were on a train going God only knew where. There were about thirty of us. Not all were orphans. One of the girls, Rose was her name, was ten. Her parents were rummies. Every day we were given a lunch bag with a sandwich and an apple.

"I remember how 'ard the seats were. Timmy cried because his bum hurt, so he sat on my lap the whole trip. Other kids slept on the floor, with no pillows or blankets. The train stopped a lot. We were forever getting on and off. At each station the head mistress marched us to a church or some other meeting place, where we were looked over by people who wanted to—adopt." Her eyebrow rose. "One by one the kids were taken. Some, like my friend Rose, were taken into good, loving homes. . . Timmy was one of the first to be picked." She stopped, closed her eyes, fighting to hold back tears, which trickled from below her lids and streamed down her cheeks. There was complete silence while the men waited for her to continue. Finally, she wiped her face and continued in a broken voice, "He was cute, you know. Nobody could resist those big puppy eyes." She broke off again, remembering how the boy had screamed when his new parents pulled him away from her. "I'm sorry," she sniffled. "Other kids were taken to be servants or farm hands. I remember a girl named Molly. She was a few years older than me and had more meat on her bones. This man comes up to her, feels her arms, and says in some accent I never 'eard: 'I think you'll do. My wife is sick, and I need somebody to cook and clean'. . . . Only three were not chosen. I was one of them." Oswald brought her a glass of water, patted her on the shoulder before he went back his stool.

"What happened to Timmy? Did you ever see him again?" the bucktoothed sailor called out.

"Three years later—-April 22, it was—-I got a letter from his new family. His adopted da was a carpenter. Timmy'd been runnin' around bare-footed when he stepped on a nail. He died the next week." Her eyes misted again.

"At least at the orphanage they taught me to read and write, and to sew," she continued, more composed. "So when I was old enough to leave I was able to get a job in a millinery shop and make my own way. . . . Until I met a handsome man who promised to marry me." Another sigh. "I got pregnant. He left me. It was downhill from there. When I couldn't hide my condition any longer, my boss fired me, and my landlord threw me out.

"I 'ad no money. Even if I did, no one would rent to me. I was *one of those girls*. It was back to the streets, sleeping in alleyways, in flop houses full a opium smokers and drunks. . . . But don't feel sorry for me. It was me own fault. Feel sorry for the innocent girls who are attacked or forced under threats a losin' their jobs, and suffer the same consequences and worse."

Without mentioning her near abortion, she talked about the young girl Anne suspected had been raped by her father, and of the women in abusive marriages who had no escape. She told them about the Magdeline Homes for Unwed Mothers, and how they treated the victimized as if they were prostitutes. She went on about Julia, and the terrible predicament she and other young girls faced.

"So—" she let out a deep breath, hardly aware that she'd been talking to a rapt audience for half an hour— "I've decided to start my own charity to help them. I want to open' a house where they'll be safe until they can get back on their feet. I know what you're thinking: 'Tis a big, silly dream. But I believe dreams can come true."

There was complete silence when she finished. Then, one by one, the men began to clap. "Dig in your pockets, boys! We're all guilty," Oswald admitted. Before she knew it, her purse was clicking with silver coins and green backs.

As she was leaving, Brian Higgins came out of his stupor and called out to her. "Annie Ryan? Is that you?"

"In the flesh."

"Well, blow me down, I ain't seen you in forever. You're looking a lot—" like Bill, he looked her up and down— "a lot classier than the last time I seen ya."

She studied him as well. "And you're lookin'—and smellin'—*mankier* than ever." She waved her hand in front of her face.

"If it's Joe you're here to see, he don't come here no more. Ever since he got married. They have their own drinking hole down by the ports. A fancy place. Called the *Tumble Inn* They serve lunch and all."

"Brian, what in God's name are you yappin' about?" she said. "All that piss water you been drinkin' finally affected your brain."

"It's true, Anne," Bill cut in. "He got married."

Anne stared at him.

"Sorry to have to tell ya. That ya have to find out like this." The bartender gave Brian a dirty look.

"But. . .he was already married," Anne said.

"Oh, ya know about the wife he left in the old country, do ya? Yeah," Brain said. "He was—" he made an obscene gesture—"you know, with his wife's cousin. He was run outta town."

"MARIE! MARIE!" ANNE SHOUTED as she burst through the door.

Julia hurried to the vestibule to meet her. "Is something wrong, Miss Anne?" The pregnant girl was dressed for bed. Her hair was down, and she was in the midst of plaiting it for the night.

"Everything is *wonderful.* She's in bed?"

Julia nodded as Anne hastened through the apartment, passing her sleeping daughter in their bed, to her friend's room with its flowered wallpaper. "Marie!" She shook her shoulder. "Marie, wake up. I have things to tell ya!"

CHAPTER 49

SYLVIA WAS LYING ON HER SIDE facing the wall, her honey brown hair splayed on a goose down pillow. It was a pleasant spring night. The window was open, and the beads on the taffeta curtains were clacking ever so slightly in the breeze. Light from an oil lamp was turning the greens and reds of the wallpaper into different shades of gray.

She'd kicked off the top sheet. Her chemise was twisted around her waist, and her full, curvaceous hips and long legs were uncovered. Joe inhaled her gardenia smell, gazed at the rise and fall of her shoulders, and stared at her lovely round bottom and polished toes. He wanted to kiss those feet, suck every toe, lick her all over, make love to her—even if he had to use a French safe that he hated but she demanded. But he dared not disturb her. She'd be furious.

The bed springs squeaked when, bathed, shaved, and doused in cologne, he slid between the satin sheets. She had insisted on his nightly toilette. He stank like their customers, she'd complain. He'd remind her that they didn't run a flower shop. She and her dead husband, not he, had bought the dive on the East River, which catered to piss-smelling drunks. She would say it didn't matter. The bar made good money. And if he wanted to live with her in her lovely apartment above the tavern, he couldn't smell like their pungent patrons. Neither would she tolerate his stubble on her delicate skin. She spent outrageous amounts of money on perfumes, scented powders, lotions, and "miracle cures" to ward off future wrinkles, and she wasn't about to let his whiskers scratch her face.

They'd been married a year. One year after her mourning period. He could hardly remember the last time they made love—-or, for that matter, had a *conversation*. She would be in bed by eleven, up by eight, and out of the house by nine. After closing and cleaning the bar, it would be past three, and he didn't get to bed before four. Then he was up at ten and back to work by noon. Fifteen hours a day. Seven days a week. Day after day. Week after week. Month after month.

They'd met two years before. Her husband had just died. Desperate for a bartender-manager-bookkeeper to replace him, she'd put ads in the *New York Times* and *New York Gazette*. But with most able-bodied men fighting in the war, the pickings were slim. Four of the six men who'd responded had not met her standards. Two were disabled veterans with missing limbs, one a Bowery bum, the other intoxicated. The two men she did approve of had refused to work for the miserly wage she offered, the long hours, and the multiple responsibilities, which consisted not only of pouring drinks, but providing security, and janitorial work.

Two weeks later, she'd walked into Paddy O'Halloran's bar. It had been a typical Manhattan summer day: hot, humid, and stinking of garbage. The door and windows had been opened to let in some air. She'd stood in the entranceway looking in. Brian Higgins had been sitting at the counter, hunched over his drink, Bill busy dusting the liquor bottles. With circles of sweat staining the underarms of his shirt, and his short, stumpy legs resting on the rung of the stool, Brian resembled a glassy-eyed troll. And Bill, having gained weight and balding, had not been much to look at either. Joe, on the other hand, fit and handsome in a clean, fashionable outfit, caught her attention.

Bill had dropped the dishrag on the wooden bar when he saw her. "Can I help you?" He couldn't imagine what a classy lady could possibly be doing there. She'd been wearing a silk mourning dress, a net veil, had her hair puffed atop her head with ringlets falling on her forehead, and carrying a parasol. Even in her bereavement attire, it was obvious she had a voluptuous figure: a tiny waist; generous, firm breasts; perfect-sized hips; and when she lifted her hem so as not to dirty her clothes on the sticky floor, they saw that her ankles were equally pleasing.

Holding a perfumed handkerchief to her nose, she'd approached Joe. ". . .I need someone to run my establishment. Would you be interested?"

Joe's glass met the counter with a thud. He'd listened to her soft voice and beheld those full, red lips. "When do you want me to start?"

The Tumble Inn was more lavish than Paddy's place. It had ten tables with padded chairs, pictures of pastoral scenes hanging on paneled walls, a fancy tin ceiling, green glass sconces, and gas lamps.

Customers were already waiting outside, lying on the sidewalk beneath the wooden sign, when he opened the metal gates. "Morning," he said as red-faced, red-nosed men reeking of alcohol, still drunk from the night before, stumbled to their regular stools at the oaken bar that ran the length of the room. One whiskey and one gin had already been poured and were ready for them. Two more customers came in behind them and dropped six cents each on the counter. The coins tinkled as they bounced on the wood. They ordered drinks and took seats near the billiard table. One had a walrus mustache and more hair in his ears than on his head. The other walked with a limp.

After Joe served them, he went into the kitchen behind the counter to fill several bowls with peanuts—adding extra salt to the already salty appetizer—which he would place along the bar, and to prepare the lunch of cold meats, pickled fish, crackers, and rye bread that would be free with two nickel beers. Of all the chores he handled (and he hated them all), he hated guarding the buffet the most. When the place got busy, it was nearly impossible to remember who had paid for liquor—and was thus entitled to the food—and who was eating for free. He'd gotten into many skirmishes and had black eyes, and an aching back, to prove it.

He heard Sylvia before he saw her. She was wearing another new dress. Her full-tiered skirt swished as she entered. She was holding a mortar filled with hot beeswax and yellow pigment. Twice a day she came down: in the morning, to mark the level of the liquor in the bottles; and at night to take the money out of the till and mark what was left on the bottles. "To calculate the number of drinks sold," she'd told him. But he knew she was checking on *him*— not only that he wasn't drinking, one more thing she would not tolerate, but that the take was correct, and he wasn't stealing. They were married, yet she kept control of the purse strings and made it known that the bar belonged to *her,* not *them*. "Find everything to your satisfaction?" he asked, folding his arms across his chest as she painted a whiskey bottle.

"Impeccable."

"I'm *so* pleased."

"I'm sure you are. A German freighter docked this morning. Do we have enough beer?" She swatted at a fly below the chignon at the nape of her neck.

"We have five full barrels. I already checked."

"And mugs?"

"Washed, dried, and ready to go." He drew her attention to the tankards lined up against the mirrored wall behind the counter. He avoided looking at his reflection. His hair seemed to be thinning by the hour. Each time he noticed, it reminded him of the toll the bartending was taking. His feet hurt. His back ached. These fifteen-hour days were killing him. Or was it his wife? He hated her. She was such a bitch. . . . And yet. "Is there anything else you'd have me do?"

"Don't be sarcastic."

"*Me? Sarcastic?*"

"Just make sure everything is ready." She turned on her heel and headed for the stairs, her new shoes clacking on the wooden planks. He watched her go, her beautiful ass swinging from side to side. It was all Shula's fault, that whore, he thought not for the first time. If she hadn't gotten herself pregnant, he would never have met Sylvia, and he'd be living a charmed life.

"Yes, your highness. Will do." He gave her a salute.

"I heard that!"

There was a sound of snickering from the men at the table.

"I'm going out for a while," she said, her back to him.

"Looking for help?" He raised his eyebrows. "Oh, no. Of course not. How stupid of me. We can't afford an extra bartender or cook or janitor or bouncer. You have too many dresses you need to buy."

She disappeared into their apartment, the door slamming behind her.

"I need a refill over here," the hairy-eared patron called out.

"Make that two," the fellow sitting beside him added.

Still grimacing, Joe poured the liquor, adding an extra jigger for spite, and brought them to the table.

"Hey, Bud," the mustached man said, "you allow that lady boss to treat you like that? I mean, I know she's a looker, and I know jobs are hard to come by these days what with the war over and so many men out of work, but no man should take that abuse."

"She's my *wife*."

"I'm sorry to hear that," the other man said, swishing the gin around the glass and then taking a healthy gulp.

"Well, like I said, she *is* a looker," the one with the mustache repeated.

"My ma used to tell me, 'Beauty is only skin deep,'" the other added.

Joe took the empty glasses away. "My mother told me the same thing. I should have listened."

THE TUMBLE INN WAS ONE OF MANY SALOONS set among dance halls, warehouses and factories facing the East River. And with two ships having docked that morning—the German freighter and a vessel from the West Indies—the pier was bustling with activity and noise, the air thick with the smell of salt and fish. Marie removed her shawl and opened the top two buttons of her dress. It had been cool when she and Anne started out that morning. But, Manhattan, with so much cement and so few trees, was much warmer than Brooklyn. Amidst whistles, stevedores shouting, and music blaring from the dance halls into the streets, they could hardly hear themselves talk. "Let me get this straight," Marie shouted over the clamor. "He has a wife across the ocean, and a wife who owns a bar. He's Marigold's father, and he left you for me. You worked for my mother—who fired you when she realized you were pregnant *and* didn't give you your pay. Do I have that right?"

"And don't forget about the one he got pregnant in the old country," Anne said, ducking beneath a groaning crane that was swinging a crate from ship to shore.

Marie stopped in mid-stride and shook her head as if to clear it. Anne stared at the barrels of sugar and molasses that lined the pavement, looked at the strong-muscled men moving boxes into warehouses.

"*Watch out*!" someone screamed.

They looked up. Above them, not more than a few feet away, a wooden crate was hanging precariously on a loosening rope. As Marie stood paralyzed, mesmerized by the groaning chain, Anne yanked her aside a moment before it crashed to the ground, bursting apart, its bottles of molasses shattering and sending glass in every direction.

The crane operator scrambled down from his machine and hurried to them, work boots making a sucking sound on the slick ground. His shirt was open, and his sleeves were rolled up. "Y'aright? Phew." He wiped the sweat that dripped from beneath his headband across his arm. "That was a close call." He seemed more shaken than Marie, who, staring at the sickeningly sweet goo that had spattered upon her skirt and shoes, appeared to be in a trance. When she came to, she began to tremble.

AND SHE WAS STILL TREMBLING when they reached the Tumble Inn. "I. . .I don't think this is a good idea." She stopped dead in her tracks and refused to move.

"Come on."

"I can't. I can't see him. What do I do? What do I say? Let's just forget it. What's the point?"

Anne huffed. "You don't 'ave ta say or do nothin'. Just follow me. Come on." And with that, she grabbed Marie's hand, pushed the heavy door open, and dragged her inside.

It was dimmer than outside and reeked from tobacco and beer.

Mumbled conversations, and the click of billiard balls, were the only sounds. The bar had been filling up since it opened earlier. Most of the tables were taken. Everyone paused and stared when the women came in. Two sailors shooting pool, one with his hair slick against his head, the other with his tied at his neck, put their cues down and followed them with their eyes. It was obvious they were not floozies who generally haunted saloons, as neither wore make-up and they were modestly clothed, the redhead in a blue voile dress with eyelet trim, the other in a school-marm dark skirt and white button-down blouse. The prettier of the pair exuded confidence, walking tall and straight: the one behind kept her gaze at her feet, stepping gingerly as though the floor was unstable beneath her.

They spotted Joe bringing drinks to a table near the bar. He had a dishtowel over his shoulder and was carrying a tray of drinks. They didn't recognize him at first. He had put on weight, had the beginning of a paunch, and walked with a lumbering gait, as if he had bunions or hemorrhoids, or both.

"Hello, Joe," Anne said in a sugary voice. "You remember us, don't ya?" She pulled Marie forward. "Your wife? Mind if we take a seat?" They sat.

They watched the color drain from his face. The tray slipped from his hands, clanging against the floor, leaving puddles of beer and broken glass at his feet.

"Y'aright, bud?" The hairy-eared customer ran over from his table a row away and pulled out a chair, which screeched against the floor. "Here. Sit down before you fall. You look like ya seen a ghost."

"Make that two ghosts," the man with the limp said watching Joe stare at the two women.

Just then, the door flew open, daylight pouring into the tavern, and a gang of boisterous sailors poured in and hightailed it to the bar.

"Hey!" one of them barked, banging the counter, as the others shouted in German. "Doesn't anybody work here?" Before Joe had time to gather his wits and respond, Silvia came down to see what was going on. She spotted her husband sitting at a table with the patrons. Hands on her hips and her face set in a scowl, she stomped over. Anne, pulling Marie behind her, moved to her side.

"You must be Joe's wife." Anne smiled at Silvia. "Meet Marie." Anne pointed to her friend, who smiled weakly. "She's Joe's wife, too. His *second*. His *first* one is in Europe.

That night, Joe slept on the park bench.

CHAPTER 50

I WISH YOU WOULDN'T LOOK AT ME the way you do," Marie said to Julia, who, not having looked at her at all, was sitting on the sofa beside Anne and Marigold, letting out the seams of her dress. It was a rainy autumn evening. A fire in the Franklin stove was warming the room, but despite rolled towels tucked around the sills, strong winds still make their way around the window frames. The sound of fog horns and snapping tree limbs penetrated the apartment. Marie stared out at the tumbling leaves, her glum reflection staring back at her.

"What way?" Julia asked.

"Like I'm a criminal."

Julia dropped the garment to her lap, pulled her scarf tighter around her shoulders, and raised her eyes. "I know it's not your fault that I have to go, Miss Marie. I'm grateful for all you've done, letting me stay as long as you have."

"I'm sorry. I'm just. . .edgy."

"That you are," Anne said, mending a sock in the dim light of the table lamp. A log crackled and hissed in the stove behind them. The smell of pine sweetened the room. She wanted to shake her friend out of that melancholy: to shout, *Get past it. Move on. Make peace with your life!* But she held her tongue.

Marie's mood had brightened when she learned she wasn't legally married. But then she'd begun to focus on how she'd been bamboozled, how stupid and gullible she was. Then there was the concern about her father. Lizzy had been coming less frequently. He hadn't always remembered too send her allowance. Lizzy would have to remind him. "'He's drinkin' so much nowadays he's losing his marbles, he is. Hardly knows what day it tis, never mind your money. Won't be long afore he's completely doddered," Lizzy had told her. And the icing on the cake: After finally getting the courage to write to Walter, the letter had come back return to sender.

"I *hate* having Julia leave," Marie said. "I really do. But it can't be put off any longer. She's showing."

"'Tis getting cool," Anne said. "When Julia goes out, a shawl can hide—"

"A *tent* can't mask that belly." Marie snapped at her friend. She took a deep breath. "When I think of you leaving too. . .and being alone—"

Anne raised her eyebrows. "Who said anythin' about puttin' her out and me leavin'?"

"You agreed—"

"Yes. I did. And I stick to me promise. But who says I'll not be startin' the charity? I've raised a fair amount of money, I 'ave."

"Not nearly enough." Marie cleared her throat. "You've been to every saloon around, twice over. It's getting to the point where they lock their doors when they see you coming."

"True. But saloons are not the only place to approach, are they? 'Ave faith, Marie. Tomorrow is another day."

The next morning at 7:00 a.m., Anne threw her cape over her shoulders, pulled her hood up, wrapped a woolen scarf around her neck, and left the house. It was barely light and early morning cold. A clean, damp earth smell filled the air. The storm had ended sometime during the night, leaving downed trees, dangling telegraph wires, and lake-sized puddles. She carefully stepped over an oak branch that blocked her path.

She didn't know where she was going. But in order not to worry Marie and Julia more than they already were, she needed to put on a happy face and appear confident. In truth, she'd lost hope.

She sighed.

Maybe Father Maloney could help, she thought. Her view of the convent and the nuns hadn't changed. But he seemed like a nice man, she reasoned. She'd never heard him yell at the children who didn't sit still during mass. Perhaps he could make a collection for her. Or if worse came to worse, maybe he knew of a family who would take Julia in.

Saint Aldan's was a small stucco church with a sloping roof, wide pine doors and steep cement steps. After stopping at the font in the vestibule to cross herself with holy water and genuflecting before the altar, where a life-size crucified Christ hung from a vaulted ceiling, she slid onto a wooden pew in the last row. Muted light filtered through stained-glass windows, and the alcoves, where statues of Saint Patrick and the Virgin Mary stood, were aglow with flickering votive candles. A line of women, heads covered in shawls and kerchiefs, was waiting to have their confessions heard. Anne's back had been turned to the confessional, and though she could only hear mumbling, she knew when someone started and ended by the creaking of knees and the soft thud of the screen opening and closing. A young woman kneeling a few rows in front of her must have had some hefty sins to report, because her rosery beads were rapidly clicking. Usually only a few Hail Marys and Our Fathers were doled out for the transgressions of the week.

When Anne heard the purple-curtained door open and saw Father Mahoney emerge, she approached him. He was middle-aged and well fed. A smell of incense and burning candle wax were not enough to drown the odor of wine on his breath. "Ah, Anne," he'd said, all smiles. "Yer needin' to give yer confession, are ya?"

"No, Father. I was hopin' you could help me." She told the white-haired pastor about Julia's predicament and her own hope to start a charity.

Before she got her last words out, his smile turned to a grimace, and he glared at her with clear loathing. "She must a done something to encourage the gentleman," he'd said in his thick Irish brogue, wagging a stubby finger in her face. "Don't you be expectin' help from me, now, or from the decent, God-fearin' people of this congregation. If you're so interested in helpin' the downtrodden, help the poor boys back from the war without their legs." And with the same stubby finger he showed her the door.

Despite that reception, she continued to appeal to all the Catholic churches in Manhattan and Brooklyn. There weren't many. And most were poor and Irish. At each one she got the same negative response.

She stood at the end of her walkway for a long time, her shoes wet and muddy from the soggy earth, not having the heart to go inside empty handed. Finally she did.

Julia and Marie looked at her expectantly when she walked through the door. Though Anne tried to smile, she could not hide her defeat. "Tomorrow is another day."

That night she prayed to St. Bridgit for guidance.

Try the Protestant churches, a voice in her head said as she opened her eyes the next morning.

There seemed to be a Protestant church on every corner: Methodist, Presbyterian, Episcopalian, Baptist. She'd never realized there were so many sects.

By five o'clock, she'd visited a dozen of them. She might as well have spent her day drinking coffee for what she accomplished, which was absolutely nothing. Saint Bridget didn't know what she was talking about. No more priests, ministers, or parishioners, Anne promised herself. It was time to face the facts. She wasn't able to do anything. Julia had to go.

Sauntering down an unpaved, tree-line street, deep in thought, about as discouraged as she'd ever been, she came upon a crowd dressed in their finest, greeting each other as they entered the Plymouth Congregational Church. *Another denomination*, she scoffed. *How many were there? . . . Plymouth Church. Plymouth Church. Why did that sound so familiar?* She was weary. Her nose was red, her legs hurt, and her fingers were numb inside her woolen gloves. *Why not go in? Sit awhile*, she told herself. *Get warm. Just sit in the back and mind your own business.* So she followed the group inside.

She'd never been inside a protestant church before that day. They'd all looked the same: clean and simple, sterile by comparison to Catholic churches. But this one was different from the rest.

This was more like a theater. Instead of a pulpit, it had a curved stage. The pews and a balcony were arranged in a semi-circle. It was packed and smelled of cologne, perfume, and powder. Sliding into a pew, she was tapped on the shoulder and told that the congregants rented their seats. Apologizing, she slipped out of the row and headed toward the door. But as she made her way to the exit, she felt another tap on the shoulder. A short, stout, clean-shaven man wearing loose fitting pants, whose wavy hair reached his shoulder, opened a folding chair. "You're new to our congregation," he said in a rich, well-articulated voice. "Welcome."

"Thank you."

"May I be so bold as to ask what brings you to our flock?"

Anne groaned. "I'm cold and tired, my feet 'urt, and I needed to sit and warm up, if you must know the truth. I saw the *flock* enterin,' and I followed."

"Ah!" he laughed. He wasn't handsome, but neither was he homely. It was unusual to see a man without a beard or muttonchops. "The truth is always good."

"Is it?" She raised an eyebrow.

"So tell me. What makes you so tired?"

"Do you have a week to listen?"

He pulled the portable seat closer to a pew and sat beside her. "I have as long as it takes."

A half-hour had passed by the time Anne finished, and during that time she realized that, while there was no sign of restlessness as people were conversing among themselves, the service had not yet begun. "I'm so sorry. I don't know what got into me to be chewin' yer ears off like that, and a perfect stranger to boot."

"No worries. It's good to talk sometimes. . . . And it's good to listen. Thank *you*." He bowed.

She smiled, feeling her cheeks flush. "I feel better now. I've warmed up." She put her arm through her purse straps and began to rise. "I'm sure the sermon will start any minute, and I've heard enough good Christian drivel for a day. Thank you for the seat."

"Don't go yet," the man said, folding his chair as he stood. "Please. It might not be as bad as you suspect."

Anne watched the long-haired man march up the aisle, stopping here and there to greet folks and shake hands, until he took the stage, faced the congregation, and raised his arms.

"Good evening and welcome!" he began in a deep, projecting voice.

"Good evening, Reverend Beecher!" the congregants called back.

Anne's hand flew to her mouth. *Oh, my God! I've just told my life story to the famous Henry Beecher. That's why the Plymouth Church sounded familiar! The abolitionist stronghold!*

"I take it you are all well and have not experienced much damage from the recent storm," he addressed his audience. The crowd assured him all was well.

Anne sat mesmerized. In all the houses of worship she'd been in, Catholic and Protestant, she'd never seen or heard members participate.

"It appears we have become a Veteran's City," he began. "Thousands of our boys in blue, from all over the Union, are looking for work—"

"And picking pockets!" a male voice exclaimed, and was answered with a few "Aye, Ayes!"

"True it is, my friends," the Reverend admitted. "But we must remember it was their sacrifice that freed our brothers and sisters. And now these brave souls can't find employment."

"Yes. That's also true," came another voice from the parishioners.

"It is our responsibility as good Christians to do our part. . ."

From there Beecher went on to the unacceptable conditions of their colored brethren, and he asked them to put their hands in their pockets. Coins could be heard jingling from every direction. He stamped his feet, marched up and down the stage, stopped several times to sip from a glass of water. And after what seemed to Anne like hours, he said, "And now, Ladies and Gentlemen, we have another sickness in our city. Yes, another. Maybe not as conspicuous as our disabled veterans lying all over the streets—"

"And picking our pockets!" came from the same gentleman as before.

"Yes. And picking our pockets," the reverend agreed. "Or the poor Negroes, who suffer indignities every day."

"Aye, aye!"

"But another sickness, no less tragic, that is in need of our attention.

"Anne Ryan! Please. Will you come up here and tell our people about the plight of the young women?"

Anne looked behind her, to her right and to her left.

"Yes. You." He motioned her forward.

She felt every eye on her. The pew creaked as she rose. Leaving her cape, shawl, and purse behind, she crept up the aisle, keeping her head down.

"Come on. Come on up." He motioned again. "No one here bites."

Laughter erupted. "Come on, Annie. Don't be shy," someone said. One person clapped, then another and another, and as she reached the front, all the people were cheering her on, some whistling and encouraging her to speak.

"What do I say? Where do I begin?" she asked the reverend, who stood beside her.

"Say exactly what you told me. Begin at the beginning." Turning to his audience, he raised his arms, and shouted: "Let us give our sister our full attention." He pumped his arms up and down. "Hold your applause till the end."

The hall quieted.

Anne felt her heart thumping inside her chest. Somehow this was harder than talking to a barroom full of drunks. "My name is Anne

Ryan, as you already know," she began. "I came upon a fourteen-year-old, an Irish lass, come here to work so she could send her pay back home to her ma. Worked as a servant, she did, for a well-ta-do family. Well, she was. . .violated by 'er boss. And when the poor thing found herself to be pregnant, 'e discharged her. Right then, on the spot. Didna even give 'er time ta get her belongings. Didna give her 'er pay. Didna even give her references for a new job. Told 'er, if she said a thing, he would accuse her a stealin' 'is wife's pearls and have 'er arrested."

"The dirty swine!" a woman's voice called out.

"A dirty swine 'e is indeed, Madam. A *bloody* swine. So now the child has no money, no place ta go, and can't get a job. . ."

There was complete silence until she finished. Then, one by one a clap, until the whole audience was standing. People surrounded her, shaking her hand, giving her money, telling her of other girls they knew. A bespectacled man, standing on the fringes, came up to her when those around her left. He was tall and thin, and walked with a limp. "Hello, Miss Ryan. It's a honor to meet you. I was impressed with your story. I think I can help."

"Really?"

"Yes. I'm a lawyer, you see. I can take care of the legalities—"

"I'm afraid I don't 'ave enough money for legal fees."

"No, no." His dark hair, plastered down with macassar oil, didn't move when he shook his head, but the scent of coconut seemed to spread with the motion. "You don't understand me. It's free of charge. I have two offices, one on Broadway, where I practice real estate law, and one in the basement of this church, where I work with those who can't afford to pay. It also happens that my father owns several buildings, and I'd be happy to work something out." He handed her his card.

Anne looked at him, looked back at the card, and looked at him again.

"Is something wrong?"

"Walter Hockenberry? Marie *Gilbert's* Walter Hockenberry?"

His eyes widened. ". . .You know *Marie*?"

"I do. She took me in when I had no place to go."

"I always knew she was a good woman." He cleared his throat. "Well, come see me about your charity. I'm here every evening from six to eight." After giving her a small bow, he turned to leave.

"You work all day and every evening. What. . .what does your wife have to say about that?"

"I'm not married," he said over his shoulder. "Give my best regards to Marie."

"Why not give them to her yourself?" she called after him.

He stopped, turned to face her. "She doesn't want to see me." He smiled timidly and tapped his shin. Anne heard the *thunk*. "Who would want to see half a man?"

"*She* would."

"Then why didn't she tell me?"

"She did. She thinks you're dead."

CHAPTER 51

JULIA SLID ONE DRESS AGAINST ANOTHER inside the armoire as, in exasperation, asked Marie whether she had anything *pretty* to wear. Marie frowned. "What's wrong with what I have?"

"You mean with these Mother Hubbard clothes?"

"And what's all the fuss, anyway?" Marie went on. "We're only going for a walk."

Anne let out a deep breath from behind Marie, where she was fixing her hair. The drapes had been pushed aside, and the silver backed brush sparkled in the bright morning sunlight. Though the few drops of vegetable oil and lemon juice Anne had rubbed into the tendrils earlier gave it a glossier texture, her friend's hair remained brittle. Anne took scissors from her pocket and snipped off the split-ends, which fell on Marie's shoulders. "The fuss, Marie love," Anne continued, "if you don't mind me saying so, is that ya been moping around the house every day, not takin' care a yaself. It's time to spruce up. 'The better ya look, the better ya feel,' Ma always said."

"Ouch!" Marie jerked her head forward. "Do you have to pull

so hard?"

"*Mama*!" Marigold called from where she was sitting cross-legged on the bed, scribbling.

"I'm sorry, sweetheart." Anne said, putting less pressure on the brush. "You know I would never hurt Aunt Marie. I'm trying to get the tangles out."

"Those are all fine garments," Marie said.

"Just because they cost a fortune don't make 'em less frowzy," Julia answered.

"Don't give me ringlets. I hate ringlets," Marie warned Anne as she felt fingers twirl her locks into curls. "Pull it into a bun."

Julia faced them with a garment in each hand. From the back, no one could tell she was expecting, but when she turned around, they could see the little belly beneath her apron. Brown patches on her forehead and cheeks, which she'd developed soon after conception, were getting more pronounced. "Which one? The blue, or the maroon?"

Anne grunted. "In one she'll look like a Quaker, and in the other a schoolmarm. Really, Marie, ya need a new wardrobe."

"*You're* telling *me* to spend money? That's funny."

"Maybe if we add a collar," Julia suggested. "And if she insists on wearing a bun, we can wrap it in a lace net."

"I guess it will have to do." The words came out jumbled past the hair pins between Anne's teeth. "It's not like we have much choice. She's so stubborn."

Once Marie was dressed, Julia sprayed her with lilac-scented toilet water.

"Why the perfume?"

"You don't want to smell like a salad, do ya?" Julia pointed at Marie's head.

"All this bother for a stroll. You'd think I was going to meet Ulysses S Grant."

"One never knows who one might meet." Anne smiled. Julia turned around to hide her giggling.

Anne was helping Marie secure the lace collar to the schoolmarm dress when they heard a knock at the door.

"I'll get it!" Julia rushed out of the room.

"Lizzy," Marie said. "Thank God. It's been weeks. I've been worried sick about Father. I'll be out in a minute, just have to stop in the washroom, to get some of this rouge off my face."

Julia pointed to the sofa. "Have a seat." She smiled and curtsied. "She'll be right with ya. I'll take that if you like and put it in a vase." She extended her hand.

"Careful," the guest said, ceding the bouquet. "Don't prick yourself with the thorns." He sat, rested his top hat and a wrapped package on the end table, and unwound his muffler. A fire in the stove was warming the parlor. Fingers trembling, he wiped perspiration from his forehead with a handkerchief he pulled from a coat pocket.

"He's exactly as you described," Julia whispered to Anne on the way back to the bedroom. "He's wearing a beautiful suit with a cashmere vest. And he brought a dozen roses."

"Marie," Anne called, "we'll meet you downstairs. Come on, Marigold." With their shoes clicking, their skirts swishing, and little Marigold running behind them, the two hurried off.

"Wait for me!" Marie called back. "I'll only be a minute!" But the door had already closed. "What's the big rush?" she was mumbling as she entered the parlor.

The man rose when he heard her voice, pressed the nonexistent wrinkles from his trousers, and patted his already patted-down hair. "Hello, Marie." He smiled timidly.

She stopped in mid-stride and leaned against the piano for fear she might faint. ". . . *Walter?*"

"I-I brought you chocolate-covered almonds. I remember they were your favorite." He studied his freshly polished shoes as he held the box out, careful not to crush the red bow.

"I-I thought you were. . .dead." Tears rolled down her cheeks. ". . .I sent you a letter. It came back. . ."

"When I didn't hear from you after I wrote, I assumed you didn't want to see me." He looked down at his wooden leg.

"Oh, Walter. I wouldn't care if you were paralyzed, God forbid. It's you who shouldn't want *me*—" her voice fell— "after what I did." Her shoulders began to shake. She covered her face with her hands and started to sob. "I'm so ashamed. How could you ever forgive me?"

"I love you."

"I'm not the same girl you knew. I have. . .a past."

"It doesn't matter."

"But you don't know—"

"I don't care." He came closer, inhaling her scent, took her hand in his, and brought it to his lips. "I love you, Marie."

THEY WERE MARRIED BY REVEREND BEECHER at the Plymouth Church. It was a quiet service, with Walter dressed in a plain suit, Marie in a simple woolen dress. Anne and Marigold threw rice. Julia hadn't attended. She'd given birth only two weeks before, and Mrs. O'Mara, the resident mid-wife at Anne's *Dare to Hope House,* old enough to remember the cholera and typhus in Ireland, hadn't thought it wise for the infant to be out before she was baptized.

The charity did well. No sooner had the welcome sign been put out than a line of desperate girls appeared on the doorstep. The three-bedroom apartment Walter had leased to Anne, at a ridiculously low rent, was already too small.

Aside from providing legal assistance and the residence, Walter had held fundraisers and assembled an army of volunteers. Anne was proving herself a competent manager. She ran the charity like a family. Once the mothers were well enough, they went to work, giving some of their pay to the household. Those still pregnant, and new moms, cared for the children, cooked, and did the chores. They were welcome to stay until they could function on their own.

It had begun to sleet while the newlyweds were inside, so they huddled beneath the doorway, waiting for it to stop. With the sky gray as far as they could see, that didn't seem likely anytime soon. They heard the hail crackling as it bounced on the pavement. They watched people slipping on the walkway, being pushed forward and back by a cold wind. Walter shielded his wife from the flying ice with his body. They were cold, wet, and feeling the sting of the needle-like rain, but happier than they'd ever been.

JOE RUBIN DIDN'T KNOW IT WAS SLEETING. His bed at Bellevue wasn't near a window. "*Sylvia!*" he screamed for the hundredth time.

And for the hundredth time, the inebriated so-called nurse took a mouthful of whiskey from the flask she hid inside a paper bag and shouted for him to shut his pie hole.

"I'll pay ya a buck if ya knock his teeth out, Sammy," Joe's neighbor, Benny, said.

But Sammy couldn't knock out Joe's teeth any more than the neighbor could pay him. Sammy was a double amputee, and Benny didn't have two coins to rub together.

"*Sylviaaaaa*!" Joe continued to call until his throat was sore.

"She ain't coming to pick ya up, ya damn fool!" The nurse left her seat at the back of the room and came hobbling toward them. She had a club foot and swayed from side to side, the keys around her neck jingling. "You know why? Because she threw ya out. And then, after getting' yaself cock-eyed drunk, ya stumbled into the street and got yaself run over by a wagon. Now both ya legs are crushed. Yer nothing but a flea-bag cripple. She don't want ya. Ya never gonna walk again. Ya ain't never gonna leave this bed. If ya want my opinion, here it is: This is home now, me lad. Until ya drop dead, which if ya keep screaming, will be sooner than later.

EPILOGUE

LEAH TUCKED A BLANKET AROUND LENA'S LEGS. It was a beautiful spring morning—-a blue sky, cotton ball clouds, and chirping birds. Though the sun was warm, Lena felt cold. Time and grief had aged her. Her joints creaked with every movement. Her hands trembled involuntarily. Wrinkles and liver spots marred her once pretty face, and her thinning hair was more silver than blonde. She patted her granddaughter's belly and smiled. Five months along with her third child, Leah was just starting to show.

"He's a fine boy," she said, watching Lena watch her son, who, playing hide-and-seek with his sister, Honey, was squatting behind a tree.

Lena raised her hand, about to speak, but Leah nodded and said what she knew the old lady was about to. "I watch him closely, Bubbe, and I make sure we read with him, so he'll be at the top of his class. Don't worry." She squeezed her grandmother's knee affectionately, feeling the bones through the homespun wool.

Ezra seemed to know they were talking about him, and he raised his head and gave them a smile that lit up his face. His teeth were white and straight, and his blue eyes—-though not as sparkling as his grandfather's—twinkled. Even at five, it was clear he was going to be a charmer.

"He's a handsome boy," Lena said.

Leah knew that what she meant was: Sometimes it's dangerous to be too handsome.

"He is, Bubbe," she said with pride. "But like I said, he's a good boy."

"It's hard to believe." Shula grinned beneath the cloth she'd wrapped around her face to lessen the odor of rendered animal fat. They'd moved their gear from the barn, where they usually worked, to outside to enjoy the lovely day.

With Shula's help, Rachel had enlarged her enterprise to include scented and herbal soaps and candle-making. Over the years, this had evolved into a full-time job, and, since her father's passing ten years earlier, the heart of the family's income. Today they were working on long-tipped tapered candles, the most popular item in the inventory. Shula dipped a bundle of wicks in and out of the vat of hot tallow while Rachel cut blocks of herbal soaps, made the week before, and placed the bars in a basket that still smelled of elderberry from the previous batch.

Rachel was wearing a light shawl, but Shula, in a sweat, had her sleeves rolled up and the top two buttons of her dress open. Her hair was damp beneath her kerchief. Beads of perspiration glistened above her lip and between her breasts. Aside from a fuller figure, she hadn't changed much since coming to live with the Rubinowitzes. She still plaited her hair, though, no longer a maiden yet never married, instead of hanging her locks down her back, she wrapped them around her head. Rachel still wore hers in a knot behind her head and hadn't gained an once. Shula wiped her face with the back of her arm.

"Look at them." Shula nudged her chin in her daughter's direction, where she had pulled up a chair beside her grandmother and was holding her hand. "If anyone had told me that she and your mother would come to love each other so, I wouldn't have believed it. With all the work that girl-girl! She'll be twenty-five. Can you believe it?" She shook her head. "All the work she has in her own house, yet she packs up the children and comes here every day because your mother loves to see them."

"Even harder to believe is you and Mother."

"I try to forget those first few months."

"How could anyone forget? It was a tough time with my mother not talking to you until the baby was born, sitting Shiva for Yussel, your uncle Mordechai threatening my father." Rachel let out a deep breath. "What's important is that it turned out well."

"Yes," Shula agreed. But did it? she wondered. It did for me and Leah. But for the rest of them? It hadn't taken long for Lena's heart to soften. That was true. She'd adored her granddaughter from the moment of her birth. And Shula herself, a hard worker, taking over many of the household chores, proved to be an asset. But for the family, the Rabinowitzes? The disgrace she brought them? Moishe, a prince among men, had not allowed a disparaging word to be spoken against her, holding his head high when his neighbors tsk-tsked about his "situation," didn't hesitate to tell them that he and his family had nothing to be ashamed of, that, in fact, they'd been blessed with beautiful new children. But he'd had to resume tailoring for the baron in order to pay Chaim's retribution, a duty about which he'd never once complained.

Perhaps, most of all, Shula felt guilty about Rachel. Personally, Shula couldn't understand what Rachel had ever seen in Avrum. He was a pompous, sanctimonious ass who wasn't fit to shine Rachel's boots. But she'd been devastated when he broke their engagement because of the family disgrace.

Six-year-old Honey stopped running after her brother and pointed to the road. "Someone is coming," she called out.

Shula shielded her eyes with her hands and looked down the dirt path. Indeed, she saw a figure hastening in their direction. It was a he, that much she could tell, because whoever it was wasn't wearing a skirt. But he was too far away to make out any other details.

"I think it's a goy," Rachel added, when he got closer.

"A goy? Here?" Shula asked.

"Well, he's wearing a loose tunic with a belt over it, and baggy pants. He's not wearing a yarmulke or a hat."

"He's got a limp, Bubbe," Haney added. "And he's got a bag tied to a pole over his shoulder."

With trepidation, they watched the stranger draw closer and closer, watched him pass the dilapidated houses on the narrow street, where the neighbors looked on from their yards, and watched as he approached their property.

Shula couldn't move. Her legs felt leaden. Her hand flew to her mouth. She saw a scar the length of his cheek, curly blond hair, streaked with gray, that came down to his ears, and the biggest, bluest eyes she could only remember seeing on one other person.

Rachel took off running.

He was standing at the gate when she reached him. ". . .No! Impossible!"

". . .Rachel. You're still as skinny as a stick," he said in a deep baritone voice.

She wrapped her arms around him, covered his face with kisses. He was all muscle. "Come." She took his hand, strong and calloused, and led him to the old lady sitting in the sun. Lena had fallen asleep.

Rachel had to tap her on the shoulder several times before she woke. "Mother!"

Lena opened her eyes and squinted, then stared at him in disbelief. ". . . Yussel?"

"Who's Yussel? I'm Layzer, your son."

ACKNOWLEDGEMENTS

I would like to thank my writing mentor, Barry Sheinkopf, at the Writing Center. I couldn't have done this book without you. Thank you also to my Wednesday night writing group classmates, who have listened patiently and given constructive criticism, and my husband's daughter, Rachel Raimi, for her expert historical input.

I have also found the following volumes helpful and illuminating. There were others as well, but they have slipped from memory. Any errors of fact or chroonology, however, remain my own: *New York Times* archives; Iver Berstein, *The New York City Draft Riots*; Yaffa Ellach, *There Once Was a World: A 900-Year Chronicle of the Shtetl of Eishyshok*; DAvid Assaf (Ed.), *Journey to a Nineteenth-Century Shtetl: The Memoirs of Yekhezkel Kotik*; Adrienne Gusoff, *Dirty Yiddish—Everyday Slang*; Fred Kogus, *A Dictionary of Yiddish Slang and Idioms*; Fred C. Wexler, *The Tammany Regiment: History of the Forty-Second New York Volunteer Infrantry 1861–1864*; Horbert Asbuy and Russel Shorto, *The Gangs of New York: An Informal History of the Underworld*; Edna Holden, *Holden's Staten Island: The History of Richmond County*; Luc Sante, *Low Life*; and Leo Tolstoy, *In the Days of Serfdom and Other Stories.*

About The Author

Rita Kornfeld lives in Staten Island, New York, with her husband, Jay, and their golden retriever, Hannah. She has two sons, Louis and Alex, a daughter-in-law, Megan, and the grandest grandson, Lev. She is a registered nurse who has worked for twenty years in psychiatry. This is her second novel.